W9-ARK-346

Guilty Pleasures

"I was enthralled—a departure from the usual type of vampire tale which will have a wide appeal to any reader hunting for both chills and fun." —Andre Norton

The Laughing Corpse

"Supernatural bad guys beware, night-prowling Anita Blake is savvy, sassy, and tough."
—P. N. Elrod, author of *The Vampire Files*

Circus of the Damned

"Ms. Hamilton's intriguing blend of fantasy, mystery and a touch of romance is great fun indeed."
—*Romantic Times*

The Lunatic Cafe

"A well-written, stylish, and imaginative work . . . a wonderful set to read." —*Kliatt*

Bloody Bones

"This fast-paced, tough-edged supernatural thriller is mesmerizing reading indeed." —*Romantic Times*

The Killing Dance

"As usual, the plot is full of red herrings . . . also as usual it's a lot of fun, with some significant new developments in Anita's personal life fans of the series won't want to miss."
—*Locus*

Burnt Offerings

"Filled with nonstop action, witty dialog, and steamy sex, this title will appeal to fans of Anne Rice and Tanya Huff."
—*Library Journal*

Blue Moon

"[This] series has to rank as one of the most addictive substances on earth . . . *Blue Moon* is the best book Laurell Hamilton has produced recently."
—*SF Site*

Obsidian Butterfly

"Just when I think that Laurell K. Hamilton can't possibly get any further out on the edge, along she comes with yet another eye-popping blend of hilarious sex, violence, and stuff that makes your hair stand on end. I've never read a writer with a more fertile imagination—and fewer inhibitions about using it!"
—Diana Gabaldon

BURNT OFFERINGS

LAURELL K. HAMILTON

ACE BOOKS, NEW YORK

This is a work of fiction. Names, characters, places, and incidents are either the product of the author's imagination or are used fictitiously, and any resemblance to actual persons, living or dead, business establishments, events, or locales is entirely coincidental.

BURNT OFFERINGS

An Ace Book / published by arrangement with
the author

PRINTING HISTORY
Ace edition / May 1998

For information address: The Berkley Publishing Group,
a division of Penguin Putnam Inc.,
375 Hudson Street, New York, New York 10014.

The Penguin Putnam Inc. World Wide Web site address is
www.penguinputnam.com

Check out the ACE Science Fiction & Fantasy newsletter
and much more on the Internet at Club PPI!

ISBN: 0-441-00524-1

ACE®
Ace Books are published by The Berkley Publishing Group,
a division of Penguin Putnam Inc.,
375 Hudson Street, New York, New York 10014.
ACE and the "A" design are trademarks
belonging to Penguin Putnam Inc.

PRINTED IN THE UNITED STATES OF AMERICA

15   14   13   12   11   10

For my grandmother, Laura Gentry,
who at 4' 11'' taught me that you could be
small, female, and still be tough.

ACKNOWLEDGMENTS

To my brother-in-law, Officer Shawn Holsapple, who should have been mentioned in these pages long ago.

Thanks for firefighter info to Paty Cockrum, who among her many talents is also a volunteer firefighter. To Bonnee Pierson, also a volunteer firefighter. To Florence Bradley, member of the Birmingham Fire and Rescue Service Department. She does this firefighting stuff for a living.

Thanks also to Dave Cockrum, who came up with the color for Asher's eyes.

As always to my writing group, the Alternate Historians: Tom Drennan, N. L. Drew, Deborah Millitello, Rett MacPherson, Marella Sands, Sharon Shinn, and Mark Sumner. I would be lost without you guys.

Here's the address for the newsletter: Laurell K. Hamilton Fan Club, P. O. Box 190306, St. Louis, MO 63119.

I look at every piece of mail personally, which explains the slow response time. I'll be getting help soon, which should speed things up.

For those on the information super highway, here's my e-mail address: Laurell_Hamilton@bigfoot.com

I don't read the computer messages. Someone else handles all the techie stuff.

1

MOST PEOPLE DON'T stare at the scars. They'll look, of course, then do the eye slide. You know, the quick look, then drop the gaze, then just have to have that second look. But they make it quick. The wounds aren't like freak show bad, but they are interesting. Captain Pete McKinnon, firefighter and arson investigator, sat across from me, big hands wrapped around a glass of iced tea that our secretary, Mary, had brought in for him. He was staring at my arms. Not the place most men look. But it wasn't sexual. He was staring at the scars and didn't seem a bit embarrassed about it.

My right arm had been sliced open twice by a knife. One scar was white and old. The second was still pink and new. My left arm was worse. A mound of white scar tissue sat at the bend of my arm. I'd have to lift weights for the rest of my life or the scars would stiffen and I'd lose mobility in the arm, or so my physical therapist had said. There was a cross-shaped burn mark, a little crooked now because of the ragged claw marks that a shapeshifted witch had given me. There were one or two other scars hidden under my blouse, but the arm really is the worst.

Bert, my boss, had requested that I wear my suit jacket or long-sleeved blouses in the office. He said that some clients had expressed reservations about my ah . . . occupationally acquired wounds. I hadn't worn a long-sleeved blouse since he made the request. He'd turned the air conditioner up a little colder every day. It was so cold today I had goose bumps. Everyone else was bringing sweaters to work. I was shopping for midriff tops to show off my back scars.

McKinnon had been recommended to me by Sergeant Rudolph Storr, cop and friend. They'd played football in college together, and been friends ever since. Dolph didn't use the word "friend" lightly, so I knew they were close.

"What happened to your arm?" McKinnon asked finally.

"I'm a legal vampire executioner. Sometimes they get pesky." I took a sip of coffee.

"Pesky," he said and smiled.

He sat his glass on the desk and slipped off his suit jacket. He was nearly as wide through the shoulders as I was tall. He was a few inches short of Dolph's six foot eight, but he didn't miss it by much. He was only in his forties, but his hair was completely grey with a little white starting at the temples. It didn't make him look distinguished. It made him look tired.

He had me beat on scars. Burn scars crawled up his arms from his hands to disappear under the short sleeves of his white dress shirt. The skin was mottled pinkish, white, and a strange shade of tan like the skin of some animal that should shed regularly.

"That must have hurt," I said.

"It did." He sat there meeting my eyes with a long steady look. "You saw the inside of a hospital on some of that."

"Yeah." I pushed the sleeve up on my left arm and showed the shiny place where a bullet had grazed me. His eyes widened just a bit. "Now that we've proven we're big tough he-men, can you just cut to the chase? Why are you here, Captain McKinnon?"

He smiled and draped his jacket over the back of his chair. He took the tea off my desk and sipped it. "Dolph said you wouldn't like being sized up."

"I don't like passing inspections."

"How do you know you passed?"

It was my turn to smile. "Women's intuition. Now, what do you want?"

"Do you know what the term firebug means?"

"An arsonist," I said.

He looked expectantly at me.

"A pyrokinetic, someone who can call fire psychically."

He nodded. "You ever seen a real pyro?"

"I saw films of Ophelia Ryan," I said.

"The old black-and-white ones?" he asked.

"Yeah."

"She's dead now, you know."

"No, I didn't know."

"Burned to death in her bed, spontaneous combustion. A lot of the firebugs go up that way, as if when they're old they lose control of it. You ever see one of them in person?"

"Nope."

"Where'd you see the films?"

"Two semesters of Psychic Studies. We had a lot of psychics come in and talk to us, demonstrate their abilities, but pyrokinetics is such a rare ability, I don't think the prof could find one."

He nodded and drained the rest of his tea in one long swallow. "I met Ophelia Ryan once before she died. Nice lady." He started to turn the ice-filled glass round and round in his large hands. He stared at the glass and not at me while he talked. "I met one other firebug. He was young, in his twenties. He'd started by setting empty houses on fire, like a lot of pyromaniacs. Then he did buildings with people in them, but everybody got out. Then he did a tenement, a real firetrap. He set every exit on fire. Killed over sixty people, mostly women and children."

McKinnon stared up at me. The look in his eyes was haunted. "It's still the largest body count I've ever seen at a fire. He did an office building the same way, but missed a couple of exits. Twenty-three dead."

"How'd you catch him?"

"He started writing to the papers and the television. He wanted credit for the deaths. He set fire to a couple of cops before we got him. We were wearing those big silver suits that they wear to oil rig fires. He couldn't get them to burn. We took him down to the police station, and that was the mistake. He set it on fire."

"Where else could you have taken him?" I asked.

He shrugged massive shoulders. "I don't know, somewhere else. I was still in the suit, and I held onto him. Told him we'd burn up together if he didn't stop it. He laughed and set himself on fire." McKinnon sat his glass very carefully on the edge of the desk.

"The flames were this soft blue color almost like a gas fire, but paler. Didn't burn him, but somehow it set my suit on fire.

The damn thing is rated for something like 6,000 degrees, and it started to melt. Human skin burns at 120 degrees, but somehow I didn't melt into a puddle, just the suit. I had to strip it off while he laughed. He walked out the door and he didn't think anyone would be stupid enough to grab him.''

I didn't say the obvious. I let him talk.

"I tackled him in the hallway and slammed him into a wall a couple of times. Funny thing, where my skin touched him, it didn't burn. It was like the fire crawled over a space and started on my arms, so my hands are fine.''

I nodded. "There's a theory that a pyro's aura keeps them from burning. When you touched his skin, you were too close to his own aura, his own protection, to burn.''

He stared at me. "Maybe that is what happened, because I threw him hard up against the wall over and over. He was screaming, 'I'll burn you. I'll burn you alive.' Then the fire changed color to yellow, normal, and he started to burn. I let him go and went for the fire extinguisher. We couldn't put the fire on his body out. The extinguishers worked on the walls, everything else, but it wouldn't work on him. It was as if the fire was crawling out of his body from deep inside. We'd dampen some of the flames, but there was just more of it until he was made of fire.''

McKinnon's eyes were distant and horror-filled as if he was still seeing it. "He didn't die, Ms. Blake, not like he should have. He screamed for so long and we couldn't help him. Couldn't help him.'' His voice trailed off. He just sat there staring at nothing.

I waited and finally said, gently, "Why are you here, Captain?''

He blinked and sort of shook himself. "I think we've got another firebug on our hands, Ms. Blake. Dolph said that if anyone could help us cut the loss of life, it was you.''

"Psychic ability isn't technically preternatural. It's just talent like throwing a great curve ball.''

He shook his head. "What I saw die on the floor of the station that day wasn't human. It couldn't have been human. Dolph says you're the monster expert. Help me catch this monster before he kills.''

"He or she hasn't killed yet? It's just property damage?" I asked.

He nodded. "I could lose my job for coming to you. I should have bucked this up the line and gotten permission from the chain of command, but we've only lost a couple of buildings. I want to keep it that way."

I took in a slow breath and let it out. "I'll be happy to help, Captain, but I honestly don't know what I can do for you."

He pulled out a thick file folder. "Here's everything we've got. Look it over and call me tonight."

I took the folder from him and sat it in the middle of my desk blotter.

"My number's in the file. Call me. Maybe it's not a firebug. Maybe it's something else. But whatever it is, Ms. Blake, it can bathe in flames and not burn. It can walk through a building and shed fire like sprinkling water. No accelerant, Ms. Blake, but the houses have gone up as if they've been soaked in something. When we get the wood in the lab, it's clean. It's like whatever is doing this can force the fire to do things it shouldn't do."

He glanced at his watch. "I'm running late. I am working on getting you on this officially, but I'm afraid they'll wait until people are dead. I don't want to wait."

"I'll call you tonight, but it may be late. How late is too late to call?"

"Any time, Ms. Blake, any time."

I nodded and stood. I offered my hand. He shook it. His grip was firm, solid, but not too tight. A lot of male clients that wanted to know about the scars squeezed my hand like they wanted me to cry "uncle." But McKinnon was secure. He had his own scars.

I'd barely sat back down when the phone rang. "What is it, Mary?"

"It's me," Larry said. "Mary didn't think you'd mind her putting me straight through." Larry Kirkland, vampire executioner trainee, was supposed to be over at the morgue staking vampires.

"Nope. What's up?"

"I need a ride home." There was just the slightest hesitation to his voice.

"What's wrong?"

He laughed. "I should know better than to be coy with you. I'm all stitched up. The doc says I'll be fine."

"What happened?" I asked.

"Come pick me up and I'll tell all." Then the little son of a gun hung up on me.

There was only one reason for him to not want to talk to me. He'd done something stupid and gotten hurt. Two bodies to stake. Two bodies that wouldn't have risen for at least another night. What could have gone wrong? As the old saying goes, only one way to find out.

Mary rescheduled my appointments. I got my shoulder holster complete with Browning Hi-Power out of the top desk drawer and slipped it on. Since I'd stopped wearing my suit jacket in the office, I'd put the gun in the drawer, but outside the office and always after dark I wore a gun. Most of the creatures that had scarred me up were dead. The majority I'd done personally. Silver-plated bullets are a wonderful thing.

2

LARRY SAT VERY carefully in the passenger seat of my Jeep. It's hard to sit in a car when your back has fresh stitches in it. I'd seen the wound. It was one sharp puncture and one long, bloody scrape. Two wounds, really. He was still wearing the blue T-shirt he'd started in, but the back of it was bloody and ragged. I was impressed he'd kept the nurses from cutting it off of him. They had a tendency to cut off clothing that stood in their way.

Larry strained against the seat belt, trying to find a comfortable position. His short red hair had been freshly cut, tight enough to his head that you almost didn't notice the curls. He was five foot four, an inch taller than me. He'd graduated with a degree in preternatural biology this May. But with the freckles and that little pain wrinkle between his clear blue eyes, he looked closer to sixteen than twenty-one.

I'd been so busy watching him squirm that I'd missed the turnoff to I-270. We were stuck on Ballas until we got to Olive. It was just before lunch, and Olive would be packed with people trying to shove food in their mouths and rush back to work.

"Did you take your pain pill?" I asked.

He tried to sit very still, one arm braced on the edge of the seat. "No."

"Why not?"

"Because stuff like that knocks me out. I don't want to sleep."

"A drugged sleep isn't the same thing as regular sleep," I said.

"No, the dreams are worse," he said.

He had me there. "What happened, Larry?"

"I'm amazed you've waited this long to ask."

"So am I, but I didn't want to ask in front of the doctor. If you start asking questions of the patient, the docs tend to wander off and treat somebody else. I wanted to know from the doctor who stitched you up just how serious it was."

"Just a few stitches," he said.

"Twenty," I said.

"Eighteen," he said.

"I was rounding up."

"Trust me," he said. "You don't need to round up." He grimaced as he said it. "Why does this hurt so much?" he asked.

It might have been a rhetorical question, but I answered it anyway. "Every time you move an arm or a leg you use muscles in your back. Moving your head and muscles in your shoulders makes muscles in your back move. You never appreciate your back until it goes out on you."

"Great," he said.

"Enough stalling, Larry. Tell me what happened." We were stopped behind a long line of traffic leading up to the light on Olive. We were stuck between two small strip malls. The one on our left had fountains and V.J.'s Tea and Spice, where I got all my coffee. To our right was Streetside Records and a Chinese buffet. If you came up Ballas at lunch time, you always had plenty of time to study the shops on either side.

He smiled, then grimaced. "I had two bodies to stake. Both vamp victims that didn't want to rise as vampires."

"They had dying wills, I remember. You've been doing most of those lately."

He nodded, then froze in mid-gesture. "Even nodding my head hurts."

"It'll hurt more tomorrow."

"Gee, thanks, boss. I needed to know that."

I shrugged. "Lying to you won't make it hurt less."

"Anybody ever tell you your bedside manner sucks?"

"Lots of people."

He made a small *hmph* sound. "That I believe. Anyway, I'd finished the bodies and was packing up. A woman rolled in another body. Said it was a vamp with no court order attached."

I glanced at him, frowning. "You didn't do a body without paperwork, did you?"

He frowned back. "Of course not. I told them, no court order, no dead vampire. Staking a vamp without a court order is murder, and I'm not going to be up on charges because someone screwed the paperwork. I told them both that in no uncertain terms."

"Them?" I asked. I eased up the line of traffic, a little closer to the light.

"The other morgue attendant had come back in. They went out in search of the misplaced paperwork. I was left with the vampire. It was morning. He wasn't going anywhere." He tried to look away and not meet my eyes, but it hurt. He ended up staring at me, angry.

"I went out for a cigarette."

I looked at him and had to slam on the brakes when the traffic just stopped. Larry was flung into the seat belt. He groaned, and when he was finished writhing on the seat, he said, "You did that on purpose."

"No, I didn't, but maybe I should have. You left a vampire body alone. A vampire that might have had enough kills to deserve a court order of execution, alone in the morgue."

"It wasn't just the cigarette, Anita. The body was just lying there on the gurney. It wasn't chained or strapped. There were no crosses anywhere. I've done executions. They plaster the vamps with silver chains and crosses until it's hard to find the heart. It just didn't look right. I wanted to talk to the medical examiner. She has to approve all vampires before execution, or somebody does. Besides the ME smokes. I figured we could have one together in her office."

"And," I said.

"She wasn't in, and I went back to the morgue. When I got there, the woman attendant was trying to pound a stake through the vamp's chest."

It was lucky we were at a dead stop in traffic. If we'd been moving, I'd have plowed into someone. I stared at him. "You left your vampire kit unattended."

He managed to look embarrassed and angry at the same time. "My kit doesn't include shotguns like yours does, so I figured, who would bother it."

"A lot of people will steal things out of the bag for souvenirs, Larry." Traffic started to creep forward and I had to watch the road instead of his face.

"Fine, fine, I was wrong. I know I was wrong. I grabbed her around the waist and pulled her off the vampire." His eyes slid downward, not looking at me. This was the part that bothered him, or the part he thought would bother me. "I turned my back on her to check the vampire. To make sure she hadn't hurt him."

"She did your back," I said. We inched forward. We were now trapped between Dairy Queen and Kentucky Fried Chicken on one side, and an Infiniti car dealership and a gas station on the other. The scenery was not improving.

"Yeah, yeah. She must have thought I was down for the count because she left me and went back to the vampire. I disarmed her, but she was still trying to get to the vampire when the other attendant came in. It took both of us to pin her. She was crazy, manic."

"Why didn't you draw your gun, Larry?" His gun was sitting in his vampire kit because a shoulder holster and his back wound did not mix. But he went armed. I'd taken him out to the shooting range, and out on vampire hunts until I trusted him not to shoot his foot off.

"If I'd drawn my gun, I might have shot her."

"That's sort of the point, Larry."

"It's exactly the point," he said. "I didn't want to shoot her."

"She could have killed you, Larry."

"I know."

I gripped the steering wheel tight enough to mottle my skin, white and pink. I let out a long breath and tried not to yell. "You obviously don't know, or you would have been more careful."

"I'm alive, and she's not dead. The vampire didn't even get a scratch. It worked out all right."

I pulled out onto Olive and started creeping towards 270. We needed to head north towards St. Charles. Larry had an apartment over there. It was about a twenty-minute drive, give or take. His apartment looked out over a lake where geese nested in the spring and congregated in the winter. Richard Zeeman, junior high science teacher, alpha werewolf, and at that time, my boyfriend, had helped him move in. Richard had really liked the geese nesting just under the balcony. So had I.

"Larry, you are going to have to get over this squeamishness or you're going to get killed."

"I'll keep doing what I think is right, Anita. Nothing you can say will change my mind."

"Dammit, Larry. I don't want to have to bury you."

"What would you have done? Shot her?"

"I wouldn't have turned my back on her, Larry. I could have probably disarmed her or kept her busy until the other attendant arrived. I wouldn't have had to shoot her."

"I let things get out of control," he said.

"Your priorities were screwed. You should have neutralized the threat before you checked on the victim. Alive, you could help the vamp. Dead, you're just another victim."

"Well, at least I've got a scar you don't have."

I shook my head. "You'll have to try harder if you want a scar I don't have."

"You let a human shove one of your own stakes into your back?"

"Two humans with multiple bites, what I used to call human servants, before I knew what the term really meant. I had one pinned and was stabbing him. The woman came at my back."

"So yours wasn't a mistake," he said.

I shrugged. "I could have shot them when I first saw them, but I didn't kill humans as easily back then. I learned my lesson. Just because it doesn't have fangs doesn't mean it can't kill you."

"You used to be squeamish about shooting human servants?" Larry asked.

I turned onto 270. "No one's perfect. Why did the woman have a hard-on to kill the vampire?"

He grinned. "You're going to love this one. She's a member of Humans First. The vampire was a doctor in the hospital. He'd tucked himself into a linen closet. It was where he always slept the day away if he'd had to stay too late in the hospital to drive home. She just popped him on a gurney and wheeled him down to the morgue."

"I'm surprised she didn't just push him out into the sunlight.

The last sunlight of the day works as well as noonday.''

"The linen closet he used was on the basement floor just in case someone opened the door at the wrong time of day. No windows. She was afraid someone would see her before she could get him up in the elevator and outside.''

"She really thought you would just stake him?''

"I guess so. I don't know, Anita. She was crazy, really crazy. She spit at the vampire and us. Said we'd all rot in hell. That we had to cleanse the world of the monsters. The monsters were going to enslave us all.'' Larry shivered, then frowned. "I thought Humans Against Vampires was bad enough, but this splinter group, Humans First, is genuinely scary.''

"HAV tries to work within the law,'' I said. "Humans First doesn't even pretend to care. They claimed they staked that vampire mayor in Michigan.''

"Claimed? You don't believe them?''

"I think someone near and dear to his household did it.''

"Why?''

"The cops sent me a description and some photos of the security precautions he'd taken. Humans First may be radical, but they don't seem very well organized yet. You'd have had to plan and be very lucky to get to that vampire during the day. He was like a lot of the old ones, very serious about his daytime safety. I think whoever did it is happy to let the right-wing radicals take the blame.''

"You tell the police what you think?''

"Sure. That's why they asked.''

"I'm surprised they didn't have you come down and see it in person.''

I shrugged. "I can't go personally to every preternatural crime. Besides, I'm technically a civilian. Cops are sort of leery about involving civilians in their cases, but more importantly, the media would be all over it. The Executioner Solves Vampire Murder.''

Larry grinned. "That's a mild headline for you.''

"Unfortunately,'' I said. "Also, I think the killer is a human. I think it's just someone he was close to. It's like any well-planned murder except for the victim being a vampire.''

"Only you would make a locked-room vampire murder sound ordinary,'' Larry said.

I had to smile. "I guess so." My beeper went off, and I jumped. I pulled the damn thing off my skirt and held it where I could see the number. I frowned at it.

"What's wrong? Is it the police?"

"No. I don't recognize the number."

"You don't give out your beeper number to strangers."

"I'm aware of that."

"Hey, don't get grumpy at me."

I sighed. "Sorry." Larry was slowly wearing me down on my aggression threshold. He was, by sheer repetition, teaching me to be nicer. Anybody else and I would have fed them their head in a basket. But Larry managed to push my buttons just right. He could caution me to be nicer and I didn't slug him. The basis of many a successful relationship.

We were only minutes from Larry's apartment. I'd tuck him into bed and answer the call. If it wasn't the police or a zombie-raising, I was going to be pissed. I hated being beeped when it wasn't important. That's what beepers are for, right? If it wasn't important stuff, I was going to rain all over somebody's parade. With Larry asleep, I could be as nasty as I wanted to be. It was almost a relief.

3

WHEN LARRY WAS safely tucked in bed with his Demorol, so deeply asleep that nothing short of an earthquake would have woken him, I made my phone call. I still didn't have the faintest idea who it was, which bothered me. It wasn't just inconvenient, it was unnerving. Who was giving out my private numbers and why?

The phone didn't even finish a ring before it was picked up. The voice on the other end was male, soft, and panicked. "Hello, hello."

All my irritation vanished in a wash of something very close to fear. "Stephen, what's wrong?"

I heard him swallow on his end of the phone. "Thank God."

"What's happened?" I made my voice very clear, very calm, because I wanted to yell at him, to force him to tell me what the hell was going on.

"Can you come down to St. Louis University Hospital?"

That got my attention. "How bad are you hurt?"

"It's not me."

My heart slid up into my throat, and my voice came out squeezed and tight. "Jean-Claude." The moment I said it, I knew it was silly. It was just after noon. If Jean-Claude had needed a doctor, they would have had to come to him. Vampires did not travel well in broad daylight. Why was I so worried about a vampire? I happened to be dating him. My family, devout Catholics, are simply thrilled. Since I'm still a little embarrassed about it, it's hard to defend myself.

"It's not Jean-Claude. It's Nathaniel."

"Who?"

Stephen's breath went out in a long-suffering sigh. "He was one of Gabriel's people."

Which was another way of saying he was a wereleopard. Gabriel had been the leopards' leader, their alpha, until I killed him. Why had I killed him? Most of the wounds he'd given me had healed. It was one of the benefits of the vampire marks. I didn't scar quite so easily anymore. There was a curl of scars high up on my buttocks and lower back, faint, almost dainty, but I would always have a little reminder of Gabriel. A reminder that his fantasy had been to rape me, to make me cry out his name, then kill me. Though knowing Gabriel, he probably hadn't been so picky on when I died, after or during—either would have worked for him. As long as I was still warm. Most lycanthropes aren't into carrion.

I sounded casual about it, even in my own head. But my fingers traced along my back as if I could feel the scars through my skirt. Had to be casual about it. Had to be. Or you start screaming, and you don't stop.

"The hospital doesn't know Nathaniel's a shapeshifter, do they?" I said.

He lowered his voice. "They know. He's healing too fast for them not to know."

"So why whisper?"

"Because I'm out in the waiting room on a pay phone." There was a sound on the other end like he'd had to take the receiver away from his mouth. He muttered, "I'll be off in just a minute." He came back on. "I need you to come down, Anita."

"Why?"

"Please."

"You're a werewolf, Stephen. What are you doing baby-sitting one of the kitty-cats?"

"I'm one of the names in his wallet in case of emergencies. Nathaniel works at Guilty Pleasures."

"He's a stripper?" I made it a question because he could have been a waiter, but it wasn't likely. Jean-Claude owned Guilty Pleasures, and he would never have wasted a shapeshifter off-stage. They were too damned exotic.

"Yes."

"The two of you need a ride?" It was my day for it, I guess.

"Yes, and no."

There was something in his voice that I didn't like. An unease, a tension. It wasn't like Stephen to be cagey. He didn't play games. He just talked. "How did Nathaniel get hurt?" Maybe if I asked better questions, I'd get better answers.

"A customer got too rough."

"At the club?"

"No. Anita, please, there's no time. Come down and make sure he doesn't go home with Zane."

"Who the hell is Zane?"

"Another of Gabriel's people. He's been pimping them out since Gabriel died. But he's not protecting them like Gabriel did. He isn't alpha."

"Pimping them out? What are you talking about?"

Stephen's voice rose high and far too cheerful. "Hello, Zane. Have you seen Nathaniel yet?"

I couldn't really hear the answer, just the buzz of all the people in the waiting room. "I don't think they want him to go just yet. He's hurt," Stephen said.

Zane must have stepped very close to the phone, very close to Stephen. A low, growling voice came through the wire. "He'll go home when I say he goes home."

Stephen's voice held an edge of panic. "I don't think the doctors will like that."

"I don't give a shit. Who are you talking to?"

For his voice to be that clear he had to have Stephen pinned against the wall. Threatening him, without saying anything specific.

The growling voice was suddenly very clear. He'd taken the phone from Stephen. "Who is this?"

"Anita Blake, and you must be Zane."

He laughed, and it sounded too low, as if his throat were sore. "The wolves' human lupa. Oh, I'm so scared."

Lupa was the word the werewolves used for their leader's mate. I was the first human so honored. I wasn't even dating their Ulfric anymore. We'd broken up after I saw him eat somebody. Hey, a girl's got to have some standards.

"Gabriel wasn't scared of me either. Look where it got him," I said.

Zane was quiet for a handful of heartbeats. He breathed over the phone like a dog panted, heavy, but not like he was doing it on purpose, more like he couldn't help it. "Nathaniel is mine. Keep off of him."

"Stephen isn't one of yours," I said.

"Does he belong to you?" I could hear cloth moving. A sense of movement on the other end of the phone that I didn't like. "He is sooo pretty. Have you tasted these soft lips? Has this long yellow hair swept over your pillow?"

I knew without seeing it that he was touching Stephen, caressing him to match the words. "Don't touch him, Zane."

"Too late."

I gripped the phone tight and forced my voice calm, even. "Stephen's under my protection, Zane. Do you understand me?"

"What would you do to keep your pet wolf safe, Anita?"

"You don't want to push that button, Zane. You really don't."

He lowered his voice to an almost painful whisper. "Would you kill me to keep him safe?"

I usually have to meet someone at least once before threatening to kill them, but I was about to make an exception. "Yeah."

He laughed, low and nervous. "I see why Gabriel liked you. So tough, so sure of yourself. Sooo dangerous."

"You sound like a bad imitation of Gabriel."

He made a sound that was somewhere between a hiss and a *bah*. "Stephen shouldn't have interfered."

"Nathaniel's his friend."

"I am all the friend he needs."

"I don't think so."

"I am taking Nathaniel with me, Anita. If Stephen tries to stop me, I'll hurt him."

"You hurt Stephen, I hurt you."

"So be it." He hung up.

Shit. I ran for my Jeep. I was thirty minutes away, twenty if I pushed it a lot. Twenty minutes. Stephen wasn't dominant. He was a victim. But he was also loyal. If he thought Nathaniel shouldn't go with Zane, he'd try and keep him. He wouldn't fight for him, but he might throw his body in front of the car.

I had no doubts at all that Zane would drive right over him. Best case scenario. Worst case scenario was Zane would take both Stephen and Nathaniel. If Zane acted as much like Gabriel as he talked, I'd rather have taken my chances with the car.

4

MY SECOND EMERGENCY room in less than two hours. It was a red-letter day even for me. Good news was that none of the injuries were mine. Bad news was that that might change. Alpha or not, Zane was a shapeshifter. They were able to bench-press medium-size elephants. I was not going to arm-wrestle him. Not only would I lose, but he'd probably pull the arm out of my socket and eat it. Most lycanthropes liked to try and pass for human. I wasn't sure Zane sweated little details like that.

Yet I didn't want to kill Zane if I didn't have to. It wasn't mercy. It was the thought that he might force me to do it in public. I didn't want to go to jail. The fact that the punishment worried me more than the crime said something about my moral state. Some days I thought I was becoming a sociopath. Some days I thought I was already there.

I carried silver-plated bullets in my gun at all times. Silver worked on humans, as well as on most supernatural beings. Why keep switching to normal ammmo that only did humans and a very few creatures? But a few months ago I'd met a fairie that had damn near killed me. Silver didn't work on fairies, but normal lead did. So I'd taken to keeping a spare clip of regular bullets in the glove compartment. I peeled off the first two rounds of my silver clip and replaced them with lead. Which meant I had two bullets to discourage Zane with, before I killed him. Because, make no mistake, if he kept coming after I'd pumped him full of two Glazer Safety Rounds, which hurt a hell of a lot even if you could heal the damage, the first silver bullet was not going to be aimed to wound.

It wasn't until I was going through the doors I realized that

I didn't know Nathaniel's last name. Stephen's name wasn't going to help me. Damn.

The waiting room was packed. Women with crying babies, children racing through the chairs belonging to no one, a man with a bloody rag around his hand, people with no visible injury staring dully into space. Stephen was nowhere in sight.

Screams, the sound of breaking glass; metal clanked to the floor. A nurse ran out of the far hallway. "Get more security, now!" A nurse behind the admittance desk punched buttons on the phone.

Call it a hunch but I was betting I knew where Stephen and Zane were. I flashed my ID at the nurse. "I'm with the Regional Preternatural Investigation Team. Can I help?"

The nurse clutched my arm. "You're a cop?"

"I'm with the police, yes." Prevarication at its best. As a civilian attached to a police squad you learn how to do that.

"Thank God." She started to pull me towards the noise.

I pulled my arm free and took out my gun. Safety off, pointed at the ceiling, ready to go. With normal ammo I wouldn't have pointed at the ceiling, not with a hospital full of patients above me, but Glazer Safety Rounds aren't called safety rounds for nothing.

The back area was like every emergency area I'd ever been in. Curtains hung from metal tracks so you could make lots and lots of little individual examining rooms. A handful of curtains were closed, but patients were sitting up, staring through the curtains, watching the show. A wall divided the room down the middle to the corridor, so there wasn't much to see.

A man wearing green surgical scrubs went flying through the air from around that wall. He smacked into the opposite wall, slid down it heavily, and lay very still.

The nurse with me ran towards him, and I let her go. What lay beyond, what was tossing doctors around like toys, wasn't a job for a healer. It was a job for me. Two more figures in surgical scrubs lay on the floor, one male, one female. The woman was awake, eyes wide. Her wrist was at a 45 degree angle, broken. She saw my ID clipped to my jacket. "He's a shifter. Be careful."

"I know what he is," I said. I lowered the gun just a touch.

Her eyes flinched, and it wasn't pain. "Don't shoot up my trauma center."

"Try not to," I said and moved past her.

Zane stepped out into the corridor. I'd never seen Zane before, but who else could it be? He was carrying someone in his arms. I thought at first, a woman, because the hair was long and shining brown, but the exposed back and shoulders were too muscular, too male. It had to be Nathaniel. He fit easily into the taller man's arms.

Zane was about six foot, stretched tall and thin. He wore only a black leather vest on his thin, pale upper body. His hair was cotton-white, cut short on the sides with the top long in moussed spikes.

He opened his mouth and snarled at me. He had fangs, upper and lower, like a great cat. Sweet Jesus.

I pointed the gun at him and let out the air in my body until I was still and quiet. I was aiming for a line of shoulder above Nathaniel's still form. At this distance I'd hit it.

"I'll only ask once, Zane. Put him down."

"He's mine, mine!" He took striding steps down the hallway, and I fired.

The bullet spun him halfway around, and staggered him to his knees. The shoulder I'd hit stopped working, and Nathaniel slid out of his arms. Zane got to his feet with the smaller man tucked under his good arm like a doll. The flesh of his shoulder was already reknitting, rebuilding itself like a fast-forward picture of a flower blooming.

Zane could have tried to rush past me, to use his speed, but he didn't. He just came walking towards me as if he didn't believe I'd do it. He should have believed.

The second lead bullet took him square in the chest. Blood exploded out of his pale skin. He fell onto his back, spine bowing, struggling to breathe with a hole the size of a fist in his chest. I went for him, not running, but hurrying.

I walked wide around him, out of arm's reach, and came up a little behind him, and to the side. The shoulder I'd shot was still limp, his other arm trapped under Nathaniel's body. Zane gasped up at me, brown eyes wide.

"Silver, Zane, the rest of the bullets are silver. I'll make it a head shot and blow your freaking brains all over this nice clean floor.''

He finally managed to gasp out, ''Won't.'' Blood filled his mouth and spilled down his chin.

I pointed the gun at his face, about eyebrow level. If I pulled the trigger, he was gone. I stared down at this man I'd never met before. He looked young, nowhere close to thirty. A great emptiness filled me. It was like standing in the middle of white noise. I felt nothing. I didn't want to kill him, but I didn't care if I did. It didn't matter to me. It only mattered to him. I let that knowledge fill my eyes. That I didn't give a damn one way or the other. I let him see it, because he was a shapeshifter, and he'd understand what I was showing him. Most people wouldn't. Most sane people anyway.

I said, ''You are going to leave Nathaniel alone. When the police arrive, you are going to do everything they tell you to do. No arguments, no fighting, or I will kill you. Do you understand me, Zane?''

''Yes,'' he said, and more blood flowed in a heavy line from his mouth. He started to cry. Tears welled down his bloodstained face.

Crying? The bad guys aren't supposed to cry.

''I'm so glad you've come,'' he said. ''I tried to take care of them, but I couldn't. I tried to be Gabriel, but I couldn't be him.'' His shoulder had healed enough that he covered his eyes with his hand so we couldn't see him cry, but his voice was thick with tears, as well as blood.

''I'm so glad you've come to us, Anita. I'm so glad we're not alone anymore.''

I didn't know what to say. Denying that I was going to be their leader seemed a bad idea with bodies littering the area. If I refused his offer, he might get nasty again and I'd have to kill him. I realized suddenly with something like a physical jolt that I didn't want to kill him. Was it the tears? Maybe. But it was more than that. It was the fact that I'd killed their alpha, their protector, and never given a thought what that might do to the rest of the wereleopards. It had never occurred to me that there was no second in command, no one to fill Gabriel's place. I certainly couldn't be their alpha. I didn't turn furry once a month. But if it would keep Zane from tearing up any more doctors, I could play along for a while.

By the time the cops arrived, Zane was healed. He'd curled around Nathaniel's unconscious body like it was a teddy bear, still crying. He stroked Nathaniel's hair and muttered over and over, "She'll keep us safe. She'll keep us safe. She'll keep us safe."

I think the "she" was me, and I was in way over my head.

5

STEPHEN LAY IN the narrow hospital bed. His curly blond hair
was longer than mine, sweeping across the white pillow. Angry
red and pink scars crisscrossed his delicate face. He looked like
he'd been shoved through a window, which is exactly what had
happened. Stephen, who didn't outweigh me by twenty pounds,
had stood his ground. Zane had finally shoved him through a
wire-mesh safety window. Like shoving someone through a wire
cheese grater. If it had been a human being, they'd be dead.
Even Stephen was hurt, badly hurt. But he was healing. I
couldn't literally see the scars fading. It was like trying to watch
a flower bloom. You knew it happened, but you never got to
see it. I'd glance back at him, and there'd be one less scar. It
was unnerving as hell.

Nathaniel was in the other bed. His hair was longer than Stephen's. Waist length, I was betting. Hard to judge since I'd only
seen him prone. It was the darkest of auburns, almost brown but
not. It was a rich, deep mahogany. The hair lay on the white
sheets like the pelt of an animal, thick and shining.

He was pretty rather than handsome, and couldn't have been
more than five foot six. The hair helped the illusion of feminin-
ity. But his shoulders were disproportionately broad, part
weightlifting, but part genetics. He had great shoulders, but they
belonged on someone about half a foot taller. He had to be
eighteen to strip at Guilty Pleasures. His face was slender, jaw
too smooth. He might have been eighteen, but he wasn't much
over. Maybe someday he'd grow into the shoulders.

We were in a semiprivate room on the isolation ward. The
floor that most hospitals kept for lycanthropes, vamps, and other
preternatural citizens. Anything they thought might be danger-

ous. Zane would have been dangerous. But the cops had carted him away, wounds nearly healed. His flesh had pushed my bullets out onto the floor like rejected bits of organ. I didn't think we needed the isolation ward for Stephen and Nathaniel. I could be wrong on Nathaniel, but I didn't think so. I trusted Stephen's judgment better than that.

Nathaniel hadn't regained consciousness. I'd asked what his injuries were, and they told me, because they still thought I was a cop, and I'd saved their asses. Gratitude is a wonderful thing.

Someone had pretty much gutted Nathaniel. I don't mean just cut open his gut with a knife. I mean opened him up and let his intestines fall onto the floor; they found bits of debris on his intestines. There were signs of severe trauma to other parts of the body. He'd been sexually abused. And yes, a prostitute can be raped. All it takes is saying no. No one, not even a lycanthrope, would agree to being raped while their insides were spilling onto the floor. The rape could have been first, then they tried to kill him. It was a touch less sick done in that order. A touch.

There were marks on his wrists and ankles like he'd been chained. The marks were rubbed bloody like he'd struggled, and they weren't healing. Which meant that they'd used chains with a high silver content so it would hurt and not just hold. Whoever had done this to him knew ahead of time they'd be getting a lycanthrope. They were prepared. Which raised some very interesting questions.

Stephen said Gabriel had been pimping the wereleopards out. I understood why people would want something as exotic as a wereleopard. I knew that sadomasochism existed. Shapeshifters could take a hell of a lot of damage. So the combination even made a certain sense. But this was beyond sex games. I'd never heard of anything this brutal outside of a serial-killer case.

I couldn't leave them alone, unprotected. Even without the threat of sexual murderers, there was still the wereleopards. Zane might have cried and kissed my feet, but there were others. If they had no pack structure, no alpha, they had no one to tell them to leave Nathaniel alone. Without a leader it might be a matter of having to back down or kill each of them individually. Not a pleasant thought. Real leopards don't sweat who's in charge much. They don't have pack structures, but shapeshifters

aren't animals, they're people. Which meant no matter how sol-
itary and uncomplicated the animal form, the people half will
find a way to screw things up. If Gabriel had hand-picked his
people, I couldn't trust that they wouldn't come and try for
Nathaniel again. Gabriel had been one sick kitty, and Zane
hadn't impressed me much either. Who you gonna call for re-
inforcements? The local werewolf pack, of course. Stephen was
a member of their pack. They owed him protection.

There was a knock on the door. I took the Browning out and
held it on my lap underneath the magazine I'd been reading. I'd
managed to find a three-month-old copy of *National Wildlife*,
with an article on Kodiak bears. The magazine hid the gun
nicely.

"Who is it?"

"It's Irving."

"Come in." I left the gun out, just in case somebody would
try to push in behind him. Irving Griswold was a werewolf and
a reporter. For a reporter he was a good guy, but he wasn't as
careful as I was. When I saw he was alone, then I would put
the gun up.

Irving pushed the door open, smiling. His frizzy brown hair
encircled his head like a brown halo with the bald spot gleaming
in the middle. Glasses perched on a small nose. He was short
and gave the impression of being round without being fat. He
looked like anything but a big bad wolf. He didn't even look
much like a reporter, which was one of the things that made
him such a great interviewer but would probably always keep
him from being on-camera material. He worked for the *St. Louis
Post-Dispatch*, and had interviewed me many times.

He closed the door behind him.

I put up the gun.

His eyes widened. He spoke low, but not in a whisper.
"How's Stephen?"

"How did you get in here? There's supposed to be a cop on
the door."

"Gee, Blake, I'm glad to see you too."

"Don't mess with me, Irving. There's supposed to be a guard
out there."

"He's talking to a very pretty nurse at the desk."

"Dammit." I was not a real cop, so I couldn't go around

yelling at them, but it was tempting. There was a law floating around Washington that might give vampire hunters federal badges soon. Sometimes I thought it was a bad idea. Sometimes, I didn't.

"Talk to me fast before I get kicked out. How is Stephen?"

I told him. "You don't care about Nathaniel?"

He looked uncomfortable. "You know that Sylvie is *de facto* pack leader while Richard is out of town working on his master's degree, right?"

I sighed. "No, I didn't know."

"I know you're not talking to Richard since you broke up, but I'd think someone else would have mentioned it."

"All the other wolves creep around me like there's been a death. No one talks about Richard to me, Irving. I thought he'd forbidden them to talk to me."

"Not to my knowledge."

"I'm surprised you didn't come in here asking for a story."

"I can't do this story, Anita. It's too close to home."

"Because you know Stephen?"

"Because everyone involved is a shapeshifter and I'm just a mild-mannered reporter."

"You really think you'd lose your job if they found out?"

"Job, hell. What would my mother say?"

I smiled. "So you can't play bodyguard."

He frowned. "You know, I hadn't thought about that. When one of the pack got hurt in public where it couldn't be hidden, Raina always used to ride to the rescue. With her dead, I don't think we have any alphas that aren't hiding what they are. No one I'd trust to guard Stephen, anyway."

Raina had been the wolf pack's old lupa before I took the job. Technically the old lupa doesn't have to die to step down, unlike the Ulfric, or King Wolf. But Raina had been Gabriel's playmate. They'd shared certain hobbies, like making pornographic snuff films starring shapeshifters and humans. She'd been helping film while Gabriel tried to rape me. Oh, yeah, Raina had made it a real pleasure to punch her ticket.

"That's the second time you've ignored Nathaniel," I said. "What gives, Irving?"

"I told you Sylvie is in charge until Richard gets back in town."

"So?"

"She's forbidden any of us to help the wereleopards in any way."

"Why?"

"Raina used the wereleopards in her porno movies a lot, along with the wolves."

"I've seen one of the films. I wasn't impressed. Horrified, but not impressed."

Irving looked very serious. "She also let Gabriel and the cats punish wayward pack members."

"Punish?" I made it a question.

Irving nodded. "Sylvie was one of the ones who got punished, more than once. She hates them all, Anita. If Richard hadn't forbid it, she'd have used the pack to hunt the leopards down and kill them all."

"I've seen what Gabriel and Raina thought was fun and games. I think I'm on Sylvie's side for once."

"You cleaned house for us, you and Richard. Richard killed Marcus and now he's Ulfric, pack leader. You killed Raina for us, and now you're our lupa."

"I shot her, Irving. According to pack law, so I'm told, using a gun negates the challenge. I cheated."

"You're not lupa because you killed Raina. You're lupa because Richard picked you as his mate."

I shook my head. "We aren't dating anymore, Irving."

"But Richard hasn't picked a new lupa, Anita. Until he does, the job's yours."

Richard was tall, dark, handsome, honest, truthful, brave. He was perfect except for being a werewolf. Even that had been forgivable, or so I thought. Until I saw him in action. Saw the whole enchilada. The meat had been raw and squirming, the sauce a little bloody.

Now I was dating just Jean-Claude. I wasn't sure how much of an improvement dating the head vampire of the city was over dating the head werewolf, but I'd made my choice. It was Jean-Claude's pale, pale hands that held my body. His black hair that curled over my pillow. His midnight-blue eyes that I stared into while we made love.

Good girls do not have premarital sex, especially with the undead. I didn't think good girls had regrets about ex-boyfriend

A, when they've chosen boyfriend B. Maybe I'd been wrong. Richard and I avoided each other when we could. Which had been for most of the last six weeks. Now he was out of town. Easy to avoid each other now.

"I won't ask what you're thinking about," Irving said. "I think I know."

"Don't be so damn smart," I said.

He spread his hands wide. "Occupational hazard."

That made me laugh. "So Sylvie's forbidden anyone to help the leopards. Where does that leave Stephen?"

"He went against her direct orders, Anita. For someone as low in the pack structure as Stephen, that took guts. But Sylvie won't be impressed. She'll tear him up, and she won't allow anyone to come down and baby-sit them. I know her that well."

"I can't do this twenty-four hours a day, Irving."

"They'll heal in a day or so."

I frowned at him. "I can't sit here for two days."

He looked away from me and went to stand beside Stephen's bed. He stared down at the sleeping man, hands clasped in front of him.

I walked over to them. I touched Irving's arm. "What aren't you telling me?"

He shook his head. "I don't know what you mean."

I turned him around, made him face me. "Talk to me, Irving."

"You aren't a shapeshifter, Anita. You aren't dating Richard anymore. You need to get out of our world, not further into it."

He looked so serious, solemn, that it scared me. "Irving, what's wrong?"

He just shook his head.

I grabbed him by both arms and resisted the urge to shake him. "What are you hiding?"

"There is a way for you to get the pack to guard Stephen and even Nathaniel."

I took a step back. "I'm listening."

"You outrank Sylvie."

"I'm not a shapeshifter, Irving. I was the new pack leader's girlfriend. I'm not even that anymore."

"You're more than that, Anita, and you know it. You've

killed some of us. You kill easily and without remorse. The pack respects that.''

"Gee, Irving, what a rousing endorsement."

"Do you feel badly about killing Raina? Did you lose sleep over Gabriel?"

"I killed Raina because she was trying to kill me. I killed Gabriel for the same reason, self-preservation. So no, I didn't lose any sleep.''

"The pack respects you, Anita. If you could find some pack members that are already outed as shifters and convince them that you're scarier than Sylvie, they'd guard them, both of them."

"I am not scarier than Sylvie, Irving. I can't beat them to a pulp. She can."

"But you can kill them." He said it very quietly, watching my face, searching my expression.

I opened my mouth, closed it. "What are you trying to get me to do, Irving?"

He shook his head. "Nothing. Forget I said it. I shouldn't have said it. Get more cops in here and go home, Anita. Just get out of it while you can."

"What's going on, Irving? Is Sylvie a problem?"

He looked at me. His usually cheerful eyes, solemn, thoughtful. He shook his head. "I've got to go, Anita."

I grabbed his arm. "You go nowhere until you tell me what's happening."

He turned back to me slowly, reluctantly. I let go of his arm and stepped back. "Talk."

"Sylvie has challenged everyone higher in the pack than she is, and won."

I looked at him. "So?"

"Do you understand how unusual it is for a woman to fight her way to second in command. She's about five foot six, small-boned. Ask how she's winning."

"You're being coy, Irving. That's not like you. I'm not going to play Twenty Questions with you. Just tell me."

"She killed the first two people she fought. She didn't have to. She chose to. The next three challenges she made just agreed she was dominant to them. They didn't want to risk being killed.''

"Very practical," I said.

He nodded. "Sylvie's always been that. She finally picked one of the inner circle to fight. She's too small to be one of the enforcers; besides I think she was afraid of Jamil, and Shang-Da."

"Jamil? Richard didn't drive him out? But he was one of Marcus's and Raina's flunkies."

Irving shrugged. "Richard thought the transition would go smoother if he kept some of the old guard in power."

I shook my head. "Jamil should have been driven out or killed."

"Maybe, but actually Jamil seems to support Richard. I think it really surprised him when he wasn't killed instantly. Richard has earned his loyalty."

"I didn't know Jamil had any loyalty," I said.

"None of us did. Sylvie fought and won the place of Geri, second in command."

"She kill for it?"

"Surprisingly, no."

"Okay, so Sylvie's tearing up the pack. She's second in command. Great, so what?"

"I think she wants to be Ulfric, Anita. I think she wants Richard's job."

I stared at him. "There's only one way to be Ulfric, Irving."

"To kill the old king," Irving said. "Yeah, I think Sylvie knows that."

"I haven't seen her fight, but I've seen Richard fight. He outweighs her by a hundred pounds, a hundred pounds of muscle, and he's good. She can't beat him in a fair fight, can she?"

"It's like Richard is wounded, Anita. The heart's gone out of him. I think if she challenged and really wanted it, she'd win."

"What are you telling me? That he's depressed?" I asked.

"It's more than that. You know how much he hates being one of the monsters. He'd never killed anyone until Marcus. He can't forgive himself."

"How do you know all this?"

"I listen. Reporters make good listeners."

We stared at each other. "Tell me the rest."

Irving looked down, then up. "He doesn't discuss you with

me. The only thing he said was that even you couldn't accept what he was. Even you, the Executioner, were horrified.''

It was my turn to look down. "I didn't want to be."

"We can't change how we feel," Irving said.

I met his eyes. "I would if I could."

"I believe you."

"I don't want Richard dead."

"None of us do. I'm afraid of what Sylvie would do without anyone to stop her." He motioned to the other bed. "First order of business would be hunting down all the wereleopards. We'd slaughter them."

I took in a deep breath and let it out. "I can't change how I feel about what I saw, Irving. I saw Richard eat Marcus." I paced the small room, shaking my head. "What *can* I do to help?"

"Call the pack and demand that they acknowledge you as lupa. Make some of them come here and guard both of them against Sylvie's express orders. But you have to give them your protection. You have to promise them that she won't hurt them, because you'll see to it that she can't."

"If I do that and Sylvie doesn't like it, I'll have to kill her. It's like I'm setting her up to be killed. That's a little premeditated even for me."

He shook his head. "I'm asking you to be our lupa. To be Richard's lupa. To show Sylvie that if she keeps pressing, Richard may not kill her, but you will."

I sighed. "Shit."

"I'm sorry, Anita. I wouldn't have said anything, but . . ."

"I needed to know," I said. I hugged him, and he stiffened in surprise, then hugged me back.

"What was that for?"

"For telling me. I know Richard won't like it."

The smile faded from his face. "Richard has punished two pack members since he took over. They challenged his authority, big time, and he nearly killed them both."

"What?" I asked.

"He sliced them up, Anita. He was like someone else, something else."

"Richard doesn't do things like that."

"He does now, not all the time. Most of the time he's fine,

but then he snaps and goes into a rage. I don't want to be anywhere near him when he loses it."

"How bad has he gotten?" I asked.

"He's got to accept what he is, Anita. He's got to embrace his beast, or he's going to drive himself mad."

I shook my head. "I can't help him love his beast, Irving. I can't accept it either."

Irving shrugged. "It's not so bad being furry, Anita. There are worse things . . . like being the walking dead."

I frowned at him. "Get out, Irving, and thanks for telling me."

"I hope you're still thankful in a week."

"Me, too."

Irving gave me some phone numbers and left. Didn't want anyone to stay too long. People might suspect him of being more than just a reporter. No one seemed to worry about my reputation. I raised zombies, slew vampires, and was dating the Master of the City. If people began to suspect me of being a shapeshifter, what the hell difference would it make?

Three names of submissive pack members who Irving thought were tough enough to play bodyguard and weak enough to be bullied. I didn't want to do this. The pack was based on obedience: punishment and reward, mostly punishment. If the pack members I called refused me, I had to punish them, or I wasn't lupa, wasn't strong enough to back Richard. Of course, he probably wouldn't be grateful. He seemed to hate me now. I didn't blame him. He'd hate me interfering.

But it wasn't just Richard. It was Stephen. He'd saved my life once and I still hadn't returned the favor. He was also one of those people that was everyone's victim, until today. Yeah, Zane had nearly killed him, but that wasn't the point. He'd put friendship above pack loyalty. Which meant that Sylvie could withdraw pack protection from him. He'd be like the wereleopards, anybody's meat. I couldn't let that happen to him, not if I could stop it.

Stephen might end up dead. Richard might end up dead. I might have to kill Sylvie. I might have to maim or kill a few pack members to make my point. Might, might, might. Damn.

I'd never killed before except in self-defense or for revenge. If I put my hat in the ring, it would be premeditated, cold-

blooded murder. Maybe not in a technical sense, but I knew
what I would be starting in motion. It was like dominoes. They
all stayed straight and neat until you hit one of them; then there
was no stopping them. I would end up with a pretty pattern on
the floor: Richard solidly in power, Stephen and the wereleopards safe, Sylvie backed down, or dead. The first three things
were going to happen. It was Sylvie's choice how the last bit
turned out. Harsh, but true. Of course, there was one other option. Sylvie could kill me. That would sort of open things up
for her again. Sylvie wasn't exactly ruthless, but she didn't let
anyone get in her way. We shared that trait. No, I am not ruthless. If I was, I'd have just called Sylvie into a meeting and shot
her on the spot. I wasn't quite sociopath enough to do it. Mercy
will get you killed, but sometimes it's all that makes us human.

I made the calls. I chose a man's name first, Kevin, no last
name. His voice was thick with sleep, gruff, like he smoked.
"Who the hell is this?"

"Gracious," I said, "very gracious."

"Who is this?"

"It's Anita Blake. Do you know who I am?" When trying
to be threatening, less is more. Me and Clint Eastwood.

He was quiet for nearly thirty seconds, and I let the silence
build. His breath had sped up. I could almost feel his pulse
quickening over the phone.

He answered like he was used to strange phone calls and pack
business. "You're our lupa."

"Very good, Kevin, very good." Condescending is also
good.

He coughed to clear his throat. "What do you want?"

"I want you to come down to St. Louis University Hospital.
Stephen and Nathaniel have been hurt. I want you to guard them
for me."

"Nathaniel, he's one of the wereleopards."

"That's right."

"Sylvie's forbidden us to help the wereleopards."

"Is Sylvie your lupa?" Questions are great, but only if you
know the answers. If you ask questions and the answers surprise
you, you look silly. Hard to be threatening when you look ill-
informed.

He was quiet for a second. "No."

"Who is?"

I heard him swallow. "You are."

"Do I outrank her?"

"You know you do."

"Then get your butt down here, and do what I ask."

"Sylvie will hurt me, lupa. She really will."

"I'll see that she doesn't."

"You're just Richard's human girlfriend. You can't fight Sylvie, not and live."

"You're right, Kevin. I can't fight Sylvie, but I can kill her."

"What do you mean?"

"If she hurts you for helping me, I'll kill her."

"You can't mean that."

I sighed. "Look, Kevin, I've met Sylvie. Trust me when I say that I could point a gun at her head and pull the trigger. I can and will kill Sylvie if she forces me to. No jokes, no bluffs, no games." I listened to my voice as I said it. I sounded tired, almost bored, and so serious it was almost frightening.

"All right, I'll do it, but if you let me down she may kill me."

"You have my protection, Kevin, and I know what that means in the pack."

"It means I have to acknowledge you as dominant to me," he said.

"It also means that if anyone challenges you, I can help you fight your battles. Seems like a fair trade."

Silence filled the phone lines again. His breathing had slowed, deepened. "Promise me you won't get me killed."

"I can't promise that, Kevin, but I can promise that if Sylvie kills you, I'll kill her for you."

Silence, shorter this time. "I believe you would. I'll be at the hospital in forty minutes or less."

"Thanks, I'll be waiting."

I hung up and made the other two calls. They both agreed to come down. I'd drawn a line in the sand with Sylvie on one side and me on the other. She wasn't going to like it, not one little bit. Couldn't blame her. If our places were reversed, I'd have been pissed. But she should have left Richard alone. Irving had said it was like Richard was wounded, like the heart had gone out of him. I'd helped put that wound there. I'd cut his heart into tiny little pieces and danced on them. Not deliberately. My intentions were good, but you know what they say about good intentions.

I couldn't love Richard, but I could kill for him. Killing was the more practical of the two gifts. And lately I'd become very, very practical.

6

SERGEANT RUDOLPH STORR showed up before the baby-sitting werewolves could arrive. I'd called him myself. He was the man in charge of the Regional Preternatural Investigation Team, RPIT, or RIP. A lot of people call us RIP, for Rest in Peace. Hey, at least they know who we are.

Dolph is six foot eight, built like a pro-wrestler, but it isn't just physical size that makes him impressive. He'd taken a squad that had been meant as a joke to appease the liberals and made it work. RPIT had solved more preternatural crimes in the last three years than any other police unit. Including the FBI. Dolph had even been invited up to lecture at Quantico. Not bad for someone who'd been given his command as a punishment. Dolph wasn't exactly an optimist, few cops are, but give him lemons and he made damn fine lemonade.

He closed the door behind him and stared down at me. "The doctor said my detective was in here. I just see you."

"I never said I was a detective. I said I was with the squad. They assumed the rest."

He shook his head. His black hair actually hid the tops of his ears. He was overdue for a hair cut. "If you were playing cop, why didn't you yell at the uniform that was supposed to be on this door?"

I smiled up at him. "I thought I'd leave that to you. I assume he knows that he was a bad boy."

"I took care of it," Dolph said.

He stayed standing at the door. I stayed sitting in my chair. I'd actually managed not to pull my gun on him. I was happy about that. He was staring at me hard enough to hurt without flashing a gun at him.

"What's going on, Anita?"

"You know everything I know," I said.

"How did you happen to be Johnny-on-the-spot?"

"Stephen called me."

"Tell me," he said.

I told him. I even put in the part about the pimping. I wanted that stopped. The cops are pretty good at stopping crime, if you tell the truth. I left out a few things, like me having killed the wereleopards' old alpha. It was the only thing I left out. For me, it was almost the same as being honest.

Dolph blinked at me and took it all down in his trusty notebook. "Are you saying that our victim allowed someone to do this to him?"

I shook my head. "I don't think it's that simple. I think he went there knowing they'd chain him up. He knew there'd be sex and pain, but I don't think he knew they'd come this close to killing him. The doctors actually had to give him blood. His body was going into shock faster than it could fix itself."

"I've heard of wereanimals healing from worse wounds than this," Dolph said.

I shrugged. "Some people heal better than others even among the shapeshifters. Nathaniel is pretty low in the power structure, so I'm told. Maybe part of being weak is not healing as well." I spread my hands wide. "I don't know."

Dolph searched back through his notes. "Someone dropped him off at the emergency entrance wrapped in a sheet. No one saw anything. He just appeared."

"No one ever sees anything, Dolph. Isn't that the rule?"

That earned me a small smile. It was nice to see the smile. Dolph wasn't too happy with me lately. He'd only recently found out that I was dating the Master of the City. He didn't like it. He didn't trust anyone that socialized with the monsters. Couldn't blame him.

"Yeah, that's the rule. Are you telling me everything you know about this, Anita?"

I raised a hand in a scout's salute. "Would I lie to you?"

"If it suited your purpose, yes."

We stared at each other. The silence grew thick enough to walk on. I let it sit there. If Dolph thought I was going to break first, he was wrong. The strain between us wasn't this case. It was his disapproval of my choice of dates. His disappointment in me was always there now. Pressing, weighted, waiting for me to apologize or say, shucks, just kidding. The fact that I was dating a vampire made him trust me less. I understood. Two months ago, even less, and I'd have felt the same way. But here I was dating who, and what, I was dating. Dolph and I, both, had to deal with it.

And yet, he was my friend, and I respected him. I even agreed with him, but if I could ever get out of this damn hospital, I had a date with Jean-Claude tonight. Regardless of my doubts about Richard, morals in general, and the walking dead, I wanted the date. The thought of Jean-Claude waiting for me made my body tight and warm. Embarrassing, but true. I don't think anything short of giving up Jean-Claude would have satisfied Dolph. I wasn't sure that was an option anymore for a lot of reasons. So I sat and looked at Dolph. He stared back. The silence grew thicker with each tick of the clock.

A knock on the door saved us. The officer, now attentively on the door, whispered something to Dolph. Dolph nodded and closed the door. The look he gave me was even less friendly, if that was possible.

"Officer Wayne says that there are three relatives of Stephen's out here. He also says that if they're all relatives, he'll eat his gun."

"Tell him to pucker up," I said. "They're fellow pack members. Werewolves consider that closer than family."

"But legally it's not family," Dolph said.

"How many of your men you want to lose when the next shapeshifter comes through that door?"

"We can shoot them just as good as you can, Anita."

"But you still have to give them a warning before you shoot them, don't you? You still have to treat them like people instead of monsters or you end up in front of the review board."

"Witnesses say you gave Zane, no last name, a warning."

"I was feeling generous."

"You were shooting him in front of witnesses. That always makes you generous."

We went back to staring at each other. Maybe it wasn't just dating a vampire. Maybe it was the fact that Dolph was the ultimate cop and he was beginning to suspect that I was killing people, murdering people. People who hurt me or threatened me did have a tendency to vanish. Not many, but enough. And less than two months ago I'd killed two people where the bodies couldn't be hidden. Self-defense both times. Never saw the inside of a courtroom. Both assassins with records longer than I was tall. The woman's fingerprints had been the answer to several political killings that Interpol had lying around. Big-time bad guys that no one really mourned, at least not the cops.

But it fed Dolph's suspicions. Hell, it did everything but confirm them.

"Why'd you recommend me to Pete McKinnon, Dolph?"

He didn't answer for so long, I thought he wasn't going to, but finally he said, "Because you're the best at what you do, Anita. I may not always approve of your methods, but you help save lives, put away the bad guys. You're better on a murder scene than some of the detectives on my squad."

For Dolph, this was a speech. I opened my mouth, closed it, then said, "Thanks, Dolph. Coming from you, that's a big compliment."

"You just spend too much time with the damn monsters, Anita. I don't mean who you date. I mean all of it. You've played by their rules so long, sometimes you forget what it's like to be normal."

I smiled. "I raise the dead for a living, Dolph. I've never been normal."

He shook his head. "Don't purposely misunderstand what I'm saying, Anita. It's not the fur or the fangs that make you a monster, not always. Sometimes, it's just where you draw the line."

"The fact that I play with monsters is what makes me valuable to you, Dolph. If I played it straight, I wouldn't be as good helping you solve preternatural crimes."

"Yeah, sometimes I wonder if I'd left you alone, not gotten you to consult with us, if you'd be . . . softer."

I frowned at him. "Are you saying you blame yourself for what I've become?" I tried to laugh it off, but his face stopped me.

"How often did you go to the monsters on one of my cases? How often did you have to make bargains with them to help put away a bad guy? If I'd left you alone . . ."

I stood up. I reached out to him, then let my hand fall back without touching him. "I'm not your daughter, Dolph. You're not my keeper. I help the police because I like it. I'm good at it. And who else you gonna call?"

He nodded. "Yeah, who else? The shifters outside can come in and . . . visit the patients."

"Thanks, Dolph."

He took in a long breath and let it out in a big rush of air. "I saw the window that your friend Stephen got shoved through. If he'd been human, he'd be dead. It's just luck that no civilians were killed."

I shook my head. "I think Zane was being careful of the humans, at least. With the strength he has, it would have been easier to kill than to maim."

"Why would he have cared?"

"Because he's in jail, and he gets a bail hearing."

"They won't let him out," Dolph said.

"He didn't kill anyone, Dolph. Since when haven't you seen someone *not* get bail for assault and battery?"

"You think like a cop, Anita. It's what makes you good."

"I think like a cop and like a monster. That's what makes me good."

He nodded, closed his notebook and slipped it into an inner pocket of his jacket. "Yeah, that's what makes you good." He left without another word. He sent in the three werewolves and closed the door.

Kevin was tall, dark, scruffy and smelled like cigarettes. Lorraine was neat and prim like a second-grade schoolteacher. She smelled of White Linen perfume and blinked nervously at me. Teddy, his preference not mine, weighed around three hundred pounds, most of it muscle. He'd buzzed his hair down to a fine dark prickle, and his head looked too small for his massive body. The men looked scary, but it was Lorraine's handshake that left power vibrating down my skin. She looked like a scared rabbit and had enough power to be the big bad wolf.

Within twenty minutes I was free to leave. The mismatched trio of werewolves had divided the shifts so that one of them would be with the boys at all times. Did I trust the new wolves to guard them? Yeah. Because if they abandoned their posts and let Stephen get killed, I really would kill them. If they tried their best and were simply not strong enough, fine, but if they just gave up . . . I'd given Stephen, and now, Nathaniel, my protection. I wasn't kidding. I made sure that all of them knew that.

Kevin said it best, "If Sylvie shows up, we'll send her to you."

"You do that."

He shook his head, playing with an unlit cigarette. I'd told him he couldn't smoke it, but even touching it seemed to comfort him. "You've pissed in her pond. I hope you can clean it up."

I smiled. "Eloquent, Kevin, very eloquent."

"Eloquent or not, Sylvie is going to bust your ass if she can."

The smile widened. I couldn't help it. "Let me worry about my own ass. My job is to keep your ass out of the sling, not mine."

The three werewolves looked at me. There was something on all their faces, almost the same expression, but I couldn't read it. "Being lupa is more than just fighting for dominance," said Lorraine in a small voice.

"I know that," I said.

"Do you?" she asked, and there was something childlike in the question.

"I think so."

"You kill us if we fail you," Kevin said, "but will you die for us? Will you risk the same price you ask us to pay?"

I liked Kevin better when he wasn't being eloquent. I stared at these three strangers. People I'd just met. Would I risk my life for them? Could I ask them to risk their lives for me if I wasn't willing to return the favor?

I looked at them, really looked at them. Lorraine's small hands clutching her purse so tightly her hands shook. Teddy, who stared at me with calm, accepting eyes, but there was a challenge in them, an intelligence that you might miss if you just looked at the body. Kevin, who looked like he should be in an alley looking for a fix, or in a bar drinking up his share of whiskey. There was something underneath the cynicism. It was fear. Fear that I'd be like all the rest. A user who didn't give a damn about them. Raina had been that, and now Sylvie. The pack was supposed to be their refuge, their protection, not the thing they feared most.

Their warm, electric power filled the room, flowed out of them, dancing over my body. They were nervous, scared. Strong emotions made most shapeshifters leak power. If you were sensitive to it, you'd feel it. I'd felt it a lot over the years. This time was different somehow. I didn't just sense the power, my body reacted to it. Not merely a shivering of skin, a line of goose bumps, but something deeper. It was almost sexual, but that wasn't it either. It was as if the power had found a part of me, caressed a part of me, that I never knew was there.

Their power filled me, touched something, and I felt it, whatever it was, open up like a switch being thrown. A rush of warm energy welled up inside of my body and spread out through my skin, as if every pore of my body was emitting a warm line of air. It brought a soft gasp to my throat. I knew the taste of the power, and it wasn't Jean-Claude. It was Richard. Somehow, I'd tapped into Richard's power. I wondered if he felt it all the way out of state, studying for his degree.

Six weeks ago to save both their lives, I'd let Jean-Claude bind the three of us to each other. They were dying, and I couldn't let them go. Richard had invaded my dreams by accident, but mostly Jean-Claude had kept us apart because anything else was too painful. This was the first time I'd felt Richard's power since then. The first time I knew for certain that the tie was still there, still strong. Magic is like that. Even hate can't kill it.

I suddenly had the words, words I couldn't have known. "I am lupa, I am the all-mother, I am your guardian, your refuge, your peace. I will stand with you against all harm. Your enemies are my enemies. I share blood and flesh with you. We are lukoi, we are pack."

The warmth cut off abruptly. I staggered. Only Teddy's hand kept me from falling to the floor. "Are you all right?" he asked in a voice as deep and impressive as the rest of him.

I nodded. "I'm fine, I'm fine." As soon as I could, I stepped back. Richard had felt the pull hundreds of miles away, and he'd cut me off. He'd slammed the door shut without knowing what I was doing, or why. A rush of rage danced down inside my head like a silent scream. He was so angry.

We were both bound to Jean-Claude. I was his human servant and Richard was his wolf. It was a painful intimacy.

''You aren't lukoi,'' Lorraine said. ''You aren't a shapeshifter. How did you do that?''

I smiled. ''Trade secret.'' Truth was, I didn't know. I'd have
to ask Jean-Claude tonight. I hoped he could explain it. He was
only the third master vampire in their long history to have bound
both a mortal and a shapeshifter into a single bond. I suspected
strongly that there wasn't a manual, and that Jean-Claude
winged it more often than I wanted to know.

Teddy went down on his knees. ''You are lupa.'' The other
two followed him. They abased themselves like good little submissive wolves, though Kevin didn't like it, and neither did I.
But I wasn't sure how much was form and how much was
necessary. I wanted them submissive because I didn't want to
have to fight anybody, or kill anybody. So I let them crawl on
the floor and run their hands along my legs, and sniff my skin
like dogs. Which is when the nurse came in.

Everybody got up off the floor. I tried to explain and finally
stopped. The nurse just stood there staring at all of us, a strange
frozen smile on her face. She finally backed out without doing
a damn thing. ''I'll send Doctor Wilson in to check on them.''
She nodded her head too often and too rapidly and shut the door
behind her. If she'd been wearing heels, I'd have bet we could
have heard her run.

So much for not being one of the monsters.

7

TUCKING IN THE baby-sitting werewolves made me late for my date. Taking time to read McKinnon's file made me later, but if there was a fire tonight, it'd be embarrassing not to be prepared. I learned two things from the file. One, that all the fires had been started after dark, which made me think instantly of vampires. Except that vampires couldn't start fires. It wasn't one of their abilities. In fact fire was one of the things they feared most. Oh, I'd seen a few vamps that could control existing flames to a small extent. Make a candle flame rise or fall, parlor tricks, but fire was the element of purity. Purity and the vamps didn't mix. The second thing I learned from the file was that I didn't know much about fires in general or arson in particular. I was going to need a book or a good lecture.

Jean-Claude had made reservations at Demiche's, a very nice restaurant. I'd had to run home, to my new rented house, to change. It had put me late enough that I'd arranged to meet him at the restaurant. The trouble with fancy dates was where to put my weapons. Women's dress clothes are the ultimate challenge to concealed-weapon carry.

Formals hid more but made grabbing the weapon harder. Anything form-fitting made it difficult. Tonight I was wearing a spaghetti-strap formal with slits so high on either side, I'd had to make sure that the hose were a matching off-black, and the underwear was lacy and black. I knew myself well enough to know that sometime during the evening I'd forget and flash the undies. And if I had to go for the gun, I'd certainly flash. So why wear it? Answer: I had a Firestar 9mm pistol tucked inside a bellyband.

The bellyband was an elastic strap that went over the underwear, but under the outerwear. It was designed to wear under a button-down dress shirt. Pull the shirt up with the free hand, pull the gun out, and violà, start shooting. The bellyband didn't work well under most formals, because you had yards of cloth to raise before you could get to the gun. It was better than nothing, but only if the bad guy was patient. But this dress, all I had to do was put my hand up through one of the slits. I had to pull the gun out, down, and out from under the dress, so it still wasn't speedy, but it wasn't bad. The bellyband also did not work with an especially form-fitting dress. Nobody gains weight in the shape of a gun.

I'd actually found a strapless bra that matched the black panties, so once I took off the gun and dress, I was wearing lingerie. The shoes were higher heels than I'd normally accept, but it was either that or hem the dress. Since I refuse to sew, heels it was.

The one major drawback to the spaghetti straps was that it showed off all my scars. I'd thought about buying a little cover-up jacket, but this wasn't a dress that was meant for a jacket. So screw it. Jean-Claude had seen the scars before, and the few people rude enough to give second glances could have an eyeful.

I was getting pretty good at makeup, eye shadow, blusher, lipstick. The lipstick was red—very, very red. But I had the coloring for it. Pale skin, black curly hair, pure brown eyes. I was all contrasts and strong colors the bright red lipstick matched. I was feeling pretty spiffy until I got a glimpse of Jean-Claude.

He was sitting at the table, waiting for me. I could see him from the entryway, though the maitre d' was two people ahead of me. I didn't mind. I enjoyed the view.

Jean-Claude's hair is black and curly, but he'd done something to it so it was straight and fine, falling past his shoulders, curled under at the ends. His face seemed even more delicate, like fine porcelain. He was beautiful, not handsome. I wasn't sure what saved his face from being feminine—some line of his cheek, bend of his jaw, something. You would never mistake him for anything other than male. He was dressed in royal blue, a color I'd never seen him in. A short jacket of a shining, almost metallic cloth was overlaid with black lace in a pattern of flowers. The shirt was his typical frilled, à la 1600's shirt, but it was a rich, vibrant blue, down to the mound of ruffles that climbed up his neck to frame his face and spill out the sleeves of the jacket to cover the upper half of his slender white hands.

He held an empty wineglass in his hand, spinning the stem of the glass between his fingers, watching the light spill through the crystal. He couldn't drink wine more than a sip at a time and mourned it.

The maitre d' led me through the tables towards him. He looked up, and seeing his face full-on made my chest tight, and it was suddenly hard to breathe. The blue so close to his face made his eyes bluer than I'd ever seen them, not the color of midnight skies, but cobalt blue, the color of a good sapphire. But no jewel ever had that weight of intelligence, of dark knowledge. The look in his eyes as he watched me walk towards him made me shiver. Not cold, not fear. Anticipation.

In the heels, and with the slits on both sides of the dress, there was an art to walking. You had to sort of throw yourself into it, a sling-back, slouching, hip-swinging walk, or the dress wrapped around your legs and the heels twisted at your ankles. You had to walk like you knew you could wear it and look wonderful. If you doubted yourself, hesitated, you'd fall to the floor and turn into a pumpkin. After years of my not being able to wear heels and dress clothes, Jean-Claude had taught me in a month what my stepmother couldn't teach me in twenty years.

He stood, and I didn't mind, though once upon a time I'd pissed off a prom date by standing every time that he did for the other girls at the table. One, I'd mellowed since then; two, I could see the rest of Jean-Claude's outfit.

The pants were black linen, clinging smooth and perfect to his body, so form-fitting that I knew there was nothing under the pants but him. Black boots climbed his legs to the knees. The boots were soft, crepe-like leather, wrinkled and pettable.

He glided towards me, and I stood there watching him come. I was still half afraid of him. Afraid of how much I wanted him. I was like a rabbit caught in headlights, frozen, waiting for death to come. But did the rabbit's heart beat fast and faster? Did its breath come like a choking thing into its throat? Was there an eager rush to the fear, or was there just death?

He wrapped his arms around me, drawing me close. His pale hands were warm as they slid over my bare arms. He'd fed on someone tonight, borrowed their warmth. But they'd been willing, even eager. The Master of the City never went begging for donors. Blood was about the only bodily fluid I wouldn't share with him. I slid my hands over the silk of his shirt, underneath the short jacket. I wanted to mold my body against his stolen warmth. I wanted to run my hands over the roughness of the linen, contrasting it to the smoothness of the silk. Jean-Claude was always a sensual feast, right down to his clothing.

He kissed my lips lightly. We'd learned that the lipstick came off. Then he tilted my head to one side and breathed along my face, down my neck. His breath was like a line of fire along my skin. He spoke with his lips just above the big pulse in my neck. "You are lovely tonight, *ma petite*." He pressed his lips against my skin, softly. I let out a shuddering breath and drew back from him.

It was a greeting among the vampires to plant a light kiss above the big pulse in the throat. It was a gesture reserved for the very closest friends. It showed great trust and affection. To refuse it meant you were angry or distrustful. It still seemed too intimate for public consumption to me, but I'd seen him use it with others and seen fights start with a refusal. It was an old gesture just coming back into vogue. In fact, it was becoming a chic greeting among entertainers and others of the same ilk. Better than kissing the air near someone's face, I guess.

The maitre d' held my chair. I waved him off. It wasn't feminism, but lack of grace. I never managed to be scooted under a table without the chair banging my legs or being so far from the table I had to finish scooting forward on my own. So the heck with it, I'd do it myself.

Jean-Claude watched me struggle into my chair, smiling, but he didn't offer to help. I'd finally broken him of that at least. He sat down in his own chair with a graceful fall. It was an almost foppish movement, but he was like a cat. Even at rest there was the potential of muscle under skin, a physical presence that was utterly masculine. I used to think it was vampire trickery. But it was him, just him.

I shook my head.

"What's wrong, *ma petite*?"

"I felt pretty spiffy until I saw you. Now I feel like one of the ugly stepsisters."

He tut-tutted at me. "You know you are lovely, *ma petite*.

Shall I feed your vanity by telling you how much?''

"I wasn't fishing for compliments.'' I gestured at him and shook my head again. "You look amazing tonight.''

He smiled, dipping his head to one side so his hair swept forward. "*Merci, ma petite.*''

"Is the hair permed straight?'' I asked. "It looks great,'' I added hastily, and it did, but I hoped it wasn't as permanent as a perm. I loved his curls.

"If it was, what would you say?''

"If it was, you'd have just said so. Now you're teasing me.''

"Would you mourn the loss of my curls?'' he asked.

"I could the return the favor,'' I said.

He widened his eyes in mock horror. "Not your crowning glory, *ma petite*, *mon Dieu*.'' He was laughing at me, but I was used to it.

"I didn't know you could get linen that tight,'' I said.

His smile widened. "And I did not know you could hide a gun under such a . . . slender dress.''

"As long as I don't hug anybody, they'll never know.''

"Very true.''

A waiter came and asked if we wanted drinks. I ordered water and Coke. Jean-Claude declined. If he could have ordered anything, it would have been wine.

Jean-Claude brought his chair over to sit almost beside me. When dinner came, he'd move back to his place setting, but picking out the meal was part of the night's entertainment. It had taken me several dinner dates to realize what Jean-Claude wanted—no, almost needed. I was Jean-Claude's human servant. I bore three of his marks. One of the side effects of the second mark was that he could take sustenance through me. So if we'd been on a long sea voyage, he wouldn't have had to feed off of any humans on the boat. He could live through me for a time. He could also taste food through me.

For the first time in nearly four hundred years he could taste food. I had to eat it for him, but he could enjoy a meal. It was trivial compared to some of the other things he'd gained through the bonding, but it was the thing that seemed to please him most. He ordered food with a childlike glee and watched me eat, tasting it as I did. In private he'd roll on his back like a cat, hands pressed to his mouth as if trying to drain every taste. It was the

only thing he did that was cute. He was gorgeous, sensual, but
rarely cute. I'd gained four pounds in six weeks eating with
him.

He slid his arm over the back of my chair, and we read the
menu together. He leaned close enough for his hair to brush my
cheek. The smell of his perfume, oh, sorry, cologne, caressed
my skin. Though if what Jean-Claude wore was cologne, then
Brut was bug spray.

I moved my head away from the caress of his hair, mainly
because the feel of him this close was all I could think about.
Maybe if I'd taken him up on his invitation to live with him at
the Circus of the Damned, some of this heat would have dissi-
pated. But I'd rented a house in record time in the middle of
nowhere so my neighbors wouldn't get shot up, which is why
I moved out of my last apartment. I hated the house. I wasn't
a house kinda gal. I was a condo kind of gal. But condos had
neighbors, too.

The lace overlay on his jacket was scratchy against my nearly
bare shoulders. He put his hand on my shoulder, smoothing his
fingertips across my skin. His leg brushed my thigh, and I realized I hadn't heard a damn thing he'd said. It was embarrassing.

He stopped talking and looked at me, gazed at me from inches
away with those extraordinary eyes. "I have been explaining
my menu choices to you. Have you heard any of it?"

I shook my head. "Sorry."

He laughed, and it hovered over my skin like his breath, warm
and sliding over my body. It was a vampire trick but low on
the scale, and had become public foreplay for us. In private we
did other things.

He whispered against my cheek. "No apologies, *ma petite*.
You know it pleases me that you find me . . . intoxicating."

He laughed again, and I pushed him away. "Go sit on your
side of the table. You've been here long enough to know what
you want."

He moved his chair dutifully back to his place setting. "I
have what I want, *ma petite*."

I had to look down and not meet his eyes. Heat crept up my
neck into my face, and I couldn't stop it.

"If you mean what do I want for dinner, that is a different question," he said.

"You are a pain in the ass," I said.

"And so many other places," he said.

I didn't think I could blush more. I was wrong. "Stop it."

"I love the fact that I can make you blush. It is charming."

The tone in his voice made me smile in spite of myself. "This is not a dress to be charming in. I was trying for sexy and sophisticated."

"Can you not be charming as well as sexy and sophisticated? Is there some rule about being all three?"

"Slick, very slick," I said.

He widened his eyes, trying for innocent and failing. He was many things, but innocent wasn't one of them.

"Now, let's start negotiating on dinner," I said.

"You make it sound like a chore."

I sighed. "Before you came along, I thought food was something you ate so you wouldn't die. I will never be as enamored of food as you are. It's almost a fetish with you."

"Hardly a fetish, *ma petite*."

"A hobby, then."

He nodded. "Perhaps."

"So just tell me what you like on the menu, and we'll negotiate."

"All that is required is that you taste what is ordered. You do not have to eat it."

"No, no more of this tasting shit. I've gained weight. I never gain weight."

"You have gained four pounds, so I am told. Though I have searched diligently for this phantom four pounds and cannot find them. It brings your weight up to a grand total of one hundred and ten pounds, correct?"

"That's right."

"Oh, *ma petite*, you are growing gargantuan."

I looked at him, and it was not a friendly look. "Never tease a woman about her weight, Jean-Claude. At least not an American twentieth-century one."

He spread his hands wide. "My deepest apologies."

"When you apologize, try not to smile at the same time. It ruins the effect," I said.

His smile widened until a hint of fang peeked out. "I will try to remember that for the future."

The waiter returned with my drinks. "Would you like to order, or do you need a few minutes?"

Jean-Claude looked at me.

"A few minutes."

The negotiation began.

Twenty minutes later I needed a refill on my Coke, and we knew what we wanted. The waiter returned, pen poised, hopeful. I'd won on the appetizer, so we weren't having one. I'd given up the salad, and let him have the soup. Potato-leek soup, hey, it wasn't a hardship. We both wanted the steak.

"The petite cut," I told the waiter.

"How would you like that prepared?"

"Half well-done, half rare."

The waiter blinked at me. "Excuse me, madam?"

"It's an eight-ounce cut, right?"

He nodded.

"Cut it in half, and cook four ounces of it well-done, and four ounces of it rare."

He frowned at me. "I don't think we can do that."

"At these prices you should bring the cow out and have a ritual sacrifice at the table. Just do it." I handed him the menu. He took it.

Still frowning, he turned to Jean-Claude. "And you, sir?"

Jean-Claude gave a small smile. "I will not be ordering food tonight."

"Would you like wine with dinner, then, sir?"

He never missed a beat. "I do not drink—wine."

I coughed Coke all over the tablecloth. The waiter did everything but give me the Heimlich. Jean-Claude laughed until tears trailed from the corners of his eyes. You couldn't really tell it in this light, but I knew that the tears were tinged red. Knew that there would be pinkish stains on the linen napkin when he was done dabbing his eyes. The waiter fled without having gotten the joke. Staring across the table at the smiling vampire, I wondered if I got the joke or was the butt of the joke. There were nights when I wasn't sure which way the grave dirt crumbled.

But when he put his hand out to me across the table, I took it. Definitely, the butt of the joke.

8

DESSERT WAS RASPBERRY-CHOCOLATE cheesecake. A triple threat to any diet plan. Truthfully, I preferred my cheesecake straight. Fruit, except for strawberries, and chocolate just muddied the pure cream cheese taste. But Jean-Claude liked it, and dessert took the place of the wine I'd refused to order with dinner. I hated the taste of alcohol. So Jean-Claude's choice of dessert. Besides, the restaurant did not serve plain cheesecake. Not artistic enough, I guess.

I ate all the cheesecake, chased the last chocolate curl across the plate, and pushed it away. I was full. Jean-Claude had laid his arm across the tablecloth, rested his cheek on his arm, and closed his eyes, swooning, trying to savor every last taste. He blinked at me, as if coming out of a trance. He spoke, head still resting on his arm, "You have left some whipped cream, *ma petite*."

"I'm full," I said.

"It is real whipped cream. It melts on the tongue and glides across the palate."

I shook my head. "I am done. If I eat any more, I'll be sick."

He gave a long-suffering sigh and sat back up. "There are nights when I despair of you, *ma petite*."

I smiled. "Funny, I think the same thing about you sometimes."

He nodded his head, making a small bow. "Touché, *ma petite*, touché." He stared off past my shoulder and stiffened. The smile didn't fade from his face. It was wiped clean. His face was its blank unreadable mask. And I knew without turning around that someone was behind me, someone he feared.

I managed to drop my napkin, and picked it up with my left

hand. With my right hand I drew the Firestar. When I sat back
up, the gun was in my hand in my lap. Though shooting up
Demiche's seemed like a bad idea. But hey, it wouldn't be the
first bad idea I'd had.

I turned to see a couple walking towards us through the tables
and crystal. The woman looked tall until you got a glimpse of
the heels she was wearing. Stiletto, four inches. I'd have broken
my ankle trying to walk in them. The dress was white, square
necked, form-fitting, and more expensive than my entire outfit,
even if you threw in the gun. Her hair was a white-blond so
pale it matched the dress and the simple white mink stole curled
around her shoulders. The hair was piled in a mound atop her
head with a sparkle of silver and the crystal fire of diamonds to
frame the hair like a crown. She was chalk-white, and despite
the expert makeup I knew she hadn't fed yet tonight.

The man was human, though there was a thrumming energy
to him that made me want to take back the human part. He was
tanned that wonderful rich brown that olive skin can manage.
His hair was a luxuriant curling brown, shaved short on the
sides, but done so it fell in curls near his eyes. The eyes were
pure brown and watched Jean-Claude steadily, joyously, but it
was a dark joy. He was dressed in a white linen suit, complete
with silk tie.

They stopped at our table like I knew they would. The man's
handsome face was all for Jean-Claude. I might as well have
not been there. He had very strong features, from high cheekbones to an almost-hooked nose. An inch either direction and
his face would have been homely. Instead, it was striking, compelling, handsome in an utterly masculine way.

Jean-Claude stood, hands loose at his side, face beautiful and
empty. "Yvette, it has been a long time."

She smiled wonderfully. "A very long time, Jean-Claude.
You remember Balthasar?" She touched the man's arm, and he
obligingly slid it around her waist. He planted a chaste kiss on
her pale cheek. He looked at me then for the first time. It wasn't
a look I'd ever gotten from a man. If it had been a woman, I'd
have said she was jealous. The vampire's English was perfect.
Her accent was pure French.

"Of course, I remember him," Jean-Claude said. "Time
spent with Balthasar was always memorable."

The man turned back to Jean-Claude then. ''But not memorable enough to keep you with us.'' He, too, sounded French, but there was an undercurrent of some other language. It was like mixing blue and red and getting purple.

''I am master of my own territory. It is what everyone dreams of, is it not?''

''Some dream of a seat on the council,'' Yvette said. Her voice was still mildly amused, but there was an undercurrent now, like swimming in dark water when you know there are sharks.

''I do not aspire to such lofty heights,'' Jean-Claude said.

''Really?'' Yvette said.

''Truly,'' Jean-Claude said.

She smiled, but her eyes stayed distant and empty. ''We shall see.''

''There is nothing to see, Yvette. I am content where I am.''

''If that is so, you have nothing to fear from us.''

''We have nothing to fear regardless,'' I said. I smiled when I said it.

Both of them looked at me as if I was a dog that had done an interesting trick. I was really beginning not to like either of them.

''Yvette and Balthasar are envoys of the council, *ma petite*.''

''Bully for them,'' I said.

''She doesn't seem very impressed with us,'' Yvette said. She turned full-face to me. Her eyes were greyish-green, with tiny flecks of amber dancing round the pupils. I felt her try to suck me under with those eyes, and it didn't work. Her power raised goose bumps on my skin, but she couldn't capture me with her eyes. She was powerful, but she wasn't a master vampire. I could feel her age like an ache in my skull. A thousand years, at least. The last vamp I'd met who was that old had cleaned my clock. But Nikolaos had been Master of the City, and Yvette would never be that. If a vamp hadn't attained master status in a thousand years, she, or he, was never going to. A vamp gained power and abilities with age, but there was a limit. Yvette had reached hers. I stared into her eyes, let her power tickle across my skin, and wasn't impressed.

She frowned. ''Impressive.''

''Thanks,'' I said.

Balthasar stepped around her and went to one knee in front of me. He put one hand on the back of my chair and leaned into me. If Yvette wasn't a master, then he wasn't her human servant. Only a master vampire could make a human servant. Which meant he belonged to someone else. Someone I hadn't met yet. Why did I get the feeling I'd be meeting that someone soon?

"My master is a council member," Balthasar said. "You have no idea what kind of power he wields."

"Ask me if I care."

Anger flared across his face, darkening his eyes, making his grip on my chair tight. He laid his hand on my leg just above my knee and started to squeeze. I'd played with the monsters long enough to know what supernatural strength feels like. His fingers dug into my flesh, and I knew he could keep squeezing until muscle popped and he bared my bones to the air.

I grabbed his silk tie and pulled him close, and shoved the barrel of the Firestar into his chest. I watched the surprise chase across his face from inches away.

"Bet I can blow a hole in your chest before you can crush my leg."

"You wouldn't dare."

"Why not?" I asked.

A touch of fear flowed through his eyes. "I am the human servant of a council member."

"Not impressed," I said. "Try door number two."

He frowned at me. "I don't understand."

"Give her a better reason not to kill you," Jean-Claude said.

"If you shoot me here in front of witnesses, you will go to jail."

I sighed. "There is that." I jerked him close enough that our faces almost touched. "Take your hand off my knee, slowly, and I won't pull this trigger. Keep hurting me, and I'll take my chances with the police."

He stared at me. "You would do it, you really would do it."

"I don't bluff, Balthasar. Remember that for future reference, and maybe I won't have to kill you."

His hand eased, then moved slowly away from me. I let him move back, his tie sliding through my hand like a fishing line. I eased back in my chair. The gun had never made it out from under the tablecloth. We'd been the soul of discretion.

The waiter came over anyway. "Is there a problem?"

"No problem," I said.

"Please bring our check," Jean-Claude said.

"Right away," the waiter said. He watched a little nervously while Balthasar got to his feet. Balthasar smoothed down the wrinkles in his linen pants, but there's only so much you can do with linen. It really isn't meant to be knelt in.

"You have won the first round, Jean-Claude. Be careful that it does not become a Pyrrhic victory." Yvette said. She and Balthasar left without ever taking a table. Guess they weren't hungry.

"What's going on?" I asked.

Jean-Claude sat back down. "Yvette is a council toady. Balthasar is the human servant of one of the most powerful council members."

"Why are they here?"

"I believe it is because of Mr. Oliver."

Mr. Oliver had been the oldest vampire I'd ever met. The oldest one I'd ever heard hinted at. He'd been a million years old, no joke, a million years, give or take. For all those with a head for prehistory, yes, that does mean he wasn't *Homo sapiens*. *Homo erectus*, and able to walk around during the day, though I never saw him cross direct sunlight. He'd been the only vamp to ever fool me for even a few moments into thinking he was human, which is nicely ironic, since he wasn't human at all. He'd had a plan to take out Jean-Claude, take over the vamps in the area, and force them to slaughter humans. Oliver had thought a slaughter like that would force the authorities to make vamps illegal again. He thought vampires would spread too quickly with legal rights and take over the human race. I'd sort of agreed with him.

His plan might have worked if I hadn't killed him. How I managed to kill him is a long story, but I'd ended up in a coma. A week unconscious, gone, so close to death that the doctors didn't know how I survived. Of course, they hadn't been too clear on why I was in a coma to begin with, and no one felt like explaining vampire marks and *Homo erectus* vampires.

I stared at Jean-Claude. "The crazy son of bitch that tried to take you out last Halloween?"

"*Oui.*"

"What about him?"

"He was a council member."

I almost laughed. "No way. He was old, older than sin, but he wasn't that powerful."

"I told you he agreed to limit his powers, *ma petite*. I did not know who and what he was at first, but he was the council member known as the Earthmover."

"Excuse me?"

"He could cause the earth to shake by his power alone."

"No way," I said.

"Yes way, *ma petite*. He agreed not to cause the earth to swallow the city because it would be blamed on an earthquake. He wanted the bloodletting to be blamed on vampires. You remember his plan was to drive vampires back to being illegal. An earthquake would not do that. A bloodbath would. No one, not even you, believes that a mere vampire can cause an earthquake."

"Damn straight, I don't." I stared at his careful face. "You're serious."

"Deadly serious, *ma petite*."

It was too much to take in all at once. When in doubt, ignore and be terribly unimpressed. "So we took out a council member, so what?"

He shook his head. "There is no fear in you, *ma petite*. Do you understand what danger we are all in?"

"No, and what do you mean the 'danger we are all in'? Who else is in danger besides us?"

"All our people," he said.

"Define 'all,' " I said.

"All my vampires, anyone that the council considers ours."

"Larry?" I asked.

He sighed. "Perhaps."

"Should I call him? Warn him? How much danger?"

"I am not sure. No one has ever slain a council member and not taken their place."

"I killed him, not you."

"You are my human servant. The council sees all that you do as an extension of my actions."

I stared at him. "You mean anyone I kill is your kill?"

He nodded.

"I wasn't your servant when I killed Oliver."

"I would keep that bit of knowledge to ourselves."

"Why?"

"They may not kill me, *ma petite*, but a vampire hunter who killed a council member would be executed. There would be no trial, no hesitation."

"Even though I'm your human servant now?"

"That might save you. It is one of our most stringent laws not to destroy another's servant."

"So they can't kill me because I'm your servant."

"But they can harm you, *ma petite*. They can harm you so very much that you may wish for death."

"You mean torture?"

"Not in a traditional sense. But they are masters at finding that which terrifies you most and using it against you. They will use your desires against you and twist everything you are into a shape of their choosing."

"I've met master vampires that could sense your heart's desire and use it against you."

"Everything you have seen of us before, *ma petite*, is like a distant dream. The council is the reality. They are the nightmare on which we are all based. The thing that even we fear."

"Yvette and Balthasar didn't seem that scary to me."

He looked at me. There was no expression on his face. It was a mask, smooth, pleasant, hidden. "If they did not frighten you, *ma petite*, it is only because you do not know them. Yvette is a toady of the council because they are powerful enough to give her a ready supply of victims."

"Victims? You aren't talking about human prey, are you?"

"It can be human. But Yvette is considered perverted even by other vampires."

I wasn't sure I wanted to know, but . . . "Perverted in what way?"

He sighed and looked down at his hands. They lay very still on the tablecloth. It was like he was pulling away from me. I could see the walls clicking back into place. He was rebuilding himself into Jean-Claude, Master of the City. It was a shock to realize that there had been a change. It had been so gradual that I hadn't realized that with me, on our dates, he was different. I don't know if he was more himself or more what he thought I wanted him to be, but he was more "relaxed," less guarded. Watching him put on his public face while I sat across from him was almost depressing.

"Yvette loves the dead."

I frowned at him. "But she's a vampire. That's redundant."

He stared at me, and it wasn't a friendly look. "I will not sit here and debate with you, *ma petite*. You share my bed. If I were a zombie, you would not touch me."

"That's true." It took me a handful of seconds to understand what he'd just said. "Are you telling me that Yvette likes to have sex with zombies, real rotting corpses?"

"Among other things, yes."

I couldn't keep the disgust off my face. "Good Lord, that's . . ." Words failed me. Then I found a word. "She's a necrophiliac."

"She will use a dead body if nothing else is available, but her true joy is the rotted animated corpse. She would find your talent most appealing, *ma petite*. You could raise her an unending stream of partners."

"I wouldn't raise the dead for her amusement."

"Not initially," he said.

"No, not under any circumstances."

"The council has a way of finding circumstances that can force you to do almost anything."

I watched his face and wished I could read it. But I understood. He was hiding from them, already. "How deep is the hole we're in?"

"Deep enough to bury us all, if the council chooses."

"Maybe I shouldn't have put the gun up," I said.

"Perhaps not," he said.

The check came. We paid. We left. I made a stop at the ladies' room on the way out and retrieved the gun. Jean-Claude took my car keys, so I wouldn't have to handle anything but the gun. It was a short walk from bathroom to door. Black gun against a black dress. Either no one noticed, or no one wanted to get involved. What else was new?

9

THE PARKING LOT was a dark expanse of shining blackness with
pools of light spotlighting gleaming cars. Jaguars, Volvos, and
Mercedes were the dominant species in the lot. I caught a
glimpse of my Jeep at the far end of a line. I lost sight of it as
we walked between the cars. Jean-Claude held my car keys
cupped in his hand so they didn't rattle as he moved. We
weren't holding hands, or anything else now. I had the Firestar
in a two-handed grip, pointed at the ground, but ready. I was
scanning the parking lot. My eyes flicking back and forth. I
wasn't coy about it. A cop would have known what I was doing
from yards away. I was searching for danger, searching for tar-
gets.

I felt both silly and nervous. The skin across my bare shoulders was trying to crawl down my spine. It was silly, but I'd
have felt better in jeans and a shirt. More secure.

"I don't think they're out here," I said softly.

"I'm sure you are right, *ma petite*. Yvette and Balthasar have
delivered their message and run back to their masters."

I glanced at him before turning my attention back to the parking lot. "Then why am I in combat mode?"

"Because the council travels with an entourage. We have not
seen the last of them tonight, *ma petite*. Of that, I can promise
you."

"Great."

We came around the last cars between us and my Jeep. There
was a man leaning against the Jeep. The Firestar was just suddenly pointing at him. No thinking, just paranoia—oh, sorry,
caution.

Jean-Claude froze beside me, utterly motionless. The old

vampires can do that—just seem to stop, stop breathing, stop moving, stop everything. As if, if you looked away, they might just disappear.

The man leaned on the back of my Jeep in profile. He was in the middle of lighting a cigarette. You'd have thought he hadn't seen us, but I knew better. I was pointing a gun at him. He knew we were there. The match flared, showing one of the most perfect profiles I'd ever seen. His hair shone golden in the light, shoulder-length, thick waves to frame his face. He tossed the match to the pavement with a practiced flick of his hand. He took the cigarette from his mouth and raised his face skyward. The street light played along his face and golden hair. He blew three perfect smoke rings and laughed.

That laugh trailed down my spine as if he'd touched me. It made me shiver, and I wondered how the hell I'd thought he was human.

"Asher," Jean-Claude said. That one word was spoken without emotion, empty of meaning. But it was all I could do not to look at Jean-Claude's face. I knew who Asher was, but only by reputation. Asher and his human servant, Julianna had traveled with Jean-Claude across Europe for a couple of decades. They'd been a ménage à trois, the closest thing Jean-Claude had had to a family since he became a vampire. Jean-Claude had been called away to his dying mother's bedside. Asher and Julianna had been taken by the Church. Read witch-hunters.

Asher turned and gave us his right profile. The street light that had caressed the perfection of his left side seemed harsh now. The right side of his face looked like melted candle wax. Burn scars, acid scars, holy water. Vampires couldn't heal damage done by holy objects. The priests had had a theory that they could burn the devil out of Asher, one drop of holy water at a time.

I kept the gun on him, solid, no wavering. I'd seen worse, recently. I'd seen a vampire whose face had rotted away on one side. An eye had been rolling in a bare socket. Compared to that, Asher was a *GQ* cover boy. The thing that made the scarring worse somehow was that the rest of him was so perfect. It made it worse somehow, more obscene. They'd left his eyes pure, and the midline of his face, so his nose, the fullness of his mouth, sat in a sea of scars. Jean-Claude had saved him before the zealots killed him, but Julianna had been burned as a witch.

Asher never forgave Jean-Claude for the death of the woman they both loved. In fact, last I'd heard, he was asking for my death. He would kill Jean-Claude's human servant as revenge. The council had refused him up until now.

"Step away from the Jeep, slowly," I said.

"Would you shoot me for leaning against your car?" He sounded amused, pleasant. The tone in his voice, the way he chose his words, reminded me of Jean-Claude when I'd first met him. Asher pushed to his feet using just his body. He blew a smoke ring at me and laughed again.

The sound slithered across my skin like the touch of fur, soft and feeling—oh, so slightly—of death. It was Jean-Claude's laugh, and that was unnerving as hell.

Jean-Claude took a deep, shuddering breath and stepped forward. He didn't block my line of sight though, and he didn't tell me to put the gun down. "Why are you here, Asher?" His voice held something I'd seldom heard, regret.

"Is she going to shoot me?"

"Ask her yourself. I am not the one holding the gun."

"So it is true. You do not control your own servant."

"The best human servants are those that come willingly to your hand. You taught me that, Asher, you and Julianna."

Asher threw the cigarette on the ground. He took two quick steps forward.

"Don't," I said.

His hands were balled into fists at his side. His anger rode the night like close lightning. "Never, never say her name again. You don't deserve to speak her name."

Jean-Claude gave a shallow bow. "As you wish. Now, what do you want, Asher? Anita will grow impatient soon."

Asher stared at me. He looked at me from head to toe, but it wasn't sexual, though that was in there. It was like he was looking me over, like I was a car he was thinking of buying. His eyes were a strange shade of pale blue. "Would you really shoot me?" He turned his head so that I couldn't see the scars. He knew exactly how the shadows would fall. He gave a smile that was supposed to melt me into my socks. It didn't work.

"Cut the charm and give me a reason *not* to kill you."

He turned his head so that a sheet of golden hair spilled over the right side of his face. If my night vision had been worse, it might have hidden the scars.

"The council extends their invitation to Jean-Claude, Master of the City of St. Louis, and his human servant, Anita Blake. They request your presence this night."

"You may put up the gun, *ma petite*. We are safe until we see the council."

"Just like that," I said. "Last I heard, Asher here wanted to kill me."

"The council refused his request," Jean-Claude said. "Our human servants are too precious to us for them to agree."

"Very true," Asher said.

The two vampires stared at each other. I expected them to try vampiric powers on each other, but they didn't. They just stood there, looking at one another. Their faces gave nothing away, but if they'd been people and not monsters, I'd have told them to hug and make up. You could feel their pain on the air. I realized something I hadn't before. They had loved each other once. Only love can turn to such bitter regret. Julianna had been their link, but it hadn't just been her they loved.

It was time to put the gun up, but irritatingly, I'd have to flash the parking lot. I was really going to have to invest in more dressy pants suits. Dresses just sucked for concealed carry.

There was no one else but the three of us in the parking lot. I turned my back on both of them and raised the dress enough to put up the gun.

"Please, don't be modest on my account," Asher said.

I smoothed the dress into place before I turned around. "Don't flatter yourself."

He smiled, and the look on his face was amused, condescending, and something else. That "something else" bothered me. "Modest. Were you also chaste before our dashing Jean-Claude found you?"

"That's enough, Asher," Jean-Claude said.

"She was a virgin before you?" He made it a question and then threw his head back and laughed. He laughed until he had to lean against the Jeep to steady himself. "You, wasted on a virgin. It is simply too perfect."

"I wasn't a virgin, not that it's any of your damn business."

The laughter stopped so abruptly, it was startling. He slid

down to the ground, sitting on the dark pavement. He stared up at me through a curtain of golden hair. His eyes looked strange and pale. "Not virginal, but chaste."

"I've had enough games for one night," I said.

"The games are just beginning," he said.

"What's that supposed to mean?" I asked.

"It means, *ma petite*, that the council await us. They will have many games for us to play, none of them pleasant."

Asher rose to his feet like he'd been pulled by strings. He stood, brushing himself off. He settled his black overcoat more solidly into place. It was hot for a long coat. Not that he would necessarily care, but it was odd. Vamps usually tried to blend in better than that. Made me wonder what was underneath the coat. You could hide a pretty big gun under an ankle-length coat. I'd never met a vampire that carried a gun, but there was always a first time.

Jean-Claude had said we were safe until we reached the council, but that didn't mean Asher couldn't pull a weapon then and blow us away. It had been beyond careless to put up my gun without patting Asher down first.

I sighed.

"What is wrong, *ma petite*?"

Asher was a vampire. How much more dangerous could he be with a gun? But I couldn't do it. "Let me test my understanding. Is Asher going to ride in the car with us to the meeting?"

"I must, to give you directions," Asher said.

"Then lean against the Jeep."

He frowned at me in an amused, condescending sort of way. "Excuse me?"

"I don't care if you're the second coming of the Antichrist, you can't sit behind me in my own car until I know you're not carrying a weapon."

"*Ma petite*, he is a vampire. If he is sitting behind you in a car, he is close enough to kill you without a gun."

I shook my head. "You're right. I know you're right, but the point isn't logic, Jean-Claude. The point is that I simply can't let him in the car behind me without knowing what's under the coat. I just can't." It was true. Paranoid, but still true.

Jean-Claude knew me better than to argue. "Very well, *ma*

petite. Asher, would you be so kind as to face towards the Jeep.''

Asher smiled brilliantly at both of us, flashing fang. ''You want to pat me down? I could rip you into pieces with my bare hands, and you're worried I have a gun?'' He chuckled, a low, skin-prickling sound. ''That is so very cute.''

Cute? Me? ''Just do it, please.''

He turned to face the Jeep, still laughing softly.

''Hands on the hood, feet apart.'' I got out the gun one more time. Maybe I should just carry it on a chain around my neck. I pressed the barrel into his spine. I felt him stiffen under my hands.

''You are serious about this.''

''Absolutely,'' I said. ''Feet further apart.''

He shifted, but it wasn't enough.

I kicked his feet apart until his balance was off-center and started searching him one-handed.

''Dominant, very dominant. Does she like to be on top?''

I ignored him. More surprising, so did Jean-Claude.

''Slower, slower. Hasn't Jean-Claude taught you not to rush?'' He drew in a breath at the appropriate moment. ''Oooh, that's nice.''

Yes, it was embarrassing, but I searched him top to bottom. There wasn't a damn thing to find. But I felt better. I stepped back until I was out of reach and put the gun up.

He was watching over his shoulder. ''Do the panties match the bra?''

I shook my head. ''You can stand up now.''

He stayed against the car. ''Don't you need to strip-search me?''

''In your dreams,'' I said.

He stood, smoothing his coat back into place. ''You have no idea what I dream, Anita.'' I couldn't read the look on his face, but the look was enough. I didn't want to know what Asher saw when he closed his eyes at the break of day.

''Shall we go?'' Jean-Claude said.

''Are you so eager to throw your life away?'' Asher asked. The anger returned with a rush, chasing out the amused teasing gallant.

''The council will not kill me tonight,'' Jean-Claude said.

"Are you so sure?"

"It is their own laws that have forbidden those of us in the United States to fight amongst ourselves until the law has passed or failed to pass in Washington. The council wants us to remain legal in this country. If they break their own rules, no one else will obey them."

Asher turned full face into the light. "There are worse things than death, Jean-Claude."

Jean-Claude sighed. "I did not desert you, Asher. What can I say to convince you of the truth? You can taste the truth in my words. I came to you as soon as I knew."

"You have had centuries to convince yourself of what you want the truth to be, Jean-Claude. Wanting it to be true doesn't make it so."

"So be it, Asher. But I would undo whatever you think I have done, if I could. I would bring her back if I could."

Asher held up his hand as if he could push the thought away. "No, no, no! You killed her. You let her die. You let her burn to death. I felt her die, Jean-Claude. I was her master. She was so afraid. To the last she thought you would come save her. I was her master and I know that her last words were your name."

Jean-Claude turned his back on Asher. The other vampire closed the distance between them in two striding steps. He grabbed Jean-Claude's arm and swung him around. The street light showed tears on Jean-Claude's face. He was crying for a woman who had been dead over two hundred years. It was a long time for tears.

"You never told me that before," Jean-Claude said softly.

Asher pushed him away hard enough that he stumbled. "Save your tears, Jean-Claude. You'll need them for yourself and for her. They've promised me my revenge."

Jean-Claude touched the back of his hand to the tears. "You can't kill her. They won't allow that."

Asher smiled, and it was most unpleasant. "I don't want her life, Jean-Claude. I want your pain." He walked around me, circling like a shark. I moved with him and knew he was too close. If he rushed me, I'd never get the gun out in time.

"You've finally given me what I need to hurt you, Jean-Claude. You love someone else at last. Love is never free, Jean-Claude. It is the most expensive emotion we have, and I am going to see that you pay in full.'' He stood in front of Jean-Claude, hands in fists by his side. He was trembling with the effort not to strike out. Jean-Claude had stopped crying, but I wasn't sure he'd fight back. In that moment I realized he didn't want to hurt Asher. Guilt is a many splendored thing. Problem was, Asher wanted to hurt him.

I stepped between them. I took a step forward. Asher was either going to have to step back or we'd be touching. He stepped back, staring down at me as if I'd just appeared. He'd forgotten me for just a second.

"Love isn't the most expensive emotion, Asher," I said. I took another step forward, and he retreated another step. "Hate is. Because hate will eat you up inside and destroy you, long before it kills you."

"Very philosophical," he said.

"Philosophy's great," I said. "But remember this: don't ever threaten us again. Because if you do, I'll kill you. Because I don't give a fuck about your tortured past. Now, shall we go?"

Asher stared at me for a few heartbeats. "By all means. I cannot wait to introduce you to the council."

He meant it to be ominous, and it was. I didn't want to go and meet the bogeymen of vampirekind, but we were going. One thing I'd learned about master vampires. You can run, but not far enough. You can even hide, but not forever. Eventually, they catch you. And master vampires don't like to be kept waiting.

10

I DROVE. ASHER gave directions. He also hung on the back of the seat. I didn't ask him to buckle up for safety. Jean-Claude sat in the passenger seat next to me, silent, not looking at Asher or me.

"Something's wrong," Jean-Claude said.

I glanced at him. "You mean besides the council coming to town?" He shook his head. "Can't you feel it?"

"I don't feel anything."

"That is the problem." He turned as far as the seat belt would let him and met Asher's eyes. "What is happening to my people?"

Asher sat so his face showed perfectly in the rearview mirror, as if he wanted me to see him. He smiled. His whole face moved when he smiled. The scarred skin had muscles underneath. Everything seemed to work just fine except for the scars. The look on his face was smug, self-satisfied. The kind of joy that cats get from tormenting mice.

"I do not know what is happening to them, but you should. You are—after all—Master of the City."

"What's going on, Jean-Claude? What else is wrong?" I asked.

"I should be able to feel my people, *ma petite*. If I concentrate, it is like . . . background noise. I can feel the ebb and flow of them. In extreme duress I can feel their pain, their fear. Now I am concentrating, and it is like a blank wall."

"Balthasar's master has kept you from hearing the cries of your vampires," Asher said.

Jean-Claude's hand lashed out in a blur of speed that was almost magical. He grabbed Asher's coat collar, twisting it into a choking ring. "I—have—done—nothing—wrong. They have no right to harm my people."

Asher didn't try to get away. He just stared at him. "There is an empty seat on the council for the first time in over four thousand years. Whoever empties that seat takes that seat. That is the law of succession."

Jean-Claude released Asher, slowly. "I don't want it."

"You shouldn't have killed the Earthmover, then."

"He would have killed us," I said.

"Council's privilege," Asher said.

"That's ridiculous," I said. "You're saying because we didn't roll over and die, we're going to be killed now?"

"No one has come here planning to kill anyone," Asher said. "Believe me, that was my vote, but I was the minority. The council just wants to make sure that Jean-Claude isn't trying to set up his own little council."

Jean-Claude and I both looked at him. I had to swing my attention back to the road before I was ready to stop being astonished.

"You are babbling, Asher," Jean-Claude said.

"Not everyone is happy with the current council's rules. Some say they are old-fashioned."

"People have been saying that for four hundred years," Jean-Claude said.

"Yes, but until now there was no alternative. Some see your refusal of the council seat as a blow for a new order."

"You know why I did not take it."

Asher laughed, a low roll that played along my skin. "Whatever do you mean, Jean-Claude?"

"I am not powerful enough to hold a council seat. The first challenger would sense that and kill me, then they would have my council seat. I would be a stalking-horse."

"Yet you killed a council member. How did you manage that, Jean-Claude?" He leaned on the back of my seat. I could feel him. He picked up a curl of my hair, and I jerked my head away.

"Where the hell are we going? You were supposed to give directions," I said.

"There is no need for directions," Jean-Claude said. "They have taken the Circus."

"What?" I stared at him, and the only thing that kept the Jeep from swerving was luck. "What did you say?"

"Don't you understand yet? The Traveler, Balthasar's master, blocked my powers and the powers of my vampires, and kept them from reaching out to me."

"Your wolves. You should have felt something from your wolves. They're your animal to call," I said.

Jean-Claude turned to Asher. "Only one vampire could have kept my wolves from calling out for help. The Master of Beasts."

Asher rested his chin on the back of my seat. I felt him nod.

"Get off my seat," I said.

He raised his head but didn't really move back.

"They must think me powerful indeed to send two council masters," Jean-Claude said.

Asher made a harsh sound. "Only you, Jean-Claude, would be arrogant enough to believe that two council masters came to this country just for you."

"If not to teach me a lesson, then why are they here?" Jean-Claude asked.

"Our dark queen wished to know how this legality is working for the vampires in the States. We have traveled from Boston to New Orleans to San Francisco. She chose what cities we would visit, and in what order. Our dark queen left St. Louis, and you, for last."

"Why would she do that?" Jean-Claude asked.

"The Queen of Nightmares can do anything she likes," Asher said. "She says go to Boston, we go."

"If she said, walk out into the sunlight, would you do it?" I asked. I glanced at him. He was close enough that turning my head was enough, no mirror needed.

His face was blank and beautiful, empty. "Perhaps," he said.

I turned back to the road. "You're crazy, you're all crazy."

"Too true," Asher said. He sniffed my hair.

"Stop that."

"You smell of power, Anita Blake. You reek of the dead." He traced his fingers along my neck.

I swerved the Jeep purposefully, sending him sliding around the back seat. "Don't touch me."

"The council thought we would find you stuffed with power.

Bloated with new-found abilities, yet you seem much the same. But she is different. She is new. And there is that werewolf. Yes, that Ulfric, Richard Zeeman. You have him bound to you, as well."

Asher pulled himself back up to the seats, though not so close to me. "It is your servants who have the power. Not you."

"Is Padma anything without his animals?" Jean-Claude asked.

"Very true, though I might not say so in front of him." He leaned on the back of the seats again, not touching me this time. "So you admit it is your servants who have given you the power to take a council member."

"My human servant and my wolf are merely extensions of my power. Their hands are my hands; their deeds, my deeds. That is council law. So what does it matter where my power comes from?"

"Quoting council law, Jean-Claude. You have grown cautious since last we met."

"Caution has served me well, Asher."

"But have you had any fun?" It was a strange question coming from someone who was supposed to hate Jean-Claude.

"Some, and you, Asher, how fares it with you? Are you still serving the council, or did you come along on this mission to torment me?"

"Yes, to both questions."

"Why have you not fled the council?"

"Many aspire to serve them," Asher said.

"You didn't."

"Perhaps revenge has changed my aspirations."

Jean-Claude laid his hand on Asher's arm. "*Ma petite* is right. Hatred is a cold fire, and it gives no warmth."

Asher jerked back, sliding as far back as the seat would let him. I glanced in my rearview mirror. He was huddled in the dark, hugging himself. "When I see you weep for your beloved, I will have all the warmth I need."

"We'll be at the Circus soon," I said. "What's the plan?"

"I am not sure there is a plan. We must assume they have all our people in thrall. So it will be only what the two of us can do alone."

"Are we going to try and take the Circus back, or what?"

Asher laughed. "Is she serious?"

"Always," Jean-Claude said.

"Fine. What are we supposed to do?"

"Survive if you can," Asher said.

"Shut up," I said. "This is what I need to know, Jean-Claude. Do we go in there kicking butt, or crawling?"

"Would you crawl to them, *ma petite*?"

"They have Willie, Jason, and who knows how many others. So, yeah, if it would keep them safe, I'd do a little crawling."

"I do not think you would be very good at it," Jean-Claude said.

"I'm not."

"But no, no crawling tonight. We are not strong enough to retake the Circus, but we go in, as you say, kicking butt."

"Dominant?" I made it a question.

"*Oui.*"

"How dominant?"

"Be aggressive, but not foolish. You may wound anyone you are capable of hurting, but do not kill. We do not want to give them an excuse."

"They think you've started a revolution, Jean-Claude," Asher said from the darkness. "Like all revolutionaries, dead you become a martyr. They don't want you dead."

Jean-Claude turned so he could see the other vampire. "Then what do they want, Asher? Tell me."

"They have to make an example of you. Surely you see that."

"If I had planned on forging a second council in America, yes, I would see their point. But I know my limitations. I cannot hold a council seat against all comers. It would be a death sentence. I want simply to be left alone."

Asher sighed. "It is too late for that, Jean-Claude. The council is here, and they will not believe your protestations of innocence."

"You believe him," I said.

He was quiet for a few seconds, then said, "Yes, I believe him. The one thing Jean-Claude has always done well is survive. Challenging the council is not a good way to do that." Asher slid forward against the seats, putting his face very near mine. "Remember, Anita, that all those years ago, he waited to save me. Waited until he knew he wouldn't be caught. Waited until he could save me at the least risk to himself. Waited until Julianna was dead, because it was too great a risk to take.''

''That is not true,'' Jean-Claude said.

Asher ignored him. ''Be careful that he does not wait to save you.''

''I don't wait around for anybody to save me,'' I said.

Jean-Claude stared out the window at the passing cars. He was shaking his head gently, back and forth, back forth. ''I tire of you already, Asher.''

''You tire of me because I speak the truth.''

Jean-Claude turned and faced him. ''No, I tire of you because you remind me of her, and that once, a very long time ago, I was almost happy.''

The two vampires stared at each other. ''But now you have a second chance,'' Asher said.

''You could have a second chance, too, Asher. If you would only let the past go.''

''The past is all I have.''

''And *that* is not my fault,'' Jean-Claude said.

Asher slid back into the darkness, huddling against the seat. I thought Jean-Claude had won the argument for now. But just call it a feeling; I didn't think the fight was over.

11

THE CIRCUS OF the Damned is in a converted warehouse. From the front it looks like a carnival with posters promoting the freak show, and dancing clowns twirling on top of the glowing sign. From the back, it's just dark.

I pulled the Jeep into the small parking lot reserved for employees. It was small because most of the help lived at the Circus. No need for a car if you never left. Here was hoping we'd be needing our car.

I turned off the engine, and silence swirled into the car. Both vampires had sunk into that utter stillness that made me have to glance at them to make sure they were still there. Mammals can freeze, but a rabbit frozen waiting for the fox to pass is a vibrating thing. It breathes fast and faster. Its heart pounds. Vampires are more like snakes. A snake will put a length of its body out, then freeze. There is no sense of movement stopped. No sense that movement will continue. In that moment of frozen time a snake seems unreal, more like a work of art, something carved rather than something alive. Jean-Claude seemed to have fallen into a well of silence where movement, even breath, was forbidden.

I glanced back at Asher. He sat in the back seat. Utterly still, a perfect golden presence, but not alive.

The silence filled the Jeep like icy water. I wanted to clap my hands, yell, anything to make noise, to startle them into being again. But I knew better. All I'd get would be a blink and a look. A look that wasn't human and maybe never had been.

The sound of my dress against the upholstery was loud. "Will they pat me down for weapons?" My voice seemed flat in the charged silence.

Jean-Claude blinked gracefully, then turned his neck to look at me. The look was peaceful rather than empty. I had begun to wonder if the stillness was a form of meditation for the vampires. Maybe if we lived through the night I'd ask.

"This is a challenge, *ma petite*. They will let us be dangerous. Though I would not flaunt your weaponry. Your little gun is fine."

I shook my head. "I was thinking of more."

He raised his eyebrows. "More?"

I turned to look at Asher. He blinked and raised his eyes to me. I hit the dome light and saw his eyes' true color for the first time. They were blue. But that didn't do them justice. They were as pale a blue as Jean-Claude's were a dark blue. Pale, cold blue, the startling color of a Husky's eyes. But it wasn't just the eyes, it was the hair. It had looked golden, but the normal gold of a dark blond. In the truer light of the car, I realized it wasn't just illusion and dim light, it *was* gold. His hair was the truest gold I'd ever seen outside of a bottle or a can of metallic paint. The combination of hair and eyes was amazing. Even without the scars he wouldn't have looked real.

I glanced from one vampire to the other. Jean-Claude was the more beautiful, and it wasn't the scars. Asher was just a trace more handsome than he was pretty. "The same vamp made you both, right?" I asked.

Jean-Claude nodded.

Asher just stared at me.

"Where'd she go?" I asked. "Unnaturally-Beautiful-Studs-R-Us?"

Asher let out a harsh bark of laughter. He dragged his fingers down the scarred side of his face, making the skin stretch, drawing it away from his eye so you could see the pale inner flesh of the eye socket. He emphasized everything into a kind of hideous mask. "Do you think I am beautiful, Anita?" He released the skin, and it snapped back into place, resilient, perfect in its own way.

I looked at him. "What do you want me to say, Asher?"

"I want you to be terrified. I want to see on your face what I've seen on every face for the last two hundred years—disgust, derision, horror."

"Sorry," I said.

He leaned into the seats, showing the scars to the light. He seemed to have an innate sense of what any light would do to the wounds, to know just how the shadows would fall. Years of practice, I guess.

I just looked at him. I met his pale, perfect eyes, gazed on the thick waves of golden hair, the fullness of his lips. I shrugged. "What can I say? I'm a hair and eye person, and you have great hair and amazing eyes."

Asher threw himself back into his seat. He gazed at us both, and there was such rage in his eyes. Such horrible rage that it scared me.

"There," he said. "There, you're afraid of me. I can see it, smell it, taste it." He smiled, pleased with himself, triumphant somehow.

"Tell him what you fear, *ma petite*."

I glanced at Jean-Claude, then back at Asher. "It's not the scars, Asher. It's your hatred that's frightening."

He leaned forward, and I think without meaning to, his hair spilled around his face, camouflaging him. It had the look of long habit, long comfort. "Yes, my hatred is frightening. Terrifying. And remember, Anita Blake, that the hatred is all for you and your master."

I knew he meant Jean-Claude, and I couldn't argue with the title anymore, though sometimes I wanted to. "Hatred makes us all ugly," I said.

He hissed at me, and there was nothing human in the gesture.

I gave him a bored look. "Come off it, Asher. Been there, done that. If you want to play big-bad-vampire, get in line."

He stripped his overcoat off in an abrupt, violent movement. A brown tweed suit jacket ended up crumpled on the seat. He turned his head so I could see that the scars marched down his neck into the collar of his white dress shirt. He started unbuttoning the shirt.

I glanced at Jean-Claude. His face was impassive, unhelpful. I was on my own. So what else was new?

"Not that I don't appreciate the offer, but I don't usually let a man strip down on the first date."

He snarled at me. He bared his chest to the light, shirt still carefully tucked into his pants. The scars dribbled down his flesh like someone had drawn a dividing line down the center of his body. One half pale and perfect, the other half monstrous. They'd been more careful of his face and neck. They had not been careful of his chest. The scars cut deep runnels. The skin so melted that it didn't even look real anymore. The scars flowed down his stomach into the belted top of his pants.

I stared because that's what he wanted me to do. When I could finally meet his eyes, I had no words left. I'd had holy water poured on a vampire bite before. Cleansed, they called it. Torture was another word for it. I'd crawled and cursed and vomited. I couldn't imagine the pain he'd survived.

His eyes were wide and fierce and fearful. "The scars go all the way down," he said.

That left a trail of visuals that I'd been trying to avoid. I thought of a lot of things to say: "Wow," but it seemed too junior high school and cruel; "sorry" was totally inadequate. I spread my hands wide, kneeling on the seat looking at him. "I asked you once before, Asher. What do you want me to say?"

He pushed himself as far away from me as he could, back against the Jeep's door. "Why doesn't she look away? Why doesn't she hate me? Why isn't she disgusted with this body?"

Like he was disgusted. It hung unsaid on the air, but it was there in his eyes, in the way he held himself. Unspoken, the words hung in the air with the weight and push of thunder.

He yelled, "Why don't I see in her eyes what I see in everyone's eyes?"

"You do not see horror in my eyes, *mon ami*," Jean-Claude said.

"No," Asher said, "I see worse. I see pity!" He opened the car door without turning around. I would have said he fell out of the car, but that isn't true. He floated upward before he could touch the ground. There was a backwash of wind that swept over me like a storm, and he was gone.

12

WE SAT IN silence for a few seconds, both of us staring at the open door. Finally, I had to fill the silence. "My, people do come and go quickly here."

Jean-Claude didn't get the movie reference. Richard would have gotten it. He liked the "Wizard of Oz." Jean-Claude answered me seriously, "Asher always was very good at flying."

Someone chuckled. The sound made me reach for the Firestar. The voice was familiar but the tone was new; arrogant, profoundly arrogant.

"Silver bullets won't kill me anymore, Anita. My new master has promised me that."

Liv appeared in the open car door, peering in at us, muscular arms propped on the sides of the door. She smiled broadly enough to flash fangs. When you pass the five-hundred mark like Liv, you only flash fangs when you want to. She was grinning like the Cheshire cat, very pleased about something. She wore a black sports bra and high-cut jogging shorts so that all that body-building muscle gleamed in the street lights. She was one of the vamps that Jean-Claude had invited into his territory recently. She was supposed to be one of his vampire lieutenants.

"What canary did you eat?" I asked.

She frowned at me. "What?"

"The cat that ate the canary," I said.

She continued to frown. Liv's English is perfect, no accent of any kind. Sometimes I forget that it's not her first language. A lot of the vamps have lost their original accents but they still don't understand all the slang. But, hey, I bet Liv knew some Slavic slang that I'd never heard.

"Anita is asking why you are so pleased with yourself,"

Jean-Claude said, "but I think I already know the answer."

I glanced at him, then back at Liv. I had the Firestar out but not pointed. She was supposed to be on our side. I was getting the feeling that might have changed.

"Did Liv say, her new master?" I asked.

"She did," Jean-Claude said.

I raised the gun and pointed it at her. She laughed. It was unnerving. She crawled into the back seat, still laughing. Very unnerving. Liv may have been six hundred years old and some change, but she wasn't powerful. Certainly not powerful enough to laugh off silver ammo.

"You know I'll shoot you, Liv. So what's the joke?"

"Can you not feel it, *ma petite*? The difference in her."

I steadied my hand on the back of the seat, gun pointed at her impressive chest. I was less than two feet from her, at this distance the bullet would take out her heart. She wasn't worried. She should have been.

I concentrated on Liv. Tried to roll her power in my mind. I'd done her before, knew what she felt like in my head. Or thought I did. Her power beat along my skull, hummed down my bones. I could feel her power like a thrumming note so deep and low it was almost painful.

I took a deep breath and let it out slowly. I kept the gun pointed at her. "If I pull this trigger, Liv, even with the boost in power you'll die."

Liv looked at Jean-Claude. It was a long, self-satisfied look. "You know I won't die, Jean-Claude."

"Only the Traveler could make such an extravagant promise, and hope to keep it," Jean-Claude said. "You are a little too feminine for his tastes, unless he has changed."

Her face was disdainful. "He is above such petty desires. He offered me only power and I accepted."

Jean-Claude shook his head. "If you truly believe the Traveler above the desires of the body, then he has been very . . . careful around you, Liv."

"He is not like the others," she said.

Jean-Claude sighed. "On that I will not argue, Liv. But be careful that his power does not become addictive."

"You seek to frighten me, but it will not work, Jean-Claude.

His power is like nothing I have ever felt before, and he can share it. I can be what I was meant to be."

"He can fill you to bursting with his power, Liv, it will not make you a master. If he has promised you that, then he has lied to you."

She hissed at him. "You would say anything to save yourself tonight."

He shrugged. "Perhaps."

"I thought Liv took an oath of loyalty to you," I said.

"*Oui.*"

"Then what's going on?"

"The council will be very careful to observe the rules, *ma petite*. The Circus is a public business, thus the council might have crossed the threshold uninvited. Instead, they found someone to invite them inside."

I stared at the smirking vamp in the back of my Jeep. "She betrayed us?"

"Yes," he said softly. He touched my shoulder. "Do not kill her, *ma petite*. The bullet would enter, but the Traveler would not allow her death. You would simply waste a bullet."

I shook my head. "She betrayed you, all of you."

"If they could not have bribed someone, they would have tortured someone else into betraying us. I much prefer this method," he said.

I stared down the barrel of the gun at Liv's smiling face. I could have pulled the trigger and not worried about it. She'd done all the damage she could do. It wasn't like I'd be killing her to save us. I didn't want, or not want, to pull the trigger. I simply thought she deserved to die for betraying us. Not anger, or even outrage, just good business. It was a bad precedent to allow anyone to betray you and survive. It set a bad example. I realized with an almost physical jolt that killing her meant nothing to me. Just good business. Sweet Jesus. I put up the gun. I didn't want to kill anyone that coldly. Killing didn't bother me, but it should mean something.

Liv leaned back in the seat, grinning, pleased I'd seen the futility of shooting her. If she only realized why I hadn't done it, she might still have been scared of me, but she was hiding behind the power of this Traveler. Confident that it was shield enough against anything. If she pissed me off enough tonight, maybe we'd test the theory.

I shook my head. If I was going to meet the bogeymen of vampirekind I needed more weapons. I had my wrist sheaths, complete with silver knives, in the glove compartment. I often carried them in the Jeep when I wore something I couldn't wear them with, like the dress. Never knew when you'd need a good knife.

"I'll tell them about any weapons I see," she said.

I finished buckling the knives in place. "Yvette and Balthasar know I have the gun. I'm not trying to be subtle here, just prepared." I opened the door and stepped out. I scanned the darkness for more company, though the really old ones could hide almost in plain sight. Some vampires had chameleons beat all to hell when it came to blending with their surroundings. I'd seen one that could wrap himself in shadows, then fling them aside like a cloak. It had been impressive.

Liv scooted out of the car to stand near me. She'd lifted a few too many weights to cross her arms comfortably but she was trying. Trying for that nonchalant bodyguard look. She was six feet tall and built like a brick outhouse; she didn't have to try hard to look intimidating.

Jean-Claude got out of the car on my side, putting himself between the two of us. I wasn't sure who he was protecting; her or me.

He had Asher's long coat in his arms. "I suggest, *ma petite*, that you wear this to cover the weapons."

"I'll tell them about the knives," Liv said.

"If the weapons are in plain sight, it is more of a challenge," Jean-Claude said. "Someone might feel compelled to take them from you."

"They can try," I said.

Jean-Claude handed me the coat, draped across his arms. "Please, *ma petite*."

I took it from him. He didn't say "please" often.

I slipped the black coat on. I was reminded of two things. One, it was too damn hot to wear a coat. Two, Asher was six foot or more, the coat was huge. I started rolling up the sleeves.

"Anita," Liv said.

I glanced at her.

She looked serious now, her strong Nordic face blank and unreadable. "Look into my eyes."

I shook my head. "What do you guys do, sit around watching old Dracula movies and stealing the dialogue?"

Liv took a threatening step forward. I just stared up at her. "Save the big-bad-vampire routine, Liv. We've done this and you can't roll me with your eyes."

"*Ma petite*," Jean-Claude said, "do as she asks."

I frowned at him. "Why?" Suspicious, who me?

"Because if the Traveler's extra power can bespell you through Liv's eyes, it would be better to know here in relative safety than inside among our greater foes."

He had a point, but I didn't like it. I shrugged. "Fine." I stared at her face, into her blue eyes, though the color was a little washed out from the street light.

Liv turned; a spill of yellow light from the open car door hit her eyes and made them that amazing violet-blue, almost purple. Her eyes were her best feature and I'd never had any trouble meeting that flower-petal gaze.

I still could. Not even a twinge.

Liv's hands balled into fists. She spoke, but I didn't think she was talking to either of us, "You promised me. Promised me enough power to roll her mind."

There was a rush of wind, cold enough to make me shiver and huddle into the long coat.

Liv laughed, a loud bray of sound. She raised her arms to the cold wind as if it were wrapping her around like drapes in the breeze.

The cold wind raised the hairs on the back of my neck, but it wasn't the temperature, it was the power in it.

"Now," Liv said, "look into my eyes, if you dare."

"Little better on the dialogue," I said.

"Are you afraid to meet my gaze, Executioner?"

The cold wind that had come from nowhere died, then faded, a last icy caress. I waited until the summer heat slid over me like plastic wrap, waited until sweat trailed down my spine; then I looked up.

Once upon a time I'd avoided looking any vamp in the eyes. I'd had some natural immunity, but even the lesser vamps were dangerous. Their gaze was one trick that almost all of them had to a lesser, or greater, extent. My powers had grown, and the vampire marks had cinched it. I was pretty much immune to vampire gaze. So why was I afraid now?

I met Liv's violet gaze solid, no flinching. At first there was nothing but their extraordinary color. A tension went out of me, my shoulders loosened. They were just eyes. Then it was as if the violet of her eyes was water, and I was something that skated over the surface tension, until something rose from her eyes and pulled me down. Always before it had been like falling, but now something had me, something dark, and strong. It sucked me under like water under ice. I screamed, and lashed out. Lashed out against that cold film of ice, reached for a surface that wasn't physical, wasn't even metaphorical, but I fought to rise. Fought against the pull of that darkness.

I came to myself, kneeling on the parking lot with Jean-Claude's hand grasped in mine. "*Ma petite, ma petite*, are you all right?"

I just shook my head. I didn't trust my voice yet. I'd forgotten how much I hated being rolled by their gaze. Forgotten how helpless I felt. My own power was making me careless around the damn things.

Liv leaned against the side of the Jeep. She seemed tired, too. "I almost had you."

I found my voice. "You didn't have anything. It wasn't your eyes I was being sucked into. It was his."

She shook her head. "He promised me the power to do you, Anita. To take your mind."

I let Jean-Claude help me to my feet, which tells you how shaky I was feeling. "Then he lied, Liv. It's not your power, it's his."

"You fear me now," she said. "I can feel your fear in my head."

I nodded. "Yeah, I'm scared. If that makes you happy, then laugh it up." I started backing away from her. More weapons. I needed more weapons.

"It does make me happy," she said. "You'll never know how happy it makes me."

"His power has left you, Liv," Jean-Claude said.

"It will return," she said.

I was on the other side of the Jeep. I was headed for the back of it, but I didn't want to be within touching range of Liv right this second. I'd broken free, but I didn't want to keep pushing my luck.

"The power may return, Liv, but Anita has broken his bond with you. She has pushed his power aside."

"No," Liv said. "He has chosen to let her go."

Jean-Claude laughed and it chased along my body, and I knew that Liv felt it, too. "The Traveler would have kept *ma petite*, if he could have held her. But he could not. She is too big a fish even for his net."

"Liar!" Liv said.

I left Liv and Jean-Claude to argue between themselves. I'd broken free of the Traveler's power, but it hadn't been pretty, or easy. Though come to think of it, as soon as I started to struggle, it had broken. The sad truth was I hadn't tried to shield myself. I'd stared into Liv's eyes empty and waiting, confident that she couldn't roll me. It had been stupid. No—arrogant. Sometimes there isn't a whole lot of difference between the two.

I walked to the rear of the Jeep. I crawled in the cargo area. Edward, assassin of the undead, had persuaded me to let an acquaintance of his remodel my Jeep. The wheel well on one side was now a secret compartment. Inside was my extra Browning and extra ammo. I'd felt silly when he'd talked me into it. I didn't feel silly now. I opened the compartment and found a surprise. A mini-Uzi complete with shoulder strap. There was a note taped to the gun.

"You can never have too much firepower."

He hadn't signed it, but it was Edward. He'd started his career as a normal assassin, but humans became too easy so he switched to monsters. He did love a challenge. I had another mini-Uzi at home. It had been a gift from Edward, too. He had the best toys.

I took off the coat and slid the Uzi's strap across my chest. When I slipped the coat back on, the Uzi hung at my back. Not perfect but not too noticeable. The second Browning Hi-Power was in the compartment, too. I put it in my pocket and two extra clips of ammo in the other pocket. When I slid to the ground, the coat hung funny, but it was so big on me that it wasn't conspicuous.

The vampires weren't arguing anymore. Liv leaned against

the Jeep looking sullen, as if Jean-Claude had had the last word, or won the argument.

I stood watching her. I wanted to shoot her. Not because she'd betrayed us, but because she'd scared me. Not a good enough reason. Besides, it had been my own carelessness that let her scare me. I tried not to punish other people for my mistakes.

"I can't let you go unpunished, Liv," Jean-Claude said. "The council would see it as a weakness."

She just looked at him. "Hit me if it will make you feel better, Jean-Claude." She pushed away from the Jeep and crossed the distance between them with three long strides. She lifted her chin like a bully daring you to take the first swing.

He shook his head. "No, Liv." He touched her face gently. "I had something else in mind." He caressed her face, rubbing his hand along her cheek.

She sighed, rubbing her face against his palm. Liv had been trying to get into Jean-Claude's pants since she hit town. She'd never hidden her plan to sleep her way to the top. She'd been very . . . frustrated that he wouldn't cooperate.

She laid a gentle kiss on his palm. "Things could have been so different if it weren't for your pet human."

I walked up behind them and it was like I wasn't there. They were in some private place that just happened to be in plain sight.

"No, Liv," Jean-Claude said, "it would not have been different. It was not Anita that kept you from my bed, it was you." His hand closed on her throat. His fingers convulsed in her flesh. He made a sharp movement and tore the front of her throat out.

Liv collapsed to the pavement, choking, blood flowing in a crimson wash down her front, out of her mouth. She rolled onto her back, hands clawing at her throat.

I came to stand beside him and stared down at her. I caught a glimpse of her spine deep in the wound. Her eyes were wide, pain-filled, frightened.

Jean-Claude was wiping his hand off on a silk handkerchief he'd pulled from somewhere. He'd flung the gobbets of flesh to the pavement, where they lay looking small and not important enough to die over.

We both watched her writhing on the pavement. Jean-Claude's face was that empty mask he wore, beautiful and distant, like trying to draw comfort from the moon. I didn't have a mirror, and my face would never be his lovely perfection, but it was just as empty. I watched Liv flop on the pavement and felt no pity.

No cold wind came to save her. I think that surprised Liv, because she reached for Jean-Claude. Reached for him, begging with her eyes for him to help her. He was motionless, sunk into that great waiting stillness, as if he was willing himself to vanish. Maybe it did bother him to watch her die.

If she'd been human, it would have been pretty fast. But she wasn't human, and it wasn't fast. She wasn't dying. I wasn't sure it was pity, but I couldn't just stand there and watch anyone in such pain, such terror.

I pulled the Browning out of the coat pocket and pointed it at her head. "I'm going to end this."

"She will heal, *ma petite*. It is a wound that her own vampire body will heal, in time."

"Why isn't her new master helping her?" I asked.

"Because he knows she will heal without his aid."

"No wasted energy, huh?"

"Something like that," he said. It was hard to tell through the blood, but it did look as if the wound was filling in; there was just so much to fill in.

"We offer our throat, or wrist, or the bend of our elbow to each other as a formal greeting. The lesser offer up their flesh to the greater as an acknowledgment of power. It is a pretty thing, a polite thing, but this is the reality, *ma petite*. Liv offered me her throat and I took it."

I stared into her wide, wide eyes. "Did she know this was a possibility?"

"If she did not, then she is a fool. Such violence is never condoned unless the lesser vampire questions the authority of the greater vampire. She questioned my dominance over her. This is the price."

Liv turned onto her side, coughing. Her breath rattled in her throat in a painful gasp. Things were re-forming. She was breathing again. When she had enough air to speak, she said, "Damn you, Jean-Claude." Then she coughed blood. Yummy.

Jean-Claude held his hand out to me. He'd wiped it off, but you never get the blood out from around the fingernails without soap and water. I hesitated, then took his hand. We'd get blood-ier before the night was over, it was almost guaranteed.

We walked towards the Circus. The coat billowed behind me like a cape. The Uzi bounced lightly against my back. I'd added one extra thing from the glove compartment. A long silver chain with a cross on it. I'd gotten longer chains when I started dating Jean-Claude. The shorter ones spilled out of my clothing at awk-ward moments. I was loaded for bear, uh, vampire, and ready to go kill something. Edward would have been proud.

13

THE SIDE DOOR of the Circus has no handle. The only way in is if someone opens the door. Security measures. Jean-Claude knocked, and the door swung inward at his touch. Open, waiting, expecting us. Ominous.

The door opened into a small storage room with a bare light bulb hanging from the ceiling. A stark room with a few boxes against one wall. A door to the right led into the main part of the Circus, where people were usually riding the Ferris wheel and eating cotton candy. A smaller door led off to the left. There were no bright lights and cotton candy in that direction.

The light swung back and forth as if someone had just hit it. The naked bulb made the shadows thicker, and the light danced until it was hard to tell shadow from light. Something glinted on the left-hand door. Something attached to its surface. I didn't know what it was, except it glinted dully in the strange light.

I shoved the door flat against the wall just to make sure no one was behind it. Then I put my back to the door and trained the Browning on the room.

"Stop the bulb from swinging," I said.

Jean-Claude reached up and touched the bulb. He had to stand on tiptoe to do it. Whoever had set it swinging was over six feet.

"The room is empty, *ma petite*," Jean-Claude said.

"What's on the door?" It was flat and thin, and my mind couldn't make a shape out of it. Whatever it was, it was hammered to the door with silver nails.

Jean-Claude let out a long sigh. "*Mon Dieu*."

I crossed the room with the Browning pointed two-handed at

the floor. Jean-Claude said the room was empty. I trusted that, but I trusted me more.

Liv staggered to the door. The front of her body was covered with blood, but her throat was perfect. I wondered if the Traveler had helped her after we walked away. She coughed, and cleared her throat so violently it sounded painful. "I wanted to see your faces when you saw the Master of Beasts' compromise," she said. "The Traveler refused to let him and his people greet you in person. This is the Master of Beasts' calling card. How do you like it?" She sounded eager in a predatory, unpleasant sort of way. What the fuck was on the door?

Even standing next to it, I didn't know what it was. Thin rivulets of blood were seeping down the door from it. The sweet metallic scent of blood warmed the stale air. The thing was almost paper thin, but had a consistency more like plastic. It curled at the edges, straining against the five silver nails.

I suddenly had an awful idea. So awful, my eyes couldn't see it even after I'd thought it. I took three steps back from the thing and tried to see the silhouette. There; there; two arms, two legs, shoulders. It was a human skin. Once I found the shape of it, I couldn't stop seeing it. I knew that when I closed my eyes tonight that it would haunt me. That thin stretched thing that used to be a person.

"Where are the hands and feet?" I asked. My voice sounded strange, distant, almost unattached. My lips and fingertips tingled with the pure horror of it.

"It is merely the back of someone's body, not the entire skin, *ma petite*. Besides, it is hard to take the living skin off of fingers and toes when your victim is still struggling," Jean-Claude said. His voice was utterly flat, carefully empty.

"Struggling? You mean whoever this was, was alive?"

"You are the police expert, *ma petite*."

"It wouldn't be bleeding this much if they hadn't been alive," I said.

"Yes, *ma petite*."

He was right. I did know that. But the sight of a human skin nailed to a door had thrown me. It was a first, even for me. "Sweet Jesus, do the silver nails mean the victim was vampire or lycanthrope?"

"Most likely," Jean-Claude said.

"Does that mean they're still alive?"

He looked at me. His look managed to be empty and eloquent all at the same time. "They were alive when the skin was removed. If vampire, or lycanthrope, the mere removal of the skin would not be sufficient to kill them."

A shudder ran through me from head to feet. It wasn't exactly fear. It was horror. Horror at the casualness of it, the callousness of it. "Asher mentioned Padma. Is he the Beast Master?"

"The Master of Beasts," Jean-Claude said. "You cannot kill him for this indiscretion, *ma petite*."

"You're wrong," I said. The horror was there like a coating of ice underneath my skin, but over that was anger. Rage. And under the rage was fear. Fear of anyone that would skin another person alive just to make a point. Told you something about a person. Told you how few rules they had. Told me, in no uncertain terms, that I should kill him as soon as I saw him.

"We cannot punish them for this tonight, *ma petite*. Tonight is about survival for all of us. Remember that and curb your anger."

I stared at the thing on the door. "I am way past anger."

"Then curb your rage. We must save the rest of our people."

"If they're alive."

"They were alive when I came upstairs to wait for you," Liv said.

"Whose skin is it?" I asked.

She laughed, and it was her usual bray. All healed, all better. "Guess," she said. "If you guess right, I'll tell you, but only if you guess right."

It took more control than was pretty not to point the Browning at her. I shook my head. "No games, Liv, not with you. The real games don't even begin until we get downstairs."

"Well said, *ma petite*. Let us go down."

"No," Liv said. "No, you'll guess. You'll guess who it is. I want to see your face. I want to see the pain in your eyes while you think about each of your friends, Anita. I want to watch the horror on your face while you picture it happening to each of them."

"What did I ever do to you, Liv?"

"You stood in my way," she said.

I shook my head and pointed the gun at her. "Three strikes and you're out, Liv."

She frowned. "What are you talking about?"

"Betraying us was one. Trying to roll me with your eyes was number two. That was partly my fault, so I would have let it go. But you took an oath to protect all of Jean-Claude's people. You swore to use that wonderful body, that strength, to protect those weaker than yourself. Whoever belongs to that skin was someone you swore to protect. Instead, you betrayed them. Delivered them over to hell. Strike three, Liv."

"You can't kill me, Anita. The Traveler will heal me, no matter what you do."

I shot her in the right kneecap. She fell to the floor, holding the shattered leg, writhing, screaming.

I felt myself smile, most unpleasant. "I hope it hurts, Liv. I hope it hurts like hell."

The temperature in the room dropped like a stone. It felt cold enough that I half expected to see my breath. Liv's screams stopped, and she stared up at me with her violet eyes. If looks could have killed, I'd have dropped on the spot.

"You cannot harm me, Anita. My master will not allow it." Liv got to her feet with the faintest of limps. She walked to the door with its awful burden. She stretched the edge of the thing, showing holes in the skin that had nothing to do with the skinning process. "I fed on him while they tortured him. I drank his blood while he screamed." Her fingers came away stained with blood. She licked them clean, sliding her fingers in and out of her mouth. "Hmm, tasty."

All I had to do was guess who it was, and she'd tell me. All I had to do was play her game. I shot her in the other knee.

She collapsed to the floor, shrieking. "Don't you understand? You can't hurt me."

"Oh, I think I can, Liv, I think I can." I shot the right knee again. She lay on her back, screaming, grabbing at her shattered knees, and recoiling, because her own touch hurt.

The Traveler's power raised the hair on my body in a shiver of goose bumps. He really was going to heal her. If I wasn't going to kill her, I needed to be somewhere else before she could walk. I knew Liv well enough to know that when she could stand she was going to be pissed. Not that I blamed her.

In fact, if I just stood there long enough for her to get to her feet, it'd be self-defense. Of course, it'd be premeditated self-defense.

"Come, *ma petite*, let her be. The Traveler does not give his blessings so easily a second time, or would this be the third? He will heal her at his own pace now. A blessing and a punishment rolled into one. As most of the council's gifts are wont to be."

He opened the door that led downstairs. His hand came away with blood on it. He held the hand out in front of him like he didn't know what to do with it. He finally walked through the door, wiping his hand along the wall, smearing the blood down the stones in a faint crimson line.

"The longer we delay, the more tortures they will think of." With that comforting line he started down the steps. I gave one last glance to Liv. She lay on her side, crying, shrieking. She was shrieking that she was going to see me dead. I should have shot her in the head until her brains leaked on the floor. If I was truly ruthless, I would have. But I didn't. I left her alive and screaming threats. Edward would have been so disappointed.

14

THE STEPS LEADING underground were taller than normal, as if whatever they were originally designed for wasn't quite human. I kicked the door shut, didn't want to touch the blood. The door cut Liv off in mid scream. I could still hear her very faintly, like the high buzzing of an insect, but the door was almost soundproof. Needed something to muffle the screams from below. Of course, tonight there was only silence on the stairs. A silence so deep that it vibrated in my ears.

Jean-Claude moved in a boneless grace, like a big cat, down the awkward steps. I had to wrap the end of the coat over my left arm to keep from tripping over it. Even then, I didn't glide down the stairs. In three-inch heels I sort of limped.

Jean-Claude waited at the bend of the stairs just before the landing. "I could carry you, *ma petite*."

"No, thanks." If I took the shoes off, the dress would be so long I'd need to hold it up. I needed one hand free for a gun. If my choices were being slow and having a gun drawn, or being fast and having my hands full of dress . . . I'd be slow.

The stairs stretched empty, wide enough to drive a small car down. The door at the base of the stairs was solid oak, iron bound like the door to a dungeon. Tonight, not a bad analogy.

Jean-Claude pulled on the heavy door, and it swung open. It was usually kept locked. He turned to me. "The council can demand that I greet every vampire within these walls, formally."

"You mean like you did with Liv?" I asked.

He gave a very small smile. "If I do not acknowledge their dominance over me, then perhaps."

"What if you do acknowledge them?" I asked.

He shook his head. "If we had gone to the council for aid of some kind, then I would not fight. I would simply acknowledge their superiority and be done with it. I am not strong enough to be council. I know that." He smoothed his hands down the ruffles of his shirt, adjusting the cuffs on his jacket so the ruffles at his wrists showed to best advantage. He often fussed with his clothes when he was nervous. Of course, he fussed with his clothes when he wasn't nervous, too.

"I hear a 'but' coming," I said.

He smiled at me. "*Oui, ma petite*. But they have come to us. They have invaded our lands. Harmed our people. If we acknowledge them as greater than ourselves without a struggle, they may set up a new master in my place. They may take all I have gained."

"I thought the only way to step down as master was to die."

"They would come to that, eventually."

"Then we go in kicking butt."

"But we cannot win by violence, *ma petite*. What we did with Liv was to be expected. She had to be punished. But in a struggle to kill or be killed, the council will win."

I frowned up at him. "If we can't just say they're bigger and badder than we are, and we can't fight them, what can we do?"

"We play the game, *ma petite*."

"What game?"

"The game that I mastered at court so long ago. It is a thing of diplomacy, bravado, insults." He raised my left hand to his lips and laid a gentle kiss on it. "You will be very good at part of the game, and very bad at others. Diplomacy is not your strong suit."

"Bravado and insults are two of my best things."

He smiled, still holding my hand. "Indeed, *ma petite*, indeed. Put the gun away. I am not saying do not use it, but have a care who you shoot. Not everything you will meet tonight can be harmed by silver bullets." He cocked his head to one side as if thinking. "Though come to that, I've never seen anyone try to kill a council member with modern silver ammunition." He smiled. "It might work." He shook his head as if to rid himself of the image. "But if it comes to trying to slay the council by bullets, then all is lost and all that will be left is to take as many of them with us as we can."

"Let's save as many of our people as we can, too," I said.

"You don't understand them, *ma petite*. If we are dead, there will be no mercy for those who are loyal to us. Any good revolution kills the loyalists first." He touched the back of my right hand lightly, reminding. I still had the gun out. Somehow, I just didn't want to put it away.

But I did. I put the safety on. I didn't want them to know the gun was there, so I couldn't keep holding it. I put the safety on because I didn't want to shoot myself in the leg. It would be embarrassing as well as painful and probably wouldn't impress the council one little bit. I didn't understand "the game," but I'd hung around vampires long enough to know that if you could impress them, sometimes you walked out alive. Of course, sometimes they killed you anyway. Sometimes a show of bravado just earned you a slower death, like it did with some American Indian tribes that only tortured enemies they thought worthy of the honor. An honor I could do without. But sometimes in the midst of being tormented you could get away. If they just tore your throat out, all options were over. We were definitely going for impressive. If we could impress them, we'd kill them. If we couldn't kill them . . . they'd kill us. Liv had just been the beginning of the evening's entertainment.

The living room was a bare stone room once again. Jean-Claude's efforts at redecorating lay in piles of black and white cloth and broken wood. The only thing untouched was the portrait above the false fireplace. Jean-Claude, Julianna, and an unscarred Asher gazed down at the ruins. I expected an unpleasant surprise to be waiting for us. There was only Willie McCoy standing in front of the cold fireplace. He had his back to us, hands clasped behind him. His pea-green suit clashed with his slicked-back black hair. One sleeve was torn and bloodstained. He turned towards us. Blood seeped from a gash on his forehead. He dabbed at it with a handkerchief covered in dancing skeletons. It was silk and had been a gift from his girlfriend, a century-old vamp who had recently joined us. Hannah was as tall, leggy, and lovely as Willie was short, badly dressed, and well . . . Willie.

He smiled at us. "So good of you to join us."

"Can the sarcasm," I said. "Where is everybody?" I started

walking towards him, but Jean-Claude stopped me with a hand on my arm.

Willie's smile was almost gentle. He stared at Jean-Claude with a look of expectancy. It was an expression I'd never seen on Willie's face.

I glanced at Jean-Claude's perfect mask of a face, closed and careful. No—fearful.

"What's going on?" I asked.

"*Ma petite*, may I introduce the Traveler."

I frowned at him. "What are you talking about?"

Willie laughed, and it was the same irritating bray he'd always had, but it ended in a low, chuckling growl that raised the hairs at the base of my neck. I looked at him and knew the shock showed on my face.

I had to swallow before I could talk, even then I didn't know what to say. "Willie?"

"He can no longer answer your call, *ma petite*."

Willie stood there staring at me. He had been an awkward person alive. Dead, he hadn't been much better. He hadn't been dead long enough to master that otherworldly movement that the others had. He walked towards us in a wave of his own liquid grace. It wasn't Willie.

"Shit," I said softly. "Is it permanent?"

The stranger in Willie's body laughed again. "I am merely borrowing his body. I borrow a great many bodies, don't I, Jean-Claude?"

I felt Jean-Claude draw me backwards. He didn't want to get closer. I didn't argue. We backed up. It was odd being backed up by Willie. Normally, he was one of the least scary vamps I knew. Now, tension sang down Jean-Claude's hand. I could taste his heart beating in my own head. He was afraid, and that made me afraid.

The Traveler stopped, hands on hips, laughing. "Afraid I will use you as my horse, Jean-Claude? If you are truly strong enough to have slain the Earthmover, then you should be strong enough to withstand me."

"I am cautious by nature, Traveler. Time has not lessened the habit."

"You always did have a smooth tongue in your head and so many other places."

I frowned at the double-entendre, not sure I caught the meaning, not sure I wanted to. "Let Willie go."

"He is not being harmed," the vampire said.

"He is still inside the body," Jean-Claude said. "He still feels, still sees. You have only pushed him aside, Traveler, not replaced him."

I glanced at Jean-Claude. His face showed nothing. "You say that like you know from personal experience."

"Jean-Claude was one of my favorite bodies, once upon a time. Balthasar and I enjoyed him very much."

Balthasar walked out of the far hallway as if he'd been waiting for his cue. Maybe he had. He was smiling, but it was more a baring of teeth than pleasure. He strode into the room looking elegant and roguish in his white suit. He stood behind Willie, hands on the shorter man's thin shoulders. Willie, the Traveler, leaned back against Balthasar's chest. The bigger man wrapped his arms around him. They were a couple.

"Will he know what they're doing with his body?" I asked.

"Yes," Jean-Claude said.

"Willie doesn't like men."

"No," Jean-Claude said.

I swallowed and tried to think reasonably, and just couldn't. Vampires could not take over another vampire's body. It wasn't possible. It just wasn't. But I looked at Willie's familiar face with a stranger's thoughts flowing through his brown eyes and knew it was true.

Those brown eyes smiled into mine. I dropped my gaze. If the Traveler could do me through Liv's eyes when he wasn't inside her, then he'd suck me down now for sure. It had been a long time since I had had to practice the trick of staring at a face without meeting the eyes. It was like tag with the vamp trying to capture my gaze, and me avoiding it. It was irritating, and scary.

Jean-Claude had said that violence wouldn't save us tonight. He wasn't kidding. If a vamp had been holding Willie against his will, forcing him sexually, I'd have shot him. But it was Willie's body, and he'd get it back. Shooting it full of holes was a bad idea. What I needed was a good idea.

"Does the Traveler like women?" I asked.

"Are you offering yourself in his place?" the vampire asked.

"No, just wondering how you'd like it if the tables were turned."

"No one else has my ability to share a body," the Traveler said.

"Would you like it if someone forced you to have sex with a woman?"

Willie's face cocked to one side, and the expression was alien to him. The sense of otherness was strong enough to make my skin crawl. "I have never felt the draw of a woman's body."

"You'd find it distasteful," I said.

Willie, the Traveler, nodded. "Yes."

"Then let Willie go. Pick someone who wouldn't mind so much."

The Traveler snuggled into Balthasar's arms and laughed at me. "Are you appealing to my sense of mercy?"

I shrugged. "I can't shoot you. You're council. I was hoping that would mean you had more rules than the rest of them. Guess I was wrong."

He looked at Jean-Claude. "Does your human servant do all your talking now?"

"She does well enough," Jean-Claude said.

"If she seeks to appeal to my sense of fair play, then you have told her nothing about your time with us at court."

Jean-Claude kept my left hand clasped loosely in his, but he stepped away from me. I felt him draw himself straighter as if he'd been hunched just a little, huddled around his panic. I knew he was still afraid, but he had rallied. Brave Jean-Claude. I wasn't that afraid yet. But then, I didn't know any better.

"I do not dwell upon the past," Jean-Claude said.

"He is ashamed of us," Balthasar said, rubbing his face against Willie's. He planted a soft kiss against Willie's temple.

"No," the Traveler said. "He fears us."

"What do you want of me, Traveler? Why has the council invaded my lands and taken my people hostage?"

Willie's body pushed away from Balthasar to stand just in front of the taller man. Willie normally looked smaller than he was, sort of hunched and rabbity, but now he looked slim and certain of himself. The Traveler had given Willie the grace and assurance he never had on his own.

"You slew the Earthmover but did not come to take his council seat. There is no other way to rise to the council except through the death of another. We have a vacancy that only you can fill, Jean-Claude.''

''I do not want it, nor am I powerful enough to keep it.''

''If not powerful enough, then how did you slay Oliver? He was a frightening force of nature.'' The Traveler walked towards us with Balthasar in his wake. ''How did you slay him?''

Jean-Claude didn't back up this time. His hand tightened on mine, but he stood his ground. ''He agreed not to call the earth against me.''

The vampire and his servant circled us like sharks. One circling left, the other right, so it was hard to keep an eye on both of them.

''Why would he limit his powers?''

''He had gone rogue, Traveler. Oliver wished to bring back the days when vampires were illegal. An earthquake might have destroyed the city, but it would not have been blamed on a vampire. He wanted to possess my vampires and cause a blood bath that would bring us back to being hunted. Oliver feared we would destroy all the humans eventually, and thus ourselves. He thought we were too dangerous to be allowed legal rights and freedom.''

''We received your report,'' the Traveler said. He stopped by me. Balthasar stopped on the other side, closest to Jean-Claude. They were mirroring each other. I wasn't sure if it was the vampire controlling his servant or just centuries of practice. ''I knew Oliver's ideas.''

I drew back against Jean-Claude. ''Is it just vamps or can he take over humans, too?''

''You are safe from his intrusion, *ma petite*.''

''Great,'' I said.

I stared at the Traveler, and it was frightening how easily I was beginning to think of this body as the Traveler and not Willie. ''Why didn't you stop Oliver, then?'' I asked.

The Traveler sidled closer and closer until only the barest inch kept us from touching. ''He was council. Council cannot fight to the death among ourselves. And nothing short of true death would have stopped him.''

''You let him come here, knowing what he planned to do,'' I said.

''We knew he had left the country but not where he fled to or what his plans were.'' The Traveler raised a hand towards my face. Balthasar did the same on his side for Jean-Claude. Willie's small hand hovered near my face.

''You had declared him rogue,'' Jean-Claude said. ''Any vampire that found him could slay him without violating our laws. That is what rogue means.''

The Traveler traced the barest of touches down my face. A trembling, tentative touch. ''So you thought we would not come to your door because you had saved us the trouble of hunting him down ourselves.''

''*Oui.*''

Balthasar had stopped caressing Jean-Claude's face. He came to stand by his master. He watched the smaller man slide his hand along my face. Balthasar seemed puzzled, surprised. Something was happening, and I didn't know what it was.

The Traveler cupped my chin in his hand. He turned my face to him. He slid his hand over my jaw, behind my neck, to run fingers in my hair.

I pulled away from him. ''I thought you didn't like girls.''

''I don't.'' He stood there, staring at me. ''Your power is amazing.'' His hand lashed out too quick to see, too quick to react. He had a handful of my hair, and his eyes, Willie's eyes, met mine. I was shielding myself this time, prepared, but my heart still fell to my feet. I waited for that cold blackness to pull me under. Nothing happened. We stood there, inches apart, and they were just eyes. I could feel his power beating down his arm like a march of icy fingers, but it wasn't enough.

He laid his hands on either side of my face almost as if he were going to kiss me. Our faces were so close that his next words seemed intimate, even though they weren't. ''I could force my gaze upon you, Anita, but it would be an expenditure of power that I might regret before dawn. You have injured Liv twice this night. I am healing her, but that too takes power.''

He stepped back from me, hugging himself as if he'd gotten more from touching me than just the feel of skin. He took three gliding steps to put himself face to face with Jean-Claude. ''Her power is a heady thing. Something to wrap around your cold skin and warm your heart for all eternity.''

Jean-Claude let out a slow breath. "She is my human servant."

"Indeed," said the Traveler. "A hundred years ago I could invade you without touching your fair skin. Now I cannot. Has she given you this power?" He reached towards Jean-Claude's face as he had mine.

I pulled Jean-Claude back, out of reach, and stepped between them. "He's mine, no sharing."

Jean-Claude slid his arm around me, holding me loosely at his side. "If you would leave us in peace, I would let Balthasar and any person you chose use me, but I will not willingly be your horse ever again, Traveler."

Willie's brown eyes stared up at Jean-Claude. There was a shrewdness, a frightening intensity, in those familiar eyes. "I am council. You are not. You will have no choice in the matter."

"Are you saying that if he took the council seat, then you couldn't hurt him?" I asked.

"If he is powerful enough to hold a council seat, then I should not be able to invade his lovely body, even were my lips pressed to him."

"Let me test my understanding here. If he takes the council seat, you'll still try and force yourself on him, because if you can force him, then he's not powerful enough to be council? But if he doesn't take the seat, you'll do it anyway."

The Traveler smiled beautifully at me, delight shining from his eyes, Willie's eyes. "Quite true."

"Why is everything with you people a freaking Catch-22? You don't do business. You just do torture," I said.

"Are you judging us?" he asked. His voice was suddenly lower and deeper than Willie's throat should have been able to hold. He took that last step forward, and I was suddenly touching them both. Their power flared over me; it was like being in the middle of two different fires, but it didn't burn. The Traveler's power was like Jean-Claude's, cool and swimming, a breath of mortality, the touch of the grave.

The power pulled a gasp from my throat and raised every hair on my body. "Back off!" I tried to shove him away from us, but he grabbed my wrist too quick to stop, almost too quick to see. The feel of his bare skin on mine sent a wave of numbing cold through my body, like a spear of ice. He jerked me away from Jean-Claude.

Jean-Claude caught my other wrist. The moment his hand touched my skin, the cold faded. His power swept through me like a flood of warm water, and it wasn't his power. I knew the taste of this warmth. It was Richard. Jean-Claude was drawing on Richard's power as I'd done earlier.

He chased the Traveler's power out of me like summer heat on ice. It was the Traveler who released me. He stepped back rubbing his hand on his coat, as if it hurt. ''Jean-Claude, you have been a very naughty boy.''

Jean-Claude drew me against him, one hand resting against my neck so that his fingers touched my skin. That electric warmth was still there playing over his skin and mine, and I knew in that moment that Richard had felt our urgency, our need.

15

A NOISE TURNED us all to the far hallway. I didn't recognize
the man. He was tall, slender, dark-skinned, maybe Hispanic,
maybe something more exotic. He wore nothing but a pair of
black satin pants with silver embroidery along the legs. He was
dragging Willie's lady love, Hannah, by one arm.

Her mascara had run in black tears down her face. Her expensive haircut still framed her face, still brought your eyes to
her strong cheekbones and full lips. But her face was like a
mask now, black tears, and burgundy lipstick smeared across
her lower face like a wound.

The Traveler said, "Why have you brought her here, Fernando?"

"My father is as much council as you are, Traveler."

"I do not dispute that."

"Yet you forbid him come to this first meeting."

"If he is council, then let him bend me to his will." The
Traveler's voice was mocking. "We are all council, but we are
not all equal."

Fernando smiled. He grabbed Hannah's beaded blue dress and
tore it down her back. She screamed.

The Traveler swayed, putting a hand to his face.

"I'm going to fuck her," Fernando said.

Balthasar strode towards them, but two leopards the size of
ponies crawled from the hallway. One black, one yellow spotted,
both big enough to tear him to pieces. They growled low and
deep, moving on huge padded feet between Balthasar and Fernando.

Fernando grabbed Hannah around the waist, pulling her dress
over her hips to expose pale blue garters. She turned and slapped

him hard enough that he rocked back. She was as feminine as they come, but she was also a vampire and could have thrown him into the solid stone wall so that he stuck there.

Fernando hit her back. Blood spattered from her mouth in shining beads. She sat half-stunned on the floor. Fernando's power boiled through the room as if he'd been holding it in check until now. Shapeshifter. Did he match the leopards that guarded his back? Maybe, but it didn't matter what flavor he was. He picked Hannah up by the front of her dress, dragging her to her knees. He drew his hand back to hit her again.

I pulled the Browning out of the coat pocket. Willie collapsed to his knees on the floor. He stared up and said, "Angel-fangs." He tried to stand and couldn't. Jean-Claude picked him up under the arms and raised him easily.

Fernando hit Hannah again. A casual slap that rocked her head back and rolled her eyes to white. "He must truly love you to fight off the Traveler's touch every time he sees you abused."

Jean-Claude's hand on my arm brought me back to myself. I had the Browning pointed at Fernando. I had to let out a breath to keep from pulling the trigger. The safety was off, and I didn't remember doing it. Why Fernando and not the kitties? The wereleopards could close the distance in the blink of an eye, but I knew who the alpha was. Take out the leader, and the cats might go play somewhere else.

Jean-Claude supported Willie with one arm, the other still lightly on my arm, as if afraid what I'd do. "Fernando," he said, "you've done what you set out to do. The Traveler is forced out, and it will take him a little time to find a second host. You can let Hannah go."

Fernando grinned at us, white teeth bright in his dark face. "I don't think so." He dragged Hannah to her feet, arms around her waist, pinning her arms to her sides. He tried to kiss her. She turned her head and screamed.

Willie was standing on his own now. He pushed away from Jean-Claude. "No, I won't let you hurt her."

The black leopard dropped to its belly, crawling closer to Willie, to us.

"If we're going to take them out, we have to do it now," I

said. Fernando first, then one of the leopards, if I had time. If not . . . one problem at a time.

"Not yet, *ma petite*. Fernando's father, Padma, will not waste precious time tormenting the little ones. The Traveler will return too soon for that."

"The Traveler won't let me taste her once he returns," Fernando said. He kept Hannah pressed to his body with one arm and raised her dress with the other.

"Does he seriously think we're going to stand here while he rapes her?" I asked.

"My father is the Master of Beasts. You won't stop me, for fear of his wrath."

"You just don't get it, do you, Fernando?" I pointed the gun very steadily at his head. "I don't give a fuck who your daddy is. Let go of her, and tell your furry buddies to back off or I'm going to make your daddy a very unhappy vampire."

"You don't want me unhappy." The voice caused my eyes to flick to the hallway beyond, but the gun didn't move.

The vampire in the doorway was Indian, as in from India. He was even wearing one of those long combo coat-tunic things. It was gold and white and shimmered on the edge of my vision as he walked further into the room. I kept my sights on his son. One monster at a time.

Jean-Claude let his hand drop away from my arm. He stepped behind me and to one side, careful not to block my shot. "Padma, Master of Beasts, greetings and welcome to my home."

"Jean-Claude, Master of the City, greetings. Your hospitality has been beyond my wildest expectations." He laughed then, but it was just a laugh. Theatrical and annoying, even sinister, but it didn't make my skin jump.

"Tell him to let Hannah go," I said.

"You must be Jean-Claude's human servant, Anita Blake."

"Yeah, nice to meet you. Now tell your son to let go of our vampire, or I'm going to put a really big hole in him."

"You wouldn't dare harm my son."

It was my turn to laugh, short, abrupt, and not very funny. "Your son said almost the same thing. You are both so wrong."

"If you kill my son, I will kill you. I will kill you all."

"Fine, let me test my understanding. If he doesn't let her go, what's he going to do with her?"

Fernando laughed, and it was low and hissing. The laugh was enough. Somewhere in that lovely body was black fur and big button eyes; wererat. "I will have her because the Traveler has forbidden it, and my father has given her to me."

"No," Willie said. He took a step forward but Jean-Claude stopped him.

"No, Willie, this is not your fight."

Fernando slid his hand over Hannah's groin. Only Jean-Claude's hand on Willie's arm kept him from rushing the shapeshifters.

Hannah said, "Master, help me."

"He can't help you, child," Padma said. "He can't help any of you."

I aimed two inches to the right of Fernando's head. The shot echoed in the big room. The bullet bit into the stone wall. Everyone froze.

"The next bullet goes in Fernando's skull."

"You wouldn't dare," Padma said.

"You keep saying that. Let's get something straight, Beast Master. Fernando is not raping Hannah. No way. I'll kill him first."

"Then I will kill you," Padma said.

"Fine, but that won't bring back your son, now will it?" I let the breath out of my body and felt that stillness spill through me. "Decide, Beast Master, decide."

"I am the Master of Beasts," he said.

"I don't care if you're Santa Claus. He lets her go or he dies."

"Jean-Claude, control your servant."

"If you can control her, Padma, be my guest. But take great care. Anita never bluffs. She will kill your son."

"Decide," I said softly, "—decide—decide—decide—decide." I wanted to shoot him. I really did, because I knew as surely as I was standing there that if I didn't shoot him now, I'd have to shoot him later. He was too arrogant to leave it alone, too blinded by his own power to leave Hannah alone, and he couldn't have her. That was a line he could not cross and live.

"Let her go, Fernando," Padma said.

"Father," the man sounded shocked.

"She will pull the trigger, Fernando. She wants to pull it. Don't you, Anita?"

"Yeah, I do."

"Silver bullets, I assume," Padma said.

"Never leave home without them," I said.

"Let her go, Fernando. Even I cannot save you from a silver bullet."

"No, she's mine. You promised."

"I'd listen to your dad, Fernando."

"Do you disobey me, my son?" There was a tone in Padma's voice that sent a rush of warm air through the room. The beginnings of anger. Something was flung over my skin, a backwash of power, but it wasn't vampiric power, not exactly. He wasn't trying to control Jean-Claude. It had a taste of warmer blood, an electric dance that said lycanthrope. Which wasn't really possible. A vampire can't be a lycanthrope, and vice-versa.

Fernando cringed, clutching Hannah to him like a doll, hiding his face in her yellow hair. "No, Father, I would never disobey you."

"Then do as I say."

Fernando flung Hannah backwards. She scrambled to Willie. He took her in his arms, touching the blood on her face, blotting at it with the silken handkerchief.

I lowered the gun.

Fernando pointed a dark hand at me. "Maybe I'll ask for you to be my pet."

"Tough talk, rat-boy. Let's see if you're man enough to back it up." I was baiting him. I realized that I wanted him to rush me. I wanted an excuse to kill him. Not good. Not good. I had to calm down or I *was* going to get us killed.

The black leopard, taller at the shoulders than my waist, started creeping towards me. It was belly to the ground, muscles tensed and rippling. The gun just shifted to it. "Don't try it."

"Elizabeth," Padma said.

The name startled me. I'd seen Elizabeth in human form once, sort of from a distance. She was one of the local wereleopards. I'd assumed, until that moment, that the leopards were part of

the entourage that Padma had brought with him. If Elizabeth
was local, the other leopard might be, too. The only thing I was
sure of was that it wasn't Zane or Nathaniel. Other than that, it
could have been anybody. But Zane acknowledging me as his
alpha had saved him from being here. If Zane had been alpha,
then beating him would have given me all the leopards, and
none of them would have been here. Or that was the theory.
With me being merely human and not a lycanthrope, the Master
of Beasts might still have called the kitties. But I would have
tried to keep them safe. I wondered if Elizabeth had tried.

She snarled at him, at me, at everyone. Her fangs were ivory-
white, and at less than ten feet, impressive as hell. This close,
even a real leopard might have gotten to me before I could fire
a killing shot. You aren't supposed to hunt big game with a
handgun.

The leopard took another belly crawl forward. "Elizabeth."
That one word flung outward burned along my skin and made
me gasp. The leopard came up short like she'd hit the end of
her leash. She rolled on the floor, struggling, slashing the air.

"She hates you, Anita," Padma said. His voice was normal
now, conversational, but whatever he was doing to the wereleopard was still happening. I could feel it like ants marching down
my skin. Ants with red hot pokers in their little hands.

I glanced at Jean-Claude, wondering if he could feel it. His
face was blank, empty, unreadable. If he felt the pain, it didn't
show.

I wasn't sure admitting I could feel it was a good idea. "Stop
it," I said.

"She would kill you if I let her. You killed the one she loved,
their leader. She would have her revenge."

"You've made your point. Let her go."

"Mercy for one who hates you so?" He glided into the room,
slippered feet barely touching the floor, as if he rode always on
tiny currents of his own power.

I should have been sensing his vampire powers. But he was
almost a blank, as if something was keeping him in check or
protecting me. I glanced at Jean-Claude again. Was he powerful
enough to keep us safe now? Had the triumvirate helped him
that much? His face told me nothing, and I didn't dare ask, not
in front of the Master of Beasts.

The leopard lay on its side, panting heavily. It watched me with pale green eyes, and it was not a friendly look.

"When I called them," Padma said. "she tried to bargain with me. They have no alpha and yet she tried to bargain. Elizabeth would bring the leopards without a struggle to do with as I like, if I would let her kill you. Help her kill you." The Beast Master motioned behind him, and a small, slender woman stepped up beside him, like she'd been waiting in the hallway for his call. Like a well-trained dog. She was nude except for a necklace that must have weighed five pounds and burned with diamonds. Her skin was that pale shade of dark that says African-American via Ireland. Bruises decorated her face, running in purple stains down her body. She was one of the most beautiful women I'd ever seen, even with the bruises. She was perfectly proportioned from forehead to slender feet. Her eyes were brown and flicked from the leopard on the floor to Jean-Claude to the rat-man. Back and forth, back and forth, until finally she settled on me.

She pleaded with her eyes, and I didn't need words to know that she was saying, Help me. That I understood, but why me?

"When Elizabeth came, she brought the others with her. I chose Vivian as my present to myself." Padma stroked her hair absently, the way you'd pet a dog. "I will give her a gift for every harm I do her. She will be rich, if she survives."

The air around her trembled like the wash of heat off a summer road. Another wereleopard that I'd never met. How many of them were there? How many people had Elizabeth delivered over to the bad guys?

"What is this, a father-son rape outing?" I asked.

Padma frowned at me. "I grow tired of you, Anita Blake."

"It's mutual," I said.

"We forced the Traveler out of his host body, but his power still shields you. He was to keep you from sensing your vampires' distress. Now he seems to be protecting you from the full rush of my powers. A pity. You would tremble at the feel of them."

Jean-Claude touched my shoulder lightly. The touch was enough. I wasn't here to trade clever repartee with the Master of Beasts. Killing him sounded like a really good idea, but I've met older vamps that you couldn't take out with silver bullets.

It would be just my luck that Padma was one of them.

Padma called the leopards to him. The yellow one rolled around his ankles like a big kitty-cat. Elizabeth sat like a well-trained dog.

Willie and Hannah were oblivious to the room. He touched her gently, as if she were glass. They kissed, and that one chaste touch of lips said it all, tenderness, love. Willie and Hannah were just plain gone on each other. It was beautiful.

"You see why I gave her to my son. Such anguish her abuse would have caused them both. But the Traveler needed their bodies."

I stared at him. It was bad enough when I thought the choice was just because Hannah was blond and lovely, but to know it was deliberate cruelty and not just lust—that made it worse.

"You son of a bitch," I said.

"Are you trying to make me angry?" Padma said.

Jean-Claude touched me again. "Anita, please."

He rarely used my real name. When he did, it was either very serious or something I wouldn't like. This time it was both.

I don't know what I was about to say, because suddenly the Traveler lifted his shield. Padma's power crashed over us. It thundered over me, filling my head, scrambling every thought I had. I fell to my knees like I'd been hit by a hammer between the eyes.

Jean-Claude stayed standing, but I felt him sway beside me.

Padma laughed. "He cannot re-enter another host and maintain his shield."

A voice came like a wind easing through the room. I wasn't sure if I heard the voice out loud or if it was just in my head. "He will need his powers in the hallway. I chose to lift the shield. Enough games, Padma. Let him see what lies beyond." There was a scent with the words; fresh turned earth, the smell of roots pulled from the ground. I could almost feel the crumble of rich black soil between my hands. I squeezed my hands around the Browning until they shook, and I still couldn't shake the sense of earth between my hands on the gun. Even staring at the gun, seeing it was clean, didn't make it go away.

"What's happening?" I asked. Surprised and pleased that I could form a coherent sentence.

"They are council," Jean-Claude said. "They have taken off, how would you say, the gloves?"

"Shit," I said.

Padma laughed. He stared at me, and I knew he was concentrating just for little ol' me. His power slammed over me, into me. It was halfway between putting your hand on a live electric wire and shoving the same hand into fire. The electric heat ate through my body. The heat gathered in the center of me. It flexed like a fist growing larger, larger. If he spread his fingers inside me, he'd tear me apart, burst me from the inside out with just his power. I screamed.

16

A COOL TOUCH slid over the heat. A wind, cool and easeful as death, swept over my body. The wind blew my hair back from my face. Blessed coolness filled me. Jean-Claude's hands caressed my shoulders. He was kneeling on the floor, cradling me in his arms. I didn't remember falling. His skin was cool to the touch. I knew that somehow he was throwing his hard-won warmth away. His warmth to cool the fire.

That awful pressure inside of me eased, then shrank. It was like Jean-Claude was a wind blowing out Padma's fire. But it cost him. I felt his heart slow. The blood in his veins flowed slow and slower. The warmth that mimicked life was leaving him, and death seeped inside to fill its place.

I turned in his arms so I could see his face. The face was pale and perfect, and you'd never have known, just by watching, what it had cost him to save me.

Hannah turned to us, her battered face set in calm lines. "My apologies, Jean-Claude. My compatriot has let your servant's defiance best his judgment."

Willie stepped away from Hannah, shaking his head. "Damn you, damn you."

Hannah's grey eyes turned to him, angry. "Do not tempt me, little one. You cannot trade insults with me and survive."

"Willie," Jean-Claude said. There was no power to the word, just a warning. It was enough. Willie stepped back.

Jean-Claude looked at the Traveler in his new body. "If he had killed Anita, I might have died with her. Is that why you have truly come? To kill us?"

"I swear it is not." Where he'd made Willie glide, Hannah was awkward on her stiletto heels. He didn't fall, but he didn't glide either. It was almost heartening. He wasn't perfect.

"To prove my sincerity," he said, "take your warmth back from your servant. We will not stop you."

"He thrust me out," Padma said. "How can you allow him to grow strong again?"

"You sound afraid," the Traveler said.

"I do not fear him," Padma said.

"Then let him feed."

I leaned into Jean-Claude's chest, resting my cheek against the mound of silken ruffles on the front of his shirt. His heart had stopped beating. He wasn't even breathing. He'd used too much of himself up.

I watched Padma from the safety of Jean-Claude's arms and knew I would kill him. I knew that Padma wanted us dead. I'd felt it. No one as powerful as he was lost control that badly. He'd nearly killed me, us, and it would all have been a tragic accident. Bullshit.

The Browning lay where I'd dropped it, but I'd tasted Padma's power now. Silver might not be enough to kill him. Wounding him seemed like a really bad idea. Kill or leave him the hell alone, like any big predator. Don't fuck with it unless you can finish the job.

"Feed from your servant," Padma said. "I will not stop you. The Traveler has spoken." That last held a touch of bitterness. Council member or not, Padma feared the Traveler, or he'd have fought him more. Compatriots but not equals.

I knelt, gripping Jean-Claude's arms through the rough lace and the glittering material of his jacket. His arms felt reassuringly solid, real. "What . . ."

He stopped me with fingers on my lips, a delicate touch. "It is not blood that I need, Padma. It is her warmth. It is only a lesser master that must needs take blood from his servants."

Padma's face had gone empty, blank. "You have not lost your knack of insulting without being insulting, Jean-Claude."

I stared up at Jean-Claude, even kneeling he was taller. His voice eased through my mind. "No questions, *ma petite*, or they will know you are not wholly mine."

Since I had a lot of questions, that pretty much sucked. But if I couldn't ask direct questions, there were other ways. "Does the Beast Master have to sink fang to jump-start his heart?"

"*Oui, ma petite.*"

"How . . . vulgar," I said. It was one of the most civilized insults I'd ever come up with. It worked, too.

Padma hissed at us. "Do not test my patience too far, Jean-Claude. The Traveler is not the head of the council. You have enough enemies here now that a vote might not go your way. Press me too hard and I will force a vote."

"Force a vote to what end?" Jean-Claude asked. "The Traveler has promised that you are not here to kill me. What else would you vote upon, Master of Beasts."

"Get on with it, Jean-Claude." Padma's voice was low with a sound that was almost a growl. It sounded more animal than vampire.

Jean-Claude touched my face gently, turning me to look at him. "Let us show the Master of Beasts how it is done, *ma petite.*"

I didn't really like the sound of that. But I knew one thing for certain, Jean-Claude needed his strength back. He'd never be able to repeat the trick of thrusting out a council member when he was so cold, so drained.

"Do it," I said. I had to trust him. Trust him not to hurt me. Trust him not to do something awful or embarrassing. I realized that I didn't trust him. That no matter how much I loved his body, I knew he was other. I knew that what he thought of as okay was not necessarily okay at all.

He smiled. "I will bathe in your warmth, *ma petite*. Roll you around me until my heart beats only for you. My breath will grow warm from your kiss." He cupped my face between the chilled skin of his hands and kissed me.

His lips were velvet, his touch light, caressing. His hands slid up the sides of my face, fingers gliding through my hair next to the scalp, kneading, massaging. He kissed my forehead and shuddered.

I tried to kiss him again, and he drew back. "Remember, *ma petite*, if any of your fair body touches mine too much, it will deaden. Do not be so eager to lose the sweet sensation of your lips for the night."

I went very still in his arms, thinking about what he'd just said. Bodies touching, bare skin needed, maybe? But if any part touched too long or too forcefully, my skin would deaden, but only for the night. Jean-Claude was really very good at giving information without seeming to. Made me wonder how often he'd had to do it in the past.

He slipped the coat off my shoulders until it hung nearly to my waist. He ran his hands over my skin, kneading his fingers into me. His hands were warm. He slid his hands over the coat, gripping my arms through it, but no bare skin. He kissed my throat butterfly light, his face rubbing up my neck, my cheek.

He drew back from me with a quick rush of breath. I put my hand over his heart, and there was nothing. I caressed his face, touching the big pulse in his throat. Nothing. I wanted to ask what we were doing wrong, but didn't dare. Didn't want the bad guys to know we didn't do things like this much. Sex we did, the otherworldly vampire shit we skipped if I could manage it.

He started unbuttoning his shirt.

I looked at him, eyes a little wide.

He bared a circle of his stomach.

I just looked at that glimpse of pale skin. "What?" I asked.

"Touch me, *ma petite*."

I glanced at the watching vampires. I shook my head. "No foreplay in front of the bad guys."

"I could simply take blood, if you would prefer," he said softly. He said it as if we did it every night. We'd done it twice voluntarily on my part. Once had been to save his life. The second time had been to save him and Richard. I did not want to donate blood. Sometimes I thought bloodletting was more intimate than sex to a vampire. I didn't want to do that in front of company either.

I stared up at him, getting angry. He was asking me to do very intimate things in front of strangers. I didn't like it, and he knew I wouldn't like it. So why hadn't he warned me? Had he really not thought we'd have to do this tonight?

"She is angry with you," Padma said. "Is she truly that modest?" He sounded doubtful. "Could it be that you cannot truly do what you say you can do?"

Hannah's body stood legs apart balancing on the unfamiliar high heels. "Are you as weak as Padma? Just another blood-sucker?" The Traveler shook his head, Hannah's hair sliding across the shoulders of her ruined dress. "What else have you been bluffing about, Jean-Claude?"

"Damn you all to hell," I said. I slid my hands inside Jean-Claude's shirt, fingers sliding over his stomach. He was cold to the touch. Dammit. I pulled his shirt out of his pants, none too gently, and ran my hands over his skin. I kneaded my fingers along the muscles of his back, and could feel heat rise up my throat into my face. Under other circumstances, in the privacy of a bedroom, it had possibilities. Now, it was just embarrassing.

He drew my arms out. "Careful, *ma petite*, or your hands will grow cold."

My fingertips were cold as if I'd been outside without gloves. I stared up at him for a second or two. "If I can't touch you with my hands, what do you suggest I use?"

Padma suggested something explicit enough to make me point a finger at him. "You stay out of this."

He laughed at me. "She is truly embarrassed. How terribly precious. Asher said she was a virgin before you. I did not believe him, until now."

I let my head drop to my chest. I was not going to say it. I did not owe the vampire council a rundown on my love life.

Jean-Claude's hand moved into view. He never touched me, but just the movement of his hand brought my face up to meet his gaze. "I would not ask this of you here and now, if it were not necessary. You must believe that."

Looking into his blue, blue eyes, I did believe him. Stupid, but true. "What do you want me to do?"

He raised his fingers and put them just above my lips, so close that if I breathed in, he'd have had to touch me. "Use your lovely mouth over my heart. If our bond is as strong as I believe it to be, there are shortcuts, *ma petite*."

I sighed and pulled his shirt up, baring his chest. In private I loved running my tongue over the cross-shaped burn scar on his chest. But this wasn't private. Hell with it.

I laid my lips against the cool skin of his stomach, and licked a quick, wet line up his chest.

He drew in a sharp hiss of breath. How could he be breathing and not have a heartbeat? No answer to that, but I'd seen it before. Vampires that breathed but did not have a pulse.

I ran my tongue over the smoothness of the cross-shaped burn scar, ending with a kiss over his heart. I felt my lips grow cold. It wasn't the tingling cold of winter, though. It was just as he'd said. His body stealing my warmth. My life seeping away into him.

I knelt back away from him, licking my lips, trying to feel them. "How's that?"

He laughed, and the sound slid down my back like an ice cube, rubbed purposefully and long to the base of my spine.

I shuddered. "You're feeling better."

He lifted me suddenly, hands on my thighs. I let out a surprised yip, putting my hands on his shoulders for balance. He wrapped his arms around my legs and stared up at me. The pupil in his eyes had bled away to a shining blue fire.

I felt his heartbeat in my throat. His pulse raced through my body. He let me slide slowly through his arms. "Kiss me, *ma petite*, as we are meant to kiss. I am warm and safe to touch."

"Warm but never safe," I said. I started to kiss him when I was inches above his forehead and continued the kiss as I slid down his body. He kissed me like he would eat me from the mouth down. Fangs pressed hard and sharp, and he had to draw away or draw blood. The kiss left me breathless, tingling, but not with cold.

I realized that he'd gotten a buzz from drinking in my warmth. That it had felt good in a more than practical way. Trust him to make a virtue out of necessity.

"Now that you have your full powers once again," the Traveler said, "I will be leaving you. You drove Padma out without my aid. Surely you can defend yourself again."

"He bested you, as well," Padma said.

Hannah's face looked at us. "Yes, he did. I would expect nothing less from the master that slew the Earthmover." Hannah turned back to Padma. "And he did what you cannot. He regained his warmth with his human servant without drawing her blood. A trick that any true master can accomplish."

"Enough of this," Padma said. He sounded angry. Having to share blood with your human servant seemed to be a real faux pas. "The night wanes. Now that you are at full strength, Jean-Claude, search for your people. See who does not answer your call."

"I will leave you now, Jean-Claude. I will await you beyond.'' Hannah suddenly sagged. Willie caught her and lowered her gently to the floor.

''Search, Jean-Claude, search for your people,'' Padma said.

Jean-Claude stood, drawing me with him. His pupils swam through the shining blue of his eyes. His eyes settled into their normal color. He stared past me, past Padma. I didn't think he was seeing anything in the room. His power crept from his hands across my skin. I think if I hadn't been touching him, I wouldn't have felt a thing. The faintest shimmer of energy, as if this was a small thing to do.

He blinked and looked at Padma. ''Damian.''

Damian was one of Jean-Claude's lieutenants. Like Liv, he was over five hundred, but would never be a master.

In Damian's case it was over a thousand years, but would never be a master. It was a frightening amount of time to have acquired so little power. Don't get me wrong, Damian was powerful. For a five-hundred-year-old he was scary. For a thousand years he was a baby. A dangerous, carnivorous baby, but still Damian had acquired all the power he might ever have. He could live until the sun expanded and swallowed the earth and he'd be no more powerful than he had been at dusk today.

He was one of the few vamps to ever fool me completely about his age. I'd underestimated his age by over half. I'd judged by power and was just beginning to learn that power was not the only thing to judge by.

Jean-Claude had bargained with Damian's old master for his freedom to come here and play second banana.

''What have you done to Damian?'' Jean-Claude asked.

''I, nothing, but is he dead?'' Padma smiled and took Vivian's hand. ''That is a question only his master may answer.'' He walked down the hallway, leading the wereleopard by the hand. Vivian looked back at me, watching me with wide, frightened eyes until they were lost to sight. The black leopard lingered, watching me.

I spoke before I thought, instinct almost. ''How could you have given them over to that thing?''

She snarled at me, tail twitching.

''You are weak, Elizabeth. Gabriel knew that and despised you for it.''

She let out a coughing roar. Padma's voice cut across the

sound like a knife blade. "Elizabeth, come to me now or I shall be very angry."

The leopard gave me a last snarl and padded out of sight.

"Did Gabriel tell you she was weak, *ma petite*?"

I shook my head. "She wouldn't have brought them here if she were stronger. He called and she came, but she should have come alone."

"Perhaps she did her best, *ma petite*."

"Then her best isn't good enough." I looked at Jean-Claude's careful, unreadable face. His body was still, calm. I laid my hand above his heart underneath his shirt. His heart was pounding.

"You think Damian's dead," I said.

"I know he is dead." He stared down at me. "Whether it is permanent, that is the question."

"Dead is dead," I said.

He laughed then and hugged me to him. "Oh, *ma petite*, you above all should know that is not true."

"I thought you said they couldn't kill us tonight," I said.

"So I thought," he said.

Great. Every time I thought I understood the rules, they changed. Why was it that the damn rules always seemed to change for the worse?

17

WILLIE CAME OVER to us, leading Hannah by the hand. "Thank you, master, Anita."

There were gashes in his thin face, part of the initial fight for the Circus, I guess. They were already healing. He looked awful, even more like the walking dead than usual. "You look like hell," I said.

He grinned at me, flashing fang. He hadn't been dead three years yet. It takes a little practice to smile without flashing fang. "I'm okay." He looked at Jean-Claude. "I tried to stop them. We all did."

Jean-Claude had tucked his shirt back in his pants. He smoothed his hands down the front of the shirt and touched Willie's shoulder. "You fought the council, Willie. Win or lose, you did well."

"Thanks, master."

Jean-Claude usually corrected anyone when they called him master, but tonight, I guess we were going formal.

"Come, we must attend Damian." He offered me his wrist, and when I didn't know quite what he wanted, he laid my fingertips over the pulse. "You touch me as if you were taking my pulse."

"Is there some significance to this?"

"It shows that you are more than my servant or my bed partner. It shows I consider you an equal."

"What will the council think about that?" I asked.

"It will force them to negotiate not only with me, but with you. It will complicate things for them and give us more options."

I rested my hand on his wrist. His pulse was steady under my fingers. "Confusion to our enemies, eh?"

He nodded, making it almost a bow. "Indeed, *ma petite*, indeed."

I walked beside him towards the hallway, my right hand in my pocket on the Browning, which I'd rescued from the floor. When we got a clear view of the hallway, Jean-Claude's pulse sped under my fingers.

Damian lay on his side curled around a sword. Blood had soaked around the blade into the dark material of the vest he wore as a shirt. The point came out his back. He'd been spitted. Hard to be a hundred percent sure, but it looked like a heart blow.

There was a new vampire standing beside him. He held a two-handed sword in his hands, point down, like a cane. I recognized the sword. It was the one Damian slept with in his coffin.

The new vamp was tall, six foot six or more, broad-shouldered. His hair was cut like a bowl of yellow ringlets around his face, leaving his ears bare. He wore a white tunic, white trousers, white on white in layers. He stood rigid, at attention, like a soldier.

"Warrick," Jean-Claude said. "I had hoped you escaped Yvette's tender mercies."

The tall vampire looked at us. His eyes flicked to my hand on Jean-Claude's wrist. He dropped to one knee and held Damian's sword across his hands. He bowed his head and offered the sword to us. "He fought well. It had been too long since I had such an opponent. I forgot myself and slew him. I would not have wished death on such a warrior. His final death is a great loss."

Jean-Claude took the sword from the vampire's hands. "Save your apologies, Warrick. I come to save Damian, not to bury him."

Warrick raised pale blue eyes to us. "But I have pierced his heart. If you were the master that had made him, then there would be a chance, but you did not call him from his grave to his second life."

"But I am Master of the City, and Damian took a blood oath."

Warrick laid the sword on the ground near Damain's still form. "Your blood may call to him. I pray that it will be enough."

I stared at him. I'd never heard a vampire say "I pray." Vampires, for obvious reasons, didn't pray a lot. I mean, who was going to answer? Oh, yeah, there was the Church of Eternal Life, but they were more a humanist religion, sort of New Wavey. I'm not sure they talked much about God.

Damian's hair was nearly blood-red, a startling color against the alabaster whiteness of his skin. I knew his eyes were a green that any cat would envy, but tonight his eyes were closed, and if things went badly, they'd never open again.

Jean-Claude knelt beside Damian. He laid his hand on Damian's chest, near the sword. "If I pull out the sword and his heart does not beat, his eyes do not open, then he is gone. One chance, and one chance only. We could put him in a hole somewhere for a hundred years and until the sword was pulled out of his heart, there would still be a chance. If we do it here and now, we risk losing him forever."

That last bit of lore is why you never ever remove a stake from a corpse's heart no matter how dead it appears to be.

I knelt beside them. "Is there a ritual for it?"

He shook his head. "I will invoke the blood oath he took. That will help call him back, but Warrick is correct. I did not make Damian. I am not his true master."

"No, he's older than you are by about six hundred years." I looked down at the vampire, spitted on the sword, lying in a pool of his own dark blood. He was wearing a pair of dress pants that matched the vest. Without a conservative shirt under the vest it looked strangely erotic. I could still feel Damian in my head. His power, the beat and the pulse of centuries flowed through him. He wasn't dead, or at least not completely dead. I could still feel his aura, something.

"I can still feel Damian," I said.

"What do you mean, *ma petite*?"

I had a horrible compulsion to touch Damian. To run my hands over his bare arms. I wasn't into necrophilia, no matter how close I walked the edge. What was going on?

"I can feel him. His energy in my head. It's like coming on

a fresh corpse before the soul has left the body. He's still intact,
I think.''

Warrick was looking at me. "How can you know that?"

I reached out towards Damian and stopped myself, hands
curling into fists. My hands ached to touch him, not sexual exactly but like seeing a really fine sculpture. I wanted to trace
the lines of his body, to feel the flow and ebb of him. To . . .

"What is wrong, *ma petite*?"

I touched my fingertips to Damian's arm, as if afraid he would
burn. My hand slid over his cool flesh, almost without me wanting it to. The force that animated Damian's body flowed through
his cooling skin, flowed over my hand, down my arm, marched
in goose bumps across my body.

I gasped.

"What are you doing, *ma petite*?" Jean-Claude was rubbing
his arms as if he, too, felt it.

Warrick put out a hand towards me like he was holding his
hand in front of fire, not sure if he could or should touch. He
pulled back, rubbing his hand on his pants. "It is true. You are
a necromancer."

"You ain't seen nothing yet," I whispered. I turned to Jean-
Claude. "When you pull out the sword, the trick is going to be
to keep the power from leaving with the opening of the wound.
To keep, for lack of a better word, his soul from fleeing, right?"

Jean-Claude was watching me, as if he'd never really seen
me before. Nice to know I could still surprise him. "I do not
know, *ma petite*. I am not a witch or a student of magical meta-
physics. I will invoke the oath, speak the ritual, and hope he
survives."

"Sometimes when I call a zombie from the grave, it's easier
to call them a second time." I slid my hands down to hold
Damian's limp hand, but it wasn't enough. My power and the
power inside the vampire needed a more immediate touch than
mere hands.

"He is not a zombie, *ma petite*."

"Warrick said you hadn't called Damian from the grave, but
I have." Once upon a time, nearly by accident I had raised three
of Jean-Claude's vampires. It was when he, Richard, and I first
invoked the triumvirate. The power had been so overwhelming

that I'd raised every true corpse near us as a zombie, but there had been too much power. I'd fed it to the vampires and they'd risen for me. Necromancers were rumored to be able to call all manner of dead to do their bidding. But that was legend. As far as I knew, I was the only living necromancer to pull off this particular trick.

"What are you asking, *ma petite*?"

I crawled around Damian's body. The blood was cool through my hose. My hand trailed up his arm, never losing contact with his body, with that power curled inside of him. The power that animated him had thrust me out once, cast me out, hurt me. But it was like once having brushed each other, we were linked.

"You're linked to Damian, but you're also linked to me. I can feel Damian in my head. I don't know if it's a link, but it's something. Use it," I said.

"You mean draw on your power to help strengthen my hold on him?" Jean-Claude said.

"Yeah." I dragged Damian into my lap, on his side, the sword still spitting him. When Jean-Claude saw what I was doing, he helped me. I cradled Damian on his side, shoulders in my lap, his head resting on my arm. I slid my hand down his chest, searching for his heart, and found the blade instead. It had pierced his heart. Even with my help, even with Jean-Claude's help, if he hadn't been over five hundred, he'd be dead. Five hundred seemed to be an age where vamps gained a great deal of power. Being over a thousand could only help him. I could feel him, through my body, my head. Through the growing power, I realized I'd turned my back to the hallway. It was hard to think, but I said, "Do we have a truce until we raise him?"

"You mean will they attack us while we save him?"

"Yes."

"I will guard you," Warrick said. He stood and took Damian's sword.

"Isn't that a conflict of interest?" I asked.

"If he does not rise, I will be punished for killing him. It is not just sorrow at my own carelessness that prompts me to help you. I fear what my mistress will do."

Jean-Claude stared down at Damian. "Padma wishes to kill us for the power the triumvirate has given us, *ma petite*. Now that he knows you have called Damian from his coffin like a zombie, he will fear you even more.''

''Is Warrick going to tell him?''

Jean-Claude gave a gentle smile. ''There is no need for Warrick to tell, is there, Traveler?''

A voice sighed around us. ''I am here.''

I stared up at the air, at nothing. ''You little son of bitch, you're an eavesdropper.''

Willie stumbled. Hannah jerked back from him. ''I am many things, Anita.'' Willie turned to us with that ancient intelligence burning in his eyes. ''Why have you withheld this information from us, Jean-Claude?''

''You see us as a threat without this bit of information, Traveler. Do you blame me for hiding it from you?''

He gave a small smile that was both gentle and condescending. ''No, I suppose I don't.''

Jean-Claude gripped the hilt of the sword. He put his hand on Damian's chest to brace himself. His fingers brushed my hand. ''You might wish to move your hand, *ma petite*. The sword is sharp.''

I shook my head. ''I'm going to make his heart beat. I can't do that if I'm not touching it.''

Jean-Claude turned his head to one side, looking at me. ''The magic grips you, *ma petite*, and you forget yourself. At least use your left hand.''

He was right. The magic, for lack of a better word, was building. I'd never felt my own power so strongly outside of a blood sacrifice. Of course, there was plenty of blood, just none that I'd spilt myself. But I could sense Damain's heart inside his chest. It was almost as if I could have reached inside and caressed the muscle. Like I was not seeing it, but feeling it, and that wasn't it either. I had no word for it. It wasn't touch or sight, but I could feel it just the same. I pulled my right hand away and slipped my left over Damian's still heart.

''Are you ready, *ma petite*?''

I nodded.

Jean-Claude rose on his knees. ''I am the Master of the City. My blood you have drunk. My flesh you have touched. You are mine, Damian. You gave yourself willing to me. Come to me now, Damian. Rise to me now. Come to my hand.'' He tightened his grip on the blade. I felt Damian's body shift boneless as the dead.

I felt his heart, caressed it and it was cold, dead. "I am master of your heart, Damian," Jean-Claude said. "I will it to beat."

"We will make it beat," I said. My voice sounded distant, strange, not like my voice at all. Power breathed through me, through Damian, into Jean-Claude. I felt it spreading outward and knew that every corpse in the place would feel the rush.

"Now," I whispered.

Jean-Claude looked at me one last time, then turned all his attention to Damian. He yanked the blade out in one harsh motion.

Damian's essence tried to follow the blade out, tried to slip away through the wound. I felt it sliding away. I called to it, pressed it into the dead flesh, and it wasn't enough. I moved my hand over his heart. The sliding blade sliced my hand. Blood, fresh and warm and human, flowed over the wound. The thing inside Damian hesitated. It stayed to taste my blood. It was enough. I didn't caress its heart. I smashed it, filled it with the power that crawled over us.

The heart thudded against his chest so that I felt it in my bones. His spine bowed, raising him out of my lap, throwing his head. His mouth opened in a silent scream. His eyes flew open wide. He slumped back into my lap.

He stared up at me, wide-eyed, frightened. He grabbed my arm. He tried to talk and couldn't speak past the thundering of the pulse in his throat. I could feel the blood in his body, the beat of his heart, the rush of him.

He reached out to Jean-Claude, grabbing the sleeve of his jacket. He finally whispered, "What have you done to me?"

"Saved you, *mon ami*, saved you."

Damian slumped suddenly. His body began to quiet. I began to lose the sense of his pulse, the taste of his heart. It slid slowly away and I let it go. But I was almost sure I could have held it. I could have kept the feel and rush of his body. I could have made it rise and fall to my touch. I was almost sure.

I ran my hand through his thick red hair and knew temptation, and it was only slightly tinged with sex. I raised my still bleeding hand where I could see it. It wasn't much of a cut; two, three stitches and I'd be fine. It hurt, but not enough. I ran the still bleeding hand through his hair. The thickness of his hair slid across the open wound, abrading it. The pain was suddenly sharper, aching and nauseating. Enough pain to bring me back to myself.

Damian stared up at me, afraid. Afraid of me.

18

"MY HOW TERRIBLY impressive." I turned, Damian still in my lap. Yvette was stalking down the hallway towards us. She'd lost the mink stole, and the white dress was very simple, very elegant, very Chanel. The rest of the scene was pure Marquis de Sade.

Jason, werewolf, flunky, sometimes voluntary appetizer to the undead, was with her. He was dressed in a cross between black leather pants and skin-tight chaps. Bare skin showed at his thighs, and what looked like a leather thong covered his groin. Around his neck was a metal-studded dog collar with a leash attached to it. Yvette was holding the leash. Fresh bruises marched down his face, neck, arms. There were cuts on his lower chest and stomach that looked like claw marks. His hands were bound behind his back, arms pulled so tight to his body that that alone had to hurt.

Yvette stopped about eight feet from us, posing. She shoved Jason hard enough in the back for him to let out a small sound, forcing him to his knees. She drew the leash tight so he was almost hanging.

She smoothed her hand through his yellow hair, adjusting it, like he was about to get his picture taken. "He's my gift while I'm here. Do you like the wrapping?"

"Can you sit up?" I asked Damian.

"I think so." He rolled off my lap, sitting up carefully, as if everything wasn't working quite right yet.

I got to my feet. "How you doing, Jason?"

"I'm okay," he said.

Yvette jerked the leash tighter, so he couldn't talk. I realized that the inside of the collar had metal spikes on it, a choke collar. Great.

"He is my wolf, Yvette. Mine to protect. You cannot have him," Jean-Claude said.

"I have already had him," she said. "But I will have him again. I have not hurt him yet. The bruises are not my doing. He got that in defense of this place. In defense of you. Ask him yourself." She eased the collar, and then the leash itself.

Jason took a long breath and looked at us.

"Did she hurt you?" Jean-Claude asked.

"No," he said.

"You have shown great restraint," Jean-Claude said to Yvette. "Or have your tastes changed since last we embraced?"

She laughed. "Oh, no, my tastes are the same as they always were. I will torment him now in front of you and you will be powerless to stop me. This way I torment several people for the price of one." She smiled. She looked better than she had at the restaurant. Not quite so pale.

"Who'd you feed off of?" I asked.

Her eyes flicked to me. "You'll see soon enough." She turned her attention to Warrick. He didn't exactly cringe, but he seemed suddenly smaller, less shining. "Warrick, you failed me."

Warrick stood against the wall, Damian's sword still in his hand. "I did not mean to hurt him, mistress."

"Oh, I don't mean that. You guarded them while they brought him back."

"You said I would be punished if he died."

"So I did, but would you really have used that great sword on me?"

He dropped to his knees. "No, mistress."

"Then how could you guard them?"

Warrick shook his head. "I did not think . . ."

"You never do." She pulled Jason in against her legs, cradling his face against her thigh. "Watch, Jason, watch and see what I do to bad little boys."

Warrick got to his feet, putting his back to the wall. He dropped the sword, clattering on the stones. "Please, mistress, please do not do this."

Yvette took in a deep breath, head back, eyes closed, caressing Jason's face. She was anticipating.

"What's she going to do?" I asked.

"Watch" was all Jean-Claude would say.

Warrick was kneeling close enough for me to touch. Whatever was about to happen, we were going to have a ringside seat. Which was the point, I suppose.

Warrick stared at the far wall, past us, ignoring us as much as he could. A white film spread across his pale blue eyes, until they were cloudy, blind. If I hadn't been standing within arm's reach, it would have been too subtle to see.

His eyes collapsed inward, crumbling with rot. His face was still perfect, strong, heroic, like an engraving of St. George, but his eyes were empty, rotting holes. Thick greenish pus trailed down his cheeks, like thick tears.

"Is she doing that to him?" I asked.

"Yes," Jean-Claude said, almost too soft to hear.

Warrick made a small sound low in his throat. Black fluid burst from his mouth, pouring down his lips. He tried to scream, and all that came out was a deep, choking gurgle. He fell forward onto hands and knees. The pus-filled liquid poured from his mouth, eyes, ears. It flowed in a puddle of liquid thicker than blood.

It should have stunk, but as so often happened with vampires that rotted, there was no odor. Warrick vomited his own rotting internal organs onto the floor.

We all began to move back from the widening pool. Didn't want to step in it. It wouldn't do us any harm, but even the other vampires stepped back from it.

Warrick collapsed onto his side. His white clothes were nearly black with gore. But underneath the mess he was still whole. His body was untouched.

His hand reached out blindly. It was a helpless gesture. A gesture that said better than words that it hurt, and he was still in there. Still feeling. Still thinking.

"Sweet Jesus," I said.

"You should see what I can do with my own body." Yvette's voice dragged our attention back to her. She was still standing there, cradling Jason against her leg. She was a white, gleaming figure, except for her hand. From the elbow down a green rot had started.

Jason noticed it. He started to scream, and she yanked the collar too tight for speech. She caressed his face with her rotting hand, leaving a smear of something thick and dark and all too real.

Jason went wild. He tore away from her. She pulled on the collar until his face turned pink, then red. He fought to stay away from her. Fought like a fish on a hook. His face turned purplish, and still he wouldn't come to her rotting hand.

Jason collapsed to the floor. He was about to choke himself into unconsciousness. "He has tasted the pleasures of rotting flesh before with other vampires, haven't you, Jason? He is so afraid. It is why Padma gave him to me." Yvette started to close the distance between herself and Jason's prone body. "I doubt his mind will survive even a night. Isn't it delicious?"

"We are *so* not doing this," I said. I took the Browning out of my pocket and showed it to her. "Don't touch him."

"You are a conquered people, Anita. Don't you grasp that yet?" she asked.

"Conquer this," I said. I raised the Browning towards her.

Jean-Claude touched my arm. "Put away your gun, *ma petite.*"

"We can't let her have Jason."

"She will not have Jason," he said. He stared down the hallway at Yvette. "Jason is mine. Mine in every way. I will not share him with you, and it is against the rules of hospitality that you do something to one of my people that will cause permanent damage. Breaking his mind is against council law."

"Padma doesn't think so," Yvette said.

"But you are not Padma." Jean-Claude glided towards them. His power began to fill the hallway like cool rising water.

"You were my toy for over a hundred years, Jean-Claude. Do you really think you can stand against me now?"

I felt her lash out, like a knife striking, but her power met Jean-Claude's and faded. It was like she was striking at mist. His power didn't fight back. It absorbed.

Jean-Claude stepped up, almost touching her, and jerked the leash out of her hand. She touched his face with her rotting flesh, smearing things worse than blood down his cheek.

Jean-Claude laughed, and it was bitter, like swallowing broken glass. It hurt to hear the sound. "I have seen you at your worst, Yvette. There is nothing new you can show me."

She dropped her hands to her side and stared up at him. "There are more delights up ahead. Padma and the Traveler await you." She didn't know that the Traveler was already among us. Willie's body remained quiet, not giving the Traveler away. Interesting.

Yvette held up her hand, and it was smooth and perfect once more. "You are conquered, Jean-Claude. You just don't know it yet."

Jean-Claude hit her, a blur of speed that sent her careening along the floor to end in a not so elegant bundle against the wall. "I may be conquered, Yvette, but not by you. Not by you."

19

JEAN-CLAUDE UNTIED Jason's hands and tore the collar from around his neck. Jason huddled into a little ball on the floor. He was making small noises in his throat more primitive than words and more piteous.

Yvette had gotten to her high heels and left us. Warrick was healing, if that was the right word. He sat up, still covered in the remains of his own bodily fluids, but his eyes were clear and blue, and he looked whole.

The Traveler in Willie's body walked up to stand by Jean-Claude. "You have impressed me more than once this night."

"I did none of it to impress, Traveler. These are my people. These are my lands. I defend them. It is not a game." He produced two handkerchiefs from somewhere. He handed me one. "For your hand, *ma petite*." He started to wipe the goop off Jason's face with the other handkerchief.

I stared down at my left hand. Blood was running in a nice steady line down my hand. I'd forgotten about it, watching Warrick rot. Some horrors were worse than pain. I took the bit of blue silk from Jean-Claude. "Thanks." I wrapped the makeshift bandage around the wound, but couldn't tie it one-handed.

The Traveler tried to help me tie the bandage. I pulled away from him.

"I offer you aid, not harm."

"No thanks."

He smiled, and again it was not Willie's thoughts that slid over his face. "It upsets you so much that I inhabit this body. Why?"

"He's my friend," I said.

"Friendship. You claim friendship with this vampire. He is nothing. A power not to be reckoned with."

"He's not my friend because he's powerful or not powerful. He's just my friend."

"It has been a very long time since someone has invoked friendship in my presence. They will beg for mercy, but never on the grounds of friendship."

Jean-Claude stood. "No one else would have thought of it."

"No one else would have been so naive," the Traveler said.

"It is a form of naiveté," Jean-Claude said. "That is true, but how long has it been, Traveler, since someone, anyone, had the courage to be naive before the council? They come before you asking for power, safety, vengeance, but not friendship, not loyalty. No, that they will not ask of the council."

Willie's head did that little turn to one side again, as if the Traveler were thinking. "Does she offer me friendship or ask it of me?"

I started to answer, but Jean-Claude beat me to it. "Can you offer true friendship without asking for it in return?"

I opened my mouth to say that I'd sooner be friends with a hungry crocodile, but Jean-Claude touched my arm gently. It was enough. We were winning. Don't blow it.

"Friendship," the Traveler said. "Now that is indeed something I have not been offered since I took my seat upon the council."

I spoke then, without thinking first. "That must be very lonely."

He laughed, and it was that same eerie mixture of Willie's loud bray and a slithering chuckle. "She is like a wind through a window long closed, Jean-Claude. A mixture of cynicism, naiveté, and power." He touched my face, and I let him. He cupped the side of my face in his hand in an almost familiar gesture. "She does have a certain . . . charm."

His hand trailed down my face, fingertips lingering against my cheek. He dropped his hand suddenly, fingers rubbing against each other as if he were trying to feel some invisible something. He shook his head. "I and this body will await you in the torture room." He answered me before I could even say no. "I do not plan to harm this body, Anita, but I do need it to walk about. I will leave this host if there is one that you would prefer I take.''

He turned and stared at the rest of the group. His gaze came to rest at last on Damian. ''I could take this one. Balthasar would enjoy that, I think.''

I shook my head. ''No.''

''Is this one also your friend?''

I glanced at Damian. ''Not my friend, no, but he's still mine.''

The Traveler turned his head to one side, staring at me. ''He belongs to you, how? Is he your lover?''

I shook my head. ''No.''

''Brother? Cousin? Ancestor?''

''No,'' I said.

''Then how is he . . . yours?''

I didn't know how to explain it. ''I won't give Damian to you to save Willie. You said it yourself. You're not hurting him.''

''And if I was? Would you trade Damian's safety for your friend?''

I shook my head. ''I'm not going to debate this with you.''

''I am merely trying to discern how important your friends are to you, Anita.''

I shook my head again. I didn't like where this conversation was going. If I said the wrong thing, the Traveler was going to start cutting Willie up. I could see it coming. It was a trap, and everything I thought to say led right into it.

Jean-Claude interrupted, ''*Ma petite* values her friends.''

The Traveler held up a hand. ''No, she must answer this one herself. It is her loyalty that I wish to understand, not yours.'' He stared at me from less than a foot away, uncomfortably close. ''How important are your friends to you, Anita? Answer the question.''

I thought of one answer that might not lead where the Traveler wanted to go. ''Important enough to kill for,'' I said.

His eyes flew wide. His mouth opened in amazement. ''Are you threatening me?''

I shrugged. ''You asked a question. I answered it.''

He threw his head back and laughed. ''Oh, what a man you would have made.''

I'd spent enough time around macho guys to know it was a

compliment, a sincerely meant one. They never understood the implied insult. And as long as we weren't cutting up people I cared for, I wasn't going to point it out. "Thanks," I said.

His face blanked instantly, the humor gone like a bad memory. Only his eyes, Willie's eyes, were still alive, glittering with a force that crept along my skin like a chill wind. He offered me his arm like Jean-Claude had done earlier.

I glanced at Jean-Claude. He gave the barest of nods. I placed my still bleeding hand on the Traveler's wrist. His pulse beat hard and fast against my hand. It felt like the small wound had a second heartbeat, pounding in rhythm to his pulse. The blood flowed faster out of the cut, called by his power. It dripped in a tickling line down my arm to the elbow to fall inside the arm of the coat, soaking into the dark cloth. Blood spread over his wrist in crimson rivulets. My blood.

My own heart sped up, feeding the fear, driving the blood faster. I knew in that moment that he could stand there and bleed me to death out of that small wound. That he could waste all the blood in me, all the power in me, to make a point.

My heart was thudding in my ears. I knew I should move my hand, but I just never seemed to get around to moving it, as if something was interfering with the screaming in my head, before it could reach my hand.

Jean-Claude reached out to me, but the Traveler spoke before he could touch us: "No, Jean-Claude. I acknowledge her as a power to be reckoned with if she can break this hold on her own."

My voice was breathy, rushed, as if I'd been running, but I could talk, think, I just couldn't move my hand. "What do I get out it?"

He laughed, pleased with himself. I think I'd finally asked a question he was comfortable with. "What do you want?"

I thought about that as the pulse in my hand beat fast and faster. Blood was beginning to soak the Traveler's sleeve, Willie's sleeve. I wanted Willie back. "Safe passage for me and all my people and friends."

He threw his head back and roared with laughter. The laughter stopped in mid-motion like a badly made film. He turned glittering eyes to me. "Break this hold, Anita, and I will grant you what you ask, but if you fail to break it, what do I gain?"

It was a trap, and I knew it, but I didn't know how to get out of it. If he kept bleeding me I'd pass out from blood loss, and it would all be over.

"Blood," I said.

. He smiled. "I have that now."

"A willing drink from me. You don't have that."

"Tempting but not enough."

Grey spots were spreading across my vision. I was sweating and vaguely nauseous. It took a long time to pass out from blood loss, but he was speeding it up. I couldn't think what to offer him. I was having trouble thinking at all. "What do you want?"

Jean-Claude let out a sigh, as if I'd said the wrong thing.

"The truth."

I collapsed slowly to my knees, and only his hand on my elbow kept me upright. My vision was going in large grey-white splotches. I was dizzy, and it was only going to get worse.

"What truth?"

"Who really killed the Earthmover? Tell me that and you are free."

I swallowed hard, and whispered, "Fuck you." I slid to the ground still holding onto him, still bleeding. He bent over me, but through my ruined vision it was just Willie. Willie's sharp-angled face. Willie with his loud suits and worse ties. Willie who loved Hannah with a gentle devotion that made my throat tight. I reached out and touched that face, ran my tingling fingertips through his slicked-back hair, cradled his jaw in my hand, and whispered, "Willie, come to me."

There was a jolt like a shiver of electricity, and I could see. My body still felt numb and distant, but my vision was clear. I looked into those glittering eyes and thought of Willie. There, deep inside was an answering spark, an answering scream. "Willie, come to me." My voice was stronger this time.

The Traveler said, "What are you doing?"

I ignored him. Willie was one of the other vampires I'd accidently called from their coffins, like Damian. And maybe, just maybe, he was mine in more than friendship. "With blood I call you, Willie McCoy. Rise and come to me."

The third heartbeat in my hand slowed. The Traveler was the one trying to get away now, trying to break the hold he had forged, but it was a two-edged blade. It cut both ways, and I wanted to make my point deep and sharp.

"Come to me, Willie. Rise to my voice, my hand, my blood. Rise and answer me. Willie McCoy, come now!" I watched Willie spill into those eyes like water filling a cup. I felt the Traveler forced out. I thrust him out, shoved him away, and slammed a door that I hadn't known I had in my head. In Willie's body. I forced the Traveler out, and he spun shrieking into the darkness.

Willie stared at me, and it was him, but there was a look in his eyes I'd never seen before. "What would you have of me, master?"

I collapsed on the floor, crying. I wanted to say, "I'm not your master," but the words died in my throat, swallowed by a velvet darkness that ate my vision and then the world.

20

I'D FALLEN ASLEEP with my head in my father's lap. He stroked
my hair. I snuggled against his lap, my cheek resting on his bare
thigh. Bare thigh? I was suddenly awake, pushing to a sitting
position before I could really see. Jason sat leaning against a
stone wall. It was his lap I'd woken up in. He gave me a very
watered-down version of his usual come-hither smile, but it left
his eyes cold and tired. He wasn't up to leering at me tonight.
Things are rough when Jason stops teasing.

Jean-Claude and Padma were arguing in French. They stood
on either side of a wooden table. A man was bound face-down
to the table with silver bands at wrist, ankles, and neck. Bands
that were bolted to the table itself. He was nude, but more than
his clothes were missing. The entire back of his body was one
raw bloody mess. I'd found the owner of the skin on the door.
Rafael's darkly handsome face was slack, unconscious. I hoped
he stayed that way for a long time.

Rafael, the Rat King, was head of the second-largest and
strongest band of shapeshifters in the city. He was no one's toy.
What the hell was he doing here like this? "What is Rafael
doing here?" I asked Jason.

He answered, voice tired, dragging, "The Master of Beasts
wants the wererats. Rafael wasn't strong enough not to come
when called, but he was strong enough to not bring any of the
other rats. He delivered himself over like a sacrifice." Jason
leaned his head back against the wall, eyes closed. "They
couldn't break him. They couldn't break Sylvie either."

"Sylvie?" I stared around the room. It was twenty by twenty,
not that big. She was across the room chained to the wall. She
sagged in the chains, full weight on her wrists, unconscious.

Most of her was hidden from view by the table that Rafael was chained to. She didn't look hurt.

"Why is she here?"

"The Master of Beasts called the wolves, too. Richard wasn't here to answer, so Sylvie came. She protected the rest of us, just like Rafael did for his people."

"What are Jean-Claude and the Beastie-Boy arguing about?"

"The Traveler granted us our freedom, but they don't want to include Rafael in the bargain. The Master of Beasts says the Rat King is not our people, nor our friend."

"He's my friend," I said.

He smiled without opening his eyes. "I knew you'd say that."

I got to my feet, pushing against the wall. I was a little unsteady, but not bad. I walked towards the arguing vampires. The French was hot and furious.

Jean-Claude turned to me. "*Ma petite*, you are awake." His English was heavily accented. It often was after he'd been speaking a lot of French.

Padma held up a hand. "No, do not influence her."

Jean-Claude gave a sweeping bow. "As you like."

I wanted to touch Rafael. I could see his back rising and falling, but I wouldn't really believe he was okay until I touched him. My hands sort of hovered over him, but there was almost no place left to touch that wasn't raw and hurting. I finally touched his hair, then drew back. I didn't want to wake him. Unconscious was better than anything else right now.

"Who is this one to you?" Padma asked.

"He's Rafael, the Rat King. He's my friend."

Hannah walked in through the open dungeon door. The moment she appeared, I knew it was the Traveler. He leaned that very feminine body against the side of the door and managed to look masculine. "You cannot be friends with every monster in the city."

I stared up at him. "Want to bet?"

He shook his head, Hannah's blond hair bouncing back and forth just like in the shampoo commercial. He laughed, and it was girlish. "Oh, no, Anita Blake, I will not bargain with you again this night." He started down the steps. He'd taken off the high heels, and glided down the stairs in stocking feet. "But there will be other nights."

"I asked for safe passage and you gave it," I said. "You can't hurt us anymore."

"I gave safe passage for tonight only, Anita."

"I do not remember a time limit being placed on your promise," Jean-Claude said.

The Traveler waved the objection away. "It was understood."

"Not by me," I said.

He stopped on the other side of the table, by Padma. He stared at me with Hannah's grey eyes and frowned. "Anyone else would have known that I meant tonight alone."

"As you yourself have said, Traveler, she is not anyone," Jean-Claude said.

"He is one council member. He cannot bargain for all," Padma said. "He can force us to let you go tonight, but the rest he cannot do. He cannot free you all without a vote of all represented here."

"Then his promise means nothing," I said.

"If I had dreamt that you meant safety for our entire stay," the Traveler said, "I would have asked for more than merely the truth of the Earthmover's death."

"We made a deal. I kept my end of it," I said.

He tried to cross his arms over his chest, but had to settle for his stomach, arms cradling the breasts. Women are just not designed to look tough. "You have given me yet another problem, Anita. It might be wise to not be so problematic."

"Threaten all you want," I said, "but for tonight you can't touch us."

"Do not let it go to your head." His voice had crawled down a few octaves, dragging out of Hannah's throat.

I moved around to stand at Rafael's head, wanting to stroke his hair and not daring to. Tears pressed like a hand against the back of my eyes. "Unchain him. He goes with us, or your word is worth shit, Traveler."

"I will not give him up," Padma said.

"You will do as you are told," the Traveler said.

I turned away from the sight of Rafael's butchered body. I also didn't want the bad guys to see me cry. Turning away from

Rafael gave me a better view of Sylvie. What I saw stopped me in my tracks.

Her pants were down around her ankles, shoes still on. I took a step towards her, then another, and was almost running by the time I got to her. I slid to my knees beside her. Blood stained her thighs. Her hands were balled into fists, eyes squeezed tight. She was whispering something, very softly, over and over. I touched her arm and she flinched. Her voice rose just enough for me to hear the one word, "No, no, no." Over and over and over like a mantra.

I was crying. I'd been talking about putting a bullet in Sylvie earlier today. Now I was crying for her. Some big tough socipath I turned out to be. I had my problems with Sylvie, but this . . . She didn't even like men under the best of circumstances. It made what they'd done worse somehow, more insulting. Or maybe it was just that I remembered her as so proud, so confident and full of herself. To see her like this was almost more than I could bear.

"Sylvie, Sylvie, it's Anita." I wanted to pull her clothes back in place, but was afraid to touch her again until I was sure she knew it was me. "Sylvie, can you hear me?"

Jason came to stand with us. "Let me try."

"She won't want a man to touch her."

"I won't touch her." He knelt on the other side of her. "I smell like pack. You don't." He very carefully slid his arm in front of her face, trying not to touch her. "Smell the pack, Sylvie. Know the comfort of our touch."

She stopped saying no, but that was it. She wouldn't even open her eyes.

I stood up and faced the room. "Who did this?"

"She could have stopped it at any time," Padma said, "given me the pack and it would all have been over. She could have gone free."

I screamed, "WHO DID THIS!"

"I did," Padma said.

I stared down at the floor, and when I came back up, the Uzi was pointed at him. "I'm going to cut you in half."

"*Ma petite*, you will hit Rafael and perhaps me."

A machine gun was not made for one target in a crowd, but

he'd survive the Browning. I shook my head. "He dies. For this, he dies."

The Traveler stepped beside Padma. "Would you slay this body?" He spread his hands wide and stepped in front of Padma. "Would you kill your Willie's lady love?"

Tears hot enough to scald trailed down my cheeks. "Damn you, damn you all."

"Padma did not personally rape your friend," the Traveler said. "Any unskilled man can rape, but it takes a true artist to skin a live shapeshifter."

"Who then?" My voice was just a little calmer. I wasn't going to use the machine gun, and we all knew it. I dropped the Uzi, letting it slide back under the coat. I wrapped my hand around the Browning and thought about it.

Jean-Claude started walking towards me. He knew me too well. "*Ma petite*, we all walk out of here in safety at least this night. You have given us this. Do not destroy us all for vengeance now."

Fernando walked through the door, and I knew. He might not be the only one, but he'd been one of them. He smirked at me. "The Traveler wouldn't let me have Hannah."

I started to tremble, a fine quivering that started in my arms and spread across my shoulders and down my body. I'd never wanted to kill anyone as badly as I wanted to kill him right that second. He glided down the steps in his bare feet, hands roving across his chest, playing in the line of hair that started on his belly. Rubbing his hands along the silk of his pants.

"Maybe I'll have you chained to a wall," he said.

I felt a smile stretch across my face. I spoke very clearly, very carefully, because if I didn't, I was going to scream, and if I lost control of my voice, I was going to shoot him. I knew that just as surely as I was standing there. "Who helped you?"

Padma stopped his son, drawing him into the circle of his arms. I saw real fear on the master vampire's face. His son was still too arrogant or too stupid to understand.

"I did it myself."

A laugh that was bitter enough to choke me came out. "You couldn't do this much damage on your own. Who helped you?"

The Traveler touched Fernando's shoulder. "Others, unnamed others. If the woman can tell you, let her. If not, you do not need to know. You will not be hunting them, Executioner.''

"Not tonight," I said. The trembling was quieting. That cold, icy center of my soul, the place where I'd given up a piece of myself, spread outward. I was calm, deadly calm. I could have shot them all and not blinked. "But you said it yourself, Traveler: there will be other nights.''

Jason was talking in a low voice and Sylvie was answering. I glanced at her. She wasn't crying. Her face was pale and strangely stiff, as if everything was held inside, tight and hard. Jason undid the locks on the chains and she slid down the wall. He tried to help her pull up her pants, but she pushed him away.

I knelt beside her. "Let me help, please.''

Sylvie tried to pull the pants up herself, but her hands weren't working right. She kept fumbling and finally collapsed to the floor in tears.

I started to dress her, and she let me. She helped where she could, but her hands were shaking so badly, she couldn't do much. Her pants were pink linen. I couldn't find the underwear. It was gone. I knew she'd been wearing some, because Sylvie wouldn't go without. She was a lady, and ladies didn't do that.

When everything was covered, she finally met my eyes. The look in her brown eyes made me want to look away, but I didn't. If she could have that much pain in her face, the least I could do was look at it. No flinching. I'd even stopped crying.

"I didn't give them the pack," she said.

"I know," I said. I wanted to touch her, reassure her, and was afraid to.

She collapsed forward, sobbing; not crying, but sobbing like she'd cry out bits and pieces of herself on the floor. I put my arms around her, tentatively. She sagged against me, holding me. I held her half in my arms, half in my lap, rocking her slowly. I leaned over next to her ear and breathed a sound into it, "He's dead. They're all dead.''

She quieted slowly, then looked up at me. "You swear it?''

"I swear it.''

She huddled against me and said softly, "I won't kill Richard.''

"Good, because I'd hate to kill you now.''

She laughed, and it turned it into more crying, but softer now, quieter, not quite so desperate.

I looked up at the others. The men, dead and alive, were staring at me. "Rafael comes with us, no more debating."

Padma nodded. "Very well."

Fernando turned to him. "Father, you can't let her do this. The wolves, yes, but not the Rat King."

"Hush, Fernando."

"He cannot be allowed to live, if he does not submit."

"You weren't rat enough to be dominant to him, were you, Fernando?" I said. "He's stronger than you'll ever be, and you hate him for it."

Fernando took a step towards me. Padma and the Traveler both held him back, a hand on each shoulder.

Jean-Claude stepped between us. "Let us be on our way, *ma petite*. The night grows long."

The Traveler stepped away from Fernando slowly. I wasn't sure who he trusted least, me or the rat-boy. He started unfastening the chains that held Rafael in place. The wererat was still unconscious, oblivious to his fate.

I got to my feet, and Sylvie came with me. She pushed away from me, tried to walk and nearly fell. I caught her, and Jason caught her other arm.

Fernando laughed.

Sylvie stumbled. She looked like she'd been slapped. The laughter cut more than any words. I laid my lips against her cheek, cradled her face against mine with my free hand, lips by her ear. "He's dead, remember that."

She leaned into me for a moment, then nodded. She straightened and let Jason help her walk towards the stairs.

Jean-Claude lifted Rafael in his arms as gently as he could, balancing the man over his shoulders. Rafael groaned, hands spasming, but his eyes stayed shut.

I stared at the Traveler. "You'll need to find another horse to ride," I said. "Hannah comes with us."

"Of course," he said.

"Now, Traveler," I said.

Arrogance spread across his face. It was a look I'd never seen on Hannah's face before. "Do not let one act of magical bravado make you foolish, Anita."

I smiled and knew it wasn't pleasant. It was bitter and arrogant and angry. "My patience is all gone tonight, Traveler. Get out of her now, or . . .'' I shoved the Browning into Fernando's groin. They were all huddled that close.

Fernando's eyes widened, but he wasn't nearly as afraid as he should have been. I pressed the barrel in a little harder; makes most men back up. He gave a small grunt but leaned into me, face bending towards me. He was going to try and kiss me.

I laughed. I laughed while his lips hovered over my mouth and the gun pressed into his body. It was the laughter, not the gun, that made him draw back.

Hannah collapsed to her knees. The Traveler had gone. Someone needed to help her to the stairs. I thought of Willie and he came. He helped her to her feet without looking at me. I kept my eyes on the bad guys. One problem at a time.

''Why are you laughing?'' Fernando asked.

''Because you are too fucking stupid to survive.'' I drew back from them, the gun still pointed at him. ''Is he your only son?'' I asked.

''My only child,'' Padma said.

''My condolences,'' I said. No, I didn't shoot him. But staring into Fernando's angry eyes, I knew there'd be other opportunities. Some people seek death through desperation. Some people fall into it out of stupidity. If Fernando wanted to fall, I was more than happy to catch him.

21

RAFAEL LAY ON an examining table. We were not in the hospital. The lycanthropes had a makeshift emergency room in the basement of a building that they owned. I'd had my own wounds tended there once. Now Rafael lay on his stomach hooked up to an IV loaded with liquids and painkillers. Painkillers didn't always work well on lycanthropes but hey, they had to try something. He'd regained consciousness in the Jeep. He hadn't screamed, but the small squeezed whimperings that clawed from his throat every time I hit a bump were more than enough.

Dr. Lillian was a small woman with salt-and-pepper hair cut in a no-nonsense style. She was also a wererat. She turned to me. "I've made him as comfortable as I can."

"Will he heal?"

She nodded. "Yes. The real danger with this type of injury once you survive the shock and blood loss is infection. We can't get infections."

"Let's hear it for the terminally furry," I said.

She smiled and patted my shoulder. "I know humor is your way of dealing with stress, but don't try it on Rafael tonight. He wants to speak with you."

"Is he . . . ?"

"Well enough, no, but he is my king and he won't let me put him under until he's spoken with you. I'll go look in on our other patient while you hear whatever he thinks is so important."

I touched her arm before she could move past me. "How is Sylvie?"

Lillian wouldn't look at me, then finally she did. "Physically, she'll heal, but I'm not a therapist. I'm not equipped to deal

with the aftereffects of an attack like this. I want her to stay
here for the night, but she's insisting that she go with you.''

My eyes widened. "Why?"

Lillian shrugged. "I think she feels safe with you. I think she
doesn't feel safe here.'' The older woman was suddenly looking
very intently at my face. "Is there a reason she shouldn't feel
safe here?''

I thought about that. "Have the wereleopards ever been
treated here?"

"Yes," she said.

"Damn."

"Why should that matter? This is a neutral place. We have
all agreed to that.''

I shook my head. "For tonight you're safe, but anything that
Elizabeth knew, the Master of Beasts knows. By tomorrow this
may not be a safe haven."

"Do you know that for sure?" she asked.

"No, but I don't know for sure that you will be safe either."

She nodded. "Very well. Take Sylvie with you, then, but
Rafael must stay here at least for one night. I will make plans
to move him by tomorrow." She looked around at all the medical equipment. "We can't take it all, but we'll do what we can.
Now go talk to our king." She left the room.

I was suddenly alone in the hush of the basement. I looked
at Rafael. They'd arranged a sort of tent of a sheet over his
body, covered but not touching. The naked skin was covered in
salve but no bandages. Anything they could put on it would hurt
worse than nothing. They were treating it sort of like a burn. I
didn't know everything they'd done to treat him because I'd
been off getting my hand stitched up part of the time.

I walked around the table so that Rafael wouldn't have to
move his head to look at me. Moving was bad. His eyes were
closed, but his breathing was fast and ragged. He wasn't asleep.

"Lillian said you wanted to talk to me."

He blinked and looked at me. His eyes rolled at an awkward
angle. He tried to move his head, and a sound came from low
in his chest. I'd never heard a sound quite like it. I didn't want
to hear it again.

"Don't move, please." I found a little stool with wheels on
it and brought it over. With me sitting, we were nearly the same

height. "You should let her pump you full of drugs. You need to sleep if you can."

"First," he said, "I must know how you freed me." He took a deeper breath, and the pain passed over his face in a flinching wave.

I looked away, then back. No flinching. "I bargained for you."

"What . . ." His hands spasmed, and he closed his full lips into a tight-pressed line. When he spoke again, his voice was lower, more careful, as if even a normal speaking voice hurt. "What did you give up for me?"

"Nothing."

"He would not . . . have given me up so easily." Rafael stared at me, his dark eyes willing me to tell him the truth. He thought I was lying, that was why he couldn't rest. He thought I'd done something noble and awful to save him.

I sighed and told him a very abbreviated version of the night. It was the easiest way to explain. "See, it didn't cost any extra to throw you in."

He almost smiled. "The wererats will remember what you did tonight, Anita. I will remember."

"Maybe we don't go shopping together or even out to the shooting range, but you are my friend, Rafael. I know that if I called you for help, you'd come."

"Yes," he said. "Yes, I would."

I smiled at him. "I'll go get Lillian now, okay?"

He closed his eyes and some piece of tension flowed out of him. It was almost as if now he could finally give himself over to the pain. "Yes, yes."

I sent Lillian into him and went to find Sylvie. She was in a small room where Lillian had hoped she could get some sleep. Sylvie had been joined by her lady friend, significant other, lover, whatever. Jason had called her. I hadn't known she existed. Gwen's voice came very clearly down the hallway. "You have to tell her, Sylvie, you have to."

I couldn't hear Sylvie's answer, but then the high heels weren't quiet. They knew I was coming. I stepped in through the open door to find Gwen looking at me, and Sylvie decidedly not. The white pillow framed her very short, very curly brown hair. She was three inches taller than me but managed to look fragile in the small bed.

Gwen sat in a straight-backed chair beside the bed, holding Sylvie's hand in both of her own. Gwen had long softly waving blond hair and big brown eyes in a delicate face. Everything about her was dainty, feminine, like a pale, finely made doll. But the intensity in her face, the intelligence in her eyes, was a vibrating thing. Gwen was a psychologist. She would have been a compelling person even without the trickle of lycanthropic energy that trailed around her like perfume.

"What do you need to tell me?" I said.

"How do you know I was referring to you?" Gwen said.

"Call it a hunch."

She patted Sylvie's hand. "Tell her."

Sylvie turned her head but still wouldn't meet my eyes. I leaned against the wall and waited. The machine gun pressed into the small of my back, forcing me to lean mostly shoulders against the cinderblock wall. Why hadn't I taken some of the weapons off? Lay a gun down somewhere, and that's when you'll need it most. I trusted the Traveler to keep his word, but not enough to bet my life on it.

Silence spilled into the small room until the whirr of the air conditioner was as loud as the blood in your own ears. Sylvie finally looked at me. "The Master of Beasts ordered Stephen's brother to rape me." She looked down, then up again, anger spilling into her eyes. "Gregory refused."

I didn't bother to hide the surprise on my face. "I thought Gregory was one of the stars of Raina's porno films."

"He was," Sylvie said softly.

What I wanted to ask was, when did he get to be squeamish? but that seemed crude. "Did he suddenly grow a conscience?" I asked.

"I don't know." She was staring at the sheet, holding onto Gwen's hands like there was worse to come. "He refused to help torture me. The Master of Beasts said he'd punish him. Gregory still refused. He said that Zane had told him that Anita was their new alpha. That all bargains made through Elizabeth weren't binding. That he needed to deal with you for them."

Sylvie withdrew her hand from Gwen's and stared up at me. Her brown eyes were furious, but it wasn't me she was angry with. "You can't be their leader and our lupa. You can't be both. He was lying."

I sighed. "Afraid not."

"But, how . . ."

"Look, it's late, and we're all tired. Let's just do the short version. I killed Gabriel, technically that makes me the were-leopards' leader. Zane acknowledged me after I put a couple of non-silver bullets in him."

"Why didn't you kill him?" Sylvie asked.

"It's sort of my fault. I didn't understand what leaving them without a leader would mean. Someone should have told me that they were meat for anybody without a leader."

"I wanted them to suffer," Sylvie said.

"I was told you wanted them all dead, that if you had your way, the pack would have hunted them down and killed them all."

"Yes," she said, "yes. I want them all dead."

"I know they helped punish you and other pack members."

She shook her head, hands in front of her eyes. It took me a second to realize she was crying. "You don't understand. There's a film of me out there. A film of the leopards raping me." She brought her hands down and stared at me with tear-filled eyes. The rage and pain in her face was raw. "I was outspoken against Raina and Marcus. It was my punishment. Raina wanted to make an example of me for the others. It worked, too. Everyone was scared after that."

I opened my mouth, closed it, then said, "I didn't realize."

"Now do you see why I want them dead?"

"Yes," I said.

"Gregory had raped me once. Why wouldn't he do it again? Why did he refuse to hurt me tonight?"

"If he really believes that I'm his leader, then he knows what I'd do to him."

"Did you mean it in the room? Did you mean it about us killing them all?"

"Oh, yeah," I said, "I meant it."

"Then Gregory was right."

I frowned at her. "What do you mean?"

"He said you were their *léoparde lionné*, their rampant leopard."

"I don't know the term," I said.

Gwen answered. "*Léoparde lionné* is a term from French heraldry. It's a leopard, or even a lion, rampant in action on a crest. It symbolizes brave and generous warriors having done some brave deed. In this case it means a protector, even an avenger. Gabriel was a *lion passant*, a sleeping lion. He led but did not protect. In effect, Gregory did not merely refuse to harm Sylvie, he also told the Master of Beasts that if he was harmed, you would save him."

"How can I be their *léoparde* what-you-call-it if I'm not a leopard?"

"*Léoparde lionné*," Slyvie said. "How can you be lupa and neither be wolf nor our Ulfric's lover?"

She had me there.

Fresh tears streamed down Sylvie's face. "Padma tried to get Vivian, his personal pet while he's here, to do things to me. Said I liked women, and maybe that would loosen my tongue. She refused, and she gave the same reason that Gregory did."

I remembered Vivian staring at me, her frightened eyes pleading for me to help her. "Shit, you mean she really expected me to rescue her tonight."

Sylvie just nodded. Gwen said, "Yes."

"Shit."

"I honestly didn't think of it until after we were in the Jeep. I swear I didn't think of it sooner," Sylvie said. "But I didn't say anything, because I wanted them to suffer. I can't stop hating them just like that. Do you understand?"

I did. "Sylvie, you and I have one thing in common. We are both vindictive as hell. So, yeah, I understand, but we can't leave them there like that, not if they were expecting to be saved."

She wiped at the tears. "You can't go up against them tonight. We can't do anymore tonight."

"I'm not planning to fight anymore tonight, Sylvie."

"But you're planning something." She sounded worried.

I smiled. "Yeah."

Gwen stood. "Don't be foolish, Anita."

I shook my head. "Foolish. I'm way past foolish." I stopped in the doorway and turned back. "By the way, Sylvie, don't challenge Richard, ever."

Her eyes widened. "How did you know?"

I shrugged. "Doesn't matter. What does matter is that I'll kill you if you kill him."

"It would be a fair fight."

"I don't care."

"You haven't seen him, Anita. He's on the edge. You can forbid me from challenging him, but there are others, and they won't be nearly as good for the pack as I am."

"Then make it carte blanche," I said. "If anyone kills Richard, I'll execute them. No challenge, no fair fight, I'll just take them out."

"You can't do that," Sylvie said.

"Oh, I think I can. I'm lupa, remember."

"If you forbid fights of succession," Gwen said, "you're undermining Richard. You're saying in effect that you don't believe he can really lead the pack."

"I've been told by two pack members today that Richard is out of control, damn near suicidal. That he's pulled his self-hatred, his loathing of his beast, and my rejection, down around his ears. I won't let him die because I chose someone else. In a few months when he's healthier, then I'll step down. I'll let him take care of himself, but not right now."

"I'll pass the word," Gwen said.

"You do that."

"You're going to try and bring out the leopards tonight, aren't you?" Sylvie said.

I kept seeing the bruises on Vivian's body. The pleading in her eyes. "They expected me to save them, and I didn't."

"You didn't know," Gwen said.

"I know now," I said.

"You can't save everyone," Sylvie said.

"Everyone needs a hobby." I started to walk out again, but Gwen called me back.

I turned in the doorway.

"Tell her the rest," Gwen said softly.

Sylvie wouldn't look at me. She spoke staring down at the sheet. "When Vivian refused to hurt me, they called in Liv." She looked up, tears glittering in her eyes. "She used things on me. Did things to me." Sylvie covered her face with her hands and rolled onto her side, crying.

Gwen met my eyes. The look on her face was frightening in its hatred. "You need to know who to kill."

I nodded. "She won't leave St. Louis alive."

"And the other one? The council member's son?" Gwen asked.

"Him either," I said.

"Promise it," she said.

"I already have," I said. I walked out then, searching for a phone. I wanted to talk to Jean-Claude before I did anything. Jean-Claude had taken everyone else to my house. They were boarding up the basement windows so that the vamps could be tucked safely away before dawn. The Traveler had refused to let them take their coffins. Besides, have you ever tried to rent a truck on a weekend after midnight?

What was I going to do about the wereleopards? Damned if I knew.

22

JEAN-CLAUDE'S VOICE floated over the phone, my phone, my house. He'd never been there before. "What has happened, *ma petite*? Jason made it sound urgent."

I told him about the wereleopards.

He was quiet for so long, I had to say something. "Talk to me, Jean-Claude."

"Are you actually thinking of endangering us all for the sake of two people, one of whom you have never met before, and the other who you once described as a waste of skin?"

"I can't leave them there if they expected me to help them."

"*Ma petite, ma petite*, you have a sense of *noblesse oblige* that does you credit. But we cannot save them. Tomorrow evening the council will come for us, and we may not even be able to save ourselves."

"Are they here to kill us?"

"Padma would kill us if he could. He is the weakest of the council, and I think he fears us."

"The Traveler's the one we have to convince," I said.

"No, *ma petite*, the council are seven in number, always an odd number so that a vote may settle a question. Padma and the Traveler will vote against one another, this is true. It has been true for centuries. But Yvette is here to vote in the place of her lord, Morte d'Amour. She hates Padma but she may hate me more. For that matter, Balthasar could persuade the Traveler against us, and we are lost."

"What about everybody else? Do they represent anybody?"

"Asher speaks for Belle Morte, Beautiful Death. It is her line that I am descended from, as is he."

"He hates your guts," I said. "We are sunk."

"I believe the choice of four was very deliberate. They wish me to take a council seat, so I am the fifth vote."

"If the Traveler votes with you, and Yvette hates Padma more than she hates you . . ."

"*Ma petite*, if I act as a voting member of the council, then they will expect me to return to France and take my place on the council."

"France?" I said.

He laughed, and it slithered over the phone like a warm touch. "It is not leaving our fair city that frightens me, *ma petite*. It is holding the seat. If the triumvirate were fully formed perhaps, perhaps, it would be possible to appear frightening enough to force would-be challengers to choose another."

"Are you saying without the fourth mark, the triumvirate is useless?"

Silence on his end, so long and deep, that I said, "Jean-Claude?"

"I am here, *ma petite*. The fourth mark will not make our triumvirate functional unless Richard heals himself."

"You mean his hatred of me."

"His jealousy of us together, yes, that is a problem, but not the only one, *ma petite*. His loathing of his beast is so intense, it weakens him. Weaken any link in a chain and it may snap."

"Did you know about what's been happening in the pack?"

"Richard has forbidden any of the wolves to tell me anything without his permission. I believe you are under the same restriction. It is, and I quote, none of my damn business."

"I'm surprised you didn't force Jason to tell you anyway."

"Have you seen Richard within the last month?"

"No."

"I have. He is on the edge, *ma petite*. I did not need Jason to tell me. It is plain for all to see. His torment will be viewed as a weakness among the pack. Weakness attracts them like blood to a . . . vampire. They will challenge him eventually."

"I've had two lukoi tell me that they don't think Richard will fight. That he'll just let someone kill him. Do you believe that?"

"Suicide by simply not defending himself hard enough. Hmm." He was quiet again, then finally said, "I had not thought of such a thing. If I had, *ma petite*, I would have told you of my concerns. I do not wish Richard harm."

"Yeah, right."

"He is our third, *ma petite*. It is in my own interest to make him healthy and happy. I need him."

"Like you need me," I said.

He laughed low and deep, and even over the phone I could feel it tickling along my body. "*Oui, ma petite*. Richard must not die. But to cure his despair he must embrace his beast. I cannot help him do that. I have tried and he will not hear me. He takes what limited help he needs to keep himself from invading your dreams, or you his, but beyond that he wants nothing from us. Nothing he will admit."

"What's that supposed to mean?" I asked.

"It is your tender mercies that he needs, *ma petite*, not mine."

"Tender mercies?" I made it a question.

"If you could accept his beast, completely, it would mean something to him."

"I can't, Jean-Claude. I wish I could, but I can't. I saw him eat Marcus. I . . ." I'd only seen Richard shapeshift once. He'd been injured from the fight with Marcus. He half-collapsed with me underneath him. I'd been trapped under him while fur flowed, muscles formed and shifted, bones broke and reknit. Clear liquid had gushed from his power, pouring over me in a near-scalding wave. Maybe if I'd just been watching, it would have been different. But trapped under him, feeling his body do things on top of me that bodies were never meant to do . . . it had been too much. If Richard had handled it differently, if I had seen him change in a nice calm way from a distance, then built up to the whole ride, maybe, maybe. But it had happened, and I couldn't forget it. I could still close my eyes and see his man-wolf shape gulping down a red, bloody piece of Marcus.

I leaned my back against the wall, cradling the receiver. I was rocking ever so slightly. It reminded me of Jason in the hallway. I made myself stand very still. I wanted to forget. I wanted to be able to accept Richard. But I couldn't.

"*Ma petite*, are you all right?"

"Fine, I'm fine."

Jean-Claude let that go. He really was getting smarter, at least about me. "I do not wish to cause you distress."

"I've done what I can for Richard on my end." I told Jean-Claude what I'd told the werewolves.

"You surprise me, *ma petite*. I thought you wanted nothing more to do with the lukoi."

"I don't want Richard to die because I broke his heart."

"You would feel responsible if he died now, is that it?"

"Yeah."

He took a deep breath and let it sigh over the phone. It made me shiver, for no particular reason. "How badly do you wish to help the wereleopards?"

"What kind of question is that?"

"An important one," he said. "What are you willing to risk for them? What would you endure for them?"

"You have something specific in mind, don't you?"

"Padma might give up Vivian in exchange for you. Gregory's freedom could be won if we gave them Jason."

"I notice you're not trading yourself in," I said.

"Padma would not want me, *ma petite*. He is neither a lover of men nor of other vampires in particular. He prefers his companions warm and female."

"Why Jason then?"

"A werewolf for a wereleopard might be an acceptable trade to him."

"Not to me. We are not trading one hostage for another, and I am certainly not giving myself to that monster."

"You see, *ma petite*, you will not endure that. You will not risk Jason to save Gregory. I ask again, what will you risk for them?"

"I'll risk my life, but only if I've got a good chance of getting out alive. No sex, absolutely not. No trading one hostage for another. Nobody else gets skinned alive or raped. How's that for parameters?"

"Padma and Fernando will be disappointed, but the others might agree. I will do the best I can within the limits you have given me."

"No rape, no maiming, no actual intercourse, no hostages, does that really tie your hands that much?"

"When we have survived all this, *ma petite*, and the council has gone home, I will tell you stories of my time at court. I have seen spectacles that even in the telling would give you nightmares."

"Nice to know you think we're going to survive."

"I am hopeful, yes."

"But not certain," I said.

"Nothing is certain, *ma petite*, not even death."

He had me there. My beeper went off. It pulled a gasp from my throat. Nervous, who me?

"Are you all right, *ma petite*?"

"My beeper went off," I said. I checked the number. It was Dolph. "It's the police. I need to return the call."

"I will begin negotiations with the council, *ma petite*. If they ask too much, I will let your leopards remain where they are."

"Padma will kill Vivian now that he thinks she belongs to me. He might have killed her before, but it would have been by accident. If we don't get her out of there, he'll do it on purpose."

"One meeting with him and you are so sure of this?"

"You think I'm wrong?" I asked.

"No, *ma petite*, I think you are exactly right."

"Get them out of there, Jean-Claude. Make the best deal you can."

"I have your permission to use your name in this?"

"Yeah." My beeper went off a second time. Dolph, impatient as usual. "I've got to go, Jean-Claude."

"Very well, *ma petite*. I will bargain for us all, then."

"You do that," I said. "Wait . . ."

"Yes, *ma petite*."

"You aren't going to go back to the Circus in person tonight, are you? I don't want you in there alone," I said.

"I will use the phone, if you prefer," he said.

"I do."

"You don't trust them," he said.

"Not hardly."

"Wise beyond your years," he said.

"Suspicious beyond my years, you mean."

"That as well, *ma petite*. If they will not negotiate over the phone?" he asked.

"Then let it go."

"You said you were willing to risk your life, *ma petite*."

"I didn't say I was willing to risk yours."

"Ah," he said. "*Je t'aime, ma petite*."

"I love you, too," I said.

He hung up first, and I dialed the police. Here was hoping whatever Dolph had in mind was some nice straightforward police work. Yeah, right.

23

THE VICTIM HAD been rushed to a hospital by the time I arrived at Burnt Offerings. It's one of my favorites of the newer vampire businesses. It was far from the vampire district. The only other vamp businesses were blocks, miles away. As you walked through the doors there was a poster from the 1970's movie *Burnt Offerings*, Oliver Reed and Bette Davis staring down at you. There was a life size waxwork of Christopher Lee as Dracula in the bar. There was one wall with framed caricatures of horror stars of the sixties and seventies, floor to ceiling, no tables allowed to obstruct the view. It wasn't uncommon to see clusters of visitors trying to identify who was who. At midnight whoever had the most correct guesses got a free dinner for two.

The place was pure schlock. Some of the waiters were real vamps, but others were just wannabes. For some it was just a job, and they specialized in plastic Halloween teeth and jokes. For others it was their chance to pretend. They had dental caps over their canines and worked very hard at being the real thing. Other waiters or waitresses were dressed up as mummies, the wolf man, Frankenstein's monster. To my knowledge the only real monsters were the vamps. If a shapeshifter wanted to come out of the closet, there was better money to be made in more exotic locales.

The place was always packed. I wasn't sure whether Jean-Claude was sorry he hadn't thought of it first or if he was simply embarrassed by it. It was a little déclassé for him. Me, I loved it. From the haunted house soundtrack to the Bela Lugosi burgers, extra rare unless otherwise requested. Bela was one of the few exceptions to the 60's and 70's movie decor. Hard to have a horror theme restaurant without the original movie Dracula.

You haven't lived until you've been there on a Friday night for Scary Karaoke. I took Ronnie. Veronica (Ronnie) Sims is a private detective and my best friend. We had a blast.

But back to the body. All right, not a body, a victim. But if the bartender hadn't been fast with a fire extinqisher, it would have been a body.

Detective Clive Perry was the man in charge. He's tall, slender, sort of Denzel Washington without the broad shoulders. He's one of the most polite people I've ever met. I've never heard him yell, and only seen him lose his composure once—when a large white cop had pointed a gun at the "nigger detective." Even then I was the one who pointed my gun at the rogue cop. I was the one that was ready to shoot while Perry was still trying to talk the situation down. Maybe I overreacted. Maybe I didn't. No one died.

He turned with a smile, soft voice. "Ms. Blake, good to see you."

"Good to see you, too, Detective Perry." He always affected me this way. He was so polite, so soft-spoken that I fell into the same pattern. I was never this nice to anyone else.

We were in the bar with its life-size waxwork of Christopher Lee as Dracula looming over us. The bartender was a vamp named Harry who had long auburn hair and a silver stud in his nose. He looked very young, very cutting edge, and could probably remember the Jamestown charter, though his British accent showed he was newer to the country than the 1600's. He was polishing the bar like his life depended on it. Even with his nice blank face, I could tell he was nervous. Couldn't blame him, I guess. Harry was part owner as well as bartender.

A woman had been attacked in the bar by a vampire patron. Very bad for business. The woman had thrown a drink in his face and lit him with her lighter. Ingenious in an emergency. Vamps burn really well. But the quiet bar in a family-oriented tourist trap didn't seem the place for such extreme measures. Maybe she panicked.

"Witnesses all say she seemed friendly until he got a little too close," Perry said.

"Did he bite her?"

Perry nodded.

"Shit," I said.

"But she lit him up, Anita. He's badly burned. He may not make it. What could she have thrown on him to get third-degree burns so quickly?"

"How quickly?"

He checked his notes. "Seconds and he went up."

I asked Harry. "What was she drinking?"

He didn't ask who, just said, "Straight Scotch. Best we had in the place."

"High alcohol content?"

He nodded.

"That would have been enough," I said. "Once you get a vamp burning, they burn until they're put out. They're very combustible."

"So she didn't come in here with some sort of accelerant?" he asked.

I shook my head. "She didn't need it. What I don't like is the fact that she knew to light the drink. If he'd been human and gotten out of hand, she'd have thrown the drink and yelled for help."

"He did bite her," Perry said.

"If she had that much problem with a vampire sinking fang in her, she wouldn't have been cuddling with him in a bar. Something's off about this."

"Yes," he said, "but I don't know what. If the vampire survives, he's going to be up on charges."

"I'd like to see the woman."

"Dolph took her to the emergency room to get the bite tended. He's got her down at our headquarters. He said to come on down if you think you need to see her."

It was late, and I was tired, but dammit, something was wrong. I walked over to the bar. "Was she trolling for vamps, Harry?"

He shook his head. "Came in to use the phone, then sat down. She's a beauty. Didn't take long for someone to hit on her. Just bad luck it was a vampire."

"Yeah," I said, "bad luck."

He kept polishing the bar in small round circles, while his eyes watched me. "If she sues us, it'll ruin us."

"She won't sue," I said.

"Tell that to the Crematorium in Boston. A woman got bit

there and sued them out of business. They had pickets going outside."

I patted his hand, and he went utterly still under my touch. His skin had that hard almost wooden feel that vamps can have when they aren't trying to be human. I met his dark eyes, and his face was as immobile and unreadable as glass.

"I'll go talk to the supposed victim."

He just looked at me. "It won't help, Anita. She's human. We're not. Nothing they do in Washington will change that."

I took my hand away and resisted an urge to wipe it on my dress. I never liked the way vamps felt when they went hard and otherworldly. They didn't feel like flesh then, almost plastic like a dolphin, but harder, as if there was no muscle underneath, nothing but solidness like a tree.

"I'll do what I can, Harry."

"We're monsters, Anita. We'll always be monsters. I've really enjoyed being able to walk the streets like everyone else, but it won't last."

"Maybe, maybe not," I said. "Let's take care of this problem before we borrow another one, okay?"

He nodded and walked away to stack glasses.

"That was very comforting of you," Perry said. Anyone else on the squad would have said it wasn't like me to be comforting. Of course, anyone else would have already given me a hard time about the dress. I was going to have to go down to RPIT headquarters. Dolph would be there and Zerbrowski, probably. They'd know just what to say about the dress.

24

THREE O'CLOCK FOUND me at the headquarters for the Regional Preternatural Investigation Team. Another squad had buttons made up for us with the abbreviation RIP bleeding down the front of the button in red or green, your choice. Zerbrowski handed them out, and we all wore them, even Dolph. The first vampire we killed after the buttons arrived came through the morgue with one of the buttons pinned to its shirt. Never did find out who did it. My money was on Zerbrowski.

Zerbrowski met me on the steps leading into the squad room. "If that dress was slit any higher, it'd be a shirt," he said.

I looked him up and down. His pale blue shirt was coming untucked from a pair of dark green dress slacks, his tie so loose, it looked like a bulky necklace. "Jeez, Zerbrowski, is Katie mad at you?"

He frowned. "No, why?"

I motioned at the tie that matched neither shirt nor slacks. "She let you wear this out where people could see you."

He grinned. "I dressed in the dark."

I touched the black-figured tie. "That I believe."

But it didn't faze him. He pushed the door open to the squad room with a flourish. He beamed at me. "Beauty before age."

It was my turn to frown. "What are you up to, Zerbrowsk?"

He gave me innocent eyes. "Me, up to something?"

I shook my head and walked through the door. There was a stuffed toy penguin on every desk. Everyone answered phones, filed, worked on their computers. No one paid me any attention. Just the penguins sitting on every desk. It had been almost a year since Dolph and Zerbrowski had seen my penguin collection. The teasing didn't start right away; I thought I was safe.

When Zerbrowski got back off sick leave after the new year, the penguins had started showing up at every crime scene. On my car seat, in my trunk. They must have spent a couple of hundred dollars on the things by now.

I still didn't know how to react. Ignore it? Pretend that there weren't a dozen penguins sitting around the room? Collect them as I went through the room and take them home? Get mad? If I could have figured out the reaction that would stop the joke, I'd have given it to them. So far, I'd tried ignoring and collecting. Neither stopped it. In fact, it seemed to be getting worse. I suspected that they were building to some grand climax. I had no idea what and wasn't sure I ever wanted to find out.

"Glad to see everybody's so energetic at three A.M."

"No effort too great, no hour too late," Zerbrowski said.

"Where's Dolph?"

"In the interview room with our victim."

There was something about the way he said it that made me look at him. "Dolph called her the 'supposed' victim over the phone. Why doesn't anyone believe her?"

He smiled. "Dolph would be mad if I spoiled it." He crooked his finger at me. "Come along, little girl. We have someone we want you to meet."

I scowled at him. "If this is some elaborate joke, I am going to be pissed."

He held the door for me. "Did we interrupt your date with Count Dracula?"

"None of your damn business."

A chorus of "ooohs" went through the squad room. I went through the door with everyone calling after me. Some of the suggestions were rude, one physically impossible even with a vampire. Sexual harassment or just being one of the guys, it was always a thin line.

I peeked back through the door and said, "You're all just jealous." That brought more catcalls.

Zerbrowski was waiting on the stairs for me. "I don't know whether you'll flash me more leg if I walk in front of you, looking back, or behind you. I think in front."

"Push it too far, Zerbrowski, and I'll tell Katie on you."

"She knows I'm a lech." He walked down the stairs looking back at me.

I walked down the stairs and let the dress fall where it might. When you wear a dress slit nearly to your hips, even if it is to have a gun handy, you are either comfortable with men looking or you wear something else. "How did you ever convince Katie to date you, let alone marry you?"

"I got her drunk," he said.

I laughed. "I'll ask her next time I'm over for dinner."

He grinned. "She'll give you this cock-and-bull story about something romantic and stupid. Don't believe her." He stopped in front of the first interview room and knocked softly.

Dolph opened the door. He filled the doorway very completely. He isn't just tall, he's bulky like a pro-wrestler. His tie was knotted perfectly, white-starched collar tight to his neck. His grey dress slacks still had a sharp crease. His only concession to the heat and the lateness of the hour was the long white sleeves of his shirt. No jacket. I could count on one hand the times I'd seen Dolph in shirt sleeves.

All cops perfect a bored face or a blank face, some even a mildly amused face. But they all eventually have a face that keeps everything inside. An emptiness settles in their eyes that keeps all their secrets. Dolph gave great blank face when questioning suspects. The look on his face now was angry. I'd never seen him so obviously pissed questioning a suspect.

"What's up?" I asked.

He closed the door behind him, stepping into the hallway. He shook his head. "I don't know why this one's getting to me."

"Tell me," I said.

His eyes flicked to my clothing, as if he'd just noticed. The frown softened into something close to a smile. "Somebody has become a bad influence on your wardrobe."

I frowned at him. "I've got a gun in a bellyband, okay? With the slits, it's easier to get to." I would never have explained my dress to Zerbrowski, but to Dolph . . .

"Ooh," Zerbrowski said. "Flash us, flash us."

Dolph's smile widened enough that his eyes were shiny. "If you're going to flash that much leg, at least it's in a good cause."

I crossed my arms over my stomach. "Is there really a suspect in there or did you call me down here just to yank my chain?"

The smile faded, and the angry frown returned. "She's not

the suspect. She's the victim. I know you talked to Perry at the scene, but I want you to hear her story, then tell me what you think." With that, he opened the door. That was Dolph, never liked to influence his people. But frankly, it was a little abrupt. I didn't have time to put my professional face on. I made eye contact with the woman while I still looked sort of surprised.

I had an impression of huge blue eyes, silky blond hair, delicate features, and yet she was tall. Even with her sitting down, I could tell that. Very few women can be both tall and dainty, but she pulled it off.

"Ms. Vicki Pierce, this is Anita Blake. I'd like you to tell her your story."

Ms. Pierce blinked big blue eyes, tears welling in them—not falling, mind you, but glittering. She dabbed at them with a Kleenex. There was a bandage on the side of her neck. "Sergeant Storr, I've told you what happened. I've told you and told you." A single tear slid down her cheek. "I'm so tired, and it's been such a traumatic night. Do I have to tell it all over again?" She leaned towards him in the chair, arms held protectively in front of her, almost pleading with him. A lot of men would have buckled under the sweet pressure of those eyes. Too bad the performance was wasted on Dolph.

"Just one more time for Ms. Blake," he said.

She looked past me to Zerbrowski. "Please, I'm so tired."

Zerbrowski leaned against the wall. "He's the boss."

She'd tried using her womanly wiles, but it wasn't working. She switched to sisterly unity with only a blink of her baby blues. "You're a woman. You know how it is, being so alone among all these—" her voice dropped to a hush—"men." She stared down at the table top, then back up with real tears trailing down her perfect skin.

It was an Oscar-worthy performance. I wanted to applaud, but I'd try sympathy first. There was always time for sarcasm later.

I walked around the table to her and leaned against it without really sitting. I was only inches from her, definitely an invasion of personal space. I patted her shoulder and smiled, though I wasn't a good enough actress for it to reach my eyes. "You're not alone now, Ms. Pierce. I'm here. Please just tell me your story."

"Are you a lawyer?" she asked.

If she asked for a lawyer and was insistent, the interview was over. I knelt in front of her, taking her still trembling hands in mine. I stared up at her. I couldn't manage to look sympathetic but I was interested. I gave her all my attention. I stared at her face like I'd memorize it and said, "Please, Vicki, let me help you."

Her hands had gone very still under mine. She stared at me with her big eyes like a deer that had scented the gun, but thought if it held very still, the gun wouldn't fire. She nodded almost to herself more than to me. She gripped my hands, and her face was utterly sincere.

"I had car trouble, and I went into the bar side of a restaurant to use the phone." She ducked her head, not meeting my eyes. "I know I shouldn't have gone in there. A woman in a bar alone is just asking for trouble. But there weren't any phones anywhere else."

"You have a right to go anywhere you want, anytime you want, Vicki. Being a woman doesn't take away that right." I didn't have to pretend to sound outraged.

She looked at me again, eyes studying my face. I could almost see the wheels in her head turning. She thought she had me. God, she was young.

Her fingers tightened on my hands, a fine tremor going up her arms. "I called a friend of mine to come look at the car. I'm in college and don't have a lot of money, so I didn't want to call a garage right away, not until my friend had seen the car. I hoped he could fix it."

She was volunteering too much information. Already justifying herself. Or maybe she'd just told the story too many times. Naw. "I'd have done the same thing," I said. And I might have.

She squeezed my hands and leaned towards me, a little eager, getting into her story. "There was this man at the bar. He seemed nice. We talked, and he asked me to sit with him. I told him I was waiting for my friend. He said, fine, we'd just talk." Again she looked down. "He said I had the most beautiful skin he'd ever seen." She looked back at me, eyes wide. "I mean, it was so romantic."

It was so rehearsed. "Go on."

"I let him buy me a drink. I know I shouldn't have." She

dabbed at her eyes. "I asked if he minded me smoking, and he said no." There was a full ashtray at her elbow. Neither Dolph nor Zerbrowski smoked, which meant little Vicki was damn near a chain smoker.

"He had his arm around me and leaned in to kiss me, I thought." The tears came faster, she hunched over a little, back shaking. "He bit me, on the neck. I swear until that second I didn't realize he was a vampire." She looked at me, from inches away vibrating with sincerity.

I patted her arm. "A lot of people can't tell vampires from humans. Especially if they've fed first."

She blinked at me. "Fed first?"

"If a vampire is full of blood, then he looks more human."

She nodded. "Oh."

"What did you do when he bit you?"

"I threw my drink at him and lit it with my lighter."

"Lit it?" I said, "It, the liquor, or it, the vampire?"

"Both," she said.

I nodded. "Vamps are very combustible. He burned real good, didn't he?"

"I didn't know he'd go up in flames like he did," she said. "A person just doesn't burn like that."

"No," I said, "they don't."

"I started to scream and run away from him. My friend came in the door then. People were shouting and screaming. It was awful."

I stood up. "I bet it was."

She stared up me, blue eyes sincere but not full of horror for what she'd done. There was no remorse. She gripped my arm suddenly, very tight, as if she could will me to understand. "I had to protect myself."

I placed my hand over hers and smiled. "What made you think of lighting the liquor once you'd thrown it?"

"I remembered that vampires were afraid of fire."

"But if you threw a drink in a human's face and lit it, it would only burn until the liquor was gone. A whoosh and it would be all over. A human would leave you alone after that, though they'd be hurt. Weren't you afraid that you'd just make the vampire more angry?"

"But vampires are very combustible, you said it yourself," Vicki said.

My smile widened. "So you knew he'd go up in flames?"

"Yes," she said, clutching me, willing me to understand her plight.

Dolph said, "I thought you didn't know the vampire would go up in flames, Ms. Pierce."

"I didn't, not until he burned like that," she said.

I patted her hand. "But, Vicki dear, you just said you knew he was combustible."

"But you said it first."

"Vicki, you just said you knew he'd go up in flames when you lit him up."

"I didn't."

I nodded. "Yes, you did."

She drew her hands away from me, sitting very straight in her chair. "You are trying to confuse me."

I shook my head. "No, Vicki, you're doing that all on your own." I moved away from her while still maintaining eye contact.

"What's that supposed to mean?" she asked. A little bit of anger peeked through her helpless-damsel act.

"What restaurant was it?" I asked as if I hadn't been there twenty minutes earlier. Interrogations are so often repetitive.

"What?" she asked.

"What was the name of the bar?"

"I don't remember."

"Dolph?" I asked.

"Burnt Offerings," he said.

I laughed. "A notorious vampire hangout."

"It's not in the vampire district," she said. "How was I to know that it was a vampire bar?"

"How about the picture of Christopher Lee as Dracula on the sign outside?," I said.

"It was quite late and nothing else was open."

"In University City on Delmar on a Friday night? Come on, Vicki. You can do better than that," I said.

She touched the bandage on her neck with a delicate, trembling hand. "He bit me." Her voice shook, and more tears trailed down her face.

I walked back to her. I put a hand on either side of her chair and leaned my face into hers. "You're lying, Vicki."

She burst into tears, hiding her face. I put a finger under her chin and lifted her face. "Damn, you're good, but not good enough."

She jerked away from me, standing so suddenly, the chair crashed to the floor. "I was attacked, and you're making me feel like the bad guy. You're a woman. I thought you'd understand."

I shook my head. "Can the universal sisterhood appeal, Vicki. It don't wash."

She jerked the bandage from her neck and threw it to the floor. "Look, look what he did to me!"

If she expected me to flinch, she had the wrong girl. I walked up to her, turning her head to one side. It was vampire fang marks, pretty fresh. A neat, nice bite, but there was no bruising, no hickey mark spreading across her creamy flesh. It was just two neat fang marks.

I stepped back from her. "You threw your drink into his face as soon as he bit you?"

"Yes, I didn't want him touching me."

"A filthy vampire," I said.

"A walking corpse."

She had a point. "Thank you, Vicki, thank you for talking to me." I walked to the door and motioned Dolph to follow. Zerbrowski stayed behind with Ms. Pierce.

Dolph closed the door behind us. "What did you see in the bite that I didn't?" he asked.

"If a vamp plunges fang into you but doesn't have time to feed much, it leaves a hickey. Just like a human sucking on your neck. The fangs aren't hollow, they just pierce the skin so that the vamp can suck the blood. One of the reasons they're so small. If the vamp feeds long enough, he takes blood away from the area and you don't get much marking. No way did a quick bite and suck leave her clean like that. She had someone else do it ahead of time, and it took a lot more time than a few seconds."

"I knew she was lying," Dolph said, and shook his head. "But I thought she'd thrown more on him than a drink. I thought she'd come into the bar with some sort of accelerant."

I shook my head. "Once you get a vamp burning, they burn until they're put out or burned to ash. You may get a few bone fragments left, but vamps burn more completely than any human. Dental records won't even help you."

"The bartender used a fire extinguisher from behind the bar. Witnesses say he was quick."

I nodded. "Yeah, good ol' Harry. It's a miracle the vamp is still alive. I know there's some hardcore opposition to a vampire business outside the vampire district. There's a petition and some sort of city meeting scheduled. Ms. Pierce will make a great witness to the dangers of vampires being outside the district."

"The restaurant owner said the bad publicity could ruin him."

I nodded. "Oh, yeah. It could also be a personal motive against the vampire. Not little Miss Blue Eyes but someone she knows that wanted him dead."

"She could be a member of Humans First. They'd love all the vamps to burn."

"A fanatical vampire hater wouldn't let a vamp do their neck like that. No. Humans First might have paid her to discredit the bar. She may be a member of Humans Against Vampires, HAV, or even Humans First, but she doesn't really believe. The bite proves that."

"Could the vamp have captured her mind?"

"I don't think so, but I've got some better questions for your other witnesses now."

"Such as?" he asked.

"Are they sure the vampire in question even got a taste of her? Are they positive that he bit her? Ask them if she smelled of blood when she came in."

"Explain," Dolph said.

"If she came in with the bite, then some of them might have smelled it. Might not, the wound was pretty clean, which was probably why the vamp did it that way. If he'd just bitten her and brought the blood to the surface, the vamps would have all scented it."

Dolph was writing it all down in his trusty notebook. "So a vamp's involved?"

"He may not know what she was planning to do. I'd check

for a vamp boyfriend, maybe, or at least one she's dated. Boyfriend may be too strong a word for Ms. Pierce. I'd see if she has some background in acting. Check out her major in college, maybe.''

"Already done," Dolph said. "She's got a background in theater arts.''

I smiled. "Why did you need me? You had it all solved.''

"The bite, the fact that vampires burn that easily . . .'' He shook his head. "None of this shit is in the literature.''

"The books aren't designed for police work, Dolph.''

"Maybe you should do a book,'' he said.

"Yeah, right. Do you have enough to get a warrant for her bank records?''

"If I'm careful what judge I ask, maybe.''

"You know, even if she is charged and convicted, the damage is done. The petition and the meeting are scheduled for next week. All they'll have is rumors of an attack, and it will grow in the telling.''

Dolph nodded. "Nothing we can do about that.''

"You could go down there and tell them what you've learned about Vicki in there.''

"Why don't you do it?''

"Because I'm the whore of Babylon to the right-wingers. I'm boffing the head bloodsucker. They wouldn't believe a damn thing I said.''

"I don't have time to attend civic meetings, Anita.''

"You think the vampire businesses should be segregated?'' I asked.

"Don't go there, Anita. You won't like the answers.''

I dropped it. Dolph thought vampires were monsters that the public needed to be protected from. I even agreed with him to an extent. But I was sleeping with one of the monsters. It made it hard to stay on the same bandwagon as Dolph. We agreed to disagree. It kept the peace and kept us working together.

"If you hate vamps so much, why didn't you buy Ms. Pierce's story?'' I asked.

"Because I'm not stupid,'' Dolph said.

"Sorry,'' I said. "Sorry that I thought even for a second that personal feelings might interfere with your job. You'd never allow it, would you?''

He smiled. "I don't know. You're not in jail yet."

"If you had proof of wrongdoing, I might be."

"You might," he said. The smile faded from his face. His eyes went empty, cop eyes. "What happened to your hand?"

I glanced down at the bandaged hand as if it had just appeared. "Kitchen accident," I said.

"Kitchen accident," he said.

"Yeah."

"What happened?"

"Sliced my hand with a knife."

"What were you doing?" he asked.

I never cook at home. Dolph knew that. "Slicing a bagel." I gave empty eyes back to him. Once, not long ago, my face showed everything. Every thought plain to see, but not now. I stared at Dolph's suspicious face and knew my face gave him nothing. Only the blankness itself was a clue that I was lying. But he knew I was lying. I wasn't going to waste his time or mine by coming up with a really good lie. Why bother?

We stared at each other. "There's blood on your hose, Anita. That must have been some bagel," he said.

"It was," I said, then couldn't help smiling. "I would have said I was mugged, but you'd want me to fill out a report."

He sighed. "You little shit. You're wrapped up in something else right now. Right this minute." His large hands balled into fists nearly the size of my face. "I'd yell at you, but it wouldn't do any good. I'd throw you in a cell overnight." He laughed, and it was bitter. "For what's left of the night, but I don't have any charges, do I?"

"I haven't done anything, Dolph." I raised the injured hand. "I was doing a favor for a friend, raising some dead. I got cut for more blood. That's it."

"The truth?" he asked.

I nodded. "Yeah."

"Why didn't you just tell me?" he asked.

"Because it was a favor, no money. If Bert finds out I'm raising the dead for free, he'll have a heart attack. He'll believe the bagel story."

Dolph laughed. "He won't ask how you got hurt. He doesn't want to know."

I nodded. "Very true."

"Just in case the kitchen gets any hotter, remember to call if you need help."

"I'll keep it in mind, Dolph."

"You do that." He put up his notebook. "Try not to kill anyone this month, Anita. Even in clear self-defense you pile up too many bodies, and you're going to get locked up."

"I haven't killed anyone in over six weeks—hell, nearly seven. I'm cutting down."

He shook his head. "The last two were the only two we've ever been able to prove, Anita. Both self-defense. One with witnesses out the ass, but we've never found Harold Gaynor's body. Just his wheelchair in that cemetery. Dominga Salvador is still missing."

I smiled at him. "People say the señora went back to South America."

"There was blood all over that chair, Anita."

"Was there?"

"Your luck is going to run out, and I won't be able to help you."

"I didn't ask for help," I said. "Besides, if the new law goes through, I'll have a federal badge."

"Being a cop, no matter what kind, doesn't mean you can't be arrested."

It was my turn to sigh. "I'm tired, and I'm going home. Good night, Dolph."

He looked at me for another second or two, then said, "Good night, Anita." He walked back into the interview room and left me standing in the hall.

Dolph had never been this grumpy before he found out I was dating Jean-Claude. I wasn't sure he was aware of how much his attitude had changed towards me, but I certainly was. A little undead nookie and he didn't trust me anymore, not completely.

It made me sad and angry. What was really hard was the fact that less than two months ago I'd have agreed with Dolph. You can't trust anyone who sleeps with the monsters. But here I was, doing it. Me, Anita Blake, turned into coffin bait. Sad, very sad. It wasn't any of Dolph's business who I dated. But I couldn't blame him for the attitude. I didn't like it, but I couldn't bitch about it. Okay, I could bitch, but it wasn't fair of me to do it.

I walked out without going through the main squad room

again. I wondered how long they'd keep the penguins on their desks waiting for me to come back. The thought of all those silly-looking toy birds sitting forlornly waiting for me to return brought a smile to my face. But it didn't last. It wasn't just that Dolph mistrusted me. He was a very good cop, a good investigator. If he really started digging, he might get proof. Heaven knew I'd done enough unsanctioned kills to put me in prison. I'd used my animating powers to kill humans. If it could be proved, it was an automatic death sentence. A death sentence for someone who had used magic to kill was not the same sort of sentence as, say, an axe murderer got. A guy could chop up his family and spend the next fifteen years on death row with appeals. There are no appeals for magic-induced murder. Trial, conviction, death within six weeks, usually less.

The prisons are afraid of magic and don't like to keep witches and such around long. There was a sorcerer in Maine who called down demons while in his cell. How anyone left him alone long enough for that particular ritual, I don't know. The people who had goofed all ended up dead, so they couldn't be questioned. They never did find the heads. Even I couldn't raise enough of them as zombies to get them to talk or write down what had happened. It was a mess.

The sorcerer escaped, but was later recaptured with the help of a coven of white witches and, strangely, a group of Satanists. Nobody who performs magic likes it when someone goes rogue. It gives us all a bad name. The last witch burned alive by a mob in this country was only in 1953. Her name was Agnes Simpson. I'd seen the black-and-white photos of her death. Anyone who studied preternatural anything had to have her picture in at least one textbook. The photo that stayed with me was one in which her face was untouched, pale, even from a distance terror plain on her face. Her long brown hair moving in the heat but not yet burning. Only her nightgown and robe had caught fire. Her head thrown back, screaming. The photo won the Pulitzer Prize. The rest of the photos aren't seen as often. A progression of photographs that ends with her burned and blackened and dead.

How anyone could stand there and keep taking pictures, I don't know. Maybe the Pulitzer Prize was a charm against nightmares. Then again, maybe not.

25

I PULLED INTO the lot of the apartment building with its secret hospital in the basement. It was nearly five. Dawn pressed like a cool hand against the wind. The sky was grey, caught between darkness and light. That trembling edge where the vampires are still moving, and you can get your throat ripped out moments from sunrise.

A taxi drew up in front of the building. A tall woman with very short blond hair got out. She was wearing a very short skirt and a leather jacket, no shoes. Zane got out next. Someone had paid his bail, and it wasn't me. Which meant he had been in the Beast Master's tender care. Just luck that he hadn't been part of Sylvie's torment. If he'd refused, he'd have been hurt worse than he appeared to be. If he'd done it, I'd have had to kill him. That would have been damned awkward.

He saw me walking towards them. I put the long coat and its weaponry back on. Zane waved to me, smiling. He was wearing nothing but shiny black vinyl pants, tight enough to be skin, and boots. Oh, and a nipple ring. Mustn't forget the jewelry.

The tall woman stared at me. She didn't look happy to see me. Not hostile exactly, but not pleased. The driver said something, and she got a wad of bills out of her jacket pocket and paid him.

The taxi drove away. Vivian, the Beast Master's pet while he stayed here, hadn't gotten out. Gregory, Stephen's brother with his new conscience, hadn't gotten out either. I was short at least two wereleopards. What was going on?

Zane walked towards me like we were old friends. "I told you, Cherry, she's our alpha, our *léoparde lionné*. I knew she'd save us." He dropped to his knees in front of me. My right hand was in my pocket, gripping the Browning, so he had to settle for my left hand. I'd spent enough time around the werewolves to know that being alpha was a touchie-feelie sort of thing. Like the animals they sometimes were, shapeshifters seemed to need the reassurance of touch. So I didn't fight it, but I did let the safety off the Browning.

Zane took my hand gently, almost reverently. He laid his cheek against my knuckles, then rolled his face from side to side like a cat chin-marking me. His tongue gave one slow lick to the back of my hand, and I gently withdrew it. It took a lot of willpower not to wipe my hand on the coat.

The tall woman, Cherry I presumed, just looked at me. "She didn't save all of us." Her voice was an almost startling low contralto. It purred, even in human form.

"Where are Vivian and Gregory?" I asked.

She pointed back the way they'd come. "Back there, they're still back there."

"The deal was that all my people got out."

Zane bounced to his feet. The movement was so quick it caught my heart and my throat, and my finger went from trigger-guard to trigger. I set the safety on the Browning and eased my hand out. They weren't going to hurt me but if Zane kept bouncing around like a punk version of Tigger I might accidently fire the gun. My nerves were usually better than this.

"The Master of Beasts said that anyone who wished to ac-knowledge your dominance could leave, if they could walk out. But he'd already made sure that Gregory and Vivian couldn't walk."

Something cold and tight filled my stomach. "What do you mean?"

"Vivian was unconscious when we left." Cherry looked at the ground when she spoke the next words. "Gregory tried to crawl after us, but he was hurt too badly." She raised her eyes, and there were tears trembling in them. She kept her eyes very wide. "He cried after us. Begged us not to leave him." She wiped at the tears with an angry swipe of her hand. "But I left him. I left him screaming, because I wanted out of there more than anything else in the world. Even if it meant leaving my friends to be tortured and killed and raped." She hid her face with both her hands and cried.

Zane came up behind her and hugged her. "Gabriel could never keep us all safe either. She did her best."

"Like hell," I said.

Zane looked at me. He rubbed his cheek against the side of Cherry's neck, but his eyes were serious. He was glad to be alive, but he hadn't wanted to leave them.

"I'm going to make a phone call." I walked into the building and after a few seconds they followed me. I used the same phone I'd called Jean-Claude on earlier. I only had moments before true dawn, and he would be down for the count.

He answered the phone like he'd been expecting the call. "*Oui, ma petite.*"

"Gregory and Vivian didn't make it. I thought you negotiated for them."

"The others forced Padma to agree, but he set up one rule, that whoever wished to leave had to walk out. I knew what he meant to do, but it was the best bargain I could make. Please believe that."

"Fine, but I won't leave them. If they can split hairs this finely, so can we."

"What do you plan, *ma petite*?"

"I'm going back and help them walk out. Padma didn't say anything about walking out under their own power, did he?"

"No." Jean-Claude gave a long sigh. "Dawn is frightfully near, *ma petite*. If you must do this thing, wait at least two hours. Time enough for even the most powerful of us to be asleep, but do not wait much longer. I do not know how much sleep the council members need. They may awaken very early."

"I'll wait two hours."

"I will send some of the wolves to you. With Padma asleep they will be useful to you."

"Fine."

"I must go." The phone went dead, and I felt the sun burst above the horizon. I felt it like a great weight, and for just an instant I couldn't breathe, my body felt heavy, so heavy. Then the sensation was gone, and I knew that Jean-Claude was gone for the day. Even with three shared marks, I'd never felt anything like that before. I knew he protected me from things that the third mark would let me feel. He even protected Richard. Of the three of us, Jean-Claude knew more about the marks, how to use them, how not to use them, and what they really meant. Months into it all, and I hadn't asked many questions. Sometimes, I wasn't sure I wanted to know. Richard seemed equally reluctant, according to Jean-Claude. The vampire just seemed patient with us, like a parent with a backward child.

Cherry leaned against the wall, arms crossed over her stomach. She wasn't wearing anything under the leather jacket. Her eyes were cautious, like she'd been disappointed often and badly.

"You're going in after them. Why?"

Zane was sitting by her legs, back against the wall. "Because she's our alpha."

Cherry shook her head. "Why would you risk yourself for two people you don't know? I accepted your dominance because I wanted out of there, but I don't believe it. Why would you go back in there?"

I wasn't sure how to explain it. "They expect me to save them."

"So?" she said.

"So, I'm going to try."

"Why?"

I sighed. "Because . . . because I remember Vivian's pleading eyes and the bruises on her body. Because Gregory cried and screamed for you not to leave him. Because Padma will hurt them worse now than he would have before, because he thinks that by hurting them, he hurts me." I shook my head. "I'm going find a bed for a couple of hours. I suggest you do the same. But you don't have to come with me. This thing is strictly volunteer."

"I don't want to go back there," she said.

"Then don't," I said.

"I'll come," Zane said.

It almost made me smile. "Somehow I knew you would."

26

I LAY IN the narrow hospital bed in one of the spare rooms. The evening dress was folded on the room's only chair. The chair was shoved up under the doorknob. Flimsy lock. The chair wouldn't keep out someone truly determined, but it would give me a few seconds to aim. I'd showered and thrown the blood-soaked hose away. I was wearing just my panties. They didn't even have a spare hospital gown. I fell asleep in a strange bed with sheets clutched to my naked breasts, and the Firestar under my pillow. The machine gun was under the bed. I didn't think I'd need it, but where else was I going to stash it?

I was dreaming. Something about being lost in an abandoned house, searching for kittens. The kittens were crying, and there were snakes in the dark, eating the kittens. You didn't have to be Freud to interpret this one. The moment I thought that clearly, that it was a dream and what it meant, the dream melted away and left me awake in the dark. I woke staring upwards, sheets spilled down my body so that I was nearly nude in the black-ness.

I could feel my body pulsing. It was like I'd been running a race in my sleep. There was sweat under my breasts. Something was wrong.

I pulled the sheet up over me as I sat up, even though I wasn't cold. As a child I'd thought that the monsters in the closet and under the bed couldn't get me if I was covered. After waking from a nightmare I still reached for the sheet, no matter how hot it was. Of course, I was in a basement with air-conditioning. It wasn't hot. So why did my body feel almost fevered?

I reached under the pillow and got the Firestar out. I felt better with it gripped in my hand. If I'd just been spooked by a dream, I was going to feel silly.

I sat in the dark and strained to hear anything before I hit the lights. If there was someone out in the hall, they'd see the light under the door. If they were trying to ambush me, I didn't want them to see the light. Not yet.

I felt something coming down the hallway towards me. A roil of energy, heat, that played over my body like a hand. It was like a storm was rushing towards me, with that prickling brush of lightning growing like weight in the room. I clicked the safety off on the Firestar, and suddenly knew who it was. It was Richard. Richard striding towards me. Richard coming like an angry storm.

I clicked the safety back on but didn't put up the gun. He was mad. I could feel it. I'd seen him toss a solid oak four poster king-size bed around like it was nothing when he was angry. I'd keep the gun, just in case. I didn't like keeping it, but the moral dilemma didn't bother me enough to put it away. I hit the lights. I sat blinking in the sudden brightness, a hard knot forming in my stomach. I did not want to see him. I hadn't known what to say to him since the night I'd first slept with Jean-Claude. The night I'd run from Richard, run from what he was on the night of the full moon. Run from the sight of his beast.

I padded barefoot to the chair and gathered my clothes up. I was struggling into the strapless bra, gun beside me on the bed, when I smelled his after-shave. I felt the air move under the door and knew it was his body disrupting the currents of air. His after-shave wasn't that strong. I shouldn't have smelled it. I knew suddenly as if it had been whispered in my ear that Richard could smell me through the door, that he knew I'd worn Oscar de la Renta parfume for Jean-Claude.

I felt his fingertips press to either side of the door in a small push up motion, felt him draw a breath and scent my body deep into him.

What the hell was going on? We'd been bound for two months, and I'd never felt anything like this, not with Richard, and not with Jean-Claude.

Richard's voice, achingly familiar: "Anita, I need to talk to you.'' The anger was in his voice; in his body, rage. He was like thunder pressed against the door.

''I'm getting dressed,'' I said.

I heard him pace in front of the door. ''I know. I can feel you in there. What's happening to us?''

That was a loaded question if ever I'd heard one. I wondering if he could feel my hands as I'd felt his a moment ago. ''We haven't been this close at dawn since we were bound. Jean-Claude isn't here to act as a buffer.'' I hoped that was it. The only alternative I could think of was that the council had done something to our marks. I didn't think that was it, though. But we wouldn't know for sure until we could ask Jean-Claude. Damn.

Richard tried the door handle. ''What's taking so long?''

''I'm almost done,'' I said. I slipped the dress on. It was actually the easiest piece of clothing to get into. The shoes were not comfortable without hose, but I would have felt even less prepared barefoot. Can't explain it, but shoes make me feel better. I moved the chair and unlocked the door. I stepped back, a little too quick, until I was on the far side of the room. I put my hands behind me, still holding the gun. I didn't think he'd hurt me, but I'd never felt him like this. His anger was like a burning knot in my gut.

He opened the door carefully, as if he was having to think before each movement. His control was a trembling line between his rage and me.

He was six foot one, broad-shouldered, with high-sculpted cheekbones, and a wide soft mouth. There was a dimple in his chin, and he was altogether too handsome. His eyes were still perfect chocolate brown; only the pain in them was new. His hair fell in thick waves around his shoulders, a brown so full of gold and copper highlights that there should have been a different word for it. Brown is a dull word, and his hair was not dull. I'd loved running my hands through his hair, grabbing fistfuls of it when we kissed.

He was wearing a blood-red tank top that left his muscular shoulders and arms bare. I knew that every inch of him you could see, and what you could not, was tanned a nice soft brown. But it wasn't really tanned, just his natural skin color.

My heart was beating in my throat, but it wasn't fear. He

stared at me in the black dress. Face scrubbed clean of makeup, my hair uncombed, and I felt his body react to the sight of me. I felt it like a twist in my own body. I had to close my eyes to keep from looking at his jeans to see if what I was feeling was visible.

When I opened my eyes, he hadn't moved. He just stood there in the middle of the room, hands balled into fists, breathing a little too hard. His eyes were wild, showing too much white like a horse about to bolt.

I found my voice first. "You said you wanted to talk, so talk." I sounded breathless. It was like I could feel Richard's heart, his chest rising and falling, like it was my own. I'd had moments of this with Jean-Claude, but never with Richard. If we'd still been seeing each other, it would have been intriguing. Now, it was just confusing.

He relaxed his hands, flexing them, fighting not to make fists. "Jean-Claude said he was protecting us from each other. Keeping us from getting too close until we were ready. I didn't believe him, until now."

I nodded. "It's awkward."

He smiled, and shook his head, but the smile never took the anger out of his eyes. "Awkward? Is that all it is to you, Anita? Just awkward?"

"You can feel what I'm feeling, right now, Richard. Answer your own damn question."

He closed his eyes and pressed his hands together in front of his chest. He pressed his palms together until his arms trembled with the effort and the muscles corded, straining against his skin all the way up to his shoulders.

I felt him withdraw from me. Though that doesn't cover how it felt. It was like he built a wall between us. He was raising mental shields between us. Someone had to. I hadn't thought to try. The sight and feel of him in my mind had turned me into a pulsing hormone. It was too embarrassing for words.

I watched his body relax, a muscle at a time, until he opened his eyes, slowly, almost sleepily, his body quiet, at peace. I'd never been that good at meditation.

He lowered his arms and looked at me. "Better?"

I nodded. "Yes, thank you."

He shook his head. "Don't thank me. It was either control it or run screaming."

We stood there, staring at each other. The silence was uncomfortably thick. "What do you want, Richard?"

He gave a choking laugh that brought heat in a rush up my face. "You know what I meant," I said.

"Yes," he said, "I know what you meant. You invoked your status as lupa while I was out of town."

"You mean protecting Stephen?"

He nodded. "You had no right to go against Sylvie's express orders. She was the one I left in charge, not you."

"She'd removed pack protection from him. Do you know what that means?"

"Better than you do," he said. "Without protection of a dominant you're anybody's meat that wants you, like the wereleopards after you killed Gabriel."

I pushed away from the wall. "If you had told me what was happening to them, Richard, I'd have helped them."

"Would you?" he asked. He motioned to the gun in my hand. "Or would you just have killed them?"

"No, that's what Sylvie wanted to do, not me." But I stood there with the gun in my hand and didn't know a graceful way to put it down.

"I know how much you hate shapeshifters, Anita. I didn't think you'd give a damn, and no one else did either or they'd have told you. They all thought you wouldn't care. I mean if you could reject someone you supposedly loved because they turned into a monster once a month, what chance did strangers have?"

He was being deliberately cruel. I'd never seen him do anything just to hurt, just to try and dig the knife in a little deeper. It was petty, and that was one thing Richard was not.

"You know me better than that," I said.

"Do I?" he said. He sat down on the bed, grabbing two handfuls of sheet. He raised the cloth to his face and took a long deep breath. He watched me with angry eyes while he did it. "The smell of you still moves me like some kind of drug, and I hate you for it."

"I just spent a few minutes inside your head, remember. You don't hate me, Richard. It'd be less painful if you did."

He crumpled the sheet in his lap, hands balling the cloth into tight fists. "Love doesn't conquer all, does it?" he asked.

I shook my head. "No, it doesn't."

He stood in an almost violent movement, pacing the room in a tight circle. He came to stand in front of me. There was no "magic" now, just two people. But it was still hard to stand so close to him. Still hard to know I wasn't allowed to touch him anymore. Dammit, it shouldn't have been this hard. I'd made my choice.

"You were never my lover, now you're not even my girl-friend. You are not a shapeshifter. You cannot be my lupa."

"Are you really angry that I protected Stephen?"

"You ordered pack members to guard him and a wereleopard. You told them you'd kill them if they didn't obey you. You don't have that right."

"You gave me that right when you made me lupa." I held up a hand to keep him from interrupting. "And whether you like it or whether you don't, it was a good thing that I had some clout to throw around. Stephen might be dead now if I hadn't been there for him. And Zane would have caused an even worse mess at the hospital. Lycanthropes don't need any more bad press."

"We're monsters, Anita. You can't have good press if you're a monster."

"You don't believe that."

"You believe we're monsters, Anita. You proved that. You'd rather sleep with a corpse than let me touch you."

"What do you want me to say, Richard? That I'm sorry I couldn't cope? I am sorry. That I'm still embarrassed that I ran to Jean-Claude's bed? I am. That I think less of myself for not being able to love you even after what I saw you do to Marcus?"

"You wanted me to kill Marcus."

"He was going to kill you if you didn't. So yeah, I wanted you to kill Marcus. But I didn't tell you to eat him."

"When a pack member is killed in a dominance struggle, we all feed. It's a way to absorb their energy. Marcus and Raina aren't really gone as long as the pack remains."

"You ate Raina, too?"

"Where did you think the bodies went? Did you think your

friends on the police force had hidden all the corpses?''

"I thought Jean-Claude had arranged it.''

"He did, but it was the pack that did the dirty work. The vampires don't care about a body once it's cold. If the blood isn't warm, they don't want it.''

I almost asked if he preferred warm flesh to cold, but didn't. I didn't really want to know. This entire conversation was going nowhere that I wanted to be. I looked at the watch on my wrist. "I've got to go, Richard.''

"Go rescue your wereleopards.''

I looked at him. "Yes.''

"That's why I'm here. I'm your backup.''

"Was that Jean-Claude's idea?''

"Sylvie told me that Gregory refused to harm her. Regardless of what they did under Gabriel, they're lycanthropes and we help our own even if they aren't lukoi.''

"Do the wereleopards have a fancy name for themselves?'' I asked.

He nodded. "They call themselves pard. The werewolves are the lukoi. The leopards are the pard.''

I walked past him, shoulder brushing his bare arm. That one touch raised the hairs on my body like he'd touched something much more personal. But I'd get used to it. I'd made my choice, and no matter how confused I was, I wasn't that confused. So I still lusted after Richard, even loved him. I'd picked the vampire, and you can't have your vampire and your werewolf, too.

I got the machine gun out from under the bed and slid the strap across my chest.

"Jean-Claude said that we weren't supposed to kill anybody,'' Richard said.

"He knew you were coming here?'' I asked.

He nodded.

I smiled, but it wasn't happy.

"He didn't tell you?'' Richard asked.

"No.''

We were left looking at each other again. "You can't trust him, Anita, you know that.''

"You're the one who let him give you the first mark voluntarily. What I did, Richard, I did to save your lives, both of you.

If you really thought he was so damn untrustworthy, why'd you bind us to him?''

Richard looked away then, and spoke very softly, ''I didn't think I'd lose you.''

''Go wait in the hall, Richard.''

''Why?''

''I've got to finish getting dressed.''

His gaze slid to my legs, very white against the blackness of the dress and the heels. ''Hose,'' he said, softly.

''A new holster, actually,'' I said. ''The hose got trashed last night. Now, please get out.''

He did. He didn't even make a last cutting remark. It was an improvement. When he closed the door behind him, I sat down on the bed. I did not want to do this. Going back in for the leopards was a bad idea. Going in with Richard as backup was worse. But we'd do it. I couldn't tell him to stay home. Besides, I needed the backup. No matter how emotionally painful it was to be around him, he was one of the most powerful shapeshifters I'd ever met. If he hadn't been crippled by a conscience the size of Rhode Island, he'd have been dangerous. Of course, Marcus would probably have said Richard was plenty dangerous just as he was. And he'd be right.

27

RICHARD DROVE HIS 4 X 4 to the Circus. I sat beside him, but in some ways I might as well not have been there at all. He never looked at me, let alone spoke. But the tension in his body was enough. He knew I was there.

Cherry and Zane rode in the back seat. It had surprised me when Cherry slid into the car. Her eyes flashed white, eyelids fluttering like a nervous tick. She looked like she was going to faint. Zane was his usual self; smiling, eyes secret. His usual self? That was almost funny. I'd known him less than twenty-four hours. I didn't know what the hell was "usual" for him.

Cherry had sunk down on the seat, hugging herself. She was slowly curling into a little ball. I'd known her less time than I'd known Zane, but this wasn't normal for anybody.

I turned as far as the seat belt would allow and said, "What's wrong, Cherry?"

Her eyes rolled to me, then closed, tight. She shook her head and huddled further into herself. There was a fresh bruise forming on her cheek. She might have had it when I first saw her. I just wasn't sure.

"Zane, what's wrong with her?"

"She's scared," he said. His voice was neutral, but there was something in his face that was angry.

"I told her this was strictly voluntary. She doesn't have to come."

"Tell that to Mr. Macho," he said. He was staring at the back of Richard's head.

I turned in the seat until I was staring at his profile. He wouldn't look at me. "What's going on, Richard?"

"She's coming," he said, voice very quiet.

"Why?"

"Because I said so."

"Bullshit."

He glanced at me then. He tried for it to be a cool look, but it was angry. "You're my lupa, but I am still Ulfric. My word is still law."

"Fuck that. You are not dragging her into this because you're mad at me."

The muscle in his jaw clenched tight enough for me to see it. "They both deserted their people. Now they are both going to make it right." His voice was still quiet, low, and careful, like if he wasn't very careful he'd lose control. He spoke like people talk when they want to yell.

"Look at her, Richard. She'll be worse than useless. She'll just be one more victim we have to keep safe."

He shook his head. "You don't leave one of your own behind, not for any reason. It's the law."

"Pack law, but she's not pack."

"Until you stop being my lupa, Anita, what belongs to you, belongs to me."

"You arrogant prick."

He smiled, but it was just a baring of teeth, more snarl than humor. "Everyone has to do something to take the edge off."

It took me a second to realize what he meant, then I was embarrassed. But I'd be damned if I'd sit there and explain that I hadn't meant it literally. He knew I hadn't meant it literally. He was trying to embarrass me. Fuck it. "Did you hit Cherry?"

He was suddenly very interested in the road, but his hands smoothed on the steering wheel. He didn't like that he'd hit her. Neither did I.

"You wanted me to be strong. Well, you got your wish."

"There is a difference between being strong and being cruel, Richard."

"Really? I never could tell the difference."

I think that last was meant for me. But you can only make me feel guilty for so long, and then I just get mad. "Fine, if what belongs to me belongs to you, then it works the other way too."

He glanced at me, frowning. "What do you mean?"

I liked the unease in his face. I enjoyed turning his logic back on him. In my own way, I was just as angry at him as he was at me. I didn't have his moral high ground, but I hadn't turned cannibal either. Maybe I did have some moral high ground, after all.

"If you can force Cherry to go with us, then I can order the pack to guard Stephen. I can order them to do any damn thing I'm dominant enough to make them do."

"No," he said.

"Why not?" I asked.

"Because I said so."

I laughed then, and even to me it sounded bitchy.

He screamed, a long ragged yell of frustration and anger. "God, Anita, God."

"We're going to cut each other up if we don't work something out," I said.

He glanced at me again. His eyes weren't angry anymore. They were almost panic-stricken. "You're sleeping with the vampire. There's nothing to work out."

"The three of us are bound to each other for what could be a very, very long time, Richard. We're going to have to find a way to live together."

He laughed, and it was bitter. "Live together? You want a house for three with Jean-Claude down in the basement and me chained out in the yard?"

"Not exactly, but you can't keep hating yourself like this."

"It's not me I hate. It's you."

I shook my head. "If that were true, I'd leave you alone. But you hate your beast and your beast is you."

He pulled in front of the Circus. "We're here." He turned off the engine and silence filled the car. "Cherry can wait here."

"Thank you, Richard," I said.

He shook his head. "Don't thank me, Anita." He smoothed his hands over his face into his hair, combing his fingers through it. The gesture showed his arms and chest to wonderful advantage. He'd never been aware of how much the simplest thing he did had moved me. "Don't thank me." He got out of the car.

I told Cherry to stay low. I didn't want them to get any ideas about taking her while we were inside rescuing the others. It would sort of defeat the purpose of the entire trip.

Zane kissed her on the forehead the way you'd calm a child. He told her everything would be all right, that I'd keep them safe. God, I hoped he was right.

28

A MAN HAD walked up to meet Richard. He'd been waiting for him. I reached in the coat pocket and clicked off the safety on the Browning because I knew him.

Zane, who was very close behind me asked, "Is something wrong?"

I shook my head. "Hello, Jamil."

"Hello, Anita." He was just shy of six feet, wearing a white tank top almost the twin of the one Richard wore. Except that Jamil had cut out the neck, arms, and chopped out the middle of the shirt so that his slender waist and cobblestone abs showed. The white tank top was in startling contrast to the rich solid brown of his skin. His hair was waist-length, worked in thin corn rows intertwined with bright beads. He was wearing white sweat pants and looked like he'd just come from the gym.

The last time I'd seen Jamil he'd been trying to kill Richard. "What are you doing here?" Even to me it didn't sound friendly.

He smiled, a quick baring of teeth. "I'm Richard's enforcer."

"So?"

"They allowed us each one backup, plus the wereleopards," Richard said. He spoke without looking at me, staring at the front of the Circus rising into the bright sunlight.

"I'm short one wereleopard and a backup," I said.

He did look at me then. His face was as closed and guarded as I'd seen it. "I thought Jean-Claude had told you, and you'd just decided against any backup."

"I'd take backup into hell, Richard. You know that."

"Don't blame me if your boyfriend forgot to mention it."

"He probably thought you'd mention it."

He just looked at me with his angry eyes.

"Is there anything else you forgot to tell me?"

"He just said to tell you, don't kill anyone."

"He mention anyone in particular not to kill?" I asked.

Richard frowned then. "As a matter of fact, he did." He said the next in a bad French accent. " 'Tell *ma petite* not to kill Fernando no matter what the provocation.' "

It brought a tight smile to my face. "Fine."

Jamil was staring at me. "The look on your face, babe. That is the most evil little smile I've ever seen. What did this Fernando do to you?"

"To me personally, nothing."

"He raped your Geri, your second in command," Zane said.

Both of the werewolves stared at him, a sudden flash of hostility that made Zane step back. He moved a little behind me, which didn't quite work since he was nearly a foot taller. Hard to cower behind someone who's shorter than you are.

"He raped Sylvie?" Richard asked.

I nodded.

"He has to be punished," Richard said.

I shook my head. "I told Sylvie I'd kill him. That we'd kill them all."

"All?" Richard made it a question.

"All," I said.

He looked away then, not meeting my eyes. He asked without turning around, "How many?"

"Two that she's told me about. There may be more, but if there is, she's not ready to talk about it yet."

"You're sure there was more than just this Fernando?" Richard looked at me, eyes hopeful, almost like he wanted me to tell him it wasn't really as bad as it seemed.

"It was gang rape, Richard. They took great pride in telling me that."

"Who was the second one?" he asked.

He asked. I answered. "Liv."

He blinked at me. "She's a woman."

"I'm aware of that."

He just stared at me. "How?"

I raised eyebrows at him. "You really want me to get that technical?"

Richard shook his head. He looked ill. Jamil didn't. He met my eyes without flinching, his face thinned into tight angry lines. "If they can take one of our highest wolves and use her like that, then the pack's threat means nothing."

"That, too," I said. "But I'm not going to kill someone just to keep the pack's rep in good repair."

"Then why?" Jamil said.

I thought about that for a second. "Because I gave my word I'd do it. They dug their grave when they touched her. All I'm doing is filling in the dirt."

"Why?" Jamil said. "You hated Sylvie." It seemed important to him that I answer, as if the question meant more than it should have, at least to him.

"They didn't break her. All that they did to her, and they couldn't break her. She could have stopped the torture by giving up the pack. She didn't give them up." I tried to put it all into words. "That kind of loyalty and strength deserves the same in return."

"What do you know about loyalty?" Richard asked.

"That's it," I said. I turned to him and poked a finger in his chest. "We can have one knock-down-glorious fight after we save Gregory and Vivian. They gang-raped Sylvie. Do you really think they're doing less to two shapeshifters that they thought had no alpha to protect them?" I was spitting every word into his face, voice squeezed tight and low, because if I let go, I'd be screaming. "We are going to get them out and take them some place safe. When we do all that, then you can go back to being pissed at me. You can wrap your jealousy and self-hatred around us both until we choke. But right this second, we have work to do. Okay?"

He looked at me for a heartbeat or two, then gave the barest of nods. "Okay."

"Great," I said. I'd abandoned my purse at the hospital, but I had the key to the front door in my coat pocket along with ID What else did a girl need?

"You have a key to the front door?" Richard asked.

"Drop it, Richard," I said.

"You're right. You're right, and I'm wrong. I haven't been paying attention to business for two months. Sylvie told me that.

I didn't listen. Maybe if I had, she . . . Maybe if I'd been listening, she wouldn't have gotten hurt.''

"Jesus, Richard, don't pull another guilt trip on me. You could be Attila the Hun, and the council would still have come. No show of strength would have kept them out.''

"What would have?'' he asked.

I shook my head. "They are the council, Richard. The stuff of nightmares. Nightmares don't care how strong you are.''

"What do they care about?'' he asked.

I shoved the key into the lock. "Scaring you.'' The big double doors pushed inward. I drew the Browning out of my pocket.

"We aren't supposed to kill anybody,'' Richard said.

"I remember,'' I said, but I kept the gun out. I couldn't kill anybody, but Jean-Claude hadn't said I couldn't maim someone. It might not be as satisfying, but when you need to back up your threat, someone writhing on the floor in pain is almost as good as a body. Sometimes it's better.

29

I STOOD WITH my back to the closed door, the others fanned out around me. Soft filtered light came down from the high, high windows. The midway looked dark and tired in the morning sunlight. The Ferris wheel towered over the haunted house and mirror maze and the game booths. It was a complete traveling carnival that didn't travel. It smelled like it was supposed to: cotton candy, corn dogs, funnel cakes.

Two men stepped out of the huge circus tent that took up one entire corner. They walked towards us side by side. The taller man was about six foot, square-shouldered, with hair that was somewhere between blond and brown. The hair was straight, thick, and just long enough to trail the edge of his shirt collar. White dress shirt tucked into white jeans, complete with white belt. He wore white loafers, no socks. He looked like he should have been walking along a beach in a credit-card commercial, except for his eyes. Even from a distance there was something odd about his eyes. They were orange-ish. People didn't have eyes that color.

The second man was about five foot seven, with dark gold hair cut very short. A brownish mustache graced his upper lip and curved back to meet brownish sideburns. Nobody had worn a mustache like that since the 1800's. His white pants were tight and slid into polished black boots. A white vest and a white shirt peeked out from beneath a red jacket. He looked like he should have been riding to the hounds, chasing small furred animals.

His eyes were a nice normal brown. But the first man's eyes just got stranger the closer he came to us. His eyes were yellow—not amber, not brown—yellow with orange spikes radiating from the pupil like a pinwheel of color. They were not human eyes, no way, nohow.

If it hadn't been for the eyes, I wouldn't have recognized him as a lycanthrope, but the eyes gave it away. I'd seen pictures of tigers with eyes like that.

They stopped a little distance from us. Richard moved up beside me, Zane and Jamil at our backs. We all stood looking at each other. If I hadn't known better, I'd have said that the two men looked uncomfortable or embarrassed.

The smaller man said, "I am Captain Thomas Carswell. You must be Richard Zeeman." His voice was British and upper-crust, but not too upper-crust.

Richard took a step forward. "I'm Richard Zeeman. This is Anita Blake. Jamil, and Zane."

"I am Gideon," the man with the eyes said. His voice was almost painfully low, as if even in human speech he growled. The sound was so low that it made my spine thrum.

"Where are Vivian and Gregory?" I said.

Captain Thomas Carswell blinked and looked at me. He didn't look happy about the interruption. "Nearby."

"First," said Gideon, "we need your gun, Miss Blake."

I shook my head. "I don't think so."

They exchanged glances. "We cannot allow you to go forward with a gun in your hand, Miss Blake," Carswell said.

"Every time someone wants to take my gun, it means either they don't trust me or they're planning to do something I don't like."

"Please," Gideon said in his gravelly voice. "Surely you must understand our reluctance. You do have a certain reputation."

"Anita?" Richard said, half-question, half-something else.

I clicked the safety on the gun and held it out to Gideon. I had two more guns and two knives left. They could have the Browning.

Gideon took the gun from me and stepped back to stand beside Carswell. "Thank you, Miss Blake."

I nodded. "You're welcome."

"Shall we go?" Carswell said. He offered me his arm as if he were escorting me to dinner.

I stared at him, then back at Richard. I raised my eyebrows, trying to ask what he thought without asking.

He gave a half-shrug.

I slid my left arm through Carswell's arm. "You're being very civilized about this," I said.

"There is no reason to lose all good manners just because things have become . . . somewhat extreme."

I let him lead me towards the tent. Gideon fell into step with Richard. They were almost the same height, and the roil of energy that came off them made the hair on my neck stand up. They were trying each other's power, tasting each other without doing anything at all but lowering their hard-won control. Jamil and Zane brought up the rear like good soldiers.

We were almost at the tent when Carswell stopped, hand tightening on my arm. I slid my right hand behind my back, under the coat, touching the machine gun.

"There is something heavy on your back, Miss Blake. Something that is not a purse." His grip on my left arm grew tighter, not hurting, but I knew he wouldn't let go, not without a fight.

I swung the machine gun around on its strap with my right hand and put the barrel into his chest, not shoving, just there, like his hand on my other arm.

"Everybody be calm," I said.

The other men were suddenly very, very still. "We are going to give you your people, Miss Blake," Gideon growled. "There is no need for this."

"Thomas here asked what I had on my back. I'm showing him."

"You do not know me well enough to call me by my Christian name, Miss Blake," Carswell said.

I blinked at him. There was no fear in him. He was human— one pull on the trigger and he was gone—but there was no fear. I stared into his brown eyes and saw only . . . sadness. A tired sorrow as if he'd almost welcome it.

I shook my head. "Sorry, Captain Carswell."

"We cannot possibly let you go inside the tent with this weapon." His voice was very calm, matter of fact.

"Be reasonable, Anita," Richard said. "If things were reversed, you'd want them without weapons."

The trouble was I had to take off the coat to take off the

machine gun. If I took off the coat, they'd see the knives. I didn't want to lose the knives. Of course, I'd still have the Firestar.

I let the machine gun slide back out of sight. "I'll have to remove my coat."

Carswell released my arm cautiously and stepped back, still close enough to grab me. I stared at his careful clothing. The jacket was too tailored for a shoulder holster, the pants had no pockets, but he could have had something at the small of his back.

"I'll remove my coat if you remove yours," I said.

"I have no weapons, Miss Blake."

"Remove your coat and I'll believe you."

He sighed and slid out of the red jacket, then turned in a full circle, arms spread to his sides. "As you see, no weapons." To be really sure I'd need to pat him down, but I didn't want him returning the favor, so I let it go.

I slipped out of the coat and watched his eyes widen at the wrist sheaths. "Miss Blake, I am impressed and disappointed."

I let the coat fall to the floor and slipped the strap over my head. I hated giving up the machine gun, but . . . I did understand. They'd been doing awful things to Gregory and Vivian. I wouldn't necessarily trust me with a gun if I were in their place. I took the clip out of the gun and handed the weapon to Carswell.

His eyes widened a little. "Fearful that I will turn on you and your friends?"

I shrugged. "Can't blame a girl for being cautious."

He smiled, and it almost reached his eyes. "No, I suppose I cannot."

I slid one of the knives out of its sheath and handed it to him hilt-first.

He waved it away. "You may keep your knives, Miss Blake. They will only be protection if someone gets very close, very personal. I think a lady should be allowed to defend her honor."

Damn, he was being nice, gentlemanly. If I kept the second handgun and he found out later, he might not be so nice. "Damn," I said.

Carswell frowned.

"I have one more gun."

"It must be very well concealed, Miss Blake."

I sighed again. "Inconveniently so, yes. Do you want it or not?"

He glanced back at Gideon, who nodded. "Yes, please, Miss Blake."

"Everybody turn their backs."

Amused or bemused looks all around.

"I have to raise the dress and flash the room to get the gun. I don't want anyone peeking." All right, it was stupid and juvenile, but I still couldn't just raise the dress in front of five men. My daddy brought me up better than that.

Carswell turned without being asked a second time. I got some very amused looks, but everyone turned, except for Gideon. "I would be a poor bodyguard if I allowed you to shoot us in the back while we were defending your modesty." He had a point.

"All right, I'll turn my back." Which I did, fishing the gun out for the last time. The bellyband was a good idea, but the Firestar was going in the other coat pocket when I got it back. I was tired of messing with it.

I handed the gun to Gideon. He took it, still looking amused. "Is that everything except for the knives?"

"Yes," I said.

"Your word of honor?"

I nodded. "My word."

He nodded, too, as if that was enough. I knew already that Carswell was someone's human servant. He was the genuine article, a British soldier of Queen Victoria's army. But until that moment I hadn't known that Gideon was as old. Lycanthropes don't age that slowly. He was getting help from somewhere or he was more than just a shapeshifter.

"Lycanthrope," I said, "but what else are you?"

He smiled then, flashing small fangs top and bottom. The only other lycanthrope I'd seen with fangs like that had been Gabriel. You get things like that if you spend too much time in animal form.

"Guess," he said in a whisper so low and rumbling it made me shiver.

Carswell said, "May we turn around, Miss Blake?"

"Sure," I said.

He slid his jacket back on, smoothing it in place, and offered me his arm once more. "Shall we, Miss Blake?"

"Anita, my name's Anita."

He smiled. "Then you may call me Thomas." He said it as if he didn't let a lot of people call him by his first name.

It made me smile. "Thank you, Thomas."

He tucked my arm more securely in the crook of his own. "I do wish . . . Anita, that our meeting could be under better circumstances."

I met his sad eyes and said, "What's happening to my people while you delay me here with your polite smiles?"

He sighed. "I am hoping he will be finished before we walk in upon them." A look almost like pain crossed his face. "It is not a sight fit for a lady."

I tried to pull my arm free, and he gripped it more tightly. His eyes weren't sad anymore. They were full of something I couldn't read. "Know that this is not my choice."

"Let go of me, Thomas."

He let me draw my arm free of him. I was suddenly afraid of what was inside the tent. I'd never spoken with Vivian, and Gregory was a perverted piece of shit, but I suddenly didn't want to see what had happened to them.

Gideon said, "Thomas, should she . . . ?"

"Let her," he said. "She has only the knives."

I didn't exactly run, but I was close when I reached the closed flap of the tent. I heard Richard say, "Anita . . ."

I felt him coming up behind me, but I didn't wait. I flung the flap aside and stepped inside. The tent had just one ring, the center ring. Gregory lay in a naked heap in the center of that ring, hands bound behind his back with thick grey tape. His body was a mass of bruises and cuts. I could see bone glistening in his legs, jagged and wet where they'd broken his legs. Compound fractures are very nasty things. That was why he couldn't walk out on his own power. They'd broken his legs.

There was a small sound that drew me down the aisle to the railing around the ring. Vivian and Fernando were in the ring, too. I'd missed them because they were too close to the side of the railing, hidden from view.

Vivian raised her face up from the ground, tape across her mouth, one eye bloody and swollen shut. Fernando shoved her face back to the ground, showing her hands bound with tape. Showing what he was doing to her. He drew himself out of her, wet and finished at last. He patted her bare butt, giving her a small slap. "That was nice."

I was already walking towards them across the sand of the ring. Which means I'd gotten over the railing in spike heels and a floor-length skirt. I didn't remember doing it.

Fernando stood, fastening his pants, smiling at me. "If you hadn't bargained for her freedom, I'd have never been allowed to touch her. My father doesn't share."

I kept walking. I had one of the knives out, held to the side of the dress. I wasn't sure if he'd noticed, or if I cared. I held my empty left hand out to him. "You're a big man when the lady's tied and gagged. How are you when the lady's armed?"

He smiled, and it was mocking. He touched Vivian with his foot, casually, like you'd poke a dog. "She's beautiful but a little too submissive for my tastes. I like them with a little more fight to them like your wolf-bitch." He finished fastening his pants, running his hands up his chest as if remembering. "*C't'une bonne bourre.*"

I knew enough French to know that he'd said Sylvie was a good lay. I balanced the knife. It wasn't made for throwing, but in a pinch it'd do.

There was the faintest shadow in his eyes, as if for the first time he realized that there was no one here to save him; then something leaped over the railings. A blur of speed and motion that hit Fernando hard enough to roll him across the ground. When they came up, Richard was on top of him.

I yelled, "Don't kill him, Richard! Don't kill him!" I ran for them, but Jamil got there first. Jamil knelt by Richard, grabbing his arm, saying something to him. Richard grabbed Jamil by the throat and flung him across the ring. I ran to Jamil, kneeling beside him, but it was too late. His throat was crushed. His eyes were wide, frightened; he tried to breathe but it wasn't working. His legs spasmed, spine bowing, as he fought to breath. He grabbed my hand, his eyes screaming at me. There was nothing I could do. Either he'd heal it or he'd die.

I screamed, "Shit, Richard, help him!"

Richard plunged his hand into Fernando's stomach. He didn't have claws yet. It was only human fingers digging in the flesh, searching for the heart. He was strong enough that he'd dig it out unless we stopped him.

I stood and Jamil's hand slid out of mine. He let me go, but his eyes would haunt me. I ran for Richard, screaming his name: "Richard!"

He looked at me with amber wolf eyes in his human face. He reached towards me with one bloody hand, and the mental shields that kept us safe from one another crashed.

My vision went black, and when I could see again, I was kneeling in the ring. I could feel my body but I could also feel Richard's fingers pushing their way through thick flesh. The blood was warm but there wasn't enough of it. He wanted to use teeth to open the belly and was fighting the urge.

Thomas knelt beside me. "Use your marks to calm him before he kills Fernando."

I shook my head. My fingers were tearing through flesh. I had to press my hands against my eyes to remember what body I was in. I found my voice and that helped separate us. Helped me know who I was, what I was. "Shit, I don't know how."

"Then take his rage, his beast." Thomas touched my hands, gripping them tight, not to hurt but to help me anchor myself in this body. I gripped his hands and stared into his face like a drowning woman.

"I don't know how, Thomas."

He made an exasperated sound. "Gideon will have to intervene until you can calm him." It was almost a question.

I nodded. Sure, I'd been about to kill Fernando myself, but I knew that if we killed him, we would never see another dawn. Padma would kill us. Kill us all.

I kept looking at Thomas's face, but I felt Gideon grab Richard. Felt him pull him off Fernando. Richard twisted and hit Gideon, knocking him to the ground, then leaped on him. They rolled over and over on the ground, each trying to get on top. The only thing that kept it from being a killing fight was that both held onto their human forms and still tried to fight like they had claws. But Richard's beast was growing inside him. If he shifted, short of killing him we'd never keep him from killing someone else.

Thomas touched my face, and I realized that I hadn't been seeing his face. I was seeing Gideon's strange eyes from inches away as my hands tried to crush his throat. But they weren't my hands.

"Help me," I said.

"Just open to his beast," Thomas said. "Simply open and it will fill you. The beast is seeking a channel of escape. Give it one and it will flow into you." I knew in that instant that Thomas and Gideon were part of a triumvirate just like we were.

"I'm not a lycanthrope," I said.

"It does not matter. Do it, or we will have to kill him."

I screamed and did what he said. But it wasn't just opening to it. I reached out to that rage. That power that he called his beast came at my touch. I smelled like home to it, somehow, and it poured into me, over me, through me, like a blinding storm of heat and power. It was similar to the times I'd raised power with Richard and Jean-Claude, but this time there was no spell to use the power on. Nowhere for the beast to run. It tried to crawl out my skin, tried to expand inside my body, but there was no beast to call. I was empty for it, and it raged inside me. I felt it growing until I thought I would burst apart in bloody fragments. The pressure built and built and had nowhere to go.

I screamed, one long, ragged shriek after another, as fast as I could get breath. I felt Richard crawling towards me, felt his hands and legs move over the ground, felt the muscles in his body that turned crawling into a sensuous art, a stalking thing. He appeared above me, just his face, staring down. His long hair fell around his face like a shadowing curtain. Blood glistened at the corner of his mouth. I felt him want to lick the blood away but stop himself, and bound this closely, I knew why he stopped. For me. Fear that I would think he was monstrous.

His power was still trying to find a way out of my body. It wanted the blood, too. It wanted to lick the blood off his face and taste at his mouth. Wanted to wrap the warmth of his body around itself and become one. His power cried out like a frustrated lover for him to open his arms, his body, his mind, to it, and embrace it. Richard gave it a name apart from himself, his beast, but it wasn't separate. In that moment I realized why Richard ran so hard and so long from the power. It was him. Just as the furred shape of him was pulled from the matter of his own human body, so the rage, the destruction, was pulled from his very human psyche. His beast was formed of that part of our brains we bury, only dragging into our consciousness in the worst of our nightmares. Not the dreams where we are hunted by the monsters, but the dreams where we are the monsters. We raise bloody hands to the sky and scream, not from fear, but from joy. The pure joy of slaughter. The cathartic moment when we plunge our hands into the hot blood of our enemies and there is no civilized thought to stop us from dancing on their graves.

The power flared inside me like a hand stroking from the inside out, reaching out towards him as he knelt over me. Fear filled his eyes, and it wasn't fear for me or of me. It was the fear that the beast was the reality and that all the careful morals, everything he was or ever had been, was the lie.

I stared up at him. "Richard," I whispered, "we're all creatures of light and darkness. Embracing your darkness won't kill the light. Goodness is stronger than that."

He dropped from his knees, flat to the ground, only propping himself on his elbows. His hair brushed my face on either side, and I had to fight the urge to rub my face back and forth in it. This close I could smell his skin, after-shave, but underneath that was him. The warm scent that was his body. I wanted to touch that warmth, to wrap my mouth around it and try and hold it forever. I wanted him. The power flared at the thought, primitive thoughts excited it, made it harder to control.

He whispered, blood still trickling from his mouth, "How can you say goodness is stronger? I want to lick the blood off my own body. I want to press my bleeding mouth onto yours. I want you to feed off my wound. That is evil."

I touched his face, the barest trace of fingertips, and even that made power jump between us. "It's not evil, Richard. It just isn't very civilized." Blood was building into a single trembling drop on the edge of his face. It fell against my skin and it was burning hot. His power flared upward and took me with it. It wanted to—I wanted to—lick the blood off Richard's face. Part of me was still saying no while I raised my head just enough to run lips, my tongue, and lightly my teeth along his face. I lay back down with the salty taste of him in my mouth and wanted more. The *more* scared me. I was just as scared of this part of him, of me, as he was. That was why I ran from him

the night of the full moon. It wasn't that he ate Marcus, though
that hadn't helped, or that he'd handled it all so badly. The
memory that haunted was the moment I'd been carried away by
the pack's power, and for just an instant I'd wanted to drop to
my knees and feed with them. I was afraid that Richard's beast
would take what was left of my humanity. I was afraid for the
same reason Richard was afraid. But what I'd said was true. It
wasn't evil, just not very human.

He laid his lips against mine in a trembling kiss. A sound
came from low in his throat, and he was suddenly pressing his
mouth against mine, until it either bruised or I opened my mouth
to him. I opened, and his tongue plunged inside me, his lips
feeding on mine. The cut inside his mouth filled my mouth with
the taste of him, salty, sweet. I held his face in my hands, my
mouth searching his, and it wasn't enough. A small high keening
sound crawled out of my mouth into his. The sound was made
up of need, frustration, a desire that wasn't civilized and never
had been. We'd been playing Ozzie and Harriet, but what we
wanted from each other was more Hustler and Penthouse.

We moved to our knees, mouths still pressed together. My
hands slid over his chest, his back, and something deep inside
me clicked and relaxed. How could I ever be this close to him
and not touch him?

His power tried to spill outward, but I held it back. I held it
like I could hold my own magic, letting it build until I couldn't
hold any longer.

Richard's hands slid up my legs finding the lace top of the
black panties. His fingers traced my naked spine and I was un-
done.

The power spilled upward, outward, filling us both. It flared
over us in a rushing wave of heat and light, until my vision
swam in pieces, and we both cried out with one voice. His beast
slid inside of him. I felt it crawl out of me, pulled like a large,
thick string, spilling inside of Richard, coiling into his body. I
expected to feel the last bit of it spill between us, like draining
the last drop of wine from a cup, but that drop remained.

Somewhere in that rush of power, I'd felt Richard take control
of his beast and send that pulsing warmth outward into Jamil. I
wouldn't have known how to do it, but Richard did. I'd felt
Jamil heal under the thundering rush of power.

Richard knelt with me in his arms, my face pressed to his chest. His heart beat against my cheek like a living thing. Sweat had broken over his body in a light dew. I licked the sweat from his chest and stared up at him.

His eyes were heavy-lidded, dazed. You'd almost have mistaken the look for sleep, but not quite. He cupped his hands on both sides of my face. The wound on his mouth was healed. The rush of power, his beast, had healed it. He lowered his soft lips to mine and just barely brushed my mouth. "What are we going to do?"

I held his hands against my face. "We're going to do what we came to do."

"Then what?" he asked.

I shook my head, rubbing my face against his hands. "Survive first, Richard. Worry about the niceties later."

Something filled his eyes with a sudden rush of panic. "Jamil, I could have killed him."

"You also healed him."

He let that take some of the panic from his face, but he still got to his feet and went to his fallen enforcer. An apology at the very least was needed. I couldn't really argue with that.

I stayed kneeling, not sure I could walk yet, for a variety of reasons.

"Not the way Gideon and I would have done it," Thomas said, "but in a pinch it will do."

I felt heat rush up my face. "Sorry."

"Don't apologize," Gideon growled. "It was a lovely show." He crawled towards us, one arm cradled against his body. Blood dripped down the arm and shoulder. The red showed brilliantly against the white shirt. I had absolutely no desire to lick the blood off his body. I was grateful for that.

"Richard did that?" I asked.

"He was beginning to change form when you called him. You drank his beast and he calmed." He sat leaning to one side, bleeding a little puddle on the floor, but he never asked for help, not by word or expression. But Thomas reached out to him. Touched his shoulder in a neutral, almost brotherly gesture. Their power strengthened in a skin-prickling rush that oozed over me like a cold wind, but if I hadn't been able to sense it, I'd have never known.

"Is this just European reserve," I asked, "or are Richard and I doing something terribly wrong?"

Thomas smiled, but it was Gideon who answered. "You do nothing wrong. In fact, I feel quite cheated." He patted Thomas's hand and smiled flashing fangs. "There are ways to share power that are quieter, and less . . . showy. But for today you did what needed to be done. It was a desperate thing and called for desperate measures."

I let it go. No need to explain how often being around Richard ended in such "desperate measures." Across the ring Jamil sat up with Richard's help. Zane had untied both the wereleopards. He'd led Vivian over to Gregory. They both knelt by him, Vivian hugging Zane and crying.

I got my feet under me and found that I could walk. Great. Richard got there before I did. He stroked Gregory's tangled hair out of his face until the wereleopard looked up at him. "We have to set these legs."

Gregory nodded, lips in a thin tight line that reminded me of Cherry.

"We need a hospital for this," I said.

Richard looked up at me. "The legs have already begun to reknit like this, Anita. Every minute the bones are out of alignment is another minute that they heal, badly."

I stared down at Gregory's legs. He was totally nude, but the wounds were so fearful that it wasn't embarrassing; it was just piteous. His legs from the knees down bent the wrong way. I had to close my eyes and look away. If it had been a corpse, I could have looked at it, but Gregory was still bleeding, still hurting. Made it worse somehow.

I looked back. "You mean the legs would heal like that?"

"Yes," Richard said.

I stared down into Gregory's frightened eyes. They were still the surprised cornflower-blue of Stephen's. They looked even bluer from the mask of blood that covered his face. I tried to think of something to say, but he spoke first.

His voice was thin, scratchy, as if he'd screamed until he was hoarse. "When you left without me the first time, I thought you were going to let them keep me."

I knelt beside him. "You're not something to keep. You're a person. You deserve to be treated . . ." To say, "better than this'' seemed too obvious. I tried to hold his hand the way you'd comfort a child, but two of the fingers were broken so badly, I didn't even know how to touch him.

Vivian spoke for the first time. "Is he dead?" Her voice was breathy, husky, somewhere between that of a little girl and a seductress. She would be great on the phone. The look in her eyes was neither childish nor seductive; it was frightening. She stared past us to where Fernando lay, and her hatred was a hot, scalding thing.

Not that I blamed her. I went to check on our little rapist. Gideon and Thomas got to him first. I noticed that they hadn't gone near him until I did. Why did I think that they didn't like him much better than we did? Fernando just had a way of pissing people off. It seemed to be his only talent.

His bare stomach was a bloody mess where Richard had tried to dig his intestines out, but the wound was healing. Filling itself in like a fast-forward motion picture. You could actually see his body rebuild itself.

"He'll live," I said. Even to me, I sounded disappointed.

"Yes," Thomas said, and that one word sounded as disappointed as I felt. He visibly shook himself, and turned sad brown eyes to me. "If he had died, then Padma would have destroyed the city, seeking you. Make no mistake, Anita, Padma loves his son, but more than that, he is his only son. The only chance he has of having an heir."

"I wouldn't think a vampire would sweat that," I said.

"He comes from a time and a culture where a son is an incredibly important thing. No matter how long we live or what we are in the end, we start out as people. We never quite lose all that we were during life. It haunts us over the centuries, our humanity."

"You're human."

He smiled and shook his head. "Once, perhaps."

I opened my mouth to ask something, but he held his hand up. "If there is time, Gideon and I would enjoy speaking with you and Richard at length on what a triumvirate can be, but now, you must leave before Fernando awakes. During daylight hours he is in charge of us."

My eyes widened, and I looked at Gideon. "But he's not alpha enough to take on Gideon."

"Padma is a harsh master, Anita. We obey or we suffer."

"Which is why," Gideon said, "you must all leave as soon as possible. What the *petit bâtard* would order us to do to you if he awoke now is best left unsaid."

He had a point. Gregory screamed, a high shrieking, that ended in whimpering. Richard had said the legs had begun to heal, bent backwards. I suddenly realized what that meant. "If the legs had healed broken, Gregory would have been crippled," I said.

"Yes," Gideon said. "It was Padma's idea of punishment."

Fernando groaned, eyes still shut. We had to get out of here. "I need my guns back," I said.

They didn't even argue. They just gave them all back. Either they trusted me or they figured I wouldn't shoot Fernando while he was unconscious. They were right, though he'd earned it. I'd killed people for a lot less than what the rat-boy had done, a lot less.

Gregory had mercifully passed out. Richard held him as carefully as he could in his arms. They'd found wood from somewhere and used Richard's shirt to tie the makeshift splints to Gregory's legs. Vivian leaned heavily on Zane as if her legs weren't quite working. She was also trying to cover her lower extremities. So hurt she could barely walk and she was embarrassed about her nudity. We were sort of out of clothes to offer her. The coat I'd brought was in the outer area.

Thomas saved the day by giving her his spiffy red jacket. It was large on her and covered enough. Just making it outside the tent to the midway made my shoulders relax a notch. I picked up the coat and put a gun in each pocket. The machine gun was already across my chest.

Thomas held the door for us. I went through last. "Thank you," I said. We both knew I didn't mean the door.

"You are most welcome." He closed the door behind us, and I heard it lock.

I stood in the hot summer sunlight and felt my body sink into the heat. It was good to be outside in the daylight. But night was coming, and I still didn't know what price Jean-Claude had bargained away to get Vivian and Gregory out of there. But the thought of Gregory's lovely body deliberately crippled forever, and Vivian passed around like so much meat, made me glad we'd bargained. I wouldn't say that whatever the price, it would be worth it, but close. Jean-Claude had said no rape, no actual intercourse, no maiming, no skinning alive. The list had seemed safer and more complete an hour ago.

30

WE PULLED INTO the driveway of my rented house with two wounded wereleopards, two unwounded wereleopards, two very silent werewolves, a partridge in a pear tree, and enough equipment for Richard to rig up a pair of traction splints in my bedroom. Gregory needed to be in traction splints for twenty-four hours according to Dr. Lillian. The hospital was being evacuated. If Fernando was in charge for the day, the evacuation wasn't just a precaution, it was a necessity. The rat-boy hadn't wanted to free Rafael, and he'd certainly want revenge on Richard for beating him, so both the wererats and the werewolves were in danger. The thought of what he'd do if he got his paws back on Gregory and Vivian was too scary to think about. The best we could do was keep them with us and try not to be anywhere Fernando would think to go.

I was half-trusting Thomas and Gideon to keep the rat-boy from searching too hard. I don't usually trust people that easily, but Gideon had called him the *petite bâtard*. The little bastard. They didn't like him any better than we did. Hard to believe, but maybe true.

Besides, where could we go where we'd be safe? We couldn't go to a hotel. That would endanger everyone in the place. Same thing with most houses. One of the main things I'd been looking for in a rental was isolation. Frankly, I liked a little city around me, but my life had turned into a free-fire zone lately. No apartments, no condos, no neighborhoods; something with lots of ground and no neighbors to get shot up was what I'd wanted. I got it. Though the isolation was about all I'd gotten that I wanted.

The house was too big for just me. It was a house that cried out for a family with walks in the woods and a dog running circles around the kiddies. Richard had never seen the house. I would have been more comfortable with him seeing it before we'd had our little make-out, oh, umh, make-up session. Before Jean-Claude had interfered, Richard and I had been engaged. We'd been planning the kind of future that went with this kind of house. I don't know if Richard had woken up and smelled the blood-soaked coffee, but I had. The future that included a picket fence and 2.5 children just wasn't in the cards for me. I didn't think it was in the cards for him either, but I wasn't going to burst his bubble. Not as long as his bubble didn't include me. If it did . . . we had a problem.

The house had a medium-sized rectangular flower bed that got full sun almost all day. It had been a rose garden, but the last owners had dug up the plants and tried to take them with them. It looked like the far side of the moon, complete with craters. It had looked so barren that I'd spent a weekend planting the damn thing. Rose moss for the border just because I loved the bright little flowers. Zinnias behind that because the flower colors echoed each other. It was a riot of color, nothing subtle. Butterflies and hummingbirds were attracted to the zinnias. I'd planted cosmos behind the zinnias, towering, feathery and tangled at the same time, with lovely pale open flowers that the butterflies loved and the hummingbirds weren't so fond of. The colors of the cosmos were a little too pastel compared with the other colors, but hey, it still worked. In the fall the cosmos would have seed heads for the goldfinches.

The flower bed had been some sort of admission to myself that I might be here awhile. That I couldn't go back to an apartment or a condo. That my life didn't allow me the luxury of close neighbors.

Richard had remarked as we drove up, "Nice flowers."

"I couldn't just leave it bare."

He made a noncommittal noise. Nearly three months away from each other and even without the marks, he knew me well enough to know when not to say something. It bugged me that I had been unable to leave the flower bed barren and ripped. I hated the fact that I'd been driven to make it pretty. No, I am not comfortable with my feminine side.

Richard and Jamil carried Gregory in on the stretcher that the hospital had loaned us. Lillian had pumped the wereleopard so full of painkillers that he was feeling no pain. I was grateful for that. Awake, he had a tendency to whimper and scream.

Strangely, Cherry turned out to be a nurse. She'd taken one look at Gregory and suddenly turned into a professional. A layer of confidence and competence crawled out of nowhere. She was like a different person. Once Gregory let her touch him, didn't reject her help, Cherry was calm. Though truthfully, it wasn't until Dr. Lillian had seemed to trust Cherry that I did, too. Lillian was confident that she could help us put Gregory into traction and not injure him further. I trusted Lillian's opinion, but I still didn't trust Cherry. I might not have approved of Richard smacking her around, but I agreed that anyone who left you behind to die wasn't trustworthy. No shame in being weak, but I'd never trust her at my back.

Vivian wouldn't let Zane carry her into the house, even though walking was obviously painful. She clung to my arm with both her small hands. Truthfully, her hands weren't any smaller than my own, but somehow she seemed fragile. It wasn't size, or even just the rape, but something about Vivian herself. Even wrapped in the borrowed red coat and a scruffy blue robe that Lillian had loaned her, Vivian looked delicate, feminine, lovely in an almost ethereal sort of way. It's hard to look lovely and ethereal with half your face swollen tight with bruises, but she managed it.

She stumbled on the rock walkway to the house. I caught her, but her knees buckled and I came damn near dropping her on the rocks.

Zane tried to help me, but Vivian let out a small sound and hid her face against my shoulder. Once we hit the car she hadn't wanted any man to touch her. It had been Zane who untied her, but it seemed to be me she looked upon as her rescuer. Or maybe I was just the only female rescuer, and female was safe right now.

I sighed and nodded my head. Zane backed off. If I'd been in jogging shoes or even flats, I'd have just carried Vivian into the house, but I was wearing three inch spike heels. I could not carry someone nearly my own body weight wearing these shoes. If I kicked the shoes off, then the dress would be so long I'd trip. I was beginning to really hate this outfit.

"Vivian." She didn't respond. "Vivian?" She was still sliding towards the ground. I braced my legs far enough apart to get as much leverage as I was going to get in the shoes, and was ready for her when her legs collapsed completely. I might have been able to carry her in a firemen's-carry even with the heels, but I'd seen her body and there were deep bruises on her stomach. Slinging her over my shoulders would hurt. I managed to lift her in my arms, but I knew better than to try and walk.

"Get Cherry," I said.

Zane nodded and went into the house.

I stood there holding Vivian, waiting for help to arrive. The July sun beat down on my back through the black coat. Sweat trickled down my spine. Cicadas filled the heat with their buzzing song. There was a small army of butterflies feeding on the flowers. Don't tell, but I drank at least one cup of coffee every day out here watching the stupid things. It was all very picturesque, but I was getting impatient. How long did it take for Zane to tell Cherry to get her butt out here? Of course, maybe she was busy with Gregory and his fearful injuries. If she was, it could be a while. It wasn't that I couldn't stand there holding her. It was that I felt stupid wearing heels so high that I couldn't carry her into the house. It made me feel girlish in the worst way.

I tried to wait by counting how many different species of butterflies were visible. Tiger swallowtail, spicebrush swallowtail, greater frittilary, giant sulphur, black swallowtail, redspotted purple, and painted lady. A trio of tiny blue hairstreaks spun into the air like glittering bits of sky. Beautiful, but where the hell was Cherry? Enough of this. I started very carefully forward, my ankle twisted and I had to throw myself backward to keep from dumping Vivian to the rocks. I ended up on my butt in the flower bed, crushing the border of rose moss flat and taking a few zinnias with me. The cosmos towered over me, some of them as tall as six feet.

Vivian gave a small moan, blinking her one good eye open. "It's all right," I soothed. "It's all right." I sat there holding her, half rocking her, with my butt in the flowers and my feet almost straight out in front of me. I'd managed to keep my feet through vampires, shapeshifters, human servants, and arsonists, but a pair of high heels had set me back on my ass. Vanity, thy name is woman. Though whoever wrote that had never seen an issue of *GQ*.

A tiger swallowtail nearly as big as my outstretched hand fluttered near my face. It was pale yellow with sharp brown stripes on its wings. It hovered over Vivian, then finally settled on my hand. Butterflies will lick the sweat from your skin for the salt, but usually you have to hold still for it. If you move, they float away. This insect seemed determined. Its proboscis is not much thicker than a straight pin, a long curved tube, but you can feel it like a tickling line.

It was maybe the third time in my life that I'd had a butterfly feed off my skin. I didn't try to chase it away. It was cool. Its wings pulsed up and down very slowly as it fed, its tiny feet almost weightless against my hand.

Cherry walked out the door, eyes widening when she saw me. "Are you hurt?"

I shook my head, still careful not to scare away the butterfly. "Just can't get the leverage to get back up."

Cherry knelt by us, and the butterfly glided away. She watched it for a moment. "I've never seen a butterfly do that."

"It was after the salt in my skin. Butterflies will feed on dogshit or spoiled fruit, too," I said.

Cherry made a face. "Thanks for ruining another idyllic image." She took Vivian out of my arms, wobbling on one knee. Vivian moaned in her arms as Cherry stood, trying to get the balance of it all. Lifting isn't just strength. It's balance, and an unconscious body is not the best thing for balance. "You need a hand up?" she asked.

I shook my head, getting to my knees.

Cherry took me at my word and just walked towards the house. She was smarter than I'd first thought. Of course, if I'd spent the night in Padma's tender care, maybe I wouldn't have made a good first impression either.

I was trying to fluff up the crushed flowers when the butterfly came fluttering back. With it hovering around my face I felt the first prickling brush of power. If it had been dark, I'd have said "vampire," but it was broad daylight.

I stood up and slipped the Browning out of the coat pocket. The bright yellow-and-brown insect batted at my face with paper-thin wings. What had been fun a moment before was suddenly ominous. For the first time in my life I brushed a butterfly away as if it had been something loathsome. And maybe it was.

I am not implying that the butterfly was literally a vampire. They couldn't shapechange, not to my knowledge. Of course, they couldn't be out in full daylight either. They were the council. Did I really know what they were capable of?

The butterfly floated away from me towards the woods on the far side of the driveway. It fluttered back and forth, back and forth, like it was waiting for me. I shook my head. I felt silly holding the gun with just the butterfly there by the woods. But something else was out there. I stood in the summer heat, feeling the sun beat down on the top of my head. I should have been safe. At least from vampires. It wasn't fair that they changed the rules.

I was about to go into the house and yell for backup, when I saw a figure. Tall with a thick hooded cloak pulled around him. Even with the cloak I knew it was a him. Shoulders that broad and that height, and I even knew it was Warrick. Except it couldn't be him. He wasn't even close to powerful enough to be out in daylight.

I stared at that tall shape in the shimmering white cloak. He stood so still, as if he were carved from marble. Even Mr. Oliver, the oldest vamp I'd ever seen had avoided direct sunlight. But there Warrick stood like a ghost that had learned the trick of walking about in daylight. Of course, he wasn't walking. He stood in the wavering shadows of the trees. He didn't try and come out into the direct light of the clearing. Maybe he couldn't. Maybe that thin band of shade was all that kept him from bursting into flames. Maybe.

I walked towards him. I stretched my senses, but his was the only power I felt. It could be a trap, an ambush, but I didn't think so. If they meant to trap me, it wouldn't have been this blatant. But just in case, I stopped a good distance back from the woods. If I saw any movement I'd yell for help and run for the house. Might even get off a shot or two.

Warrick stood with his head bowed so low, the hood completely hid his face. He stood immobile, as if he didn't know I was there. Only the wind making a soft folding line in the white cloth showed any movement. He was like a statue with a cloth thrown over it.

The longer he stood there motionless, the more eerie it seemed. I had to fill the silence. "What do you want, Warrick?"

A shiver went through him and he raised his head slowly. Rot had spread across that strong face. His skin was green and black as if that thin layer of tissue were holding in centuries of death. Even his blue eyes had dulled with a film, like a fish that had been dead too long to eat.

My mouth was hanging open. You'd think after what I'd seen Yvette do to him, it wouldn't have shocked me, but it did. Some sights you don't grow jaded about.

"Is Yvette punishing you?" I asked.

"No, no, my pale mistress sleeps in her coffin. She knows nothing of this visit." His voice was the only thing that remained "normal." The voice was still strong and firm. It didn't match what was happening to his body.

"What's happening to you, Warrick?"

"When the sun rose I did not die. I thought it was a sign from God. That He was giving me permission to end this foul existence. That He had given me the chance to walk into the light for one last time. I walked into the rising sun and did not burn, but this happened." He raised his hands out of the cloak, showing me the greying flesh. The fingernails were blackened, even the ends of the fingers seemed shriveled.

"Will it heal?" I asked.

He smiled and even with that horrific visage, it was a smile full of hope. His rotted face showed a light that had nothing to do with vampire powers. The butterfly hovered above his face. "God will call me to his arms soon. I am after all a dead man."

I couldn't argue with him there. "Why did you come here, Warrick?"

A second butterfly joined the first, then a third. They fluttered above his head like a carousel. Warrick smiled up at them. "I have come to warn you. Padma fears Jean-Claude and your triumvirate. He will see you dead if he can."

"That's not news," I said.

"Our master, Morte d'Amour, has given Yvette orders to destroy you all."

That was news. "Why?" I asked.

"I don't believe that any of the council truly believes that Jean-Claude means to set up his own rival council in this country. But they all see him as a part of this new legal vampirism. They see him as part of a change that may sweep away our old existence. The old ones who have power enough to be comfortable do not want any change in our status quo. When the vote is taken, Anita, there will be two against you.''

''Who else gets to vote?'' I asked.

''Asher has the proxy for his mistress, Belle Morte, Beautiful Death. He hates Jean-Claude with a fine, burning hate like sunlight through glass. I do not think you can count upon his help.''

''So they have all come to kill us,'' I said.

''If they had come merely to kill you, Anita, they would have done so by now.''

''Then I'm confused,'' I said.

''Padma's fear is too strong, but I believe our master would be content if Jean-Claude gave up his seat of power here and joined the council as he was meant to.''

''The first challenger that comes along will take him out,'' I said. ''No thanks.''

''So Jean-Claude keeps saying,'' Warrick said. ''I am beginning to think that he underestimates himself, and you.''

''He's cautious, and so am I.''

A host of butterflies had formed above his head. They fluttered around him in a multicolored cloud. One landed on his hand, bright wings fanning softly as it fed off the rotting flesh.

His power thrummed along my body. It wasn't council-level power, but it was master-level. Warrick was a master vampire, and he hadn't been last night. ''Are you borrowing power from someone else?''

''From God,'' he said.

Of course.

''The longer we are away from our master, the weaker Yvette grows, and the stronger I grow. The Holy Fire of God's eternal light has entered my body once more. Perhaps He will forgive me for my weakness. I feared death, Anita. I feared the punishment of hell more than I feared Yvette. But I walk in the light. I burn with God's power once more.''

Personally I didn't believe God had a private torture chamber. Hell was being cut off from God, cut off from his power, his energy, Him. We walked through his power every day of our lives until it was like white noise, something we ignored or failed to hear. But somehow lecturing Warrick on the fact that he'd let Yvette torture him for centuries because he feared eternal damnation, which I didn't in fact believe existed, seemed pointless. Nay, cruel.

"I'm happy for you, Warrick."

"I would ask one boon of you, Anita."

"A boon is a favor, right?" I asked. Didn't want to agree to something and be wrong.

"Yes," he said.

"Ask."

"Do you have a cross upon you?"

I nodded.

"Show me, please."

I didn't think this was a good idea, but . . . I pulled the silver chain up until the cross sparkled in the sunlight. It didn't glow. It just dangled.

Warrick smiled. "The Holy Cross does not reject me."

I didn't have the heart to tell him that the cross didn't always glow around all vampires. It seemed to wait for one that meant me harm, though there were exceptions both ways. I, like Warrick, didn't question God's wisdom. I figured He knew what He was doing, and if He didn't, I really didn't want to know.

Warrick walked to the edge of the tree line. He stood there in the white cloak with its black lining, hesitating. I watched the struggle on his face. He wanted to cross into that last band of pure sunlight and was afraid to. I didn't blame him.

He stretched out his hand to the trembling edge of solid golden light, then fell back. "My courage and my faith, they still fail me. I am still not worthy. I should stride into the light and grab the Holy Cross and hold it unafraid." He covered his face with his darkened hands. The butterflies lit on every inch of naked skin, wings fanning. There was nothing to see but the white cloak and the fluttering insects. For a moment the illusion was perfect that the butterflies were all that was inside the cloak.

Warrick spread his hands slowly, carefully, so as not to disturb the insects. He smiled. "I have heard the masters speak of calling their animals for centuries but have never understood until now. It is a wondrous bond."

He seemed happy with his "animal." Me, I'd have been a little disappointed. A butterfly wasn't going to be much defense against the sort of animals that most vamps could call. But, hey, as long as Warrick was happy, who was I to bitch?

"Yvette made me swear an oath to God on some of her secrets. I have not betrayed my word, or my oath."

"Are you saying there are things I should know that you haven't told me?" I asked.

"I have told you all I am free to tell, Anita. Yvette was always clever. She manipulated me all those years ago to betray all I held dear. She bound me with oaths before we arrived on your shores. I didn't understand it at the time, but I do now. She knew I would see you as a person of honor. A person who protects the weak, and does not abandon her friends. You make the council's talk of honor and responsibility seem a pale pretense."

Saying thanks didn't seem enough, but it was all I had. "Thank you, Warrick."

"Even when I was alive there was a vast difference between the nobles that truly led and tended their people's needs, and those who just took from them."

"It hasn't changed that much," I said.

"I am sorry to hear that," he said. He glanced upward, maybe at the sun, maybe at something I couldn't see. "As the sun approaches its zenith I feel weaker."

"Do you need a place to rest for the day?" I asked. The moment I said it, I wasn't sure I should have made the offer. Did I really trust him down in the basement with Jean-Claude and the gang, without me to watch him every minute? Not exactly.

"If this would be my last day in the daylight, then I would not lose it by hiding. I will walk in your delightful woods, then I will dig among the deep leaves. I have hidden among the leaves before. They fall thick and deep in the hollows."

I nodded. "I know. Somehow I figured you for a city boy."

"I have lived in a city for many years, but my first days were among trees thicker and more lush than these. My father's lands were far from any city. Though that has changed. There are no trees now where I fished and hunted as a boy. It is all gone. Yvette allowed me a trip home, in her company. I wish I had not gone. It has tainted my memories, and made them seem like some dreams."

"The good stuff is as real as the bad stuff," I said. "Don't let Yvette take that from you."

He smiled, then shivered. The butterflies whirled into the air like autumn leaves flung into the sky. "I must go." He moved off through the trees, followed by a line of eager butterflies. I lost sight of the white cloak as he walked down the far side of a hill, but the butterflies trailed after him like tiny vultures marking the line of death.

31

I CROSSED THE yard, the driveway, and was back on the side-walk when the sound of a car coming down the gravel driveway turned me around. It was Ronnie. Shit. I'd forgotten to call her and cancel our morning jog. Veronica (Ronnie) Sims was a pri-vate detective and my best friend. We worked out together at least once a week, usually on Saturday mornings. Sometimes we went to the gym; sometimes we ran. It was Saturday morn-ing, and I'd forgotten to cancel.

I held the gun along my side, hidden in the coat. Not that she'd care. It was just automatic. If you were privileged enough to be allowed a carry permit for your gun, you didn't flash it around. Deliberately flashing your gun in public without just cause is called ''brandishment'' and can get your permit re-voked. It's like a new vampire flashing fangs. It's a sign of an amateur.

I was feeling guilty that I'd made Ronnie come all the way out here for nothing, when I realized she wasn't alone. Louie Fane, Dr. Louis Fane, who taught biology at Wash U. was with her. They spilled out of the car together, laughing, holding hands as soon as the car wasn't between them. They were both dressed for jogging. His shirt was untucked, coming down low enough on his five-foot-six frame that his short-shorts barely showed. His black hair was cut short and neat, and didn't match the oversized T-shirt.

Ronnie was wearing a pair of lavender biker's shorts that showed her long legs to perfection. A crop-top T-shirt in the same color showed flashes of flat stomach as she walked to-wards me. She never dressed this nicely just to go exercise with me. Her shoulder-length blond hair was freshly washed, blow-dried, and shiny. The only thing missing was makeup, but she didn't need it. Her face glowed. Her grey eyes had that tinge of blue they get when she wears the right color outfit. She'd chosen the color, and Louie had eyes only for her.

I stood there watching them walk hand and hand up the sidewalk and wondered when they'd notice me. They both looked up almost startled, as if I'd appeared out of thin air. Ronnie had the grace to look embarrassed, but Louie just seemed content. I happened to know for a fact that they were having sex, but just watching them together would have been enough. His fingers played lightly over her knuckles as they stood looking at me. I wasn't sure they were in love, but lust, that I was sure of.

Ronnie looked me up and down. "A little overdressed for jogging, aren't you?"

I frowned. "Sorry, I forgot to call. I just got home."

"What happened?" Louie asked. He still held Ronnie's hand, but everything else changed. He was suddenly alert, taller somehow, black eyes searching my face, noticing for the first time the bandage on my hand and other signs of wear. "You smell like blood, and"—his nostrils flared—"something worse."

I wondered if he could smell Warrick's rotted flesh on my shoes, but I didn't ask. I didn't really want to know. He was one of Rafael's lieutenants, and I was surprised he didn't know what had been happening. "Have you guys been out of town?"

They both nodded, and Ronnie's smile was gone now, too. "We were up at the cabin." The cabin had been part of her divorce settlement from a two-year marriage that ended very badly. But it was a great cabin.

"Yeah, it's nice up there."

"What's happened?" Louie asked again.

"Let's go inside. I can't think of a version short enough not to need coffee."

They followed me into the house, still touching, but some of the glow had leaked away. I seemed to have that effect on people. Hard to be bright and shiny in the middle of a kill zone.

Gregory was lying on my couch, still drugged into blissful unconsciousness. Louie stopped in his tracks. Of course, maybe it wasn't just the wereleopard. There was a large Persian rug underneath my white couch and chair. It wasn't my rug. There were bright pillows on the white furniture that echoed the colors of the rug. The colors were like jewels in the early morning sunlight.

Ronnie said, "Stephen." She even went forward as if to touch him, but Louie pulled her back.

"It's not Stephen."

"How can you tell?" I asked.

"They don't smell the same."

Ronnie was just staring. "This is Gregory?"

Louie nodded.

"I knew they were identical twins but . . ."

"Yeah," I said. "I have got to get out of this dress, but let me make one thing clear. Gregory is mine now. He's a good guy. No abusing him."

Louie turned to me, and his black eyes had bled across the pupil so that his eyes were like black buttons, rat's eyes. "He tortured his own brother."

"I was there, Louie. I saw it."

"Then how can you defend him?"

I shook my head. "It has been a long night, Louie. Let's just say that without Gabriel to force the wereleopards to be evil, they've been choosing different paths. He refused to torture one of the wolves, and that's why they broke his legs."

The look on Louie's face said he didn't believe it. I shook my head and made shooing motions. "Go in the kitchen, make coffee. Let me slip out of this damn dress and I'll tell you everything."

Ronnie pulled him towards the kitchen, but her eyes watched me, full of questions. I mouthed, "Later" to her, and she went into the kitchen. I trusted her to keep Louie busy until I got changed. I didn't really think that he'd harm Gregory, but the wereleopards had pissed off so many people. Better to be safe than sorry.

Richard was up on a stepladder drilling holes in the ceiling above my bed. So much for my security deposit. My bedroom was the only one on the first floor. I'd given it up so they wouldn't have to get Gregory up the stairs. Little flakes of ceiling covered his bare torso in a fine white powder. He looked very handy-mannish in just jeans. Cherry and Zane were on the bed, holding pieces of the traction apparatus for him, helping him measure.

The drill stopped, and I asked, "Where's Vivian?"

"Gwen took her to see Sylvie," Richard said. His eyes were very neutral as he looked at me, voice careful. We hadn't said much to each other since our moment in the ring.

"Nice to have a trained therapist in the house," I said.

Cherry and Zane were both watching me. They reminded me of golden retrievers in the obedience ring, eyes earnest, intent on every word and gesture. I didn't really like people looking at me like that. Made me nervous.

"I just came in to get clothes. I want out of this dress." I moved past them to the chest of drawers. Jean-Claude had been busy in here, too. It just wasn't as obviously not my taste. At the far end was a bay window complete with window seat. It was full to overflowing with my toy penguin collection. There was a new penguin sitting on the bed with a large red bow on its neck and a card leaning against its furry belly. Bits of ceiling had already rained down on its black fur.

The drill stopped, and Richard said, "Go ahead, check the card. That's what he meant for you to do."

I looked up at him, and there was still anger in his eyes and pain, but underneath that there was something else. Something I had no words for, or perhaps didn't want words for. I took the penguin off the bed, dusting it off, and opened the card with my back to him. The drill didn't start up again. I could feel him watching me while I read the card.

It said, "Something to sleep with when I am not with you." It was signed simply with an elegant J.

I shoved the card back in the envelope and turned to face Richard, penguin clutched to my stomach. His expression was very careful, as neutral as he could manage it. He looked at me, fighting to keep his face empty and finally failing. A rawness spilled into his eyes, of need and words and things unsaid.

Zane and Cherry backed off the bed, gliding towards the door. They didn't leave, but they made a point of not standing between us. I didn't think we were going to have a full-out battle, but I couldn't blame them for getting out of the way.

"You can read the note if you want. But I'm not sure it will help."

He made a small abrupt sound, not quite a laugh. "Should

you be offering your boyfriend's love letters to your ex-boyfriend?''

"I don't want to hurt you, Richard. I really don't. If seeing the note will make it better, you can see it. Except for that first time, I've never done anything you didn't know about. I don't intend to start now.''

I watched the muscles in his jaw clench until the tension swelled his neck and shoulders. He shook his head. ''I don't want to see it.''

"Fine.'' I turned around, penguin and card in one arm, and opened the dresser drawer. I grabbed what was on top, not really paying attention. I just wanted out of the suddenly silent room, away from the weight of Richard's eyes.

"I heard someone come in with you,'' he said, voice quiet. ''Who was it?''

I turned, penguin and clothes clutched in a mass. ''Louie and Ronnie.''

Richard frowned. ''Did Rafael send Louie?''

I shook my head. ''They were off in a love nest together. Louie doesn't know what's been happening. He seems really pissed at Gregory. Is it personal, or what he did to Stephen?''

"Stephen,'' Richard said. ''Louie is very loyal to his friends.'' There was something in the way he said that last that seemed to imply that maybe not everyone in the house was as loyal. Or maybe I was just reading things into an otherwise innocent statement. Maybe. Guilt is a many-splendored thing. But meeting Richard's true-brown eyes, I didn't think I was hearing anything he didn't mean for me to hear.

If I'd known what to say to him, I'd have sent the wereleo-pards out of the room so we could talk. But God help me if I knew what to say. Until I had time to think about things, the talk could wait. In fact, it had better wait. I hadn't expected to still be able to feel something for Richard, or him for me. I was sleeping with another man, in love with another man. It complicated things. Just thinking that made me smile and shake my head.

"What's so funny?'' he asked. His eyes were so hurt, so confused.

"Funny?'' I said. ''Nothing, Richard, absolutely nothing.'' I fled to the downstairs bathroom to change. This was the biggest

bathroom in the house, the one that had a sunken marble tub.
It wasn't as big as the one Jean-Claude had at the Circus, but
it was close. White candles encircled the head and foot of the
tub. Untouched, fresh, new, waiting for nightfall. He'd chosen
peppermint candles. He loved scented candles that smelled ed-
ible. His food fetish was showing.

There was a second card taped to the stem of a silver can-
dlestick. There was nothing on the outside of the envelope, but
call it a hunch. I opened it.

The note said, "If we were alone, *ma petite*, I would have
you light them at dusk. And I would join you. *Je rêve de toi*."
The last was French for "I dream of you." This one wasn't
even signed. He was such a confident little thing. According to
him, I was the only woman in nearly four hundred years to ever
turn him down. And even I had finally lost the battle. Hard not
to be confident with a track record like that. Truthfully, I'd have
loved to fill the tub, light the candles, and been waiting naked
and wet for him to rise for the night. It sounded like a very,
very good time. But we had a house full of guests, and if Richard was staying the night, we were going to behave ourselves.
If Richard had dumped me for another woman, I wouldn't have
taken it quite as badly as he was taking it, but I couldn't have
stayed in a house and listened to him have sex with the other
woman. Even my nerve wasn't that strong. I certainly wasn't
going to put Richard into that position. Not on purpose.

I had to make two trips back and forth into the bedroom from
the bathroom. First, I forgot a normal bra. A strapless bra was
just not meant to be worn this long. Second, I traded the shorts
I'd grabbed first for jeans.

I was very aware of Richard watching me as I came and went.
Zane and Cherry watched both of us like nervous dogs that
expect to be kicked. The tension was thick enough to walk on
and the leopards could feel it. The tension was more than physical awareness. It was like he was thinking very hard, and I
could feel it, a building pressure that had a lecture at the end of
it, or a fight.

I ended up dressed in a pair of new jeans in that wonderful
dark blue color that never lasts, a royal blue tank top, white
jogging socks, and white Nikes with a black swoosh. I shoved
most of the old clothes into the dirty clothes hamper and folded

the dress on top of it. The dress was, of course, "dry clean only." I tucked the Firestar down the front of the jeans. I had an inner pants holster for it, but it was in the bedroom. I didn't want it badly enough to go back in there right this second. I felt like I was tempting fate every time Richard and I passed each other. Eventually, he'd insist on talking, and I wasn't ready. Maybe for this particular talk, I would never be ready.

I folded the borrowed coat over my arm with the Browning hanging heavy in one pocket. The machine gun I kept on my shoulder like a purse. When the bedroom cleared out, I'd put the machine gun in the closet. The trick about having this many loaded guns is that you don't dare leave them lying around. Lycanthropes are great in a fight, but most of them don't seem to know one end of a gun from the other. There's something about a gun just lying around, especially one as nifty as a sub-machine gun, that tempts people. There is an almost physical itch to pick it up, point it, go bang-bang. You either make a gun safe, unloaded or locked up, or you keep it on your body where you can control it. Those are the rules. Deviating from the rules is what lets eight-year-old kids blow the heads off their baby sisters.

I went into the living room. Gregory was gone from the couch. I started to assume he'd been carried to the bedroom, then walked into the bedroom to make sure. Be damn silly to let Gregory get snatched from my living room and not notice it.

Cherry and Richard were tucking him into the bed with Zane's help. Gregory had woken enough that he was whimpering. Richard caught me peeking in the doorway.

"Just making sure Gregory was all right," I said.

"No, you were making sure that the bad guys hadn't gotten him," he said.

I looked down, then up. "Yeah," I said.

We might have said more, but Gregory woke up as they put his legs in traction. He started screaming. Lycanthropes metabolized drugs incredibly quickly. Cherry readied a needle full of a clear liquid. I fled. I don't like needles. But truthfully, I didn't want Richard to lecture me over the guns. His being a lycanthrope wasn't our only problem. Richard thought I killed too easily. Maybe he was right, but I'd saved his ass more than once with my quick trigger finger. And he'd endangered me more than once with his squeamishness.

I went back down the stairs, shaking my head. Why did we even bother? We had too many important areas that we disagreed on. It wouldn't work. So we lusted after each other, even loved each other. It wasn't enough. If we couldn't find a way to compromise on the rest of it, we'd just end up cutting each other apart. Better to just make the break as cleanly as possible. My head agreed with the logic. Other body parts weren't so sure.

I followed the smell of coffee into the kitchen. It was a lovely kitchen, if I ever cooked or entertained. It was all dark wood cabinets with a large island in the middle with hooks above it for cooking pots and pans. I didn't own enough kitchen stuff to fill one whole cabinet let alone the rest of the gleaming expanse. Of all the rooms in the new house this was the one that made me feel most like a stranger. It was so *not* what I would have chosen.

Ronnie and Louie were sitting at my small two-seater kitchen table. It sat on a raised platform in a three-sided bay of windows. The area was meant for a full-sized dining room table. My little breakfast-nook set looked like a temporary measure. Except for the flowers. The flowers took up most of the small table. The flowers were another addition.

I didn't have to count to know that there were a dozen white roses and one lone red one. Jean-Claude had been sending me white roses for years, but ever since we made love for the first time there had been a thirteenth rose. Red, crimson, a spot of passion lost in a sea of white purity. There was no card, because there was no need for a card.

Jamil leaned against the wall near Ronnie and Louie, sipping coffee. He stopped talking when I entered the room, which meant he'd probably been talking about me. Maybe not, but the silence was thick, and Ronnie was very busy not looking at me. Louie looked at me a little too hard. Yep, Jamil had been spilling the beans.

I didn't even want to know before I had some caffeine in me. I poured coffee into a mug that said "Warning: The Surgeon General has determined that bothering me before I've had my first cup of coffee is hazardous to your health." The mug had been at the office until my boss accused me of threatening the clients. I hadn't picked out a new mug yet. I had to find something suitably irritating.

There was a sparkling new espresso machine on the cabinet by the coffeemaker, with another card. I took a sip of coffee and opened this one.

"Something to warm your body and fill this empty *cuisine*." The last was French for "kitchen." He often did that in notes, as if even after a hundred years in this country he still sometimes forgot the correct English phrase. His speech was flawless, but many people speak a second language better than they write it. Of course, it could be his backhanded way of teaching me French. It was working. He'd write a note, and I'd hunt him down and ask what it meant. Having French sweet-nothings whispered in your ear is great, but after a while you wonder exactly what he's whispering, so I asked. There had been other lessons, but nothing much that I could share in public.

"Nice flowers," Ronnie said. Her voice was neutral, but she'd made herself very clear on the subject of Jean-Claude. She thought he was a pushy bastard. She was right. She thought he was evil. I didn't agree on that one.

I sat down at the far end of the octagon, back to the wall, head below the level of the windows. "I don't need any more lectures today, Ronnie. Okay?"

She shrugged and sipped her coffee. "You're a big girl, Anita."

"That's right, I am." It sounded petulant even to me. I settled the submachine gun beside me on the floor with the coat. I breathed in the coffee, black and thick. Sometimes I added cream and sugar, but for the first cup of the day, black would do.

"Jamil's been filling us in," Louie said. "Did you and Richard actually raise power in the middle of the Circus?"

I took a sip of coffee before answering. "Apparently."

"There is no equivalent among the wererats for the wolves' lupa, but is it common to be able to call power like that?"

Ronnie was glancing back and forth from one to the other of us. Her eyes were a little wide. I'd been telling her what was happening in my life. She'd been hanging around with me and the monsters long enough to meet Louie, but it was still a strange new world for her. Sometimes I thought she'd be better off keeping further away from the monsters, but like she'd said, we were both big girls. Sometimes she even carried a gun. She could make her own decisions.

Jamil answered, "I have been a werewolf for over ten years. This is my third pack. I have never even heard of a lupa that could help her Ulfric raise power outside of the lupanar, our place of power. Most lupas can't even do that. Raina was the first I'd met that could call power within the lupanar. She could do small powers without the full moon to boost her power, but nothing like what I felt today."

"Jamil says you helped Richard raise enough power to heal him," Louie said.

I shrugged, carefully so the coffee wouldn't spill. "I helped Richard control his beast. It raised . . . something. I don't know. Something."

"Richard went into one of his rages, and you helped bring him back?" Louie asked.

I looked at him then. "You've seen him when he loses control?"

He nodded. "Once."

The memory made me shiver. "Once is enough."

"But you helped him control it."

"She did," Jamil said. He sounded pleased.

Louie looked at him and shook his head.

"What's going on?" I asked.

"I've been telling Richard that he won't get better unless he gets you completely out of his system. I thought he had to forget you to heal himself."

"You sound like you've changed your mind," I said.

"If you can help Richard regain control of his beast, then he needs you. I don't care what arrangement you work out, Anita. But if he doesn't do something soon, he's going to end up dead. To stop that from happening, I'd do almost anything."

For the first time I realized that Louie didn't like me anymore. He was Richard's best friend. I guess I couldn't blame him. If he'd dumped Ronnie as badly as I'd dumped Richard, I'd be pissed, too.

"Even encouraging Richard to see me again?" I made it a question.

"Is that what you want?"

I shook my head and wouldn't meet his eyes. "I don't know. We're bound to each other for eternity. That's a long time to bitch at each other."

Richard appeared in the doorway. "A very long time," he said, "to watch you in his arms." He didn't sound bitter then. He sounded tired. His thick hair and muscular upper body were covered in fine white dust. Even his jeans were coated. He looked like something out of a porno movie where the handyman consoles the lonely housewife. He walked over to stand in front of the roses. "Forever to see white roses with your name on them." He touched the single red rose, and smiled. "Nicely symbolic." His hand closed around the crimson flower; when he opened his hand, red petals scattered across the table. A drop of blood fell to the pale table top. He'd found a thorn.

Ronnie's eyes were wide, staring at the ruined rose. She glanced at me, eyebrows raised, but I didn't even know what expression to give her in return. "That was childish," I said.

Richard turned to me, hand stretched out towards me. "Too bad our other third isn't here to lick the blood off."

I felt an unpleasant smile curl my lips, and spoke before I could stop myself, or maybe I was just tired of trying. "There are at least three people in this room that would love to lick the blood off your skin, Richard. I'm not one of them."

He balled his hand into a fist. "You are such a bitch."

"Woof, woof," I said.

Louie stood. "Stop it, both of you."

"I will if he will," I said.

Richard just turned away, speaking without looking at anyone. "We changed the sheets on the bed. But I'm still a mess." He opened his hand. Blood had spread along the lines in his hand like a river following its banks. He turned to me with angry eyes. "Can I use one of the bathrooms to clean up?" He raised the hand slowly to his mouth and licked the blood very slowly, very deliberately, off his skin.

Ronnie made a small sound, almost a gasp. I managed not to faint; I'd seen the show before. "There's a full bath with shower upstairs. Door across the hall from the bedroom."

He put one finger in his mouth in slow motion, like he'd just eaten some finger-lickin' good chicken. His eyes never moved from my face. I was giving my best blank look, empty, nothing. Whatever he wanted from me, blankness was not it.

"What about the fancy tub downstairs?" he asked.

"Help yourself," I said. I sipped coffee, the picture of non-chalance. Edward would have been proud.

"Wouldn't Jean-Claude be upset if I used your precious tub? I know how much you both like water."

Someone had told him that we'd made love in the tub at the Circus. I'd have loved to know who and hurt them. Heat rose up my face; I couldn't stop it.

"A reaction at last," he said.

"You've embarrassed me, happy?"

He nodded. "Yes, yes I am."

"Go take your shower, Richard, or your bath. Light the damn candles, have a ball."

"Are you going to join me?" There was a time when I'd wanted an invitation like that from Richard more than almost anything in the world. The anger in his voice when he said it brought something very close to tears to my eyes. I wasn't ex-actly crying, but it hurt.

Ronnie stood, and Louie put a hand on her arm. Everyone stood or sat and tried to pretend they weren't witnessing some-thing painfully personal.

A couple of deep breaths and I was okay. I wasn't about to let him see me cry. No way. "I didn't join Jean-Claude in the tub, Richard. He joined me. Maybe if you hadn't been such a frigging boy scout, it'd be you I was with right now and not him."

"Was one good fuck all it would have taken? Was it just that easy for you?"

I pushed to my feet, coffee sloshing down my hand onto the floor. I set the mug on the table, which put me within touching distance of Richard.

Ronnie and Louie had moved back from the table, giving us room. I think they'd have left the room if they had been sure we wouldn't come to blows. Jamil had set his coffee down as if he was getting ready to jump in and save us from ourselves. But it was too late to save us, far too late.

"You bastard," I said. "It took us both to get where we are, Richard."

"Three of us," he said.

"Fine," I said. My eyes were hot, my throat tight. "Maybe one good fuck would have done it. I don't know. Do your high ideals keep you warm at night, Richard? Does your moral high ground make you less lonely?"

He took that last step that put us almost touching. His anger flowed over me like an electric current. "You cheated on me, but you have him in your bed, and I have no one."

"Then find someone, Richard, find anyone, but let it go. Let it the fuck go."

He stepped back so abruptly, it made me sway. He left the room striding, his rage trailing after him like the smell of disturbing perfume.

I stood there for a second, then said, "Get out, everyone out."

The men left, but Ronnie stayed. I wouldn't have cried, honest, but she touched my shoulders, hugged me from behind, and whispered, "I'm so sorry." I could have withstood anything except sympathy.

I cried with my hands covering my face, still hiding, still hiding.

32

THE DOORBELL RANG. I moved as if to answer it, but Ronnie said, "Let someone else get it."

Zane called from the living room. "I'll get it." Which made me wonder where Jamil and Louie were. Comforting Richard, maybe?

I pushed away from Ronnie, scrubbing at my face. "Who could it be out here? We're in the middle of nowhere."

Jamil and Louie were suddenly back in the room. Either they'd heard me, or they were just as suspicious as I was. I picked the machine gun off the floor and stood in the doorway with the gun held at my left side, out of sight. The Firestar was in my right hand, also out of sight. Louie and Jamil moved into the living room to either side.

"Don't cross my line of sight," I said.

They both moved a little farther apart. Ronnie said, "I didn't bring my gun."

"The Browning is in the coat on the floor."

Her grey eyes were just a touch wide, her breathing just a little fast, but she nodded and went for the gun.

Zane was looking back at me with wide eyes. He looked a question at me, and I nodded. He checked the peephole. "Looks like a delivery guy with flowers."

"Open it," I said.

Zane did, blocking my view of the man. The man's voice was too soft to hear. Zane turned back to me. "Says you have to sign for the flowers."

"Who are they from?"

The man peered around Zane, raising his voice to say, "Jean-Claude."

"Just a minute." I laid the machine gun on the floor out of sight and kept the Firestar hidden behind my leg as I moved for the door. Jean-Claude kept me supplied with flowers, but he usually waited for the old ones to start to die, or at least fade. Of course, he had turned on the romantic overtime today.

He was a small man, holding the box of roses in his arm, his left hand on top of the box with a clipboard and a pencil with one of those strings on it.

Zane stepped away from the door to let me move up, but I got my first look in the little plastic window of the box. Yellow roses. I stopped moving forward and tried to smile. "You'll need a tip. Wait there while I get my purse."

The man's eyes flicked around the room, watching Jamil move up to his left and Louie to his right. I stepped to one side trying not to be directly in front of him. He followed me with the box, with his hand under the box.

Jamil had the best angle. I made his name a question, "Jamil?"

"Yes," was all he said, but it was enough.

"I don't need a tip," the man said, "but I'm running behind. Could you just sign for it so I could get going?"

"Sure," I said. Jamil had picked up on what was going on, but Zane was still looking puzzled. Ronnie was somewhere behind me. I didn't dare look for her, but I moved just a little more off-line and the man followed me with the hand I couldn't see, with the hand that Jamil had confirmed had a gun in it.

I was almost even with Louie. He'd stopped moving, waiting for me to come to him. He'd figured it out, too. Great, now what?

It was Ronnie who decided it. "Drop the gun, or I drop you." Her voice confident—certain. I spared a glance to see her standing feet apart, Browning in a two-handed grip pointed at the man in the doorway.

Jamil yelled, "Anita!"

I turned and pointed the Firestar in one movement. The man was already raising the hand and the box. I got a glimpse of the gun. He ignored Ronnie completely, pointing the gun at me. If he'd just fired from his hip, he'd have had time for one shot, but he tried for a better shooting stance and that was that.

Zane finally reacted, when what he should have done was

stay out of the way, which just goes to show that super strength and super speed are not enough. You got to know what to do with it. He slapped the box and clipboard out of the man's hand, making his first shot ring into the floor.

Ronnie's first shot went wide into the doorjamb. Zane was blocking my line of fire. I watched the gun come back up, pointed towards Ronnie this time.

Zane grabbed for the gun, and the gun went off twice more. Zane's body jerked, falling in slow motion to the floor. I had the gun pointed so that when Zane's body cleared the way, I was ready. Ronnie's second shot took the man in the shoulder, pushing him backwards. He fired at me, slumped in the doorway. His bullet went wide. Mine didn't.

Blood blossomed on his chest. He stared at me, eyes wide and almost puzzled, as if he didn't understand what was happening to him. Even with that first touch of death filling his eyes, he started to raise the gun, trying for one last shot.

Two shots went off like thunderous echoes. My shot took him in the chest. Ronnie's shot took the top of his head off. Glazer Safety Rounds will do that to unprotected flesh.

I walked up to the man, gun pointed at him, ready to shoot him again, but it was over. His chest was a mass of blood, and his head looked like someone had scalped him and gone a little too deep. Heavier fluids than blood were leaking all over my porch step.

Ronnie came up beside me, gun pointed at him. She took one look and stumbled outside, nearly tripping over the dead man's legs. She fell into the grass, wretching and crying.

Zane just lay there, bleeding. Louie was checking his pulse. "He's dying." He wiped the blood on his T-shirt and went out into the sunlight to take care of Ronnie.

I stared down at Zane's pale chest. One bullet had taken him low in the lungs. Red bubbles filled the wound, making that horrible sound that sucking chest wounds make that says, without a medic or a doctor, the person is dead. Just a matter of when, not if.

33

W E'D CALLED THE ambulance and found that they weren't coming right away. Too many other emergencies ahead of us. It was Louie who pried the phone out of my hands and apologized to the nice operator.

Cherry ran to the kitchen. I could hear her opening and shutting drawers, cabinets banging.

I walked into the kitchen.

She was standing in the middle of the room with a drawer pulled all the way out in one hand. Her eyes were almost wild. Before I could say anything, she said, "I need a Ziploc bag, masking tape, and scissors."

I didn't ask stupid questions. I opened the small drawer beside the stove and handed her the tape and scissors. The Ziploc bags were one of the few things in the roomy pantry closet.

Cherry snatched them from my hands and headed for the living room. I had no idea what she had in mind, but she had the medical training. I didn't. If it would give Zane a few more minutes, then I was for it. The ambulance would come eventually. The trick was having him alive for it to matter.

As far as I could tell, she didn't use the scissors. She taped the bag over his chest, plastering it with tape except for one corner. It was very obviously meant to be left that way, but I had to ask. "Why is the one corner untaped?"

She answered without looking up from her patient. "The open corner lets him breathe, but when he sucks in air the bag collapses and seals the wound. It's called an inclusive bandage." She sounded as if she was lecturing. I wondered, not for the first time, what Cherry was like outside the monster stuff. She was almost like two different people. I'd never meant anyone, monster or not, who seemed so divided.

"Will it keep him alive long enough for the ambulance to get here?" I asked.

She finally looked up at me—eyes very serious. "I hope so."

I nodded. It was better than I could have done. I was great at putting holes in people. Not so good at keeping them alive.

Richard brought a blanket and folded it over Zane's legs, letting Cherry take the upper part of the blanket to fix the way she wanted around the wound.

Richard was wearing nothing but a towel around his waist, his tanned skin beaded with water as if he hadn't even taken time to dry off. The towel clung in a smooth tight line to his butt as he folded the quilt over Zane. His thick hair hung in heavy strands, so wet that water trickled from it in fine lines down his back.

He stood up, and the towel flashed a lot of thigh.

"I have larger towels," I said.

He frowned at me. "I heard gunshots. I wasn't really worried about the size of the towel."

I nodded. "You're right. Sorry." My anger with Richard seemed to shrink in direct proportion to his clothes. If he really wanted to win the war, all he had to do was strip. I'd have put up a white flag and applauded. Embarrassing, but almost true.

He ran his hand through his hair, smoothing it back from his face and squeezing out the excess water. That small movement showed his arms and chest to wonderful advantage. He arched his back just a little, which stretched the rest of his body in one long muscled line. It was the back arch that did it. I knew he was showing his body off on purpose. He'd always seemed unconscious of the effect his body had on me until now. Now, staring into his angry eyes, I knew he'd shown me his body very deliberately. His way of saying, without words, see what you passed on, see what you lost. If it had just been the great body I'd lost out on, it wouldn't have hurt so much.

I missed Sunday afternoons watching old musicals. Saturday hiking through the woods, bird-watching, or entire weekends of rafting on the Meramec. I missed hearing about his day at school. I missed him. The body was just a very nice bonus. I wasn't sure there were enough roses in the world to make me forget what Richard had almost been to me.

He stalked away towards the stairs and his interrupted shower. If I'd been as strong of will as I liked to think, I wouldn't have watched him walk away. I had a sudden vivid image of licking water off his chest and jerking that tiny white towel away. The image was clear enough that I had to turn away and take a few deep breaths. He wasn't mine anymore. Maybe he never had been.

"I don't mean to interrupt the stud watch," Jamil said, "but who is the dead guy, and why did he try to kill you?"

If I thought I'd been embarrassed before, I was wrong. The fact that I'd let the shit with Richard distract me from the much more vital question of the would-be murderer just proved that I wasn't up on my game. It was too careless for words. The sort of carelessness that can get you killed.

"I don't know him," I said.

Louie lifted the sheet that someone had thrown over him. "I don't recognize him either."

"Please," Ronnie said. She was looking somewhere between grey and green again.

Louie let the sheet fall back, but it was flatter somehow and clung to the top of his head. The blood soaked up the cotton like oil to a wick.

Ronnie made a small sound and ran for the bathroom.

Louie watched her run out. I watched him watch her. He caught me looking and said, "She's killed people before." The implied "why is this worse?" went unsaid.

"Once before," I said.

He stood up. "Did she react like this?"

I shook my head. "I think it was the sight of his brains leaking all over the porch that did it."

Gwen walked into the room. "A lot of people who can take the sight of blood don't like to see other things leaking out."

"Thank you, Ms. Therapist," Jamil said.

She turned to him like a small blond storm, her otherworldly energy spiraling through the room. "You are a homophobic bastard."

I raised eyebrows. "I miss something?"

"Jamil is one of those men who believes that every lesbian

is just a heterosexual woman waiting for the right man. He was persistent enough to me that Sylvie kicked his ass.''

''Such language from a trained therapist,'' Jason said. He'd rushed up from the basement where the vampires were stored for the day when the shooting started. When the excitement died down, he'd gone back to check on everybody.

''All quiet down below?'' I asked.

He gave me that grin of his that managed to be both mischievous and just a touch evil. ''Quiet as a tomb.''

I groaned because he expected it. But the smile left my face before it left his. ''Could it be the council?'' I asked.

''Could what be the council?'' Louie asked.

''Whoever sent the hit man,'' I said.

''Do you really think he was a hit man?'' Jamil asked.

''You mean was he a professional assassin?''

Jamil nodded.

''No,'' I said.

''Why wasn't he a professional?'' Gwen asked.

''Not good enough,'' I said.

''Maybe he was a virgin.'' Jamil said.

''You mean a first timer?''

''Yes.''

''Maybe.'' I glanced at the sheet-covered lump. ''He picked the wrong career.''

''If it had been some suburban housewife or an investment banker, he'd have done okay,'' Jamil said.

''Sounds like you know.''

He shrugged. ''I've been an enforcer since I was fifteen. My threat's not worth anything unless I'm willing to kill.''

''How does Richard feel about that?'' I asked.

Jamil shrugged again. ''Richard's different, but if he wasn't, then I'd be dead. He'd have killed me right after he killed Marcus. It's standard op for a new Ulfric to kill the old leader's enforcers.''

''I wanted you dead.''

He smiled and it was tight, but not altogether unpleasant. ''I know what you wanted. You're closer to being one of us than he is sometimes.''

''I just don't have a lot of illusions, Jamil. That's all.''

''You think Richard's morality is an illusion?''

"He nearly crushed your throat earlier today. What do you think?"

"I think he also healed me. Marcus and Raina couldn't have done that."

"Would they have hurt you that badly by accident?" I asked.

He smiled, a quick baring of teeth. "If Raina had gone for my throat, it wouldn't have been by accident."

"On a whim," Gwen said, "but not by accident."

The werewolves all had a moment of perfect understanding. None of them mourned Raina, not even Jamil, who had sort of been on her side.

I shook my head. "I just don't think the council would send out some amateur with a gun. They've got enough daytime muscle to do the job without hiring outsiders."

"Then who?" Jamil asked.

I shook my head again. "I wish I knew."

Ronnie came back into the living room. We all watched her as she made her shaky way back to the couch. She sat down, eyes red-rimmed from crying and other things. Louie brought her a glass of water. She sipped it very slowly and looked at me. I expected her to talk about the dead man. Maybe to accuse me of being a horrible friend. But she'd decided to ignore the dead body and work on the live ones.

"If you had slept with Richard when you first started dating, all this pain could have been avoided."

"You're so sure of that," I said. I let Ronnie change the subject. She needed something else to concentrate on. I'd have preferred the topic to be something besides my love life, but . . . I owed her.

"Yes," she said, "the way you look at him, Anita. The way he looks at you when he's not being cruel. Yeah, I'm sure."

Part of me agreed with her, part of me . . . "There'd still be Jean-Claude."

She made an impatient sound. "I know you. If you'd had sex with Richard first, you still wouldn't be sleeping with that damn vampire. You think sex is a commitment."

I sighed. We'd had this talk before. "Sex should mean something, Ronnie."

"I agree," she said. "But if I had your scruples, I'd still just be holding hands with Louie. We're having a wonderful time."

"But where is it going?"

She closed her eyes and leaned her head against the back of the couch. "Anita, you make your life harder than it has to be." She opened her eyes and moved just her head so she could look at me and still slump. "Why can't a relationship just be what it is? Why does everything with you have to be so damn serious?"

I folded my arms over my stomach and stared at her. If I thought I was going to stare her down, I was wrong. I looked away first. "It is serious or should be."

"Why?" she said.

I was finally reduced to shrugging. If I hadn't been having sex with a vampire out of wedlock, I'd have had some moral high ground to stand on. As it was, I had nothing to fight back with. I'd been virtuous for so long, but when I lost it, I lost it big time. From celibacy to fucking the undead. If I'd still been Catholic, it would have been enough to get me excommunicated. Of course, being an Animator was enough to get me excommunicated. Lucky for me I was Protestant.

"You want some advice from your Auntie Ronnie?"

That made me smile, a small smile, but it was better than nothing. "What advice?"

"Go upstairs and join that man in the shower."

I looked at her, suitably scandalized. The fact that I'd been pretty much fantasizing about doing just that not ten minutes ago only made it more embarrassing. "You saw him in the kitchen, Ronnie. I don't think he's in a co-ed shower sort of mood."

A look came into her eyes that suddenly made me feel young or maybe naive. "You strip off and surprise him, and he won't kick you out. You don't get that kind of anger without heat. He wants you as badly as you want him. Just give into it, girlfriend."

I shook my head.

She sighed. "Why not?"

"A thousand things, but mainly, Jean-Claude."

"Dump him," she said.

I laughed. "Yeah, right."

"Is he really that good? So good that you couldn't give him up?"

I thought about that for a minute and didn't know what to say. It finally boiled down to one thing, and I said it out loud. "I'm not sure there are enough white roses in the world to make me forget Richard." I held up a hand before she could interrupt. "But I'm not sure there are enough cozy afternoons in all eternity to make me forget Jean-Claude."

She sat up straight on the couch, staring at me. A look almost of sorrow filled her eyes. "You mean that, don't you?"

"Yeah," I said.

Ronnie shook her head. "Jesus, Anita, you are screwed."

That made me laugh, because she was right. It was either cry or laugh about it, and Richard had gotten all the tears he was getting from me for one day.

34

THE PHONE RANG, and I jumped. Now that the danger was over, I could be jumpy. I went into the kitchen and picked up the phone. Before I could even answer, I heard Dolph's voice. "Anita, you okay?"

"The police grapevine is even faster than I thought," I said.

"What are you talking about?"

I told him what I'd told the 911 operator.

"I didn't know," Dolph said.

"Then why did you want to know if I was okay?"

"Nearly every vampire-owned business or house in the city was hit about the same time this morning. They fire-bombed the Church of Eternal Life, and we've had one-on-one hits on non-vamps all over the city."

Fear rushed through me like fine champagne, useless adrenaline with nowhere to go. I had a lot of friends that were undead, not just Jean-Claude. "Dead Dave's, has it been hit?"

"I know Dave resents being kicked off the force after he . . . died, but we take care of our own. His bar's got a uniformed guard until we find out what the hell is going on. We got the arsonist before he could do more than smoke up an outside wall."

I knew that only the bad vamps were at the Circus, but Dolph didn't. He might find it strange if I didn't ask. "The Circus?"

"They defended themselves against a couple of arsonists. Why didn't you ask about the love of your life, first, Anita? Isn't he home?"

Dolph asked like he already knew, which could mean he knew or it could mean he was fishing. But I was pretty sure the council flunkies wouldn't have told the whole truth. Half-truth, it was. "Jean-Claude stayed over last night."

The silence this time was even thicker than before. I let it build into something thick and unpleasant enough to choke on. I don't know how long we listened to each other breathe, but it was Dolph who broke first. "Lucky for him. Did you know this was coming?"

That caught me off guard. If he thought I'd held out on something this big, no wonder he was pissed at me. "No, Dolph, I swear I had no idea."

"Did your boyfriend?"

I thought about that for a second. "I don't think so, but I'll ask him when he gets up."

"Don't you mean when he rises from the dead?"

"Yeah, Dolph," I said, "that's what I mean."

"You think he could have known about all this shit and not told you?"

"Probably not, but he has his moments."

"Yet you still date him . . . I just don't understand that, Anita."

"If I could explain it so that it made sense to you, Dolph, I would, but I can't."

He sighed. "You got any ideas why someone's hitting all the monsters today?"

"You mean, why monsters or why this date?" I asked.

"Either," he said.

"You've got some suspects in custody, right?"

"Yes."

"They haven't talked."

"Only to ask for a lawyer. A lot of them ended up dead like yours."

"Humans Against Vampires, or Humans First, maybe," I said.

"Would either of them hit shifters?"

My stomach clenched into a nice tight knot. "What do you mean?"

"A man walked into a bar in the loop with a submachine gun with silver ammo."

For a minute I thought Dolph meant the Lunatic Cafe, Raina's old restaurant, but it wasn't an openly lycanthrope hangout. I tried to think what was up there that was openly shifter. ''The Leather Den?'' I made it a question.

''Yeah,'' he said.

The Leather Den was the only bar in the country, to my knowledge, that was a hangout for sadomasochistic gay men who happened to be shapeshifters. It was a triple threat to any hatemonger. ''Geez, Dolph, if it wasn't happening with everything else, I'd say it could be almost any right-wing fruitcake. Did you get the machine gunner alive?''

''Nope,'' Dolph said. ''The survivors ate him.''

''Bet they didn't,'' I said.

''They used teeth to kill him, Anita. That's eating him in my book.''

I'd seen shapeshifters eat people, not just attack them, but since most of those were illegal kills, i.e. murders, I let Dolph win the fight. He was still wrong, but hard to show him my proof without getting people in trouble.

''Whatever you say, Dolph.''

He was quiet for long enough that I had to say, ''You still there?''

''Why do I think you're holding back on me, Anita?''

''Would I do that?''

''In a heartbeat,'' he said.

His asking about the date had triggered some vague memory. ''There is something about today's date.''

''What is it?'' he asked.

''I don't know—something. Do you need me to come in?''

''Since almost all this shit is preternatural-related, every uniform and his K9 is asking for us. So yeah, we need everybody in the field today. They've been hitting the monster isolation wards of most of the major hospitals.''

''Jesus, Stephen,'' I said.

''He's all right, they all are,'' Dolph said. ''A guy with a 9mm tried for them. The cop at the door got hit.''

''He all right?'' I asked.

''He'll live.'' Dolph didn't sound happy, and it wasn't just the hitter or a wounded cop.

''What happened to the shooter?'' I asked.

He laughed, an abrupt, harsh sound. ''One of Stephen's 'cousins' threw him up against a wall so hard, his skull cracked.

Nurses say the shooter was about to put a round right between the uniform's eyes when he was . . . stopped.''

"So Stephen's cousin saved the cop's life," I said.

"Yeah," Dolph said.

"You don't sound happy about that."

"Leave it alone, Anita."

"Sorry. What do you want me to do?"

"The detective in charge is Padgett. He's a good cop."

"No small praise coming from you," I said. "Why do I hear a 'but' coming?"

"But," Dolph said, "he gets freaked around the monsters. Someone needs to go down there and hold his hand so he doesn't get carried away with the murderous shapeshifters."

"So I'm a babysitter?"

"It's your party, Anita. I can send someone else. I thought you'd want this one."

"I do, and thanks."

"Don't stay all day, Anita. Make it as quick as you can. Pete McKinnon just called me to ask if he could borrow you."

"Was there another arson?"

"Yes, but it wasn't his firebug. I told you they bombed the Church of Eternal Life."

"Yeah."

"Malcolm is in there," he said.

"Shit," I said. Malcolm was the undead Billy Graham, founder of the fastest-growing denomination in the country. It was the vampire church, but humans could join. In fact, they were encouraged. Though how long they stayed human was debatable.

"I'm surprised his daytime retreat was that obvious."

"What do you mean?"

"Most master vamps spend a lot of time and energy hiding their daytime address so that shit like this doesn't happen to them. Is he dead?"

"You are amusing as hell today, Anita."

"You know what I mean," I said.

"No one knows. McKinnon's going to call you with more details. Hospital first, then his scene. When you get done there call me. I'll figure out where to send you next."

"Have you called Larry?"

"You think he's up to this much solo action?"

I thought about that for a second. "He knows his preternatural stuff."

Dolph said, "I hear a 'but' coming."

I laughed. "We have worked together too damn long. Yeah, but he's not a shooter. And I don't think that's going to change."

"A lot of good cops aren't shooters, Anita."

"Cops can go twenty-five years and never clear leather. Vampire executioners don't have that luxury. We go in planning to kill things. The things we're planning to kill know that."

"If all you have is a hammer, Anita, every problem begins to look like a nail."

"I read Massad Ayoob, too, Dolph. I don't use my gun as the only solution."

"Sure, Anita. I'll call Larry."

I wanted to say, "don't get him killed," but I didn't. Dolph wouldn't get him killed on purpose, and Larry was a grownup. He'd earned the right to take his chances like everyone else. But it hurt something inside of me to know he'd be out there today without me as backup. They call it cutting the apron strings. It feels more like amputating body parts.

I suddenly remembered why today's date was important. "The Day of Cleansing," I said.

"What?" Dolph said.

"The history books call it the Day of Cleansing. The vampires call it the Inferno. Two hundred years ago the Church joined forces with the military in Germany, England, oh, hell, almost every European country except France—and burned out every vampire or suspected vampire sympathizer in a single day. The destruction was complete and a lot of innocent people went up in the flames. But the fire accomplished their goal, a lot fewer vampires in Europe."

"Why didn't France join with everyone?"

"Some historians think the King of France had a vampire mistress. The French Revolutionaries put out propaganda that the nobility were all vampires at one point, which wasn't true of course. Some say that's why the guillotine was so popular. It kills both the living and the undead."

Somewhere during the mini-lecture I realized that I could ask

Jean-Claude. If he missed the French Revolution, it wasn't by much. For all I knew, he'd fled the Revolution by coming to this country. Why hadn't I thought to ask? Because it still freaked me out that the man I was sleeping with was nearly three hundred years older than I was. Talk about a generation gap. So sue me if I tried to be as normal in some areas as possible. Asking my lover about events that happened when George Washington and Thomas Jefferson were still alive was definitely not normal.

"Anita, are you all right?"

"Sorry, Dolph, I was . . . thinking."

"Do I want to know about what?"

"Probably not," I said.

He let it go. Not more than a handful of months ago Dolph would have pushed until he thought I'd told him everything about everything. But if we were going to stay co-workers, let alone friends, some things were best left unsaid. Our relationship couldn't survive full disclosure. It never had, but I don't think Dolph understood that until recently.

"Day of Cleansing, okay."

"If you talk to any vampires, don't call it that. Call it the Inferno. The other phrase is like calling the Jewish Holocaust a racial cleansing."

"You've made your point," he said. "Remember while you're out there doing police work that you're still on some-one's hit parade."

"Gee, Dolph, you do love me."

"Don't push it," he said.

"Watch your own back, Dolph. Anything happens to you, Zerbrowski's in charge."

Dolph's deep laughter was the last thing I heard before the phone clicked dead. I don't think in the nearly five years I'd known Dolph that he'd ever said goodbye on the phone.

The phone rang as soon as I put it down. It was Pete Mc-Kinnon. "Hi, Pete. Just got off the phone with Dolph. He told me you wanted me down at the main branch of the Church."

"He tell you why?"

"Something about Malcolm."

"We've got nearly every human member of his Church screaming for us to make sure their big cheese didn't get toasted.

But we opened the floor up to check on some vamps on the west side and they weren't in coffins. Two of them went up in smoke. If we let Malcolm get cooked, trying to save him . . . Let's just say I don't want to do the paper work.''

''What do you want me to do?'' I seemed to be asking that a lot lately.

''We need to know if it's safe to leave him alone until he can rise on his own, or if we need to figure out how to rescue him. Vampires can't drown, can they?''

I thought the last was a strange question. ''Except for holy water, vamps don't have any problem with water.''

''Even running water?'' he asked.

''You've been doing your homework. I'm impressed,'' I said.

''I'm big into self-improvement. What about running water?''

''To my knowledge, water isn't a deterrent, running or otherwise. Why do you ask?''

''You've never been to a building after a fire, have you?'' he asked.

''No,'' I said.

''Unless the basement is airtight, it'll be full of water. A lot of water.''

Could vampires drown? It was a good question. I wasn't sure. Maybe they could, and that was why some of the folklore talked about running water. Or maybe it was like saying that vampires could shapechange, not true at all. ''They don't always breathe, so I don't think they'd drown. I mean, if a vampire woke with his coffin underwater, I think they could just not breathe and get out of the water. But, truthfully, I'm not a hundred percent sure.''

''Can you tell if he's okay without going down there?''

''Truth is, I'm not sure. I've never tried anything like that.''

''Will you try?''

I nodded, realized he couldn't see it, and said, ''Sure, but you're second on my list, not first.''

''All right, but hurry. The media is all over this thing. Between them and the Church members, we are not having a good time.''

''Ask them if Malcolm is the only vamp down there. Ask them if the basement is steel-reinforced.''

''Why would it be?''

"A lot of the basements where vamps sleep have concrete ceilings reinforced with steel beams. The church's basement doesn't have any windows, so it could mean that the lower area was specially designed with vamps in mind. I think you'd need to know that even if you decide to open the floor up."

"We do."

"Take some of the bitching faithful aside and ask them questions. You need to know the answers either way, and it'll at least give them the illusion that something's happening until I can get there."

"That is the best idea I've heard in two hours."

"Thanks. I'll be there as soon as I can, promise." I had a thought. "Wait, Pete. Does Malcolm have a human servant?"

"A lot of the people here have vampire bites."

"No," I said. "I mean a true human servant."

"I thought that was just a human with one or two vampire bites."

"So did I once," I said. "A human with just a couple of bites is what the vamps call a Renfield, as in the character from the novel *Dracula*." I'd asked Jean-Claude what they called them before the book came out. He'd said, "slaves." Ask a silly question.

"What's a human servant, then?" Pete asked. It reminded me of Dolph.

"A human who's bound to the vampire by something called marks. It's sort of mystical and magical shit, but it gives the servant and the vamp a tie that we could use to see if Malcolm is okay."

"Can any vampire have a servant?"

"No, only a master vampire, and not even all of them. I've never heard of Malcolm having one, but he could if he wanted to. Ask the faithful, though I think if he had one, the servant would be yelling louder than the rest. It's still worth a shot. If you solve it before I get there, call. Dolph says there's plenty of other shit to go around."

"He's not kidding. The city is going nuts. So far we've managed to contain the fires to just a few buildings, but if the crazies keep this up, it's going to get out of hand. There's no telling how much of the city could go up."

"We need to know who's behind this," I said.

"Yes, we do," Pete said. "Get here as soon as you can." He sounded so sure I could help. I wished I was as certain. I wasn't sure I could do shit in broad daylight. I'd been told once that the only reason I couldn't raise the dead at high noon was that I thought I couldn't. I was about to put it to the test. I still didn't think I could do it. Doubt is the greatest enemy of any magic or psychic ability. Self-doubt is a self-fulfilling prophecy.

"I'll be there as soon as I can."

"Great. I won't lie. I'm relieved that somebody with vampire experience is going to be on-site. The cops are starting to get some training on how to handle the preternatural, but no one trains firemen for this kind of shit."

It had never occurred to me that firemen have to deal with the monsters almost as much as the police. They don't hunt them down, but they enter their houses. That can be just as dangerous, depending on if the monster in question realizes you're there to help or not.

"I'll be there, Pete."

"We'll be waiting. See ya."

"Bye, Pete."

We hung up. I went for my shoulder holster and a different shirt. The shoulder holster would chafe with just a tank top on.

35

I CHANGED INTO a navy polo shirt and didn't run into Richard. The water had stopped running, but he hadn't come out. I did not want to see him again, especially not half naked. I wanted away from him. Lucky for me the shit had hit the fan, professionally speaking. Police work, lots of it, maybe enough to keep me out of the house all day. Fine with me. The ambulance arrived, and Zane was loaded in. Cherry went with him. I felt guilty not going with him, but she could do more good than I could. The police had still not shown up for the corpse. I hated leaving the others to talk to the cops without me, but I had to go. The fact that I was relieved to go caused me a few moments of guilt, but not much.

Ronnie had gone back to sitting on the couch. She asked just before I walked out the door, "Am I going to jail tonight?"

I knelt in front of her, taking her strangely cold hands in mine. "Ronnie, you didn't kill him."

"I shot the top of his head off. What kind of ammo do you have in that gun of yours anyway?"

"I shot him twice in the chest. There isn't enough left of his heart to scrape up with a spoon," I said.

She closed her eyes. "His brains are leaking out all over the porch. Don't tell me that wouldn't have killed him all by itself."

I sighed and patted her hands. "Please, Ronnie, you did what you had to do. Maybe it will take a medical examiner to decide which bullet did him in, but when the cops get here, make sure you don't take credit."

"I've been here before, Anita, remember. I know what to say and what not to say." She looked at me and it wasn't an entirely friendly look.

I released her hands and stood. "I'm sorry, Ronnie."

"I've only shot two people and both times I was with you."

"Both times you did it to save my life," I said.

She looked up at me with bleak eyes. "I know."

I touched her face and wanted to pat her on the head or something, comfort her the way you'd comfort a child, but she wasn't a child. "I am sorry this happened, Ronnie. Truly, but what else could you have done?"

"Nothing," she said, "and that makes me wonder if I'm in the right business."

Something inside of me tightened. "Don't you mean, wondering if you have the right friends? This didn't happen because of your business. It happened because of mine."

She gripped my hand tight. "Best friends, Anita, forever."

"Thanks, Ronnie, more than you'll ever know. I don't think I'd ever get over losing you as a friend, but don't decide to stay with me because of loyalty. Think about it, Ronnie, really think about it. My life doesn't seem to be getting any safer. If anything, it's getting more dangerous. You might want to think about whether you want to be in the line of fire." Just making the offer made my eyes burn. I squeezed her hand and turned away before she could see that the scourge of vampirekind was tearing up.

She didn't call me back and profess undying friendship. I'd half wanted her to, but the other half was glad she was really thinking about it. If Ronnie got herself killed because of me, I just might pull the guilt down over my ears and crawl into a hole. I caught Richard watching me from the doorway below the stairs. Maybe he and I could share a hole together. That'd be punishment enough.

"What's happened now?" he asked. He'd dried his hair into a shining mass of waves that slid over the top of his shoulders as he moved into the room. He'd put his jeans back on and found a shirt that fit him. It was a large T-shirt with a caricature of Arthur Conan Doyle on it. I used it for sleeping. It was a little snug on Richard through the shoulders and chest. Not small, mind you, just tight. On me the shirt hung nearly to my knees.

"See you found the blow dryer and the T-shirt drawer. Help yourself," I said.

"Answer my question," he said.

"Ask Jamil. He's got all the details."

"I asked you," Richard said.

"I don't have time to stand here and tell it twice. I've got to go to work."

"Police or vampire?"

"You used to ask that because you worried more if I was out on a vampire execution. You were always relieved if it was just police work. Why the hell do you want to know now, Richard? What do you care?" I walked out without waiting for an answer.

I had to step over the dead man on my porch. I hoped the cops got there soon. It was a typical July day in St. Louis—hot and claustophobically humid. The body would start to smell if it didn't get carried away soon. Just another of the many joys of summer.

My Jeep was in the garage, where it should have been. I'd let Jean-Claude use it to ferry everyone here. Though he hadn't driven. I'd never met an older vamp that drove. The older ones tended to be a bit technophobic. I was actually backing out of the garage when I saw Richard in the rearview mirror. He looked angry. I thought very seriously about just continuing out. He'd move. But just in case he'd be stupid enough not to, I waited for him to come up to the driver's-side window.

I pressed the button and the window whirred down like it was supposed to. "What?" I asked. I let that one word be as hostile as his eyes.

"Three of my pack in danger. Three of my people may be under arrest, and you didn't tell me."

"I'm taking care of it, Richard."

"It's my job to take care of my wolves."

"You want to go down there in person and announce that you're their Ulfric? You can't even go down there and be their friend because that might jeopardize your precious secret."

He gripped the edge of the window hard enough for his fingers to grow pale. "Most pack leaders have secret identities, Anita. You know that."

"Raina was your public alpha, Richard. She would have gone down to the hospital for them. But she's dead. You can't go. Who's left?"

Something popped in the door.

"I will be pissed if you break my car," I said.

He moved his hands slowly as if he needed something to hold just to keep his hands busy. "Don't get too comfortable as lupa, Anita. I am going to replace you."

We stared at each other from less than a foot away. Once he'd have come out to the car for one last goodbye kiss. Now it was one last fight.

"Fine, but until you find someone else, I'm all you've got. Now I've got to go and see if I can keep our wolves out of jail."

"They wouldn't be in police custody if you hadn't put them in harm's way."

He had me there. "If I hadn't put guards on Stephen and Nathaniel, they'd be dead right now." I shook my head and started easing the Jeep back. Richard stepped out of the way so I could do it without risking his toes.

He stood there and watched me drive away. If he'd asked, I would have found him a shirt, but it wouldn't have been that one. One, it was a favorite; two, it reminded me of a particular weekend. There'd been a Sherlock Holmes movie marathon, starring Basil Rathbone. Not my favorite, mainly because they make Dr. Watson out to be a buffoon, but still good. I wore the shirt that weekend even though it was too big to wear outside the house. The fashion police didn't get me, but Richard loved the shirt. Had he just grabbed a shirt and not even remembered? Or had he worn it to remind me of what I'd given up? I think I preferred it as a vindictive gesture. If he could wear the shirt and not remember that weekend, I didn't want to know. We'd managed to spill popcorn all over me and the couch. Richard wouldn't let me get up and dust myself off. He'd insisted on cleaning me up himself. Cleaning up seemed to involve no hands at all and a lot of mouth. If the memory meant nothing to him, then maybe we'd never been in love. Maybe it had all been lust and I just confused the two. God, I hoped not.

36

ANOTHER CRIME SCENE, another show. At least, the body had been removed. That was an improvement from my house. I'd left three werewolves behind to guard Stephen and Nathaniel. Two of those werewolves were in the hallway. Lorraine was still dressed like the ideal second-grade school teacher except for the handcuffs, which didn't seem to match the outfit. She was sitting in one of those straight-backed chairs that all hospitals seem to have. This one was in a horrid orange color which matched none of the soft pastel walls. She was sobbing with her hands covering her face. Her wrists looked small in the handcuffs. Teddy knelt beside her like a small weightlifting mountain, patting her thin back.

There was a uniformed cop on either side of them, at attention. One of the uniforms had his hand sort of casually resting on the butt of his gun. The strap that held the gun in the holster was already unsnapped. It pissed me off.

I walked up to the cop in question, way too close, invading the hell out of his personal space. "Better snap up the weapon there, Officer, before someone takes it away from you."

He blinked pale eyes at me. "Ma'am?"

"Use your holster the way it's meant to be used or get away from these people."

"What's the problem here, Murdock?" A tall, lanky man with a headful of dark curls walked towards us. His suit hung so loose on his thin body that it looked borrowed. His face was taken up by a huge pair of blue eyes. Except for the height, he looked like a twelve-year-old who had borrowed his daddy's clothes.

"I don't know, sir," Murdock said, eyes front. I was betting that he'd been in the military or wanted to be. He just had that taste to him of a wannabe.

The tall man turned to me. "What seems to be the problem, Detective . . . ?" He left a long blank space for me to put a name in.

"Blake, Anita Blake. I'm with the Regional Preternatural Investigation Team."

He held out a large-knuckled hand to me. He pumped my hand a little too vigorously but he didn't squeeze hard. He wasn't trying to test me, just glad to see me. His touch made my skin tingle. He was psychic. A first among the police I'd met, except for a witch they'd hired on purpose.

"You must be Detective Padgett," I said.

He nodded and dropped my hand, smiling wonderfully. Smiling made him look even younger. If he hadn't been nearly Dolph's height, he'd have had real trouble with being authoritative. But a lot of people mistake height for in charge. I've struggled against the opposite reaction most of my life.

He put a hand across my shoulders and led me away from the werewolves. I didn't much care for the hand on my shoulders. If I'd been a guy, he wouldn't have done it. I let him herd me to one side, then stepped out of the circle of his arm. Didn't make a point of it, just did it. Who says I haven't mellowed?

"Fill me in," I said.

He did. It was pretty much what Dolph had told me. The only addition was that it had been Lorraine who slammed the man into the wall, which explained her tears. She probably thought she'd be going to jail. I couldn't promise she wouldn't be. If she'd been a human female that had just saved a policeman's life by inadvertently killing a bad guy, she wouldn't go to jail, not today. But she wasn't human, and the law isn't even-handed, or blind, no matter what we'd like to believe.

"Let me test my understanding here," I said. "The officer on the door was down. The shooter had the gun pointed at the officer's head and was about to deliver the coup de grâce when the woman dived into him. Her momentum carried them both back into the far wall, where he hit his head. That about right?"

Padgett glanced at his notes. "Yeah, that's about right."

"Why is she in handcuffs?"

His eyes widened, and he gave me his best little boy smile.

Detective Padgett was a charmer. Didn't matter that he looked like a scarecrow, he was accustomed to getting by on charm. At least with women. I was betting his act had worked even less well on Lorraine.

"She's a lycanthrope," he said smiling, as if that explained it all.

"She tell you that?" I asked.

He looked startled. "No."

"You assumed she was a shapeshifter because why?"

The smile wilted, replaced by a frown that made him look petulant rather than angry. "She threw a man into a wall hard enough to crack his skull."

"Little old ladies lift cars off their grandchildren. Does that make them lycanthropes?"

"No, but . . ." His face closed down, defensive.

"I'm told you don't like shapeshifters much, Padgett."

"How I feel personally doesn't interfere with my job."

I laughed, and it startled him. "Padgett, how we feel personally always affects our job. I came here pissed because I'd had a fight with an ex-boyfriend, so I got in Murdock's face about his holster. Why don't you like lycanthropes, Padgett?"

"They give me the creeps, okay."

I had an idea. "Literally?" I asked.

"What do you mean, literally?"

"Does being around shapeshifters actually make your skin creep?"

He glanced up towards where the other cops were clustered. He bent forward and lowered his voice, and I knew I was right. "It's like bugs crawling on my skin every time I'm around them." He didn't look twelve now. The fear and the loathing in his face showed lines that put him closer to thirty than twenty.

"You're feeling their energy, their aura."

He jerked back from me. "The hell I am."

"Look, Padgett, I knew you were psychic the second I shook your hand."

"You're full of shit," he said. He was scared, scared of himself.

"Dolph's put the word out for any cops that have talent in this area. Why didn't you apply?"

"I am not a freak," he said.

"Ah, the truth comes out. You're not afraid of lycanthropes. You're afraid of you."

He raised a large fist, not to hit me, but just somewhere for his anger to go. "You don't know anything about me."

"They make my skin crawl, too, Padgett."

That calmed him, a little. "How can you stand to be near them?"

I shrugged. "You get used to it."

He shook his head, almost shivering. "I'd never get used to this."

"They aren't doing it on purpose, Detective. Some shape-shifters are better at hiding what they are than others, but all of them give off more energy during strong emotions. The more you questioned them, the more distressed they got, the more energy they gave off, and the creepier you felt."

"I had the woman in a room alone and I thought my skin was going to crawl off my body."

"Wait, alone? Did you Mirandize her?"

He nodded.

"Did she tell you anything?"

He shook his head. "Not a damn word."

"What about the others?"

"The men didn't do anything."

"Are they free to go?"

"The big one won't leave her and the other one is in room with the two injured ones. Says he can't leave them unguarded. I told him that we could take care of it. He said, apparently not."

I agreed with Kevin. "You've got witnesses that say she didn't mean to hurt the man. He isn't even dead yet. Why is she still here in handcuffs?"

"She has already killed one man today. I think that's enough," he said.

"Two things, Detective. First, she could snap those cuffs any time she wanted to. Second, if she were human, you'd have let her go home by now."

"That's not true," he said.

I looked at him. He tried to stare me down, but he flinched first. He said, looking at a spot above my head, "The man is dying. If I let her go, she could skip out."

"Skip out on what? She saw a cop about to get his head blown off and jumped an armed man to save him. She didn't cut him up. She pushed him into a wall. Trust me, Detective, if she'd meant to kill him, it would have been a more thorough job. She risked her life to save one of your own."

"She didn't risk anything. Bullets don't hurt lycanthropes."

"Silver bullets do. They work just like real ammo on a human. Every hit that they've investigated today had silver ammo, Padgett. Lorraine could have been killed, but she didn't hesitate. If she had, we'd have a dead cop on our hands. How many citizens would risk their lives to save a cop?"

He finally looked at me, eyes so angry they'd darkened two shades of blue. "You've made your point."

"Have I?"

He nodded. "Yes." He walked back down towards the waiting uniforms and the sobbing werewolf. "Uncuff her."

Murdock said, "Sir?"

"Do it, Murdock," Padgett said.

He didn't question it again, just knelt in front of Lorraine and unlocked the cuffs. His partner on the other side unsnapped his holster and took two big steps back. I let it go. We were winning, no need to fight.

As soon as her hands were free, Lorraine threw herself at me. I knew she didn't mean any harm, but I could hear the leather clearing down the hallway. I raised my voice and said, "It's okay, guys. She's okay. Ease down."

Lorraine was on her knees, arms locked around my legs, sobbing full out, loud and messy. I held a hand pointed palm out to either end of the hallway. Teddy stood and half the guns swiveled to cover him. We were on the verge of having things go really wrong.

"Padgett, get a hold of your men." I spared a glanced back at him and found his gun out, pointed at Teddy. Shit.

"Padgett, put up your gun and they'll follow your lead."

"Have him sit down," Padgett said, voice even and very serious.

"Teddy," I said softly, "sit back down, very slowly, no sudden moves."

"I haven't done anything," he said.

"Doesn't matter, just do it, please."

He sat back down under the watchful eyes of half a dozen guns. He put his big hands on his knees, palms down showing he was unarmed. Like he'd had practice trying to look harmless. "Now put your gun up, Detective," I said.

Padgett looked at me for a second. I thought he wasn't going to do it. I looked into those big blue eyes and saw something dangerous. A fear so deep and wide that he needed to destroy the thing he feared. He put the gun up, but that one moment of nakedness in his eyes had been enough. I'd talk to Dolph and see if Padgett had any shapeshifter kills to his credit. I'd almost have bet that he did. Cleared of charges didn't always mean innocent.

I patted the top of Lorraine's head. "It's all right. Everything's all right." I had to get them out of here. The good guys were almost as big a threat as the bad ones.

She looked up at me, eyes puffy, nose running. Real crying is like real sex. If you really do it, it isn't pretty. "I didn't mean to hurt him," she whispered.

"I know." I glanced at the police up and down the hallway. Some of them avoided my eyes. I shook my head and helped her stand. "I'm taking them into Stephen and Nathaniel's room with me, Detective Padgett. Any objections?"

He just shook his head.

"Great. Come on, Teddy."

"I can stand up?" he asked.

I looked at Padgett. "You think you and your people can hold the Rambo routine?"

"If he behaves himself, sure." Padgett wasn't trying to be charming anymore. I think he was embarrassed about the show. I knew he was still angry, maybe at me, maybe at himself. I didn't care as long as he didn't start shooting.

"You got a uniform inside the room?" I asked.

He gave one curt nod.

"Is he as trigger-happy as the rest of you, or can I open the door without being shot at?"

Padgett strode to the door and knocked on it. "Smith, it's Padgett. Detective coming in." He opened the door with a flourish and ushered Lorraine and me in.

I looked at the young uniform seated just inside the door. Kevin was slumped down in a chair across from him, an unlit

cigarette in the corner of his mouth. The werewolf looked at
me, and one look was enough—not a happy camper. It wasn't
just nicotine withdrawal either.

I half-pushed Lorraine into the room, then walked back to
Teddy. I held my left hand out to him, and he took it. I helped
him stand, though he didn't need the help. "Thank you," he
said, and he didn't mean for helping him stand up.

"No problem," I said. I escorted him back to the room. Once
they were both safely inside, I turned to Padgett.

"We need to talk. I'd prefer private if I could be guaranteed
no one will get shot while I'm gone."

"You okay in here, Smith?" he asked.

The young cop said, "I'm fine. I like animals."

The look on Teddy's face was scary even to me. That otherworldly energy was rising like a warm, stinging tide. "If the
nice policeman behaves himself, then so do the rest of you," I
said.

Teddy stared right at me. "I know how to follow orders."

"Great, shall we find some place private, Detective Padgett?"

His breath was coming fast, almost a pant. He was feeling
the rising energy, too. "We can talk right here. I'm not leaving
one of my men alone with these things."

"I'm okay, boss," the young cop said.

"You're not afraid?" Padgett asked. It was a question that
cops seldom ask each other. They ask, are you all right. They
admit to being nervous. Never scared.

Officer Smith's eyes widened a little, but he shook his head.
"I know Crossman. He's a good guy. She saved his life." Smith
sat up a little straighter in his chair, said softly, "These aren't
the bad guys."

A tic started in Padgett's cheek. He opened his mouth, closed
it, then turned abruptly on his heel and left. The door slid shut
behind him. We all stood in the suddenly thick silence.

Stephen said, "Anita." He held his hand out to me. His face
was flawless, no scars, no marks of any kind. I took his hand
and smiled.

"I know you guys heal fast, but it's still impressive. You
looked pretty bad last time I saw you."

"I looked worse," a soft male voice said. Nathaniel was
awake in the other bed. His long auburn hair hung like a shining

curtain around his face, maybe longer than waist-length. I'd never seen a man with hair that long. I couldn't see his face because I was too busy staring at his eyes. They were the color of lilacs, a wonderful pale lavender that was a genuine show-stopper. It took me a few seconds of staring to be able to see the rest of his face. He looked a few years older awake than he had unconscious—nineteen instead of sixteen, maybe. He still looked drawn and tired, ill, but there was a vast improvement.

"Yeah, you looked worse," I said.

Stephen turned to Officer Smith like they were old friends. "Can we have a few minutes alone?"

Smith looked at me. "Okay with you?"

I nodded.

He stood. "I don't know how Padgett's going to like it, so if you want to exchange secret codes or anything, make it fast."

"Thanks," I said.

"Don't mention it." He stopped in front of Lorraine before he left. "Thank you. Crossman has a wife and two daughters. I know they'd thank you if they could."

Lorraine blushed and nodded, mumbling, "You're welcome."

Smith left, and I walked over to Nathaniel's bed. "Nice to meet you while you're conscious."

He tried to smile, but the effort showed. He held out his left hand to me, the right hand was still hooked up to an IV drip.

I took his hand. His grip was tremblingly weak. He drew my hand towards his mouth as if to kiss it. I let him do it. The effort made his hand shake.

He pressed his lips to my hand, eyes closed, almost as if he were resting. For a second I thought he'd passed out, but his tongue flicked out, a quick wetness.

I jerked back, fighting the urge to wipe my hand on my jeans. "Thanks, a handshake would have been fine."

He frowned up at me. "But you're our *léoparde lionné*," he said.

"So people keep telling me," I said.

He turned his head so he could see Stephen. "You lied to me." Tears trembled in his pale, pale eyes. "She won't feed us."

I looked at Stephen. "I have missed part of this conversation, haven't I?"

"Have you seen Richard share blood with the pack?"

I started to say no, then, "I saw him let Jason feed off of a knife wound once. Jason seemed almost drugged from it."

Stephen nodded. "That's it. Gabriel could share blood."

My eyes widened. "I didn't think he was strong enough to do that."

"Neither did we." This from Kevin. He came to stand near me, cigarette transferred, still unlit, to his left hand. "It's been very interesting listening to Nathaniel talk about Gabriel. Nathaniel was addicted to heroin and a street whore when Gabriel rescued him, gave him a second life."

"Bully for him, getting him off drugs, but Gabriel still pimped him out. To a sicker clientele."

Kevin patted Nathaniel's leg under the sheet, a casual gesture, like you'd pat a dog. "But Nat here likes it, don't you, boy?"

Nathaniel looked at him and said softly, "Yes."

"Please, tell me you didn't enjoy being gutted."

He closed his eyes. "No, not that. But until then it was . . ."

"That's all right," I said. Something occurred to me. "Have you told the police who did this to you?"

"He doesn't know," Kevin said. He put the ever-present cig back in his mouth, as if just the taste of the paper was sweet.

"What do you mean, he doesn't know?" I asked.

Stephen answered, "Zane chained and blindfolded him, then left. That was the deal. Nathaniel never saw them."

"Them?" I made it a question.

Stephen nodded. "Them."

I took in a deep breath and let it out slowly. "Do you remember anything unique or different that might help identify them?"

"Perfume like gardenias, and a sickly smell."

Great, I thought, that was helpful.

He looked full at me, and suddenly his eyes weren't just dull with illness. I realized they were dull with experience. It went beyond jaded, as if Nathaniel had looked into the lower rungs of hell. He'd lived to tell the tale, but he hadn't really survived, not intact.

"I remember the perfume. I'd recognize it again if I smelled it."

"Okay, Nathaniel, okay." In the bottom of the awful emptiness of his eyes was panic. He was scared, unbelievably scared. I patted his hand, and when his fingers curled around mine, I held on. "No one will ever hurt you like that again, Nathaniel. I promise you that."

"You'll take care of me?" He looked up at me with a need in his eyes that was so raw, so primitive, I would have promised him anything to chase that look away.

"Yes, I'll take care of you."

His whole body relaxed. A tension running out of him like water from a cracked cup. I felt it run down his arm into his hand into me like a jolt of energy. It made me jump, but I didn't pull away.

He smiled up at me, lying back against the pillows. He looked a little better somehow, stronger.

I slid my hand out of his slowly, and he let me go. Great. I turned to the rest of the room. "We need to get you all out of here."

"I could go home now," Stephen said, "but Nathaniel still can't be moved."

"I don't trust the cops without me here to act as a buffer."

"Padgett is very afraid of us," Teddy said.

I nodded. "I know."

"Feed me," Nathaniel said. "Give me your strength, and I will go with you."

I frowned at him, then looked back at Stephen. "He's not seriously suggesting I open a vein for him, is he?"

"Richard could do it," Stephen said.

"Richard couldn't feed one of the leopards," Lorraine said, "only us."

"Raina could have fucked him back to health," Kevin said.

That earned him a long stare from me. "What are you talking about?"

"Raina could share energy without sharing blood," he said. His face registered both distaste and lust, as if he'd enjoyed some of Raina's shows in spite of himself. "She'd run her hands over you, then her body. It always ended with her fucking you.

The more hurt you started out, the better she liked it, but you'd be healed when she was finished.''

I turned to Stephen, because I didn't believe it. He nodded. ''I've seen her do it.''

''You're not suggesting that she . . .'' Lorraine let the awful thought go unsaid, but I was with her.

''I am not opening a vein, and I am most certainly not going to have sex with him.''

''You don't want me.'' Nathaniel's voice was tear-filled, heartbroken.

''It's nothing personal,'' I said. ''I'm just not into casual sex.'' This entire conversation was too weird even for me.

''Then Nathaniel has to stay here at least another twenty-four hours,'' Kevin said. He rolled the cigarette between his fingers while he talked.

Stephen nodded. ''That's what the doctor said. We asked when he told me I could go home today.''

''Don't leave me, Stephen.'' Nathaniel reached out across the space between them, as if he could touch him.

''I won't leave you alone, Nathaniel, not without someone to take care of you.''

Teddy spoke. ''Just because it ended in sex for Raina doesn't mean it has to end that way.''

We all looked at him. ''What do you mean?'' Kevin asked.

''Everything ended in sex for Raina. But it was the touching that healed. I think my injuries were healed before we got down to basics.'' Just listening to him talk like that with a sixty-inch chest of pure muscle made my brain hurt. It was like finding out your golden retriever talked. You just didn't expect to get brains in such a bulky package.

Kevin shrugged. ''I don't know. All I know is she healed me. I don't remember when I was better. I just remember her.''

''Is there anyone in this room that didn't sleep with Raina?'' I asked.

The only person who raised their hand was Lorraine, and knowing Raina, that had been debatable. ''Sweet Jesus.''

''I think Anita could heal him without sex, just bare skin,'' Teddy said.

I started to say no, then remembered sharing energy with Jean-Claude. Bare skin had been important there, too. Maybe it was the same. ''Did Raina seem to feel tired after healing you?''

All the men shook their heads. The consensus was it seemed to energize her, not weaken her. Of course, that was Raina and she had been an unusual puppy even for a werewolf.

I didn't want to leave Nathaniel here, not even with werewolves to guard him. I didn't trust Padgett. There was also no guarantee that the zealots, whoever they were, wouldn't try for another hit. Either we all went or we all stayed. I had more crime scenes to visit. I couldn't sit here all bloody day.

''Okay, let's try it, but I don't have the faintest idea how to begin.''

Nathaniel settled back into the pillows with something like a smile of expectation on his face. Like a child who's about to get the ice cream he was promised. Trouble was, I was the ice cream.

37

KEVIN PUT A chair under the door handle and we were as secure as we were likely to get. I'd told Smith, who was now manning the door, that I needed to get a feel for things, and I'd be done when I was done. I was being treated like a detective, so the uniforms would stay out. The only worry was Padgett. He'd only stay out until his ego recovered. I half expected him to try and barge in on us. The only thing that might save us from him was the fact that he'd want to break the door in because he'd be sensing what we were doing, and he wouldn't want to admit that.

I stood by the bed. Nathaniel looked up at me with a look that was so trusting, it made me nervous. I turned away and found everyone else looking at me, too. "Okay, guys, now what? I've never even seen this done."

There was an exchange of looks all the way around. Stephen said, "I don't know if we can explain it to you."

I nodded. "I know, magic is like that. You either get it, or you don't."

"Is this magic?" Teddy asked. "Or is it just psychic ability?"

"I'm not sure there is a difference," I said. "Sometimes I think the only difference is that psychic ability is something you do without thinking about it, and magic requires a ritual to get your juices going."

"You do more of this kind of shit than we do," Kevin said. "We're just werewolves, not witches."

"I'm not a witch. I'm a necromancer."

He shrugged. "Same diff to me." He sat down in the chair he'd started out in, crushing the cigarette into the palm of his hand as if it were lit and his flesh were an ashtray. He scowled up at me. I didn't know him well enough to be sure, but he seemed nervous.

Me, too. I only knew two ways to raise energy: ritual or sex. The sex took the place of ritual when I was with Jean-Claude or Richard. But I had no bond with Nathaniel. No marks, no emotion, nothing. I wasn't his *léoparde lionné*, not really. It was all lies. I couldn't do this without some feeling towards him. Pity wasn't enough.

Teddy loomed up behind me. "What's wrong, Anita?"

I would have walked across the room and whispered, but I knew Nathaniel would hear anywhere in the small room. "I need some emotion to work from, something."

"Emotion?" he asked.

"I don't know Nathaniel. I don't feel anything for him except pity, obligation. Neither of those is enough to even get started."

"What do you need?" His eyes were very serious. The intelligence in them was almost touchable.

I tried to put it into words and ended up saying, "I need something to take the place of a ritual."

"Raina didn't use a ritual," Kevin said from the chair. "She used sex. Sex can take the place of the ritual."

"You raised power at the lupanar that one night with Richard," Stephen said. "You didn't have sex, but you still raised power."

"But I . . . I wanted Richard sexually. It's a sort of energy all of its own."

"Nathaniel is handsome," Stephen said.

I shook my head. "It's never been that easy for me. I need more than a pretty face."

Stephen slid out of the bed in one of those wraparound gowns, but it didn't gape as he moved. It was wrapped around him like a sheet, more cloth than he needed, just like it would have been on me. One size never really fits all.

He tried to take my hand, and I wouldn't let him. "Let me help you."

"Define help." Suspicious, who me?

He smiled, and it was almost condescending. The smile men get around girls when they're doing something sort of cute and girlish. The smile alone pissed me off. "What is your problem?" I asked.

"You," he said softly. "You know I would never hurt you, don't you?"

I looked into his cornflower-blue eyes and nodded. "Never on purpose," I said.

"Then trust me now. Let me help you call the power."

"How?" I asked.

He took my hand in both of his, and this time I let him. He drew my hand to Nathaniel. He rested my fingertips on Nathaniel's forehead. His skin was cool. Just the touch of his skin, and you knew he wasn't well.

"Pet him," Stephen said.

I looked at him, shaking my head. I drew my hand back. "I don't think so."

Nathaniel started to say something, but Stephen put his fingers across his mouth. "No, Nathaniel." It was almost like he knew what the other man was going to say. But he couldn't know, not for sure, could he? I might have believed it if Nathaniel was pack, but he wasn't.

"Close your eyes," Stephen said.

"Uh-huh," I said.

"We don't have time for this," Kevin said.

"He's right," Teddy said. "I understand your natural reluctance, but the police are going to knock on the door eventually."

If Nathaniel couldn't leave with us, that meant leaving people behind to guard him, which put people in danger again. If we were all somewhere together, at least we wouldn't be endangering innocent policemen, though most cops would wince at being called innocent.

I took a deep breath and blew it out. "Fine, what's your idea?"

"Close your eyes," Stephen said.

I frowned at him. He looked patient, long-suffering even, and I closed my eyes. He took my hand in his, and it wasn't until he began to gently open my fist that I realized I'd clenched up. He started to massage my hand.

I said, "Stop that."

"Then loosen up," he said. "It won't hurt."

"I'm not afraid it will hurt," I said.

He moved around to stand in back of me, so close the hem of his gown brushed my legs. "But you're still afraid." His voice had dropped almost to a whisper. "Can you use that fear to call power?"

My pulse was hammering in my throat, and I was afraid, but it wasn't the right kind of fear. The fear that overwhelms you in the midst of an emergency can call power almost without effort. This was the kind of fear that keeps you from jumping out of perfectly good airplanes even though you'd decided to do it. Not an unhealthy fear, but it would hold you back.

"No," I said.

"Then let go of the fear," he said. He touched my arms gently and sat me on the edge of the bed.

Nathaniel made a small protesting sound, as if it had hurt.

I opened my eyes and Stephen said, "Close them." It was the closest thing to an order I'd ever heard him give. I closed them.

He took my hands and laid the tips of my fingers on either side of Nathaniel's face. "The skin just over the temples is so soft." He drew my fingers in a soft feathery line down Nathaniel's face, fingers gliding on either side, as if I were blind and trying to memorize his features.

He slid my hands into Nathaniel's hair. It was silken, unbelievably soft. His hair had the texture of satin. I balled my hands into that soft warmth, lowered my face towards his hair and smelled it. There was a faint medicinal smell. I buried my face in the satin brush of his hair and found his scent under it all. He smelled like vanilla, and under that was the scent of wood and field and fur. He wasn't pack, but the scent was similar. He smelled like home. Something clicked deep inside me, like a switch being thrown.

I opened my eyes and knew what to do, how to do it, wanted to do it. Like a distant thought, I realized that Stephen's hands had fallen away long ago.

I stared down into Nathaniel's lilac eyes and bent towards that amazing gaze. I touched his lips with mine, a chaste kiss, and that one soft brush brought the power in a warm, skin-tingling rush. It spilled out of me like water, warm, soothing, filling. But power alone wasn't enough. It needed direction, guidance, and I knew how to do it, as if I'd done it before. I didn't question it, didn't want to.

I tried to run my hand down his chest, but the gown covered him. He was like Stephen, like me, small. The gown was fastened in front, not in back. My hand sought the opening and slid along bare skin. Slid until I felt the incision.

I straddled Nathaniel's legs. He made another small hurting sound and I liked it. I rose up on my knees so only the sides of my legs touched his body. I slid the sheet down around his body and opened the gown, exposing him. The stitches were a thin dark line across the paleness of his skin that ran nearly from one hip to the other. A fearful wound, a killing wound.

He wore nothing below the waist. Hospitals are always stripping us down, leaving us as vulnerable as possible. The sight of him naked should have stopped me in my tracks. Dimly, it shocked me. I hadn't expected it, but it was too late. The power didn't care. I ran my fingers lightly over the stitches.

Nathaniel cried out, only half from pain. He was half-erect before I lowered my face to the stitches. I licked the wound like a dog would, long, slow caresses. He was more than half-erect when I raised my face to see his eyes staring down at me. I knew in that moment that I could have him, that he wanted me to take that last step.

I could feel the others in the room like a hum of energy, a vibrating backdrop to the energy inside me. I'd never been interested in casual sex, but the smell and feel of Nathaniel's body was almost overwhelming. I'd never been so tempted by a stranger. But temptation is just tempting. You don't have to give in. I rose on my knees over him, placing my hands on the smooth bones of his hips, drawing my hands towards the middle of the incision. When my hands touched, I put one on top of the other and pressed. Not with muscle or flesh but with power. I thrust that warm, rising power into his body.

He gasped, spine bowing underneath me, hands grabbing my arms, fingers convulsing against my bare skin.

It was like smoothing out the imperfections in a zombie except this flesh was warm and alive, and I couldn't see what I was fixing with my eyes. But I could feel it. I could feel his body smooth and firm, caressing places that no hand was meant to touch. Rolling them between my fingers, filling him up with the rising, rushing heat inside me. It spilled down my arms, my hands, into him. The heat spread through his body, through my body, until it was like fever, running over the skin, through the body, forming our bodies into a single thing of heat and flesh, and a rush of power that just kept building. It built until I closed my eyes, but even the darkness was shot with brightness, white flowers exploding on my vision.

My breath came in pants, too quick, too shallow. I opened my eyes and watched Nathaniel's face. His breathing matched mine. I forced us slower, forced his breathing to slow. I could feel his heart as if I caressed it, held in my hands. I could touch any part of him. I could have any part of him. I could smell the blood under his skin and wanted a taste.

He was healed when I lowered myself on top of him, pressed my mouth to his. I turned his face to one side and ate down the side of his neck until I felt the pulse under his skin. I licked the skin, but it wasn't enough. I laid my mouth over the beating pulse, bit gently into the skin until I could hold the throbbing of him in my mouth. I wanted to bite down harder and harder until blood flowed. I wanted it. Dimly, I knew that Jean-Claude had awakened for the day. It was his hunger that I felt, his need. But it wasn't his need that had me straddling Nathaniel's body. It wasn't even mine.

I remembered Nathaniel's body, and I'd never met him before. I knew the taste of him. The feel of him as only an old lover can. Not my memories. Not my energy.

I slid off Nathaniel, tried to crawl out of the bed, and fell to my knees. I couldn't stand, not yet. Richard had said as long as the pack existed, Raina wasn't gone. I hadn't understood what he meant, until now. I was channeling the bitch from hell, channeling her, and having a very good time doing it.

But I knew something else, something that Raina hadn't done. Couldn't blame her for this one. I knew how to heal Nathaniel's body, but I also knew how to tear it apart. Anything that you can fix, you can break. When I held his heart in my metaphysical hand, I'd had a split second, a dark urge, to close that hand, to crush that pulsing, throbbing muscle until blood flowed and his life stopped. A moment, the blink of an eye, of an urge so evil, it scared even me. I'd have liked to blame the bitch from hell, but something told me that this little bit of darkness was all mine. Stephen's hand on my mouth was all that kept me from screaming out loud.

38

STEPHEN'S HAND HELD the screams to a whimper. He held me
against his body, hard, as if afraid of what I'd do if I got loose.
I wasn't so sure myself. Running seemed like a good idea. Running until I outran the thought of it, the feel of it, all out of me.
But like Richard, I couldn't run from myself. That thought made
me stop struggling and just sit in the circle of Stephen's arms.

"Are you all right?" he asked softly.

I nodded.

His hand slid away from my mouth, slowly, as if he wasn't
sure I'd heard him or understood him.

I sagged against him, almost sliding to the floor.

He stroked my face, over and over, like you'd comfort a sick
child. He didn't ask what was wrong. None of them did.

Nathaniel knelt beside us. He didn't just look healed, he
looked healthy. He was smiling, handsome in a boyish, unfin-
ished sort of way. If you cut the hair and changed the eyes, he
looked like he should have been playing halfback on the high-
school football team and dating the homecoming princess.

The fact that I'd almost gone down on him two minutes ago
brought a rush of heat that made me hide my face against Stephen's shoulder. I did not want to look into that youthful, handsome face and realize how close I'd come to doing him. The
fact that I could still remember his body in details that I'd personally never touched, didn't help. Raina was gone, but not
forgotten.

I felt movement. The vibrating energy of the shapeshifters
was getting closer. I knew without looking that they were
crowding around me. The energy tightened like a circle drawing
closed. It was hard to breathe.

I felt someone's cheek brush my face. I moved my head enough to see Kevin inches from me. I'd expected Nathaniel. Teddy's large hands stroked down my bare arms. He brought his hands to his face. "You smell like pack."

Lorraine was on her back staring up at me with eyes gone strange and wolfish. "She smells like Raina." She rolled her face so that her lips brushed the knee of my jeans.

I knew that if I allowed it, we could sleep in one big communal heap like a litter of puppies, that touching was part of what kept the pack together, like the mutual grooming that primates do. Touching, comforting, it didn't have to be sexual. That had been Raina's choice. They were wolves but they were also people and that made them primates. Two animals really, not just one.

Kevin laid his head in my lap, cheek resting on my legs. I couldn't see his eyes, to tell if they'd gone wolf on me. His voice came thick and low, "Now I do need a cigarette."

It made me laugh. Once I started laughing, I couldn't stop. I laughed until tears ran down my face. The werewolves ran their hands up and down me, faces rubbing my bare skin. They were taking my scent, rolling in the lingering scent of Raina. Marking me with their scent.

Stephen kissed my cheek, the way you'd kiss your sister. "Are you all right?" It was hard to remember, but I think he'd asked that before.

I nodded. "Yes." My voice sounded tinny and distant. I realized I was on the edge of shock. Not good.

Stephen shooed the wolves away from me. They moved languorously, as if the energy we'd raised had been some sort of drug, or maybe sex was a better analogy. I didn't know. I wasn't even sure I wanted to know.

"Richard said that Raina wasn't truly gone as long as the pack lived. Is this what he meant?" I asked.

"Yes," Stephen said, "though I've never heard of a non-pack member being able to do what you just did. The spirits of the dead should only be able to enter lukoi."

"Spirits of the dead," I said. "You mean you don't have a fancy name for them?"

"They are munin," Stephen said.

That almost started me laughing again. "Memory, Odin's raven."

He nodded. "Yes."

"What exactly was it, *is* it? It wasn't a ghost. I know what a ghost feels like."

"You've felt one of them," Stephen said. "It's the best explanation I can give you."

"It's energy," Teddy said. "Energy is neither created nor destroyed. It exists. We have the energy of everyone that has ever been pack."

"You don't mean all lukoi, do you?"

"No," he said, "but from the first member of our pack to now, we have them all."

"Not all," Lorraine said.

He nodded. "Sometimes one of us will be lost to accident and the body cannot be recovered and shared. Then all they were, all their knowledge, their power, is lost to us."

Kevin had gone back to the chair, still sitting on the floor, leaning his shoulders against the chair seat. "Sometimes," he said, "we decide not to feed. It's sort of like excommunication. The pack rejects you in death as in life."

"Why didn't you reject Raina? She was a twisted sadistic bitch."

"It was Richard's choice," Teddy said. "By rejecting her body that last time, he thought it would have angered some of the other pack members who aren't wholeheartedly on his side yet. He was right, but . . . now we have her inside us."

"She's powerful," Lorraine said, and she shivered. "Powerful enough to possess a lesser wolf."

"Old wives' tales," Kevin said. "She's dead. Her power survives but only when called."

"I didn't call her," I said.

"We might have," Stephen said softly. He lay back on the floor, hands covering his eyes as if it was too horrible to look at.

"What do you mean?"

"I mean that we've never seen anyone but Raina do what you just did. I was thinking about her, remembering."

"So was I," Kevin said.

"Yes," Teddy said. He had moved back to the far wall, as if he didn't trust himself near me.

Lorraine had moved back with him, sitting so that their bodies touched lightly. A comforting closeness. "I, too, was thinking about her. Glad she was not here. Happy it was Anita." She hugged her arms as if cold, and Teddy put a muscular arm around her, hugging her close, resting his chin in her hair.

"I wasn't thinking about Raina," Nathaniel said. He crawled towards me.

"Don't touch me," I said.

He rolled onto his back, for all the world like a big pussy cat wanting its belly rubbed. He stretched, straining from toes to finger tips. He laughed and rolled onto his stomach, propped on his elbows. He looked up at me, long, rich brown hair like a curtain across his face. His lilac eyes stared out at me, feral and almost frightening. He lay down in a pool of hair and energy. His gaze stayed on my face, and I realized he was being playful. Not exactly seductive, but playful. It was different and almost more disturbing. Nathaniel managed to be childlike, catlike, and still be an adult. You didn't know whether to pat him on the head, rub his belly, or kiss him. All three seemed to be up for grabs. It was too confusing for me.

I used the far bed to get to my feet. When I was sure I could walk without falling down, I let go of the bed. I swayed just a touch, but not too bad. I could walk. Great, because I wanted out of here.

"What do you want us to do?" Stephen asked.

"Go to my house. Jean-Claude's there, and Richard was there."

"What about him?" Kevin asked.

Nathaniel raised his head enough to look at us all. He said nothing, asked for nothing, but I could taste his pulse in my mouth. I knew he was scared. Scared to be left alone again. I hoped this empathy with me wasn't permanent. I had quite enough men running around in my head without adding another one.

"Take him with you," I said. "The leopards are mine as you are mine."

"He is to be protected and treated as pack?" Kevin asked.

I rubbed my temples. I was getting a headache. "Yes, yes.

I've given him my protection. Any of the leopards that want my protection can have it."

"As our lupa that binds us to protect them," Lorraine said, "even to give our life for them. Will they do the same?"

I wasn't getting a headache, I had one.

Nathaniel rolled to his feet in a movement that was too graceful to be real and almost too quick to see. He sat on the foot of Stephen's bed, watching me with bright, eager eyes. He said, "My body is yours. My life, if you want it, is yours to take." He said it almost matter-of-factly—no, joyously, like it was a good thing.

I stared at him. "I don't want anyone's life, Nathaniel, but if the pack is willing to risk their lives to protect you, I expect you to do the same."

"I will do anything you want," he said. "All you have to do is tell me."

He didn't say, "ask me." He said, "tell me." I'd never heard it phrased quite like that. It implied he didn't have the right to say no. I asked, "Does everyone here know they have the right to argue a point with me? I mean, when I say jump, you don't just say how high, right?"

"We don't," Stephen said. His face was guarded, careful.

"How about you?" I asked, turning to Nathaniel.

He rose to his knees, leaning his upper body out towards me, but with both hands still on the bed railing. He didn't try to touch me, just get closer. "How about me, what?" he asked.

"You do understand that you have the right to refuse me? That my word is not like from on high?"

"Just tell me what you want me to do, Anita, and I'll do it."

"Just like that, no questions, you'll just do it?"

He nodded. "Anything."

"Is this a custom among the leopards, the pard?" I asked.

"No," Stephen said, "it's just Nathaniel's way."

I shook my head, literally waving my hands in the air as if I'd just erase it all. "I don't have time for this. He's healed. Take him with you."

"Do you want me to wait in your room?" Nathaniel asked.

"If you need to rest, help yourself to a bed. I won't be there."

He smiled happily and I had the oddest feeling that what I was saying wasn't what he was hearing. I wanted out of the room, away from them all. I'd tell Padgett I was sending them all to a safe house, and he'd buy it because he wanted off this detail. He wanted away from them more than I did.

The doctor was amazed at Nathaniel's recovery. They released him, though they started talking about wanting to run more tests. I vetoed that. We had places to go, people to meet. They all piled into Kevin's and Teddy's cars, and I went for my Jeep. Happy to be rid of them for a while. Happy even if it meant another crime scene. Happy even if I still didn't know how to tell if Malcolm was alive down there in the dark. Nathaniel watched me through the back window of the car, his lilac gaze on me until the car turned a corner. He'd been lost, and now he thought he'd been found. But if he expected me to be more than friends, he was still lost.

39

I FELT LIKE shit and didn't have a bruise to show for it. I concentrated on the next problem, pushing what I'd done, and almost done, to the back burner. Nothing I could do about it until I talked to Richard and Jean-Claude. I'd worried about tying myself to the vampire, but I'd never really worried about being tied to the werewolf. I should have known I'd get shit from both sides.

I got beeped three times in about three minutes. McKinnon first, Dolph second, and an unknown number. The unknown number called back twice in ten minutes. Damn. I pulled off into a service station. I called Dolph first.

"Anita."

"How do you always know it's me?"

"I don't," he said.

"What's up?"

"We need you at a new location."

"I'm on my way to the church site for McKinnon."

"Pete's here with me."

"That sounds ominous."

"We've got a vamp on his way to the hospital," he said.

"In his coffin?"

"No."

"Then how . . . ?"

"He was on the stairs covered in blankets. They don't think he's going to make it. But this is one of the halfway houses for the Church. We've got a two-biter here that says the vamp we took was the guardian for the younger vamps still inside. She seems worried about what the vamps will do when they wake and the guardian isn't there to calm them down or feed them."

"Feed them?" I asked.

"Says that they each take a small drink from the guardian to start the night. Without it, she says the hunger grows too strong, and they may be dangerous."

"Isn't she a font of information."

"She's scared, Anita. She's got two freaking vampire bites on her neck, and she's scared."

"Shit," I said. "I'm on my way, but frankly, Dolph, I don't know what you want me to do."

"You're the vampire expert, you tell me." A little hostility there.

"I'll think about it on the way. Maybe I'll have come up with a plan by the time I get there."

"Before they became legal, we'd have just burned them out ourselves."

"Yeah," I said, "the good old days."

"Yeah," he said. I don't think he got the sarcasm. But with Dolph it was always hard to tell.

I dialed the third number. Larry answered, "Anita." His voice sounded strained, pain-filled.

"What's wrong?" I asked, my throat suddenly tight.

"I'm all right."

"You don't sound all right," I said.

"I've just been moving around too much with the stitches and stuff. I need to take a pain pill, but I won't be able to drive."

"You need a lift?"

He was quiet for a second or two, then, "Yes."

I knew how much it had cost him to call me. This was one of his first times in the field on a police job without me. The fact that he needed my help for anything must have griped his ass. It would have bugged the hell out of me. In fact, I wouldn't have called. I'd have toughed it out, until I passed out. This wasn't a criticism of Larry, it was a criticism of me. He was just smarter than I was sometimes. This was one of those times.

"Where are you?"

He gave me the address, and it was close. Lucky us. "I'm less than five minutes away, but I can't take you home. I'm on my way to another crime scene."

"As long as I don't have to drive, I'll be okay. It's starting to take all my attention just to stay on the road. Time to stop driving when it's this hard.''

"You really do have a higher wisdom score than I do.''

"Which means you wouldn't have asked for help yet," he said.

"Well . . . yeah.''

"When would you have asked for help?''

"When I drove off the road and had to call a tow truck.''

He laughed and took a sharp breath as if it hurt. "I'll be waiting for you.''

"I'll be there.''

"I know," he said. "Thanks for not saying you told me so.''

"I wasn't even thinking it, Larry.''

"Honest?''

"Cross my heart and . . .''

"Don't say it.''

"You getting superstitious on me, Larry?''

He was quiet for a space of heartbeats. "Maybe, or maybe it's just been a long day.''

"It'll be a longer night," I said.

"Thanks," he said. "Just what I wanted to hear." He hung up then without saying goodbye.

Maybe I'd trained Dolph never to say goodbye. Maybe I was always the bearer of bad tidings, and everyone wanted to get off the phone with me as soon as possible. Naw.

=40=

I EXPECTED LARRY to be sitting in his car. He wasn't. He was leaning against it. Even from a distance I could tell he was in pain, back stiff, trying not to move any more than necessary. I pulled in beside him. Up close he looked worse. His white dress shirt was smeared with black soot. His summer-weight dress pants were brown, so they'd survived a little better. A black smudge ran across his forehead to his chin. The blackness outlined one of his blue eyes so that it seemed darker, like a sapphire surrounded by onyx. The look in his eyes was dull, as if the pain had drained him.

"Jesus, you look like shit," I said.

He almost smiled. "Thanks, I needed that."

"Take a pill, get in the Jeep."

He started to shake his head, stopped in mid-motion and said, "No, if you can drive, I can go to the next disaster."

"You smell like someone set your clothes on fire."

"You look pristine," he said, and he sounded resentful.

"What's wrong, Larry?"

"Other than my back feels like a red-hot poker is being shoved up it?"

"Besides that," I said.

"I'll tell you in the car." Underneath the sulkiness, he sounded tired.

I didn't argue with him, just started walking for the Jeep. A few steps and I realized he wasn't keeping up. I turned and found him standing very still, eyes closed, hands in fists at his sides.

I walked back to him. "Need a hand?"

He opened his eyes, smiled, "A back, actually. Hands work fine."

I smiled and took his arm gently, half expecting him to tell me not to, but he didn't. He was hurting. He took a stiff step, and I steadied him. We made slow but sure progress to the Jeep. His breath was coming in small, shallow pants by the time I got him around to the passenger side door. I opened the door, wasn't sure how to get him inside. It was going to hurt any way I could do it.

"Just let me hold your arm. I can do it myself," he said.

I offered my arm. He got a death grip on it and sat down. He made a small hissing noise between his teeth. "You said it would hurt worse the second day. Why are you always right?"

"Hard to be perfect," I said, "but it's a burden I've learned to cope with." I gave him my best bland face.

He smiled, then started to laugh, then almost doubled over with pain, which hurt more. He ended up writhing on the seat for a few seconds. When he could sit still again, he grabbed the dashboard until his fingers turned colors. "God, don't make me laugh."

"Sorry," I said. I got the aloe-and-lanolin Baby Wipes from the trunk of my car. They were great for getting blood off. They'd probably work on soot. I handed him the wipes and helped him buckle his seat belt. Yes, his wounds would have hurt less if he hadn't had the belt, but no one rides with me without a seat belt. My mom would be alive today if she'd been wearing a belt.

"Take a pill, Larry. Sleep in the car. I'll take you home after this next scene."

"No," he said, and he sounded so stubborn, so determined, that I knew I couldn't talk him out of it. So why try?

"Have it your way," I said. "But what have you been doing that you look like you've been trying to hide your spots?"

He moved just his eyes to look at me, frowning.

"Rolling in soot," I said. "Don't you ever watch Disney movies or read children's books?"

He gave a small smile. "Not lately. I've had three fire scenes where I just had to confirm the vamps were dead. Two of the scenes I couldn't find anything, just ashes. The third one looked like black sticks. I didn't know what to do, Anita. I tried to check for a pulse. I know that was stupid. The skull just exploded into ashes all over me." He was sitting very stiff, very controlled, yet his body gave the impression of hunching from pain, avoiding the blow of what he'd seen today.

What I was about to say wouldn't help things. "Vamps burn to ashes, Larry. If there were skeletal remains left, it wasn't vampire."

He looked at me then, the sudden movement bringing tears to his eyes. "You mean that was human?"

"Probably—I'm not sure, but probably."

"Thanks to me we'll never know for sure. Without the fangs in the skull you can't tell the difference."

"That's not entirely true. They can do DNA. Though truthfully I'm not sure what the fire does to DNA sampling. If they can gather it, they can at least know if it's human or vamp."

"If it's human, I've destroyed any chance they have of using dental records," he said.

"Larry, if the skull was that fragile, I don't think anything could have saved it. It certainly wouldn't have stood up to dental imprinting."

"Are you sure?" he asked.

I licked my lips and wanted to lie. "Not a hundred percent."

"You'd have known it was human. You wouldn't have touched it, thinking it was alive, would you?"

I let silence fill the car.

"Answer me," he said.

"No, I wouldn't have checked for a pulse. I would have assumed it was human remains."

"Dammit, Anita, I've been doing this for over a year, and I'm still making stupid mistakes."

"Not stupid, just mistakes."

"What's the difference?" he asked.

I was thinking that what he'd done to get his back ripped up was a stupid mistake, but decided not to say it out loud. "You know the difference, Larry. When you get over feeling sorry for yourself, you'll know the difference."

"Don't be condescending, Anita."

The anger in his voice stung more than the words. I didn't need this today. I really didn't. "Larry, I'd love to soothe your ego and make it all better, but I am all out of sugarplums and puppy-dog tails. My day hasn't been exactly a barrel of laughs either.''

"What's wrong?" he asked.

I shook my head.

"Come on. I'm sorry. I'll listen."

I wasn't even sure where to start, and I wasn't ready to tell anybody about what had happened in the hospital room, least of all Larry.

"I don't even know where to start, Larry."

"Try," he said.

"Richard is being nasty."

"Boyfriend trouble," he said; he sounded almost amused.

I glanced at him. "Don't be condescending, Larry."

"Sorry."

"It's not just that. Before this emergency came up, they wanted me at the Church of Eternal Life. Malcolm is bedded in the basement. His followers want him to be rescued. The firemen want to know if they can leave him until nightfall when he'll rise on his own."

"So?" Larry asked.

"So, I don't have the faintest idea how to find out if Malcolm is alive or dead."

He stared at me. "You're kidding."

"Wish I was."

"But you're a necromancer," he said.

"I raise zombies and an occasional vamp, but I can't raise a master vamp of Malcolm's power. Besides, what if I could? Would that prove he was alive or prove he was dead? I mean if I could raise him, it might just mean he was ready to be a zombie. Hell, Jean-Claude's awake for the day, maybe Malcolm is, too."

"A vampire zombie?" Larry said.

I shrugged. "I don't know. I'm the only person who can raise vamps like zombies, that I know of. There aren't a lot of books on the subject."

"What about Sabitini?"

"You mean the magician?"

"He raised zombies as part of his act, and he had vampires that did his bidding. I've read eyewitness accounts of it."

"First, he died in 1880. A little before my time. Second, the vampires were just dupes who went along with him. It was a way for vampires who would have normally been killed on sight to walk freely among the people. Sabitini and his pet vampires, they called them.''

''No one's ever proved that he was a fraud, Anita.''

''Fine, but he's dead and he didn't leave any diaries behind.''

''Raise him and ask,'' Larry said.

I stared at him long enough that I had to hit the brakes fast to keep from ramming a car in front of me. ''What did you say?''

''Raise Sabitini and find out if he could raise vampires like you can. He's just a little over a hundred years dead. You've raised zombies a lot older than that.''

''You missed the case last year where a vaudun priestess had raised a necromancer. The zombie got completely out of control and started killing people.''

''You've told me about it, but the priestess didn't know what he was. If you knew going in, you could take precautions.''

''No,'' I said.

''Why not?'' he said.

I opened my mouth, closed it, because I didn't have a good answer. ''I don't approve of raising the dead for curiosity's sake. You know how much money I've been offered to raise dead celebrities?''

''I'd still like to know what really happened to Marilyn Monroe,'' he said.

''When her family comes and asks, maybe I'll do it. But I am not raising the poor woman because a tabloid waved money at our boss.''

''Waved a lot of money at our boss,'' Larry said. ''Enough money that he sent Jamison out to try it. He couldn't raise her. Too long dead without a bigger sacrifice.''

I shook my head. ''Jamison is a weenie.''

''Everyone else at Animators Inc. turned it down.''

''Including you,'' I said.

He shrugged. ''I might raise her and ask how she died, but not in front of cameras. The poor woman was hounded alive. Dead, she's still being hounded. Doesn't seem fair.''

''You're a good guy, Larry.''

"Not good enough to know that vampires burn to ash and skeletal remains are human."

"Don't start, Larry. It's just experience. I should have told you before you went out today. Truthfully, you're getting so good at the job, I didn't think to tell you."

"You assumed I knew?" he said.

"Yeah."

"I have noticed the daily lectures have been in short supply lately. I used to take more notes at work with you than I ever did in college."

"Not so many notes lately, huh?" I said.

"No, I hadn't really thought about it, but no." He grinned suddenly and it lit up his eyes, chased away the horrors of the day. For a moment he was the bright-eyed, optimistic kid who had first shown up on my doorstep. "You mean I'm finally learning how to do the job?"

"Yeah," I said, "you are. In fact, if you were quicker on the trigger, I'd say you were good at it. It's just hard to learn everything, Larry. Something comes up and you find out you really don't know what the hell's going on after all."

"You, too?" he said.

"Me, too."

He took a deep breath and let it out. "I've seen you surprised a time or two, Anita. When the monsters get so strange that *you* don't know what's going either, it usually gets real nasty, real fast."

He was right. I wished he wasn't, because right now I didn't know what the hell was going on. I didn't understand what had happened with Nathaniel. I didn't know how the marks worked with Richard. I didn't know how to find out if Malcolm was still among the undead, or if he'd crossed into that more permanent state of true death. In fact I had so many questions and so few answers that I just wanted to go home. Maybe Larry and I could both take a pain pill and sleep until tomorrow. Surely tomorrow would be a better day. God, I hoped so.

41

THE HOUSE WAS still smoking when we got there. Thin greyish wisps of smoke rose from the blackened beams like miniature ghosts. Some trick of the fire had left the high cupola on top of the building intact. The lower stories were gutted and blackened, but the cupola rose like a white beacon above the wreck. It looked like a black-toothed giant had taken a great bite out of the house.

The fire truck took up most of the narrow street. There was a spread of water seeping along the street like a shallow lake. Firefighters waded through the water, rolling up miles of hose over their shoulders. A uniformed police officer stopped us well back from the action.

I eased down my window and flashed my ID. It was a little plastic clip-on card and looked official, but it wasn't a badge. Sometimes the uniforms would let me through, and sometimes they had to go ask permission. Brewster's Law was going around Washington and would give vamp executioners what amounted to federal marshal status. I wasn't sure how I felt about that. It takes a hell of a lot more to make a cop than just a badge, but for me personally I'd love to have had a badge to flash.

"Anita Blake, Larry Kirkland, to see Sergeant Storr."

The officer frowned at the ID. "I'll have to clear this with someone."

I sighed. "Fine, we'll wait here."

The uniform went off in search of Dolph, and we waited.

"You used to argue with them," Larry said.

I shrugged. "They're just doing their job."

"Since when has that stopped you from bitching?"

I looked at him. He was smiling, which saved him from the scathing comeback I had ready. Besides, it was nice to see him smiling about anything right now. "So I'm mellowing—a little. So what?"

The smile widened to a grin, a shit-eating grin, my uncle would have called it. It was like the next thing out of his mouth was almost too funny to say. I was betting I wouldn't think it was funny at all.

"Is it being in love with Jean-Claude that's mellowed you or the regular sex?"

I smiled sweetly. "Speaking of regular sex, how is Detective Tammy?"

He blushed first. I was happy.

The uniform was walking down the wet street towards us with Detective Tammy Reynolds in tow. Oh, life was good.

"Well, if it isn't your little sugarplum now," I said.

Larry saw her then. The red flush brightened to something the color of raw flame, redder than his hair. His blue eyes were a little bulgy with the effort to breathe. The soot had been wiped away, which saved his face from looking like a reddish bruise. "You won't say anything, will you, Anita? Tammy doesn't like to be teased."

"Who does?" I said.

"I'm sorry," he said, speaking very fast before they could get to us. "I apologize. It will never happen again. Please do not embarrass me in front of Tammy."

"Would I do that to you?"

"In a hot second," he said. "Please don't."

They were almost at the car. "Don't pull my leg and I won't pull yours," I whispered.

"Deal," he said.

I eased down the window, smiling. "Detective Reynolds, how good to see you."

Reynolds frowned because I was seldom glad to see her. She was a witch and the first police detective ever with preternatural abilities beyond psychic gifts. But she was young, bright, shiny, and tried just a little too hard to be my friend. She was just sooo fascinated with the fact that I raised the dead. She wanted to know all about it. I'd never had a witch make me feel like such a damned freak. Most witches were nice understanding souls. Perhaps it was the fact that Reynolds was a Christian witch, a member of the Followers of the Way. A sect going back to the Gnostics, who embraced almost all magical ability. They were all but wiped out during the Inquisition due to the fact that their beliefs don't allow them to hide their light under a bushel, but they survived. Fanatics have a way of doing that.

Reynolds was tall, slender, with straight brown hair falling around her shoulders, and eyes that I would have said were hazel but she called green. Greyish-green with a large circle of pale brown around the pupil. Cats have green eyes. Most people don't. She'd tried to be my friend, and when I wouldn't tell her about raising the dead, she'd turned to Larry. He'd been reluctant at first for the same reasons I was, but she hadn't offered me sex. It pushed Larry over the edge and into her arms.

I'd have complained about his choice of sweeties if I'd any moral high ground to stand on. It wasn't the witch part that bothered me or the cop. It was the religious-fanatic part. But when you share the sheets with the walking dead, you don't get a lot of room to bitch.

I smiled sweetly at her.

Reynold's frown deepened. I'd never been this happy to see her before. "Good to see you, too, Anita." Her greeting was cautious, but seemed sincere. Always willing to turn the other cheek. A good little Christian.

I was beginning to wonder if I was still a good Christian. I didn't doubt God. I doubted me. Having premarital sex with a vampire had shaken my faith in a lot of things.

She bent her five foot ten frame to peer in the window past me at Larry. "Hi, Larry." Her smile was genuine, too. Her eyes sparkled with it. I could feel the waves of lust, if not love, going from her to him like a warm, embarrassing current.

The blush had left Larry's face milk-pale with the sprinkling of freckles like brown ink spots. He turned large blue eyes to her, and I didn't like the way he looked at her. I wasn't sure it was just lust on Larry's part. Maybe it wasn't for Reynolds, either, but I didn't worry about her feelings the way I did Larry's.

"Detective Reynolds," he said. Was it my imagination or was his voice just a touch deeper? Nah.

"Larry." That one word was full of too much warmth.

"Where do you want us to park?" I asked.

She blinked hazel eyes at me, as if for a second she'd forgotten I was there. "Anywhere back here."

"Great."

She stepped back and let me park, but her eyes lingered on Larry. Maybe it was more than lust. Damn.

We parked. Larry undid his seat belt carefully, grimacing. I'd gotten the door for him at the gas station.

"You want me to get the door?"

He turned stiffly towards the door, trying to keep his upper body immobile. He stopped with his hand on the handle. His breath came in little gasps. "Yes, please."

Me, I'd have gotten the door myself, just from pure stubbornness. Larry really was the wiser of the two of us.

I held the door for him and offered him a hand. I pulled, he pushed with his legs, and we got him standing. He started to hunch from the pain, but that bent his back, which made the pain worse. He ended standing as straight as he could, leaning against the Jeep, trying to get his breath back. Pain will leave you breathless.

Reynolds was suddenly beside us. "What's wrong?"

"You tell her. I'll go talk to Dolph."

"Sure," Larry said, voice strained. He needed to be in bed, knocked out on painkillers. Maybe he wasn't that much smarter than me.

It wasn't hard to spot Dolph. Pete McKinnon was standing with them. It was like walking towards two small mountains.

Dolph's dark suit looked freshly pressed, white shirt crisp, tie knotted against the collar. He couldn't have been out in the heat long. Even Dolph sweats.

"Anita," he said.

"Dolph."

"Ms. Blake, nice to see you again," Pete McKinnon said.

I smiled. "Good to know someone's happy to see me."

If Dolph got the dig, he ignored it. "Everyone's waiting for you."

"Dolph always was a man of few words," Pete said.

I grinned at him. "Good to know it's nothing personal."

Dolph frowned at us. "If you two are through, we've got work to do."

Pete and I grinned at each other and followed Dolph across the wet street. I was happy to be back in my Nikes. I could walk as good as any of the men, in the right shoes.

A tall, thin fireman with a grey mustache watched me stride across the street. He was still wearing a helmet and coat in the July heat. Four others had stripped down to T-shirts with just the rubbery-looking pants on. Someone had sprayed them down with a water. They looked like an ad for a beefcake wet T-shirt contest. They were drinking Gatorade and water like their lives depended on it.

"Did a Gatorade truck just roll by or is this some arcane post-fire ritual?" I asked.

Pete answered, "It's damned hot in a fire with full gear on. You dehydrate. Water to rehydrate and Gatorade for the electrolytes so you don't pass out from the heat."

"Ah," I said.

The fireman who'd been rolling up the hose came over to us. A delicate triangle of face peered out from under the helmet. Clear grey eyes met my gaze. There was a lift to the chin, a way that she held herself that was a challenge. I recognized the symptoms. I had my own mountain-sized chip on my shoulder. I felt like apologizing for assuming she was a man, but didn't. It would have been insulting.

Pete introduced me to the tall man. "This is Captain Fulton. He's Incident Commander on this site."

I offered my hand while he was still thinking about it. His hand was large, big-knuckled. He shook hands like he was afraid to squeeze too hard, and dropped contact as soon as he could. I bet that he was just pleased as punch to have a female fireperson on his unit.

He introduced the fireperson in question. "Corporal Tucker." She offered her hand.

She had a nice firm handshake and eye contact so sincere it was aggressive.

I smiled. "Nice not to be the only woman on the scene for a change."

That brought a very small smile to her face. She gave the barest of nods and stepped back, letting her captain take over.

"How much do you know about a fire scene, Miss Blake?"

"It's Ms. Blake, and not much."

He frowned at the correction. I felt Dolph shift beside me, unhappy with me. His face wouldn't show it, but I could almost feel him willing me not to be a pain in the butt. Who, me?

Corporal Tucker was staring at me, eyes wide, face very still as if she was trying not to laugh.

One of the other firemen joined us. His damp T-shirt clung to a stomach that had required far too many sit-ups, but I enjoyed the view anyway. He was tall, broad-shouldered, blond, and looked like he should have been carrying a surfboard or visiting Barbie in her Malibu dream house. There was a smear of soot on his smiling face, and his eyes were red-rimmed.

He offered his hand without being introduced. "I'm Wren." No rank, just his name. Confident.

He held my hand just a little longer than necessary. It wasn't obnoxious, just interested.

I dropped my eyes. Not out of shyness, but because some men mistake direct eye contact as a come-on. I had about as much beefcake on my plate as I could handle without adding amorous firemen.

Captain Fulton frowned at Wren. "Do you have any questions, Ms. Blake?" He emphasized the *Ms.* so it sounded like three *z*'s at the end.

"You've got a basement full of vampires that you need to rescue without exposing them to sunlight or getting any of your people eaten, right?"

He stared at me for a second or two. "That's the gist of it."

"Why can't you just leave them in the basement until full dark?" I asked.

"The floor could cave in at any minute," he said.

"Which would expose them to sunlight and kill them," I said. He nodded.

"Dolph said one vamp was covered with blankets, and rushed to the hospital. Is that why you think the others may not be in their coffins?"

He blinked. "There's also a vampire on the stairs leading down. It's . . ." His gaze fell, then came up suddenly to grab mine, angry. "I've seen burn victims but nothing quite like this."

"Are you sure it's a vampire?"

"Yes, why?"

"Because vamps exposed to sunlight or fire usually burn completely down to ash and a few bone fragments."

"We doused it with water," Wren said. "Thought it was a person at first."

"What changed your mind?"

It was his turn to look away. "It moved. It was like third-degree burns down to cartilage and muscle, bone, and it held out its hand to us." His face looked pale, haunted. "No person could have done that. We kept coating it with water, thinking maybe we could save it, but it stopped moving."

"So you assumed it was dead?" I asked.

All three of them exchanged glances. Captain Fulton said, "You mean it might not be dead?"

I shrugged. "Never underestimate a vamp's ability to survive, Captain."

"We've got to go back in there and get it to a hospital," Wren said. He turned as if he'd walk back into the house. Fulton caught his arm.

"Can you tell if the vampire is alive or dead?" Fulton asked.

"I think so."

"You think?"

"I've never heard of a vamp surviving fire. So yeah, I *think* I can tell if it's alive. If I said otherwise, I'd be lying. I try not to do that when it's important."

He nodded twice, briskly, as if he'd made up his mind about me. "The arsonist threw accelerant all over the floor that we're going to be walking on top of, and once we're down in the basement that same floor will be above us."

"So?"

"That floor is not going to hold, Ms. Blake. I'm going to make this a strictly voluntary job for my people."

I looked up into his serious face. "How likely is the floor to fall and how soon?"

"No way of knowing. Frankly, I'm surprised it hasn't caved in by now."

"It's a halfway house for the Church of Eternal Life. If it's like the last basement I saw at a Lifer's place, the ceiling is concrete reinforced with steel beams."

"That would explain why it hasn't fallen in," Fulton said.

"So we're safe, right?" I asked.

Fulton looked at me and shook his head. "The heat could have weakened the concrete, or even weakened the tensile strength of the steel beams."

"So it could still fall down," I said.

He nodded. "With us in it."

Great. "Let's do it."

Fulton grabbed my arm and gripped it too tight. I stared at him, but he didn't flinch and he didn't let me go. "Do you understand that we could be buried alive down there or crushed to death, or even drowned if there's enough water?"

"Let go of me, Captain Fulton." My voice was quiet, steady, not angry. Point for me.

Fulton released me and stepped back. His eyes looked a little wild. He was spooked. "I just want you to understand what could happen."

"She understands," Dolph said.

I had an idea. "Captain Fulton, how do you feel about sending your people in to a potential deathtrap to save a bunch of vampires?"

Something passed through his dark eyes. "The law says they're people. You don't leave people hurt or trapped."

"But," I prompted.

"But my men are worth more to me than a bunch of corpses."

"Not long ago I'd have brought the marshmallows and wieners for the roast," I said.

"What changed your mind?" Fulton asked.

"Kept meeting too many human beings that were as monstrous as the monsters. Maybe not as scary, but just as evil."

"Police work will ruin your view of your fellow man," Detective Tammy said. She and Larry had joined us at last. It had taken Larry a long time to cross those yards. He was far too hurt to insist on going inside the house. Good.

"I'll go in because it's my job, but I don't have to like it," Fulton said.

"Fine, but if we do have a cave-in, we better get dug out before nightfall, because without the vamp chaperone we'll be facing a basement full of new vamps that may not have perfect control over their hunger."

His eyes widened, showing too much white. I would have bet

money that Fulton had had a close encounter of the fanged kind once upon a time. There were no scars on his neck, but that didn't prove anything. Vamps didn't always go for the neck, no matter what the movies say. Blood flows near the surface in lots of places.

I touched his arm lightly. Tension sang down his muscles like a string pulled too tight. "Who'd you lose?"

"What?" He seemed to be having trouble focusing on me.

"Who did the vampires take away from you?"

He stared at me, dark eyes focusing on me. Whatever horrible image was floating behind his eyes retreated. His face was almost normal when he said, "Wife, daughter."

I waited for him to say more, but the silence gathered round us in a still, deep pool made up of all the horror in those two whispered words. Wife, daughter. Both lost. No—taken.

"And now you have to go into the dark and save some bloodsuckers and risk yourself and your people. That really sucks."

He took a deep breath through his nose and let it out slowly. I watched him gain control of himself, watched him build his defenses back piece by piece. "I wanted to let it burn when I found out what was inside."

"But you didn't," I said. "You did your job."

"But the job's not done," he said softly.

"Life's a bitch," I said.

"And then you die," Larry finished for me.

I turned and frowned at him, but it was hard to argue. Today, he was right.

42

THE TWO-BITER, AS Dolph so poetically put it, was a small woman in her thirties. Her brown hair was back in a tight ponytail leaving her neck and the vampire bites painfully visible. Vampire freaks, people who just liked vamps for sexual turn-ons, hid their fang marks unless at one of their hangouts. Human members of the Church of Eternal Life almost always made sure the bites were visible. Hair worn just right, short sleeves if the marks were at wrist or elbow bend. They were proud of the bites, saw them as signs of salvation.

The upper set of fang marks were larger, the skin redder and more torn. Someone hadn't been neat with their food. The second mark was almost dainty, surgically neat. The two-biter's name was Caroline, and she stood hugging herself as if she were cold. Since you could probably fry eggs on the sidewalk, I didn't think she was cold, or at least not that kind of cold.

"You wanted to see me, Caroline?"

She nodded, head bobbing up and down like one of those dogs you used to see in the backs of cars. "Yes," she said, voice breathy. She stared at Dolph and McKinnon, then back at me. The look was enough. She wanted privacy.

"I'm going to take Caroline for a little walk. If that's okay?"

Dolph nodded. McKinnon said, "The Red Cross have coffee and soft drinks." He pointed to a small truck with a camper shell. Red Cross volunteers giving coffee and comfort to the cops and firemen. You didn't see them at every crime scene, but they hit their share.

Dolph caught my gaze and gave a very small nod. He was trusting me to question her without him, trusting me to bring him back any info that pertained to the crime. The fact that he still trusted me that much made the day a little brighter. Nice that something did.

It was also nice to be doing something useful. Dolph had been hot to get me to the scene. Now everything was stalled. Fulton just wasn't eager to risk his people for corpses. But that wasn't it. If there'd been six humans down there, we'd have already been suited up and going in. But they weren't human, and no matter what the law said, it made a difference. Dolph was right, before *Addison* v. *Clark*, they'd have gotten a fire crew in here to make sure it didn't spread to the other houses, but they'd have let it burn. Standard operating procedure.

But that was four years ago, and the world had changed. Or so we told ourselves. If the vamps weren't in coffins and the roof collapsed, they would be exposed to sunlight, and that would be it. The firemen had used an axe on the wall next to the stairs so I could see the second vamp corpse. It was crispy-crittered but not dust. I had no explanation for why the body had remained so intact. I wasn't even a hundred percent sure that come nightfall it wouldn't heal. *It*—even I still did it. But the body was so badly burned, like black sticks and brown leather, the muscles in the face had pulled away leaving the teeth, complete with fangs, in a grimace that looked like pain. Firemen Wren had explained to me that the muscles contract with the heat enough to break bones sometimes. Just when you think you know every awful thing about death, you find out you're wrong.

I had to think of the body as an "it" or I couldn't look at it. Caroline had known the vampire. I think she was having a lot more trouble thinking of the body as an it.

She got a soft drink from the nice Red Cross lady. Even I got a Coke, which meant it was pretty damn hot for me to pass on the coffee.

I led her to the front yard of a neighboring house where no one had come out to check the scene. The drapes were all closed, driveway empty. Everyone gone for the day. The only sign of life was a triangular rose bed and a black swallowtail butterfly floating over it. Peaceful. For a moment I wondered if the butterfly was one of Warrick's pets, but there was no feel of power. It was just a butterfly floating like a tiny tissue-paper kite over the yard. I sat down on the grass. Caroline joined me, smoothing her pale blue shorts down in back as if she was more accustomed to wearing skirts. She took a drink of soda. Now that she had me to herself, she didn't seem to know how to start.

It might have worked better if I'd waited for her to begin, but my patience had been used up long ago. It wasn't one of my cardinal virtues to begin with. "What did you want to tell me?" I asked.

She sat her can of soda carefully on the grass, thin hands smoothing along the hem of her shorts. She had pale pink nail polish on her short nails that matched the pink stripes in her tank top. Better than pale blue, I guess.

"Can I trust you?" she asked in a voice as fragile and pale as she seemed.

I hate being asked questions like that. I wasn't in the mood to lie. "Maybe. It depends on what you want to trust me with."

Caroline looked a little startled, as if she'd expected me to just say, sure. "That was very honest of you. Most people lie without thinking about it." Something in the way she said it made me think that Caroline had been lied to often, by people she'd trusted.

"I try not to lie, Caroline, but if you have information that'll help us here, you need to tell me." I took a drink of my own soda and tried to appear casual, forced my body not to tense up, not to show how much I wanted to simply scream at her until she told me whatever it was. Short of torture, you can't make people talk, not really. Caroline wanted to tell me her secrets. I just had to be calm and let her do it. If I was overeager or abusive, she'd either fold and tell all, or clam up and let us rot. You never knew which way it would go, so you try patience first. You can always browbeat them later.

"I've been the human liaison for this halfway house for three months now. The guardian who oversaw the younger ones was Giles. He was strong and powerful, but he was trapped in his coffin until true darkness. Then two nights ago he woke in the middle of the day. The first time for him. The one on the stairs has to be one of the younger vampires."

She looked at me, brown eyes wide. She leaned into me, lowering her soft voice even further. I had to lean into her just to catch her voice, close enough that my hair brushed her shoulder.

"None of the younger ones has been dead two years. Do you understand what that means?"

"It means that they shouldn't have risen during daylight hours. It means that the one on the stairs should have been burnt to ashes."

"Exactly," she said. She sounded relieved to finally find someone who understood.

"Was this early waking restricted to your halfway house?"

She shook her head, whispering now. We had our heads together like first-graders talking in class. I was close enough to see the fine red lines in her eyes. Caroline had been losing sleep over something. "Every house and all the churches were suddenly having vampires rise early. The hunger seemed worse on the young ones." Her hand went to her neck and the messy wound. "They were harder to control, even by the guardians."

"Anyone have any theories as to why this was happening?" I asked.

"Malcolm thought someone was interfering with them."

I had several candidates for who might be interfering with the vamps, but we weren't here to get my answers. We were here to get Caroline's answers. "He have any ideas about who?"

"You know about our illustrious visitors?" she asked, voice even lower, as if she were afraid to say the last.

"If you mean the Vampire Council, I've met them."

She jerked back from me then, shocked. "Met them," she said. "But Malcolm has not met them yet."

I shrugged. "They paid their . . . respects to the Master of the City first."

"Malcolm said they would contact us when they were ready. He saw their coming as a sign that the rest of vampirekind was ready to embrace the true faith."

I wasn't about to sit there and tell her why the council had really come to town. If the Church didn't know, they didn't need to know. "I don't think the council thinks much about religion, Caroline."

"Why else would they come?"

I shrugged. "The council has its reasons." See, not a lie, cryptic as hell, but not a lie.

She seemed to accept the statement. Maybe she was used to

cryptic bullshit. "Why would the council want to hurt us?"

"Maybe they don't see it as hurting."

"If the firemen go down in there to save the young ones and they wake without a guardian . . ." She drew her knees to her chest, hugging her legs. "They'll rise like revenants, mindless beasts, until they've fed. People could be dead before they come to themselves."

I touched her shoulder. "You're scared of them, aren't you?" I'd never met a human church member who was scared of vampires, especially not one that was donating blood as a human liaison.

She lowered the neckline of her tank top until I could see the tops of her small breasts. There was a bite mark on the pale flesh of one breast that looked more like a dog bite than one made by a vampire. The flesh had bruised badly, as if the vamp had been pulled off her almost as soon as he'd started sucking.

"Giles had to pull him off of me. He had to restrain him. Looking into his face, I knew that if Giles hadn't been there, he'd have killed me. Not to bring me over or embrace me, but just because I was food." She let her top slide back over the wound, hugging herself tight, shivering in the hot July sunshine.

"How long have you been with the Church, Caroline?"

"Two years."

"And this is the first time you've been scared?"

She nodded.

"They've been very careful around you, then."

"What do you mean?" she asked.

I unbent my left arm, showing the scars. "The mound of scar tissue at the crook is where a vamp gnawed on me. He broke the arm. I was lucky not to lose the use of it."

"What about that?" She touched the claw marks that trailed down the lower part of the arm.

"Shapeshifted witch."

"How did the cross get burned into your arm?"

"Humans with a few bites like you thought it was amusing to brand me with the cross. Just amusing themselves until their master rose for the night."

Her eyes were wide. "But the vampires in the Church aren't like that. We aren't like that."

"All vamps are like that, Caroline. Some of them control it

better than others, but they still have to feed off humans. You can't really respect something that you see as food.''

"But you are with the Master of the City. Do you believe that of him?''

I thought about that and answered truthfully. "Sometimes.''

She shook her head. ''I thought I knew what I wanted. What I was going to do for all eternity. Now I don't know anything. I feel so . . . lost.'' Tears trailed out of her wide eyes.

I put my arm across her shoulders, and she leaned into me, clinging to me with her small, carefully painted hands. She cried soundlessly, only the shakiness of her breathing betraying her.

I held her and let her cry. If I took the nice firemen down into the darkness and six newly dead vampires rose as revenants, either the firemen were dead or I'd be forced to kill the vampires. Either way, not a win-win situation.

We needed to find out if the vamps were alive, needed some control over them. If the council was causing the problems, maybe they could help fix it. When big bad vampires come to town to kill me, I don't generally turn to them for help. But we were trying to save vampire lives here, not just human. Maybe they'd help. Maybe they wouldn't, but it couldn't hurt to ask. All right, it could hurt to ask, and probably would.

43

EVEN OVER THE phone, I could tell Jean-Claude was shocked at my idea of turning to the council for help. Call it a guess. He was literally speechless. It was nearly a first.

"Why not ask for their help?"

"They are the council, *ma petite*," he said, voice almost breathy with emotion.

"Exactly," I said. "They are the leaders of your people. Leadership doesn't just mean privileges. It has a price tag."

"Tell that to your politicians in Washington in their three-thousand-dollar suits," he said.

"I didn't say that we did any better. That's beside the point. They've helped make this problem. They can, by God, help fix it." I had a bad thought. "Unless they're doing it on purpose," I said.

He gave a long sigh. "No, *ma petite*, it is not on purpose. I did not realize that it was happening to the others."

"Why isn't it happening to our vampires?"

I think he laughed. "Our vampires, *ma petite*?"

"You know what I mean."

"Yes, *ma petite*, I know what you mean. I have been protecting our people."

"Don't take this wrong, but I'm surprised you had the juice to keep the council from messing with your people."

"In truth, *ma petite*, so am I."

"So you're more powerful than Malcolm now?"

"It would appear so," he said quietly.

I thought about that for a minute. "But why the early rising? Why the increased hunger? Why would the council want that to be happening?"

"They do not want it, *ma petite*. It is merely a side effect of their proximity."

"Explain," I said.

"Their very presence will give unprotected vampires extra power: early rising, perhaps other gifts. The more voracious appetite and lack of control of the younger ones could mean that the council has decided not to feed while in my territory. I know the Traveler can take energy through lesser vampires without possessing them."

"So he takes part of the blood they drink?"

"*Oui, ma petite.*"

"Are the others feeding?" I asked.

"If all of the Church's members are experiencing this difficulty, I would think not. I think the Traveler has found a way to drain energy for all of them, though I cannot imagine Yvette going for even a night without causing pain to someone."

"She has Warrick to pick on." The moment I said it, I realized I hadn't had a chance to tell Jean-Claude about Warrick's little daytime excursion, or his warning. Jean-Claude had woken from his sleep while I was at the hospital surrounded by were-animals. Since then I'd been moving from one emergency to another.

"Warrick came to visit me while you were out for the day," I said.

"What do you mean, *ma petite*?"

I told him. All of it.

He was silent. Only his soft breathing let me know he was still there. Finally, he spoke. "I knew that Yvette gained power through her master, but I did not realize he was dampening Warrick's abilities." He laughed suddenly. "Perhaps that is why I did not realize I was a master vampire while I was with the council that first time. Perhaps my master, too, was preventing my powers from blossoming."

"Does Warrick's warning change our plans?" I asked.

"We are committed to a formal entertainment, *ma petite*. If we refuse to pay the price for your wereleopards, then we will give Padma and Yvette the very excuse they need to challenge us. Breaking faith once your word is given is an almost unforgivable sin among us."

"I've endangered us," I said.

"*Oui*, but being who you are, you could not do less. Warrick a master vampire, who would have thought it? He has been Yvette's plaything for so very long."

"How long?" I asked.

Jean-Claude was quiet for a heartbeat or two, then, "He was a knight of the Crusades, *ma petite*."

"Which crusade? There were several," I said.

"So nice to talk to someone who knows their history, *ma petite*. But you have been near him. What age is he?"

I thought about it. "Nine hundred, give or take."

"Which would mean?"

"I don't like being quizzed, Jean-Claude. The First Crusade in the late 1000s."

"*Exactement*."

"So Yvette was old even then," I said.

"Do you not know her age?"

"She's a thousand years old. But it's a soft one thousand. I've met vamps her age that scared the hell out of me. She doesn't."

"Yes, Yvette is terrifying but not because of her age, or her power. She can live until the end of the world and she will never be a master among us."

"And that gripes her ass," I said.

"Crudely but accurately put, *ma petite*."

"I'm going to ask the Traveler for help."

"We have bargained for all the aid we will ever get from them, *ma petite*. Do not put yourself further in their debt. I beg this of you."

"You've never begged anything of me," I said.

"Then heed me now, *ma petite*. Do not do this."

"I'm not going to bargain," I said.

He let out a breath as if he'd been holding it. "Good, *ma petite*, very good."

"I'm just going to ask."

"*Ma petite, ma petite*, what have I just told you?"

"Look, we're trying to save vampire lives here, not just human. Vampires are legal in this country. It doesn't just mean you get privileges. It comes with a price. Or it should."

"You are going to appeal to the council's sense of justice?"

He didn't bother to keep the incredulity out of his voice. In fact, he played on it.

Put that way it sounded silly, but . . . "The council is partially to blame for what's happening. They've endangered their own people. Good leaders don't do that."

"No one has ever accused them of being good leaders, *ma petite*. They just are. It is not a question of good or bad. We fear them, and that is enough."

"Bullshit. That isn't enough. It isn't even close to enough."

He sighed. "Promise me only that you will not bargain with them. Make your request but do not offer them anything for their aid. You must swear this to me, *ma petite*. Please."

It was the "please" that did it, and the fear in his voice. "I promise. It's their job to do this. You don't bargain to get someone to do what they're supposed to do in the first place."

"You are a wondrous combination of cynicism and naiveté, *ma petite*."

"You think it's naive to expect the council to help the vampires of this city?"

"They will ask what is in it for them, *ma petite*. What will you say?"

"I'll tell them it's their duty, and call them honorless bastards if they don't do it."

He did laugh then. "I would pay to hear this conversation."

"Would it help for you to listen in?"

"No. If they suspect it is my idea, they will demand a price. Only you, *ma petite*, could be this naive before them and hope to be believed."

I didn't think of myself as naive, and it bugged me that he did. Of course, he was nearly three centuries older than I was. Madonna probably seemed naive to him. "I'll let you know how it goes."

"Oh, the Traveler will make very certain that I know the outcome."

"Am I about to get you in trouble?"

"We are already in trouble, *ma petite*. It cannot get much deeper."

"Was that meant to be comforting?" I asked.

"*Un peu*," he said.

"That meant 'a little,' right?"

"*Oui, ma petite. Vous dispose a apprendre.*"

"Stop it," I said.

"As you like." He lowered his voice to a seductive whisper, as if it wasn't already the voice of wet dreams. "What were you doing when I awoke today?"

I'd almost forgotten about my little hospital adventure. Now it came rushing back hard enough to bring heat to my face. "Nothing."

"No, no, *ma petite*, that is not correct. You were most certainly doing something."

"Did Stephen and Nathaniel arrive at the house?"

"They did."

"Great. I'll talk to you later."

"You refuse to answer my question?"

"No, I just don't know a short version that doesn't make me feel like a slut. I don't have time for a longer version right now. So, can you wait?"

"I will wait for all eternity, if my lady asks it."

"Can the crap, Jean-Claude."

"If I wish you luck with the council, would that please you more?"

"Yeah, yeah."

"It is all right to be a lady, Anita. It is not a bad thing being a woman."

"You try being one, then talk to me," I said. I hung up. "My lady" sounded like *my dog*. Ownership. I was his human servant. Short of killing him, I couldn't change that. But I didn't belong to him. If I belonged to anybody, I belonged to me. And that was how I was going to approach the council, as me: Anita Blake, vampire executioner, police liaison for the monsters. They wouldn't listen to Jean-Claude's human servant, but they might listen to me.

44

THOMAS ANSWERED THE phone at the Circus. "They have you doing flunky work?" I asked.

"Excuse me?" he said.

"Sorry, this is Anita Blake."

He was quiet for a second, then, "I'm sorry, we are not open for business until nightfall."

"Is Fernando there?"

"Yes, that's right. Nightfall."

"I need to talk to the Traveler, Thomas. I'm asking this on police business, not as Jean-Claude's human servant. We've got some vampires in trouble, and I think he can help."

"Yes, we do take reservations," he said.

I gave him the number of Dolph's car phone. "We don't have a lot of time, Thomas. If he won't help me, I've got to go in with cops and firemen on my own."

"I look forward to seeing you tonight." He hung up.

Life would be so much easier if Fernando were dead. Besides, I'd promised Sylvie we'd kill him. I always tried to keep my promises.

Dolph was leaning in the door wanting to know what was taking so long, when the phone rang. I looked at him. He nodded and moved away. I picked up.

"Yes."

"I am told you needed to speak with me."

I wondered whose lips he was using, whose body. "Thank you for calling me back, Traveler." A little politeness couldn't hurt.

"Thomas was surprisingly eloquent on your behalf. What do you wish of me?"

I explained as briefly as possible.

"And what do you wish me to do about this problem of yours?"

"You can stop taking energy through them. That would help."

"Then I must feed on live humans. Is there someone you would offer in their place for each of us?"

"No, no offers, no bargains. This is police business, Traveler. I'm speaking with the authority of human law behind me, not Jean-Claude."

"What is human law to me? To us?"

"If we go down there and they attack us, I'll end up killing some of them. They may kill policemen, firemen. That's bad publicity with Brewster's Law to be decided this fall. The council has stopped all vampires in this country from fighting amongst themselves until the law is finalized. Surely slaughtering policemen is forbidden, too?"

"It is," he said. His voice was so careful. He gave me nothing. I couldn't tell if he was angry or amused or gave a damn either way.

"I'm asking you to help me save the lives of your vampires."

"They belong to this Church of yours. They are not mine," he said.

"But the council is the overall leadership of the vampires, right?"

"We are their ultimate law."

I didn't like the phrasing, but I plowed ahead. "You could find out case by case if the vampires were alive or dead in the burned-out buildings. You could keep the vamps from rising early and attacking us here."

"I think you overestimate my powers, Anita."

"I don't think so," I said.

"If Jean-Claude will supply us with . . . food, I will be more than happy to cease borrowing from the others."

"No, you get nothing for this, Traveler."

"If you give me nothing, I give you nothing," he said.

"Dammit, this isn't a game."

"We are vampires, Anita. Do you not understand what that means? We are apart from your world. What happens to you does not affect us."

"Bullshit. Some fanatics are out here trying to duplicate the Inferno all over again. That affects you. Thomas and Gideon have had to repel invaders while you slept. It does affect you."

"It doesn't matter. We are in your world, but not of it," he said.

"Look, that may have worked in the 1500's or whenever, but the minute vampires became legal citizens, it changed. A vampire got taken to the hospital in an ambulance. They are doing their best to keep him alive, whatever the hell that means for you guys. Firemen are risking their lives to go into burned-out buildings to save vampires. The fanatics are trying to kill you, but the rest of us humans are trying to save you."

"Then you are fools," he said.

"Maybe," I said, "but we poor humans have taken oaths to protect and serve. We honor our promises."

"Are you implying I do not?"

"I'm saying that if you don't help us here, today, then you aren't worthy to be council. You aren't leaders. You're just parasites feeding on the fear of your followers. True leaders don't leave their people to die, not if they can save them."

"Parasites. May I tell the rest of the council your so high opinion of us?" He was angry now. I could hear it like heat across the line.

"Yeah, tell them all. But mark me on this, Traveler, vampires can't just gain privileges with legal citizenship. They also gain responsibilities to the human law that made them legal."

"Is that so?"

"Yeah, that's so. This mysterious 'in your world but not a part of it' may have worked in the past. But welcome to the twentieth century, because that's what legal status means. Once you're citizens who pay taxes, own businesses, marry, inherit, have children, you can't hide in some crypt somewhere and count the decades. You are a part of our world now."

"I will think upon what you have said, Anita Blake."

"When I get off the phone with you, I'm going inside the house. We're going to start bringing out the vamps in body bags to protect them in case the floor caves in. If they rise as revenants while we're doing it, it'll be a bloodbath."

"I am aware of the problems," he said.

"Are you aware that it's the presence of the council that's

giving them the energy to possibly rise this early in the day?''

"I cannot change the effect our presence has on the lesser vampires. If this Malcolm wishes to claim the status of master, then it is his duty to keep his people safe. I cannot do it for him.''

"Can't or won't?" I asked.

"Can't," he said.

Hmmm. "Maybe I have overestimated your powers. My apologies if I have.''

"Accepted, and I understand how rare it is for you to apologize for anything, Anita.'' The phone went dead.

I hit the button that turned off the buzzing line.

Dolph walked back as I got out of the car. "Well?" Dolph asked.

I shrugged. "Looks like we go in without vampire backup.''

"You can't depend on them, Anita, not for backup.'' He took my hand, something he'd never done, squeezing it. "This is all you can count on. One human to another. The monsters don't give a shit about us. If you think they do, then you are fooling yourself.'' He dropped my hand and walked away before I could think of a comeback. Just as well. After talking to the Traveler, I wasn't sure I had one.

=====45=====

AN HOUR LATER I was dressed in a Hazardous Materials suit—
Haz-Mat for short. It was bulky, to say the least, and turned
into a portable sauna in the St. Louis heat. Heavy tape was
wrapped around my elbows and wrists, securing the seal between gloves and sleeves. I'd walked out of the boots twice, so
they taped my legs, too. I felt like an astronaut who had gone
to the wrong tailor. Insult to injury, there was a Self-Contained
Breathing Apparatus, SCBA, strapped to my back. Add Underwater and you got SCUBA, but we weren't planning to go
underwater. I was grateful for that.

There was a mask that covered the entire face instead of a
mouthpiece with regulator, but other than that, it was damn close
to SCUBA gear. I had my diving certification. Got it back in
college and keep it updated. If you let it slide, you have to take
the whole damn training course over again. Updating was less
painful. I was delaying putting on the mask as long as possible.
Due to a diving accident in Florida, I've got claustrophobia now.
Not bad enough for elevators to be a problem, but enclosed in
the suit, with a mask about to cover my face and the Haz-Mat
helmet going over my entire head—I was panicking and didn't
know what to do about it.

"Do you really think all this is necessary?" I asked for the
dozenth time. If they'd just give me a regular fire helmet with
the SCBA, I could handle it.

"If you go in with us, yes," Corporal Tucker said. Her three
inches of extra height didn't help much. We both looked like
we were wearing hand-me-downs.

"There's the possibility of disease contamination if there are
bodies floating in the basement," Lieutenant Wren said.

"Will there really be that much water in the basement?"

They exchanged glances. "You've never been in a house after a fire, have you?" Tucker asked.

"No."

"You'll understand once we're in," she said.

"Sounds ominous."

"It's not meant to," she said.

Tucker didn't have much of a sense of humor, and Wren had too much. He'd been entirely too solicitous while we were wriggling into the suits. He'd made sure he taped me up and was even now wasting a brilliant smile on me. But it was nothing too overt. Nothing obvious enough for me to say, look I have a boyfriend. For all I knew, he was always like this and I'd look an ass for taking it personally.

"Put the mask on, and I'll help you fit the hood over it," Wren said.

I shook my head. "Just give me a regular helmet and I'll use the SCBA."

"If you fall in the water without the hood sealed, Anita, you might as well not have the suit at all."

"I'll take my chances," I said.

Tucker said, "You had trouble walking from the Haz-Mat truck to here. You'll get better with practice, but in deep water, even we'll have trouble keeping our feet."

I shook my head again. My heart was pounding so hard, I was having trouble breathing. I put the mask on my face. I took a breath, and that horrible sound began. It was like Darth Vader breathing except it was yours. In the water, in the dark, your breath was the only sound. It could become thunderously loud while you waited to die.

"Strap needs tightening," Wren said. He started to adjust the strap as if I were five and being bundled off to play in the snow.

"I can do it." My voice came over the open radio line in the mask.

He raised his gloved hands skyward, still smiling. He was a hard man to insult, because I'd been trying. He had this sort of cheerful goodwill that seemed to deflect everything. Never trust people who smile constantly. They're either selling something or not very bright. Wren didn't strike me as stupid.

Insult to injury, I couldn't get the strap adjusted on the

damned mask. I always hated trying to work with anything bulk-ier than surgical gloves. I pulled the mask off and my first breath of real air was too loud, too long. I was sweating, and it wasn't just the heat.

I had the Browning and the Firestar lying on the side of the fire truck. There were enough pockets on the outside of the suit to hold half a dozen guns. I had a sawed-off shotgun from my vampire kit in a makeshift pack across my back. Yeah, it's il-legal, but Dolph had been with me once upon a time when we went after a revenant vampire. They were like PCP users: im-mune to pain, stronger even than a normal vamp. A force of hell with fangs. I showed him the shotgun before I got it out. He okayed it. We'd ended with two dead security guards and one rookie officer spread all over the hallway the last time. At least Dolph and his men had silver ammo now. He and Zer-browski nearly getting killed because they didn't have it was what pushed the paperwork through. I gave them a box of ammo for Christmas before they got official silver ammo. I never wanted to watch any of them bleed their lives away for lack of it.

I'd left the knives in their wrist sheaths. Carrying naked blades in the pockets of a suit that was air- and water-tight seemed sort of defeatist. If I lost both handguns and had to scramble for the knives under the suit, then we were probably toast. No need to worry about it. My silver cross hung naked around my neck. It was the best deterrent I had against baby vamps. They couldn't force their way past a bare cross, not when it was backed up by faith. I'd only met one vamp that could force his way past a blazing cross and harm me. And he was dead. Funny how so many of them ended up that way.

Tucker came over to me. "I'll help you adjust the mask."

I shook my head. "Leave me till last. The less time I'm in this get-up the better."

She licked her lips, started to say something, stopped, then said, "Are you all right?"

Normally, I would have said sure, but they were depending on me, maybe for their lives. How scared was I? Scared. "Not exactly," I said.

"You're claustrophobic, aren't you?" she said.

I must have looked surprised, because she said, "A lot of

people want to be firemen, but in the middle of a fire with the mask down and smoke so thick you can't see your hand in front of your eyes, you don't want to be claustrophobic.''

I nodded. ''I can understand that.''

''There's a part of training where they cover your eyes completely and make you do the equipment by touch as if the smoke had blacked out the world. You learn who doesn't like it close.''

''I could take the suit without the SCBA. It's the combination of the suit and listening to myself breathe. I had a diving accident just after college.''

''Can you do this?'' No accusations, just honesty.

I nodded. ''I won't leave you stranded.''

''That's not what I asked,'' she said.

We stared at each other. ''Give me a few minutes. I just didn't understand what Haz-Mat was. I'll be okay.''

''You sure?''

I nodded.

She didn't say anything else, just walked away to let me gather my scattered wits.

Wren had finally wandered over to talk to Fulton. Wren and Tucker were going in because they were both paramedics and we might need their medical training. Also, frankly, I didn't want Fulton in the dark with me and a bunch of vamps. He was simply too freaked. I didn't blame him, but I didn't want him at my back either. Of course, if I'd been watching me sweat and struggle to breathe calmly, I might not want me in there. Dammit. I could do this. I had to do this.

Detective Tammy Reynolds came slogging up in her own suit. They didn't have one big enough to fit Dolph, so she was my armed backup. Oh, joy. I couldn't send them in with Tammy as their only backup.

Tammy had managed to get her shoulder rig over the suit. She had one of those that just rode across the shoulders, no belt to put through straps. When I'd been shopping, all the holsters that just crossed the shoulders moved around on me too much. Part of it is having narrow shoulders. I'd have had to have the holster cut down. I don't buy things that have to be fussed with. Not dresses or holsters.

Reynolds smiled at me. ''Larry's really disappointed that he can't come along.''

"I'm relieved," I said.

She frowned at me. "I thought you'd want him to back you up."

"Yeah, but a gun can't help him if the ceiling caves in on us."

"You think it will?" she asked.

I shrugged. I'd concentrated on getting suited up, on small details, on Wren's quiet teasing. I'd managed not to dwell on the thought that we were about to walk across a floor that might collapse underneath us, then walk under it and wait for it to collapse on top of us, while wading through water full of coffins and vampires. What could be better?

"Let's just say I'm cautious."

"And you don't want to risk Larry."

"That's right. I don't like the idea of Larry getting hurt, by anything." I stared at her while I said it.

She blinked hazel eyes at me, then smiled. "Neither do I, Anita, neither do I."

I nodded and let it go. I'd done my parenting bit. I wasn't even sure why I didn't trust Tammy, but I didn't. Women's intuition, or maybe I just didn't trust much of anybody anymore. Maybe.

Tucker came back to us. "Time to suit up." She looked right at me.

I nodded. I let her help me adjust the mask over my face. I closed my eyes and concentrated on my breathing—in, out, in, out. In diving if you breathed too fast, you could blow your lungs. Now it was just a way to keep from hyperventilating.

She fitted the suit's hood over my head. I watched her do it and knew my eyes were a little too wide.

Wren's cheerful voice came over the radio in the mask. "Breathe normally, Anita."

"I am breathing normally," I said. It sounded odd to be able to talk normally while my own breathing was wheezing, loud and ominous in my ears. With a regulator in, you couldn't talk, though I'd learned you could scream with a regulator clenched between your teeth. Sounds echo like a son of a bitch under water.

With the helmet over the mask, visibility was not the best. I practiced turning my head, seeing just how big the blind spots were. My peripheral vision was almost gone.

Tammy's voice came over the radio. "It's hard to see in this thing."

"You'll get used to it," Tucker said.

"I hope we're not in this get-up long enough to get used to it," I said.

"If we say 'run,' run like hell," Tucker said.

"Because the floor will be caving in, right?" I said.

I think she nodded, but it was hard to tell through the layers. "Right."

"Fine, but when we get to the stairs, I have to take the lead, and if I say 'run like hell,' it means the vampires are going to eat us."

Wren and Tucker exchanged glances. "You tell us to run," Wren said, "we'll ask how fast."

"Agreed," Tucker said.

"Great," I said. Truthfully, it was a damn relief not to have to argue with anyone. No debate. What a relief. If I hadn't been sweating like a pig, listening to my own breathing echoing horrifically like *The Tell-Tale Heart*, having to relearn how to walk in metal-lined boots, I'd have said working with the fire department was a break. But it wasn't. I'd have rather rappelled down on ropes with Special Forces into a free-fire zone than shuffle along in the mummy suit trying not to lose it. It was just a phobia, dammit. Nothing was wrong. Nothing was hurting me. My body didn't believe the logic. Phobias are like that. Reason doesn't move them.

Wren stepped onto the floor. It made a noise like a giant groaning in its sleep. He froze, then stomped his feet so hard I thought my pulse was going to spill out my mouth.

"Shouldn't we be quieter?" I asked.

Wren's voice came in my ear. "Walk exactly where I walk. Don't deviate, don't spread out."

"Why?" I asked.

"Just because the floor is solid where I'm walking doesn't mean it's solid anywhere else."

"Oh," I said.

I went right behind Wren, so I got a closeup view of his little stomping dance. It was not comforting. Tucker came behind me, then Detective Reynolds bringing up the rear.

I'd given everybody a cross to put in the pockets of their suits. Why wasn't everyone wearing one like I was? Because Tucker and Wren were carrying a pack of opaque body bags apiece. Plan was to put the vamps in the bags and take them back up. Inside an ambulance in the body bags they'd be safe until nightfall. If we pulled this off and the ceiling didn't collapse before darkness, I was going to be pissed. As long as it didn't fall while we were down here. That I could pass on.

I walked where Wren walked, religiously. Though I did have to say, "Even out of this suit my stride isn't as big as yours. In the suit I'm damned near crippled. Can I take smaller steps?"

"Just as long as the steps are directly in line with mine, yes," Wren said.

Relief. The floor was covered with debris. Nails were everywhere in the blackened boards. I understood the metal insoles now. I was grateful for them, but it didn't make them any easier to walk in.

There was a line to one side going down a hole in the floor. It was a hard suction hose attached to a loud pump some distance away. They were draining the water out of the basement. If the place was watertight, it could be full to the ceiling. Comforting thought.

Fulton had called in a Haz-Mat tanker for the water. He seemed to be treating vampirism like a contagious disease. It was contagious but not in the way he seemed to think. But he was Incident Commander. I was learning that that title equated with God at a fire scene. You couldn't argue with God. You could get mad at him, but it didn't change anything.

I concentrated on moving my feet. Watching for debris. Stepping in Wren's footsteps. I let the world slide away except for moving forward. I was aware of the sun beating down, sweat trickling down my spine, but it was all distant. There was nothing but moving forward, no thinking required. My breathing was normal when I bumped into Wren's back.

I froze, afraid to move. Was something wrong?

"What's up?" I asked.

"Stairs," he said.

Oh, I thought. I was supposed to take the lead now. I wasn't ready. Truthfully, I wasn't sure how good I could walk on stairs in the damn suit. I just hadn't appreciated how hard it would be to walk in it.

"Stairs are the most dangerous part of a building like this," Wren said. "If anything is going to collapse it'll be the stairs."

"Are you trying to make us feel better?" Reynolds asked.

"Just prepared," he said. "I'll test the first few steps. If it seems solid, I'll move back and let Blake take it." He wasn't teasing anymore. He was all business, and we were suddenly on a last-name basis.

"Watch the body on the stairs," he said. He moved onto the first step, stomping hard enough that I jumped.

The body on the stairs was black, charcoaled. The mouth gaped open in a soundless scream. You had to look close to see the fangs. Real vamp fangs just aren't that big. Tendons were stretched naked looking like they'd snap if you touched them. The body looked fragile, as if one touch and it would be dust. I remembered Larry and the skull that had turned to powder at his touch. This body looked tougher than that, but not by much. Could it be alive? Was there some spark inside it that with nightfall it would move, live? I didn't know. It should have been ash. It should still have been burning in the sunlight, no matter how much water they poured on it.

Wren's voice startled me. "You can take the lead now, Anita."

I looked down the steps and found Wren several steps below, almost halfway. The darkness down below spilled around his feet like a pool. He was far enough down that a really ambitious vamp might have grabbed a leg and pulled him down. I hadn't been concentrating. My fault.

"Come back up, Wren," I said.

He did, and he was oblivious to the possible danger. Damn. "The stairs are concrete, which makes it safer. You should be okay."

"Do I still have to stomp every step?"

"It'd be safer," he said.

"If I feel it going, I yell?"

"Yes," he said. He brushed past me.

I stared down into the Stygian depths. "I need a hand for the railing in this suit. A hand for the gun. I'm out of hands for a flashlight,'' I said.

"I can try and shine a light in front of you, but it won't be where you need it.''

"Don't worry about it, unless I ask.'' It took me over a minute, maybe two, to fumble the Browning out of its pocket. The gun was definitely going in one hand. I had to use two hands to click off the safety in the bulky gloves. I slid my hand inside the trigger guard on the trigger. I'd never have carried a gun like this normally. But my gloved finger didn't want to fit inside the trigger guard. I was ready to go now. If I put safety first, I'd never get a shot off in time. I'd practiced with winter gloves on, but I'd never dreamed of having to shoot vamps in a Haz-Mat suit. Hell, I didn't know what a Haz-Mat suit was until today.

"What's the holdup?'' Fulton's voice. I'd forgotten he was monitoring everything we said. Like being spied on.

"These damn gloves aren't exactly made for shooting.''

"What's that mean?'' he asked.

"It means, I'm ready to go down now,'' I said. I kept the Browning pointed up and a little forward. If I fell in the suit and accidently fired a shot, I was going to try very hard not to shoot anyone behind me. I wondered if Detective Tammy had her gun out. I wondered how good a shot she was. How was she in an emergency? I said a short prayer that we wouldn't be finding out, got a death grip on the banister, and stomped the first step. It didn't fall down. I stared ahead into the thick blackness at the middle of the stairs. The sunlight cut across the darkness like a knife.

"Here we go, boys and girls,'' I said. And down we went.

46

WATER LAPPED AT the last few steps. The basement had turned into a lake. Wren's flashlight passed over the dark water like a tiny searchlight. The water was a solid blackness, holding all its secrets close and quiet. A coffin floated about ten feet from the stairs, bobbing gently in the dark, dark water.

Even over the wheezing and whoosh of my own breathing, I could hear the water lapping. There was the sound of wood rubbing together like boats tied up at a dock. I pointed, and Wren's light followed my hand. Two coffins were bumping against one another near the far wall.

"Three coffins visible, but there should be four more. One for the guardian, one for the vamp on the stairs, and two more."

I took that last step into the water. Even through the suit I could feel the liquid like a distant coolness, a liquid weight lapping at my ankles. The feel of the water was enough to speed my breathing, send my heart pounding in my throat.

"You're going to hyperventilate," Wren said. "Slow your breathing."

I took a deep breath and let it out slowly, counting to make it slower. A count of fifteen, then another breath.

"You okay?" he asked.

"What's going on?" Fulton asked.

"Nothing," Wren said.

"I'm okay," I said.

"What's happening?" Fulton said.

"We're missing four coffins. Two could have sunk, but we still have two missing. Just wondering where they are." I said.

"Be careful down there," he said.

"Like a virgin on her wedding night," I whispered.

Someone laughed. Always good to be amusing.

I tried stomping on the next step, knee-deep in water, and my feet went out from under me. I was suddenly sliding down the steps, only my grip on the banister keeping me from going under. I sat in water up to my chin, feeling stupid and scared. A combination I'm not fond of.

Wren came to stand over me, light sliding over the water while he helped me to my feet. I needed the help. I raised the Browning dripping wet into the light.

"Will your gun work now?" he asked.

"I could fire it underwater and it would still work," I said. It still amazes me how many people think a little water ruins a gun. You have to clean it really well afterwards but during the shooting, water is fine. The days of having to keep your powder dry are long past.

I eased down the remaining steps and slid slowly down into the cool water. My breathing grew ragged. Fuck it, I was scared. Flat-footed in the water, I could have gone for the flashlight in one of the pockets, or I could have slid the shotgun out of the bag across my back. But before I started changing guns, I'd let Detective Tammy get down here with her gun to cover me. I still didn't know how good she was, but it was better than nothing.

The water slid around my upper chest, not quite armpit depth, but almost. I slid very carefully out into the water, more swimming than walking, gun held two-handed and ready. Or as ready as you can be half-floating in a borrowed astronaut suit.

I didn't like the fact that we were missing two coffins with vamps inside them. They probably just sank, but my gut was tense, waiting for hands to slide over my ankles, and yank me under. My foot brushed something solid, and I couldn't breathe for a second. My foot scooted against it. Paint can maybe. I guess even vamps have crap in their basement just like the rest of us.

"I've got some debris over here," I said.

"You sound like a real fireman," Wren said.

"Coffin?" Detective Tammy asked from the stairs. She slid into the water last.

"No, just a can of some kind."

The coffin had almost floated to me. No effort. I put a hand out to touch it, keeping it floating gently in the small waves. "When Wren and Tucker get up to the coffin, I'm going to back off. Cover me while I pull out the shotgun."

"You got it," Tammy said. She had her flashlight and gun in two hands, one above the other, so the light moved with the barrel of her gun. She was sweeping the water for movement. Just seeing her do that made the tension in my shoulders ease a bit.

"Don't open the coffin until I'm ready," I said. I had a moment to realize that I wasn't worried about my breathing. The suffocating closeness had receded under the pure adrenaline rush of being chest-deep in water with vampires all around. I could be phobic later, after we survived.

Wren and Tucker took either end of the coffin. Even they were having trouble moving in the water in full suits. "I'm going for the shotgun now, Reynolds."

"You're covered," she said.

I backed off and swung the bag around. I had a moment to decide whether to try to put the Browning back in a pants pocket or in the bag where the shotgun was now. I chose the bag. I kept the bag in front though, where I could put a hand in if I needed the gun. I swung the shotgun around, settling the butt of it against my shoulder. I braced myself as much as I could in the water and said, "Open it."

Tucker steadied it, and Wren swung the lid back. He crossed my line of fire while he did it. "You've crossed my line of sight, Wren."

"What?"

"Move to your right," I said.

He did it without any more questions but that one delay could have been enough to get him hurt or dead. The vampire lay on her back, long hair spread around her pale face, one hand clasped on her chest like a sleeping child.

"Okay to move her?" Wren asked.

"Stay out of my line of fire and you can do anything you want," I said.

"Sorry," he said. Even over the mikes he sounded embarrassed.

I didn't have time to soothe his ego. I was too busy watching for vamps. I kept my attention mainly on the one in the open coffin, but I had no peripheral vision in the suit. My hearing was cut in half or more. I felt totally unprepared.

"Why aren't our crosses glowing?" Reynolds asked from just behind me.

"They don't glow around dead bodies," I said.

Wren and Tucker were having trouble getting the body into the bag. Wren finally threw the body across one shoulder and Tucker started squirming the legs into the bag. The vampire lay utterly limp across Wren's back. Her long hair trailed into the water, turning black as it absorbed the water. When they slid her the last bit into the bag, I got a glimpse of her death-pale face, strands of wet hair clinging to it, like a drowning victim.

Tucker zipped the bag and said, "There's water in the bag. I don't know how to avoid it."

Wren got the body as balanced as he could and started for the stairs. "This is going to take a long time with just two of us carrying," he said.

Fulton's voice came over the radios. "We've got two more suits, Ms. Blake. Is it safe to send more men down?"

"Speaking as one of the sacrificial lambs," I said, "yeah. Why should we have all the fun?"

Wren got to the stairs and started climbing up, one hand on the banister. He tried to do the little stomping routine like we did on the way down and nearly fell back into the water. "I'm just going up the stairs. If they collapse, try not to leave me buried until my air runs out."

"Do our best," I said.

"Thanks," he said, sarcasm traveling just fine over the mikes.

Tucker had isolated one of the other coffins. Reynolds slogged over to steady it while Tucker got the lid. She didn't have enough height to swing it back nicely like Wren had. She just shoved. The lid fell back smacking the other coffin with a loud, echoing thunk. The sound made the tips of my fingers tingle.

"Shit," Reynolds breathed.

"Everything okay?" Fulton asked.

"Yeah," I said, "just a little case of nerves."

"You okay down there, Tucker?" he asked.

"It was me," Reynolds said. "Sorry."

The second vamp was male with short brown hair and a sprinkling of freckles still clinging to his white skin. He was over six foot. He was going to be even harder to bag.

Tucker came up with the idea of dragging the coffin to the stairs and using the stairs to help leverage the body. Sounded good to me. The bottom of the stairs wasn't in sunlight, so the vamp shouldn't mind.

Reynolds and Tucker had dragged the coffin to the foot of the stairs by the time Wren came back down. He laid an unzipped bag over the length of the body. "If Reynolds and Tucker steady the coffin, I think I can just roll him into the bag."

"Sounds like a plan to me," Tucker said. She stepped lower in the water.

Reynolds looked to me, and I said, "Sure." She moved to the other side of the coffin, her gun not pointed at anything anymore, flashlight held beam-down into the water like a distant golden ball of light in the dark pool.

Wren leaned in over the body to roll it on its side. "You're in my line of sight again, Wren," I said.

"Sorry," he said, but his arms were half under the body, rolling it. He didn't move out of the way.

"Move, dammit," I said.

"I've almost got him in the bag."

The vampire's head spasmed. It happens sometimes even in their "sleep," but I didn't like it now. "Drop him and step back Wren, now." My cross and Reynolds's cross flared to life like two small white suns.

Wren did what I asked, but it was too late. The vampire turned on him, mouth wide, fangs straining. It bit into the suit with a loud hiss of released air. They were too close to trust the shotgun. "Reynolds, it's yours," I said.

Wren screamed.

Reynolds's gun made sparks in the near darkness. The vampire jerked back from Wren, a hole in its forehead. But it wasn't dead, not even close. Revenants don't die that easy. I fired into that pale face. The face exploded into blood and bits of meat; small heavy pieces rained down into the water with soft plops. It fell back against the raised coffin lid, head gone, hands still spasming in the white satin interior. Legs kicking. Wren fell to his butt on the stairs.

Tucker was saying, "Wren, Wren, answer me."

"I'm here," he said, voice hoarse. "I'm here."

I came two careful steps closer on the water-covered stairs and put another shell in the vampire's chest, blowing a hole in it and the coffin lid behind it. I pumped another shell in the shotgun and said, "Up the stairs, now!"

I knelt by Wren, hand under his arm, the other full of shotgun. Over the ringing in my ears from the guns I heard Tucker say, "Something brushed my leg."

"Out, now!" I tried to force them up the stairs with my voice. I dragged Wren to his feet and pushed him up the stairs. He didn't need much urging. When he reached sunlight, he turned back, waiting for the rest of us.

Reynolds was almost with us. Two wet, dripping arms came up on either side of Tucker.

I yelled, "Tucker!"

The arms closed and she was suddenly airborne, backwards, under the water. It closed over her like a black fist. There'd never been anything to shoot at.

Her voice was crystalline over the radio, breathing so ragged it hurt to hear it. "Wren! Help me!"

I slid down the steps, falling into the water, letting the blackness close over me. My cross flared through the water like a beacon. I saw movement but wasn't sure it was her.

I felt movement in the water seconds before arms grabbed me from behind. Teeth tore into the suit, hands ripping the helmet off like wet paper. It rolled me in the water, and I let it. I let its eager hands carry me around until I shoved the shotgun against its chin and fired. I watched its head vanish in a cloud of blood by the glow of my cross. I still had the breathing mask on, which was why I wasn't drowning.

Tucker's screams were continuous now. Her screaming was everywhere, in the radio, in the water, echoing and constant.

I stood up, the remnants of the suit sliding down my body. I lost some of the echoes of Tucker's screams. The water was conducting the screams like an amplifier.

Reynolds and Wren were both in the water. A bad idea. He was struggling towards something, and I saw it. Tucker's Haz-Mat suit was floating on the other side of the basement. He threw himself into the water trying to swim to her. Reynolds was trying to stay with him, gun in hand. Her cross was blindingly bright.

I yelled over the radio, ''Everyone out! Out, dammit, out!'' No one was listening.

Tucker's screams stopped abruptly. Everyone else screamed more. Everyone but me. I went quiet. Screaming wouldn't help. There were at least three vamps down here with us. Three revenants. We were going to die if we stayed down here.

The vampire exploded out of the water in front of me. The shotgun fired before I realized I'd done it. The vampire's chest exploded, and it grabbed for me anyway. I had time to jack another shell in, but not to fire. At moments like this the world goes too fast and too slow. You can't stop anything from happening, but you can see it all in excruciating detail. The vampire's fingers dug into my shoulders, painfully tight, holding me still while he reared back to strike. I had a glimpse of fangs framed by a dark beard. My cross's glow was almost frantically bright, highlighting the vampire's face like a Halloween flashlight. I fired the shotgun straight up under the chin, no time to brace, just to pull the trigger. The head exploded in a red rain all over my face mask. I was blinded by blood and thicker things. The recoil of the shotgun sat me down in the water. I went under without knowing if the thing was still coming or if it was dead.

I struggled to the surface. The water had streaked the face mask clean of blood, but heavier things clung to it, so I was still blind. I jerked the mask off my face, losing the radio but gaining my vision.

The vampire was floating in front of me, not face down, or face up. Faceless. Goody.

When Reynolds's gun fired, the shots sounded strange, and I realized I was deaf in the ear I'd fired the shotgun next to. The vampire's body reacted to the bullets, staggering, but not stopping. She was hitting it full middle body like they teach you on the range.

I yelled, ''Head shot.''

She raised the gun, and the gun clicked empty. I think she was going for extra ammo in a pocket when the thing jumped her and they both vanished into the water.

I slid out of what remained of the suit. Even with the taped joints it slipped off me like a shed skin. I exchanged hands to keep the shotgun ready and dived into the water. Swimming was faster, and if there was anything to catch, I'd caught it by now. The cross lit my way like a beacon. But it was Reynolds's cross that I swam for. That was my beacon.

I had seconds to reach her or it was all over. I had a sense of movement a second before the last vamp slammed into me. I turned, starting to point the shotgun at it, and it grabbed the gun. I think it was just grabbing anything, but it tore the gun from my hand and grabbed for me.

She was almost pretty with her long pale hair streaming behind her like a mermaid straight out of a fairy story. The cross made her skin glow as she reached for me. I had a knife ready and shoved it up under her chin. It slid in easily but didn't reach the brain. It wasn't a killing blow, not even close. She stood in the water, hands clawing at the knife. I don't think it was pain. She just couldn't open her mouth enough to feed.

I shoved the second blade under her ribs, up into her heart. Her body shuddered, eyes impossibly wide. Her mouth opened enough for me to see my knife blade impaling her. She screamed wordlessly and hit me with the back of her hand. The only thing that kept me from being airborne was the water. It absorbed some of the shock. I fell backwards, and the water closed over me. I had a second of floating, then I tried to breathe, got a mouthful of water and staggered to my feet, coughing, falling down as soon as I stood. I got my feet under me and felt something warmer on my face than water. I was bleeding. My vision was going grey with little white flowers in it.

The vampire was still coming for me with my last two knives in its body. There was no more screaming from across the room. I couldn't see that far, but it could only mean one thing. Reynolds, Wren, and Tucker were gone.

I was backing up in the water. I tripped over something and went down, water pouring over me. It was harder to get up this time, slower. I'd tripped over the Haz-Mat suit, and the bag with the Browning in it. My vision was full of holes. It was like watching the vampire through a strobe light. I closed my eyes, but the white flowers ate the back of my eyelids. I let myself sink into the water and found the bag by my foot. Was I holding my breath, or had I just stopped breathing? I couldn't remember.

I got the Browning out without opening my eyes. I didn't need to see to use it.

She grabbed a handful of my hair and dragged me to the surface. I fired as I came up, blowing holes in her body like a zipper until I came to that pale face. She put a hand out, over the muzzle of the gun, and that delicate hand blew into bits of bone, a bloody stump. I fired into that face until it was a red ruin and I was deaf in both ears.

The vampire fell backwards into the water, and I slid to my knees. The water poured over me. I tried to push to the surface again and couldn't. I think I got one last mouthful of air, then the grey and white spots were everywhere. I couldn't see the glow of the cross or the black water. When darkness swallowed my vision, it was smooth and perfect. I had a moment of floating, a dim thought that I should be scared, then nothing.

47

I WOKE UP on the grass where Caroline and I had been sitting. Vomiting water and bile, feeling like shit, but alive. Alive was good. Almost as good was Detective Tammy Reynolds standing over me, watching the EMTs work on me. Her arm was taped to her side, and she was crying. Then nothing, like someone changed the channel, and I woke up to a different show.

Hospital this time, and I was afraid I'd dreamed Reynolds, and that she was really dead. Larry sat in a chair by my bed, head back, asleep or knocked out on painkillers. I took his presence as a sign I hadn't hallucinated Reynolds. If his sweetie had been dead, I didn't think he'd be sitting here, at least not asleep.

He blinked awake, eyes unfocused, from drugs I think. "How are you?"

"You tell me."

He smiled, tried to stand and had to take a deep breath before he could do it. "If I wasn't hurt, I'd be out helping Tammy rescue vamps right now."

Something tight in my chest loosened. "She is alive, then. I thought I'd dreamed it."

He blinked at me. "Yeah, she's alive. So is Wren."

"How?" I asked.

He grinned at me. "A vampire known as the Traveler seems able to inhabit bodies of other vamps. Says he's a member of their council and he's here to help. Says you enlisted his aid." Larry was watching me very closely, the painkillers sliding away from his eyes as he tried to will me to tell the truth.

"That's essentially it," I said.

"He took over the body of the vamp attacking Tammy and

Wren. He saved them. She shoved her arm into the vamp's mouth, and it's broken, but it'll heal.''

''What about Wren?''

''Okay, but he's pretty broken up over Tucker.''

''She didn't make it,'' I said.

He shook his head. ''She was torn up, nearly yanked in half. All that was holding her together was the Haz-Mat suit.''

''So you didn't have to stake her,'' I said.

''The vamps did the job themselves,'' he said. ''They got Tucker's body up but not the vamps you did in. They're still down there.''

I looked at him. ''Let me guess, it caved in—didn't it?''

''Not five minutes after they pulled Tucker's body out, and laid you on the grass, the whole thing went. The vamp body that the Traveler was using started to burn. I've never seen one of them burn before. It was impressive and scary. The rubble covered the vamp. They couldn't dig him out until dark because that would have exposed him to sunlight again. He dug his own way out while they were still getting started.''

''He attack anyone?'' I asked.

Larry shook his head. ''He seemed pretty calm.''

''You were there?''

''Yep.''

I let it go. No sense worrying over what might have happened if the vamp had clawed his way to freedom pissed. I also found it very interesting that the Traveler couldn't stand the sunlight, and Warrick could. Surviving sunlight, even dim sunlight, was the rarest of talents among the walking dead. Or maybe Warrick was right. Maybe it was God's grace. Who was I to know?

''Is it my imagination or are you just moving better, with less pain?'' I asked.

''It's been another twenty-four hours. I'm starting to heal.''

''Excuse me?'' I said.

''You've been out for over a day. It's late Sunday afternoon.''

''Shit,'' I said. Had Jean-Claude met with the council without me? Had the ''dinner,'' whatever it was, already happened? ''Shit,'' I said again.

Still frowning, he said, ''I've got a message from the Traveler for you. Tell me why you suddenly look so scared and I'll give it to you.''

"Just give it to me, Larry, please."

Still frowning, he said, "The dinner is postponed until you feel well enough to attend."

I settled back against the pillows and couldn't keep the relief off my face, my body.

"What the hell is going on, Anita?"

Maybe it was the concussion. Maybe it was the fact that I didn't like to lie to Larry face to face. Whatever it was, I told him truth. I told him all of it. I told him about Richard and the marks. He knew about that, but not what I'd discovered recently. I left out a few things, but not much. When I was done, he sat back in the chair looking stunned.

"Well, say something."

He shook his head. "Sweet Mary Mother of God, I don't know where to start. Jean-Claude had a press conference last night with the Traveler at his side. They talked about vampire and human unity in the face of this awful event."

"Whose body did the Traveler use?" I asked.

Larry shivered. "That is one of the creepiest vamp powers I have ever seen. He used some vamp from Malcolm's Church. Malcolm was at the press conference, too. The Traveler used his powers to help rescue the other vamps, including Malcolm."

"Who acted as intepreter while the sun was up?" I asked.

"Balthasar, his human servant."

"Balthasar as a public servant, that is creepy," I said.

Larry frowned. "He told me he had a thing for men with red hair. Was he kidding?"

I laughed, and it made my head hurt. I was suddenly very aware of a growing headache, as if it had been there all the time, just masked by drugs. Modern chemistry, there is no substitute.

"Probably not, but don't worry. You're not on the menu."

"Who is?" Larry asked.

"I don't know yet. Has Dolph found out who's behind the bombings and stuff?"

"Yes." He said that one word like it was enough.

"Tell me or I will get out of this bed and hurt you."

"It was Humans First. The police raided their headquarters earlier today, got most of the leaders."

"That is wonderful." I frowned, which hurt, then closed my

eyes and said, ''How did Humans First know where all the monsters were? They hit private homes, secret daytime lairs. They shouldn't have known where everyone was.''

I heard the door open a moment before Dolph's voice said, ''The vampires had a traitor in their midst.''

''Hey, Dolph.''

''Hey, yourself. Good to see you awake.''

''Good to be awake,'' I said. ''What traitor?''

''Remember Vicki Pierce—and her little scene at Burnt Offerings?''

''I remember.''

''She had a boyfriend that was with Humans First. She gave him up when we questioned her a second time.''

''Why'd you bring her in?''

''Seems she got paid for her little acting assignment. We threatened to charge her with assault and attempted murder. She folded like a cheap card table.''

''What does little Miss Blue Eyes have to do with a vampire traitor?''

''She's been dating Harry, the bartender and part owner of Burnt Offerings.''

I was confused. ''Then why stage the scene at his business? Why give himself grief?''

''Her human boyfriend wanted to pay her to do it. She didn't want him to know she was seeing Harry. Harry went along with it because he thought it would look funny if his place was the only vamp-owned business not hit by the fanatics. ''

''So Harry knew what she was using the information for?'' I said. I was finding it hard to believe that any vamp would do it, let alone one as old as Harry.

''He knew. He took his cut of the money,'' Dolph said.

''Why?''

''When we find him, we'll ask.''

''Let me guess. He's vanished.''

Dolph nodded. ''Don't tell your boyfriend, Anita.''

''The vampires may be your only hope of catching Harry now.''

''But will they turn him over to us or kill him?''

I looked away, not meeting his eyes. ''They're going to be pretty pissed.''

"I can't blame them for that, but I want him alive, Anita. I need him alive."

"Why?"

"We didn't get every member of Humans First. I don't want them out there with some new nasty surprise waiting."

"You have Vicki. Won't she tell you?"

"She asked for a lawyer, finally, and now she's suddenly developed amnesia."

"Damn."

"We need him to tell us if there's one last big nasty coming our way."

"But you can't find him," I said.

"That's right."

"You don't want me to tell Jean-Claude."

"Give us twenty-four hours to locate Harry. If we fail, then you can put out a vampire all-points. Before they kill him, try to get information from him."

"You say that like I'll be there when he dies," I said.

Dolph just looked at me.

I met his eyes this time. "I don't kill for Jean-Claude, Dolph, no matter what the street says."

"I wish I believed that, Anita. You don't know how much I wished I believed that."

I lay back against the pillows. "Believe what you like, Dolph. You will anyway."

He walked out then without another word, as if what he wanted to say was too painful, too final. Dolph kept pushing against us, against me. I was beginning to worry that he was going to keep pushing until he pushed us apart. We'd be working together but we wouldn't be friends. The headache was getting worse, and it wasn't just the drugs wearing off.

48

I WAS GIVEN a clean bill of health. The doctors were amazed at my recuperative powers. If only they knew. Pete McKinnon called late in the day. He'd found that there were fires similar to those set by our firebug in New Orleans and San Francisco. It took a moment for me to remember why those particular cities were important. When I remembered, I asked, "How about Boston?"

"No, no fires in Boston. Why?"

I don't think he believed me when I said, "nothing," but unlike Dolph, he let it go. I wasn't ready to point the finger at the Vampire Council. Just because the mysterious fires happened in cities they'd been visiting didn't mean it had to be them. There'd been no fires in Boston. Just because there were now mysterious fires in St. Louis, and the council was here, didn't prove anything. Yeah, and the Easter Bunny brings me goodies every year.

I told Jean-Claude about my suspicions. "But why would the council wish to burn empty buildings, *ma petite*? If one of them could call fire to their hands, they would not waste it on empty real estate. Not unless the real estate being burned gained them something."

"You mean a financial motive?" I said.

He shrugged. "Perhaps, though a personal motive would suit them better."

"I can't find out much more information without giving the council up to the authorities as suspects," I said.

He seemed to think about that for a second or two. "Perhaps you could wait upon committing absolute suicide for us until after we have survived this evening."

"Sure," I said.

True darkness found me in a short form-fitting black velvet dress with a V-neck and no sleeves. The waist of the dress was open lace. My skin showed pale and enticing through it. Black thigh-high hose that actually came up a bit higher than mid-thigh, like all the way up until the black lace stretch top brushed against the black satin panties with their lace edgings. The hose were a size too large. Jean-Claude had purchased them, and done it deliberately. I'd tried thigh-highs before and had to agree that the longer length was more flattering for my shorter legs. It sort of framed the right area. If we'd been planning extracurricular activities, I'd have loved to see his face when I was standing in nothing but the stockings. As it was, it was just frustrating, and a little scary.

I'd vetoed the high velvet heels he'd picked out. Instead I used my own black pumps. Not as spiffy. Maybe not even more comfortable, but the heels were low enough that I could run in them, or carry fainting wereleopards if the need arose.

"You are perfection, *ma petite*, except for the shoes."

"Forget it," I said. "You're lucky to have gotten me in the hose. The thought that I'm dressing just in case the rest of the party sees my underwear is just creepy."

"You talked to the Traveler of price and responsibility. Well, tonight we pay the price for your wereleopards. Are you regretting it now?"

Gregory was still trussed up in my bedroom, pale and fragile-looking. Vivian was tucked in a guest room speaking in monosyllables.

"No, no I don't regret it."

"Then let us gather the rest of our party and be on our way." But he didn't move. He stayed lying on his stomach on the white couch, head resting on his folded hands. If it had been anyone else, I'd have said they were sprawled on the couch, but Jean-Claude did not sprawl. He posed, he lounged, but he did not sprawl. He lay full length, his long body stretched out, only the tips of his black boots over the edge of the couch.

He was wearing an outfit I'd seen before, but repetition didn't make it less lovely. I loved his clothes; loved watching him dress, and undress.

"What are you thinking?" I asked.

"I wish we were staying home tonight. I want to undress you one piece of clothing at a time, enjoying your body between every unveiling."

Just the suggestion made my body tight. "Me, too," I said, and knelt on the floor in front of him. I folded the short skirt under so it wouldn't wrinkle or ride up. He didn't teach me that, my Grandma Blake did, over a lifetime of Sunday church services where what I looked like seemed more important than the sermon.

I laid my chin on the couch near his face. My hair spilling around me, brushing the sides of his folded hands, curling against his face.

"Do your undies look as nice as mine?" I asked.

"Brushed silk," he said softly.

I had a sensory memory so strong it made me shiver. The feel of him through the thick silk, the almost living texture that the brushed fabric had over the hardness of his body. I had to close my eyes to keep from letting him see it in my face. The image was so vivid it made me clench my hands.

I felt him move a second before he kissed my forehead. He spoke with his lips still touching my skin. "Your thoughts betray you, *ma petite*."

I raised my face upward, sliding his lips down my face. He was utterly passive as I moved against him, until our lips met. Then his mouth pressed against mine, lips and tongue working. Neither of us used our hands, only our mouths touching. Our faces pressed together.

"Can I cut in?" The familiar voice was so heavy with anger that it made me draw back from Jean-Claude.

Richard stood at the end of the couch staring down at us. I hadn't heard him come up. Had Jean-Claude? I was betting he had. Somehow I never thought that even in the throes of passion Jean-Claude would ever let anyone sneak up on him. Or maybe I just didn't think I was that distracting. Poor self-esteem, who me?

I sat back on my heels and looked up at Richard. He was dressed in a black tux, complete with tails. His long hair slicked back into a ponytail so tight it gave the illusion of short hair. You always knew Richard was handsome but it was only when you got rid of the hair that you realized how perfect his face

was. The high-sculpted cheekbones, the full mouth, the dimple.
He stared down at me with that handsome, familiar face, and
he looked arrogant. He knew the effect he had on me, and
wanted to turn the knife a little more.

Jean-Claude sat up on the couch, his mouth smeared with my
lipstick. The red so vivid against his pale skin it looked like the
surprised scarlet of blood. He ran his tongue around the outside
of his mouth, then ran his finger across his upper lip, slowly,
until it came away red. He put the finger in his mouth and
sucked the lipstick off of it, very slowly, very deliberately. His
eyes were on me, but the show was for Richard.

I was both grateful for it, and angry about it. He knew Richard
was trying to hurt me, so he was hurting Richard. But he was
also baiting him, rubbing the proverbial salt in the wound.

The look on Richard's face was so raw I had to look away.
"That's enough, Jean-Claude," I said, "that's enough."

Jean-Claude looked amused. "As you like, *ma petite.*"

Richard looked down at me again. I met his eyes. Maybe
there was something in my face that was too raw to look at,
too. He turned abruptly and left the room.

"Go freshen your tasty lipstick, then we must leave." Jean-
Claude's voice held regret, the way it sometimes held joy, or
sex.

I took his hand, raising it gently to my mouth. "Are you still
frightened of them, even after all the good publicity? Surely if
they were planning to kill us, they wouldn't have appeared on
camera with you." I touched his leg, running my fingers over
the cloth, feeling his thigh underneath. "The Traveler shook
hands with the mayor of St. Louis, for heaven's sake."

He touched my face, cradling my cheek in his hand. "The
council has never before tried to be, what you would call, main-
stream. It is their first foray into a very new arena. But they
have been the stuff of nightmares for thousands of years, *ma
petite.* One day of human politics does not make them into
something else."

"But . . ."

He touched fingers to my lips. "It is a good sign, *ma petite.*
That I will agree to, but you do not know them as I do. You
have not seen them at their worst."

My mind flashed on Rafael's raw, bloody body; Sylvie sagging in the chains, voice small and broken; the sight of Fernando using Vivian. "I've seen them do some pretty awful things since they hit town," I said. "You set up the rules, Jean-Claude. They can't maim us, or rape us, or kill us. What's left?"

He kissed me lightly on the lips, and stood, offering me his hand. I took it, let him pull me to my feet. He was wearing his amused mask, the one that once upon a time I'd thought was his normal face. Now I knew it meant he was hiding things. He looked like that a lot when he was scared and didn't want people to know.

"You're scaring me," I said softly.

He smiled. "No, *ma petite*, they will do that for me, for us all." With that comforting shot, he went off to round up the others. I went for my purse and the tasty lipstick. The council had laid down some conditions of their own. No weapons tonight. Which was why I was dressed like I was; one glance was enough to know I wasn't carrying anything. Jean-Claude thought this would keep them from having an excuse to pat me down. When I asked what the big deal was, all he would say was, "You don't want to give them a reason to touch you, *ma petite*. Trust me on this."

I did trust him. I didn't want any of the council touching me, ever. It was going to be a long night.

49

WHAT HAD ONCE been Jean-Claude's living room and Nikolaos's throne room before that, had been turned into a banquet
room. They'd found a table that was over ten feet long. What
you could see of the table was heavy clawed feet with lions'
mouths carved in bold relief. A tablecloth so thick with gold
embroidery that it shimmered under the lights covered the table.
If they had meant for us to actually eat off it, I'd have been
worried we'd trash it, but there was no food. There were no
chairs. There were no plates. There were white linen napkins
with gold rings, crystal wineglasses, and one of those industrial-
size warmers with blue gas flames under its gleaming surface.
There was a man hanging by his wrists, feet dangling helplessly
over the gleaming table. He was hanging directly over the empty
warming pan. His name was Ernie. His muscular upper body
was bare. A gag cut across his face, trapping part of his long
ponytail. His hair was shaved to nothing on either side of his
face. The council hadn't done it as torture. He'd done it to
himself. He was one of Jean-Claude's newest hangers-on, a human who wanted to be a vampire and was serving his appren-
ticeship acting as a sort of maid and errand boy. Now,
apparently, he was the appetizer.

　　Richard, Jean-Claude, and I stood with Jamil, Damian, Jason,
and surprisingly, Rafael, at our backs. The Rat King had insisted
on accompanying us. I hadn't argued too hard. We were allowed
one person apiece plus Jason. Yvette had requested him especially. By taking him, we gained a werewolf, but his blue eyes
were wide and his breathing a little too quick. Yvette was Jason's idea of hell, and hell had sent out an invitation.

　　Ernie stared at us all, kicking his feet and struggling, trying to talk through the gag. I think he was trying to say, "Get me down," but I couldn't swear to it.

"What is the meaning of this?" Jean-Claude said. His voice filled the huge room, hissing and tumbling until the shadows gave his words back in harsh, sibilant echoes.

Padma stepped out of the far hallway. He was dressed in a suit that glittered as gold as the tablecloth. He was even wearing a golden turban with peacock feathers and a sapphire bigger than my thumb. He looked like someone had called down to central casting for a maharaja.

"You have offered us no hospitality at all, Jean-Claude. Malcolm and his people have offered us refreshment. But you, the Master of the City, have offered us nothing." He motioned upward at Ernie. "This one walked in without our permission. He said he was yours."

Jean-Claude walked until he stood by the table and could look up into Ernie's face. "You came home two days early from your family visit. The next time, if there is a next time, call first."

Ernie stared at him, eyes wide, making small *hmmm* sounds through the gag. He kicked his legs enough that he started to swing.

"Struggling will just make your shoulders hurt more," Jean-Claude said. "Be at peace." As he said it, Ernie slowly grew limp. Jean-Claude had captured him with his eyes and was lulling him to, if not sleep, peace. The tension drained from him, and he stared at Jean-Claude, brown eyes empty, waiting. At least he wasn't scared anymore.

Gideon and Thomas came up to stand on either side of Padma. Thomas was in full uniform, boots polished like a black mirror. The helmet was white with a long tassel on top that was probably horsehair. The coat was red, the buttons brass, white gloves, even a sword.

Gideon was pretty close to naked. A white thong was all he wore on his body. It barely covered him. A heavy gold collar encrusted with small diamonds and huge emeralds covered almost his entire neck. His carefully combed golden hair fanned over it. A chain led from the collar to Thomas's hands.

Padma put his hand out, and Thomas gave the chain to him.

Neither Thomas nor Gideon exchanged so much as a glance. They'd seen the show before.

The only thing that kept me from making some scathing remark was that I'd pretty much given my word to let Jean-Claude do the talking tonight. He thought I might say something to piss someone off. Who, me?

Jean-Claude walked around the table. Richard and I fell two steps back, mirroring Padma and his pets. The symbolism wasn't lost on anyone. Thing was, Richard and I were pretending. I didn't think the others were.

"I suppose you mean to slit his throat into the warmer, then serve his blood to all?" Jean-Claude said.

Padma smiled and gave a gracious nod of his head.

Jean-Claude laughed that wonderfully touchable laugh of his. "If you really meant to do that, Master of Beasts, you'd have hung him by his ankles."

Richard and I did exchange glances behind his back. I turned and looked at Ernie's peacefully hanging figure. How had Jean-Claude known you'd have to hang him by his ankles? Ask a silly question.

"Are you saying we are bluffing?" Padma asked.

"No," Jean-Claude said, "merely grandstanding."

Padma smiled, and it almost reached his eyes. "You always did play the game well."

Jean-Claude gave a small bow, never taking his eyes from the other vampire. "I am honored that you think well of me, Master of Beasts."

Padma gave a sharp laugh. "A honeyed tongue, Master of the City." The humor died abruptly, gone, poof. His face was suddenly harsh, empty, except for anger. "But the point remains you have been a poor host. I have fed through my servants." He slid a dark hand caressingly down Gideon's bare shoulder. The weretiger never reacted. It was as if Padma were not there. Or maybe as if he, Gideon, were not there.

"But there are others who are not so blessed as I. They hunger, Jean-Claude. They stand in your territory as your guests and know hunger."

"The Traveler was feeding them," Jean-Claude said. "I thought he was feeding you as well."

"I do not need his cast-off energy," Padma said. "He was

sustaining the others until that one ''—he pointed at me with his free hand—''told him to stop.''

I started to say something, almost asked permission, and thought, screw it. ''Asked him to stop,'' I said. ''No one tells the Traveler what to do.'' There, that was so diplomatic, my teeth hurt.

His laughter entered the room ahead of him. The Traveler's new body was young, male, handsome, and so newly dead he still had a good tan. Balthasar came at his side, hands sliding over the other man's body possessively. A new toy to explore. I'd been told that Malcolm was loaning the Traveler a church member. I wondered if Malcolm really knew what the Traveler and Balthasar were doing with the body.

I would have said they were both wearing togas, but that wasn't quite it. The Traveler wore a rich purple cloth pinned at one shoulder with a ruby-and-gold brooch. His left shoulder was bare, showing the smooth tanned skin to good advantage. The garment was gathered at the waist with two woven red cords. It fell nearly to his ankles, giving glimpses of sandals tied around his ankles.

Balthasar wore red with an amethyst-and-silver brooch at one shoulder. His bare shoulder showed just enough chest to prove he was muscular, as if there'd been any doubt. The red garment was bound at the waist with purple cords.

''You guys look like the Bobbsey Twins,'' I said.

Jean-Claude cleared his throat.

I stopped talking, but if everyone had such nifty clothes, I wasn't sure I could stop myself from making remarks. I mean, it was just too easy.

The Traveler threw his head back and laughed. It was a joyous laugh with an edge underneath like the hissing of snakes. He turned brown eyes to me, but down in the depths it was him. I'd have known him no matter whose eyes he was looking out of.

Balthasar was actually shorter than the new body by an inch or two. He stood close enough for the Traveler to take him under his arm, like a tall man will walk with a woman, cradled against his body, protected.

''I saved your humans today, Anita. I saved many vampires. Is that not enough for you?''

"Jean-Claude?" I made his name a question.

He let his breath out in a long sigh. "It was pointless to make you promise. Be yourself, *ma petite*, but try not to be too insulting." He stepped back so that we were all even with each other. Maybe he hadn't liked the symbolism either.

"I'm thrilled that you saved my friends today," I said. "I'm ecstatic that you saved all the trapped vampires. But you got a lot of good press out of it without any risk to yourself. I thought you agreed that you guys needed to modernize a little, come into the twentieth century."

"But I do agree, Anita, I do agree." The Traveler rubbed his cheek against Balthasar's face, staring at me hard enough that I was glad he wasn't heterosexual.

"Then what is this medieval shit?" I jabbed a thumb backwards at Ernie.

His eyes flicked to the man, then back to me. "I would have let it go, but the others voted and it is true that Jean-Claude has been a lax host."

Jean-Claude touched my arm. "If you had come at my invitation or even requested permission to enter my territory, I would have been more than happy to grant you hunting rights. Though you will find one of the other benefits to legality is an amazing number of willing victims. People will even pay you to quench your thirst on their bodies."

"It is an old law among us," The Traveler said, "not to feed in another's lands without their permission. I sustained the others, but then your human servant showed me that my powers were having serious side effects on your local population." He stepped away from Balthasar, coming within touching distance of Jean-Claude.

"But none of your vampires were affected. I could not steal their energy, or give them extra energy. You prevented that. That has surprised me more than anything else you have done, Jean-Claude. It smacks of a power that I would never have credited you with, not now, not a thousand years from now." He paced to stand in front of Richard. And the new body was still taller, six foot four at least.

He stood so close that the purple cloth brushed the length of Richard's body. He moved around him so closely that the cloth never stopped touching, sliding over the tailored tux like a cloth

hand. "Padma has not gained such power from his joining."
He ended standing between Jean-Claude and Richard. He raised
a hand to stroke Richard's face, and Richard caught his wrist.

"That's enough," Richard said.

The Traveler drew his wrist slowly downward so that his hand
brushed Richard's. He turned to Balthsar with a smile. "What
do you think?"

"I think Jean-Claude is a lucky man," Balthsar said.

A red flush crept up Richard's face, his hands curled into
fists. He was placed in the position usually reserved for women.
If you deny that you're sleeping with someone, they won't believe you. The harder you deny it, the surer everyone is that
you're guilty.

Richard was smarter than I was. He didn't try to deny it. He
just turned and looked at the Traveler. He stared him nearly eye
to eye and said, "Get away from me."

All the bad guys laughed. None of us did. Us included Gideon
and Thomas, strangely enough. What were they doing with
Padma? What series of events had trapped them with him? If
we all survived, maybe I'd get a chance to ask them, but it was
doubtful. If we killed Padma, they would probably die, too. If
Padma killed us, well, there you go.

The Traveler walked over to me in a cloud of purple cloth.
"Which brings us to you, Anita." His new body towered over
me, over a foot taller, but hey, you get used to it.

"What?" I said, staring up at him.

He laughed again. He was so damn happy. I realized what it
was—afterglow. He and Balthsar had been polishing the family
jewels.

I stared up into that smiling face and said, "Is this new body
double-jointed or something, or does Balthsar just like a change
of menu?"

The laughter faded from his eyes, his face, like the sun sinking below the horizon. What was left was cold and distant and
nothing you could talk to.

Maybe I did talk too much.

Jean-Claude touched my shoulders and moved me back. He
started to move in front of me, but I stopped him. "I pissed him
off. Don't protect me from him."

Jean-Claude let me stay in front, but at some unseen signal

the rest of our entourage moved up, fanning out behind us.

Yvette and Warrick came out of the hallway with Liv. "You all look good enough to eat." She laughed at her own joke. She was dressed in a simple white formal. Her bare shoulders were whiter than the cloth. As soon as I saw her, I knew she hadn't fed. Sleeves that were not attached to the dress covered her from armpit to wrist. The fitted bodice flared into a full white skirt with layers that were mirrored in the layers of the strange un-attached sleeves. Her white-blond hair fell in braided loops and whorls around her face. No period costume for Yvette, only the cutting edge of fashion would do. Her makeup was just a little dark against the paper whiteness of her skin, but it was hard to get that understated look when you were so terribly drained.

Warrick wore a white suit with one of those round collars so there was no place to put a tie. It was a lovely suit that matched Yvette's dress so well, they looked like the top of a fashion wedding cake.

Yvette wore the dress like it had been made just for her. Warrick looked chokingly uncomfortable.

Liv glared at all of us impartially. She was dressed in a blue formal that was meant for a woman with softer edges and less muscle. It had been cut down or up for her, and she wore it badly.

This was the first time I'd seen Liv since I learned that she'd helped torture Sylvie. I expected to regret not having killed her when I had the chance. But there was an uncertainty in her eyes, an unease in her body, that said, maybe, she'd seen another side of the council since then. She was afraid. I was glad.

"You look like you're wearing hand-me-downs, Liv," I said. "Like someone's poor relative."

"Has the Traveler given you to Yvette as her handmaiden?" Jean-Claude asked. "Has he given you away so quickly?"

"Yvette merely helped me dress," she said head high, but her hands were trying to smooth the dress into place. Nothing helped.

"You had much more attractive outfits in your own closet," Jean-Claude said.

"But no dresses," Yvette said. "For a formal occasion you must have dresses for the women." She smiled sweetly.

It made me regret wearing a dress. "I know what you did to

Sylvie, Liv. I was regretting not blowing your head off when I did your knees. But you know what, Liv, a few years with the council and you may be regretting it too.''

''I regret nothing,'' she said. But there was a tightness around the eyes, a flicker through those lovely eyes. Something had spooked her good and solid. Part of me wanted to know what had been done to her, but it was enough just to see how scared she was.

''I'm glad you're enjoying yourself, Liv,'' I said.

Asher walked out in the middle of the scene. His hair had been pulled back in a tight braid. His hair was still nearly the color of the metallic thread in the tablecloth, an unearthly color even if he'd been human. The hair pulled back left the scars on his face naked. It was hard not to look at them, hard not to stare. The rest of the outfit didn't make it any easier.

His naked upper body was a wonderment of contrasts. It was like his face, half angelic beauty, half melted nightmare. His pants were black leather with a line of bare flesh showing from hip to mid-calf, where boots covered the rest. The flesh glimpsed on the right side of his thigh was scarred. The scars seemed to stop about mid-thigh. It left the big question. Had his torturers made him a eunuch or left him whole? It was like a car crash. You wanted to know, and you didn't.

''Jean-Claude, Anita, so good of you to join us.'' He made the polite words a mockery, filling them with a hissing warmth of threat.

''Your presence is the same pleasure it has always been,'' Jean-Claude said. Those words were blank, utterly neutral, compliment or snide putdown. It was the listener's choice.

Asher glided towards us, a smile curling his perfect lips. Again both sides of his mouth worked. The muscles were still whole underneath all the scars. He came to stand directly in front of me. He was about two steps closer than was comfortable, but I didn't back up or complain. I just met his smile with one of my own. Neither smile touched our eyes.

''Do you like my outfit, Anita?''

''A little aggressive, don't you think?''

He traced a fingertip down the lace at my waist. The fingertip slid inside the open lace, touching my bare skin. It brought a small gasp from my throat.

"You can touch me, anywhere you like," he said.

I moved his hand. "I can't return the offer, sorry."

"I think you can," the Traveler said.

I looked at him. "No," I said. "I can't."

"Jean-Claude was very clear on your rules," the Traveler said. "Asher needs to feed. It is within the rules for him to feed off of you, Anita. He would prefer to sink something else into you, but he will have to be content with fangs."

I shook my head. "I don't think so."

"*Ma petite,*" Jean-Claude said softly.

I didn't like the way he said my name. I turned, and one look was enough. "You have got to be kidding me."

He stepped close, taking me to one side. "The guidelines you gave me said nothing against sharing blood."

I stared up at him. "Do you really want him to feed off of me?"

He shook his head. "It is not a matter of want, *ma petite.* But if they cannot torture us or rape us, we leave them little else."

"If you wish to trade back one of my wereleopards," Padma said, "Vivian, perhaps, I would grant you safe passage for the return of my so sweet Vivian."

Fernando entered the room as if on cue. He was bruised but walking. More's the pity. He was wearing a jeweled vest and something like harem pants. The Arabian Nights maybe, instead of a maharaja.

"Did Fernando tell you he raped her?"

"I know what my son has done."

"That doesn't spoil her for you?" I asked.

Padma looked at me. "What I do with her once she is mine again is no concern of yours, human."

"No way," I said.

"Then you have no choice. You must feed one of us. If there is one among us who would please you more, someone . . . less hideous, we could arrange something. Perhaps I could take you myself. Among our own people only Yvette finds Asher attractive, but then her tastes have always run to the strange and grotesque."

Asher's face betrayed nothing, but I knew he'd heard. He was

meant to hear. He'd spent the last two centuries being treated
like a circus freak. No wonder he was cranky.

"I'd let Asher sink the whole thing into me before I'd let you
touch me."

Surprise showed for a heartbeat on Padma's face, then arrogance. But he hadn't liked the insult. Goody. "Perhaps before
the night is over, Anita, you will get your wish."

Not comforting, but Asher was having trouble looking at me,
as if he were afraid. Not of me, exactly, but that this was some
elaborate game to hurt him. He had that casual tension that
victims get when they are slapped too often for too many different things.

Jean-Claude whispered, "Thank you, *ma petite*." I think he
was relieved. I think he'd thought I might go down in flames
rather than submit. Before Padma had made his little joke, I
would have put up more of a fight. I was going to do this. If I
drew the line here and refused, that meant we fought them. We
would lose. If donating a little blood would keep us all alive
come morning, I could spare it.

A leopard screamed. It raised the hairs on my arms. Two
leopards padded into the room, jeweled collars sparkling around
their necks. The black one, Elizabeth I assumed, snarled at me
as they went past. The leopards were just leopard-size, not as
tall as a Great Dane but longer. They paced like velvet over
muscle, their energy and anger filling the room, prickling along
the other shapeshifters like a drug. The leopards sprawled at
Padma's feet.

I felt Richard's power swell. It flowed out of him in a soothing wash, willing the leopards quiet, calling them back to human
form.

Padma said, "No, no, they are mine. I will keep them in
whatever form I choose, however long I choose."

"They will begin to lose human characteristics," Richard
said. "Elizabeth is a nurse. She cannot do her job if she has
fangs or eyes that do not change back."

"She has no other job than to serve me," Padma said.

Richard took a step forward. Jean-Claude touched his shoulder. "He is baiting us, *mon ami*."

Richard shook his hand off, but nodded. "I don't think the

Master of Beasts could stop me if I forced them back to human form.''

"Is that a challenge?" Padma asked.

"The wereleopards don't belong to you, Richard," I said.

"These two don't belong to anybody," he said.

"They can be mine if they want to be," I said.

"No," Padma said. "No, I will give up nothing else. No one else to you." He stepped back against the wall, dragging Gideon with him by the jeweled collar. Thomas followed almost as closely. "Asher, take her."

Asher tried to grab my arm, but I backed up. "Hold your horses. Hasn't anyone told you anticipation adds to the experience?"

"I have been anticipating this for over two hundred years, *ma cherie*. If anticipation adds, then it will be wondrous indeed."

I stepped away from his eager eyes and went to Jean-Claude. "Any advice?"

"He will try to make it rape, *ma petite*." He stopped me before I could say anything. "Not actual rape, but the effect is surprisingly similar. Make it a seduction, if you can. Turn necessity into a pleasure. It will be the last thing he expects, and it will unnerve him."

"How unnerve?" I asked.

"That will depend, I think, upon how strong your nerve is."

I glanced back at Asher. The eagerness on his face was frightening. I was sorry he'd been picked on for centuries, but it wasn't my fault. "I don't think it's that good."

Richard had been listening. He came close enough to whisper, "You're donating blood to one vampire, what's one more?"

"*Ma petite* and I do not have to share blood to share power," Jean-Claude said.

Richard frowned at him, then at me. "Still holding back? Don't you know how to give yourself completely to anyone?"

Jean-Claude's face was very neutral, blank and beautiful. I looked from his impassive face to Richard's angry one, and shook my head. "If I could find someone else to fill our third spot, I would, Richard. But we're stuck with each other, so stop being such an ass.'' I pushed past him hard enough for him to stumble, and it was all I could do not to slap him as I went by. Being nasty in private was one thing. Doing it in front of the bad guys was against the rules.

50

ASHER DRAGGED ME to a corner, and the others gathered around on the floor like story time in elementary school. Or maybe show-and-tell was a better analogy. He jerked me roughly against him, one hand in my hair controlling my head. He kissed me roughly enough to bruise unless I opened my mouth. I did better than that. I closed my eyes and French kissed him, running my tongue between his fangs. I'd perfected the art of French kissing a vampire without bleeding, and apparently I was good at it because Asher drew back first. There was a look of astonishment, total and complete. He couldn't have looked more surprised if I'd slapped him. No, less surprised. He expected the slap.

Jean-Claude was right. If I could just outmaneuver Asher, be bolder than he was, he might never sink fang into me. It was worth a try. I didn't even let Jean-Claude feed off of me. I wasn't sure it was the lesser evil, but a girl's got to draw the line somewhere.

Asher put his face so near mine, our noses almost touched. "Look at me, girl, look at me. You don't want to touch this."

The startling pale blue of his eyes, almost a white-blue, framed by golden eyelashes, was lovely. I concentrated on the eyes. "Undo your hair," I said.

He pushed me away from him, hard enough that I stumbled. I was pissing him off, stealing his revenge. Can't rape the willing.

I went to him, stalking around him, half wishing for the heels Jean-Claude had wanted me to wear. Asher's back was pure and untouched. Only a few dribbling scars where the holy water had trailed down his side. I ran my hands up that smooth skin, and he jumped as if I'd bit him.

He whirled, grabbing my arms, holding me away from him. He searched my face almost frantically. Whatever he saw, it didn't please him. He moved his hands upward until he held my wrists, then placed one of my hands on the scarred side of his chest. "It's easy to close your eyes and pretend. Easy to touch that which is not spoiled." He pressed my hand against the rough ridges that had been his chest. "This is the reality. This is what I live with every night, what I will live with for all eternity, what he did to me."

I stepped in close, pressing my upper arm against the scars, as well as my hands. The skin was rough, ridged, like frozen, fleshy water. I looked up into his face from inches away, and said, "Jean-Claude did not do this to you. Men who are long dead did this to you." I rose up on tiptoe and kissed his scarred cheek.

He closed his eyes, and a single tear slid from his eye to trail down that rough cheek. I kissed the tear away, and when he opened his eyes, they were suddenly startlingly close. In his eyes I saw a fear, loneliness, a need so overwhelming that it had eaten his heart as surely as the holy water had eaten his skin.

I wanted to take away the hurt I saw in his eyes. I wanted to hold him in my arms until the pain eased. I realized in that moment that it wasn't me. It was Jean-Claude. He wanted to heal Asher's pain. He wanted to take away that awful emptiness. I looked at Asher through a film of emotions that I'd never had for him, a patina of nostalgia for better nights, of love and joy and warm bodies in the cold darkness.

I kissed my way down his chin, careful to touch only the scars, ignoring the perfect skin as I'd ignored the wounded skin earlier. Strangely, his neck was whole, untouched. I kissed his collar bone and its white ridge of scars. His hands eased but didn't release me. I pulled out of his grip as I moved down his body, one soft kiss at a time.

I ran my tongue across his belly where it vanished into his pants. He shuddered. I moved to the open skin on his hip and worked down. When the scars ended at mid-thigh, so did I. I stood, and he watched me, watched me almost afraid of what I would do next.

I had to stand on tiptoe to reach behind him to the braid of his hair. It would have been easier from behind, but he'd have taken it as a rejection. I couldn't turn away from the scars, not even if that wasn't what I was doing at all. I loosened the braid. I separated the strands of hair, then had to lean my body against his just to steady myself while I combed my fingers through the golden strands. There is something very personal to touching a person's hair in the right situation. I took my time, enjoying the feel of it, the extraordinary color, the thick richness of it between my fingers. When his hair fell in waves around his shoulders, I lowered myself flat-footed. My calves were cramped, too long on point.

I put into my eyes what I saw, that he was beautiful.

Asher kissed me on the forehead, a light touch. He held me against him for a moment, then stepped back. "I cannot capture you with my eyes. Without that or the throes of passion, it would only cause you pain. I can feed on anyone. What I saw in your face, no one else could give me." He looked out at Jean-Claude. They stared at each other for a long moment, then Asher stepped out of the circle, and I made my way back to Jean-Claude.

I sat down beside him, knees tucked under, skirt smoothed back. He hugged me and kissed me on the forehead as Asher had done. I wondered if he was trying to taste Asher's mouth on my skin. The thought didn't bother me. Maybe it should have, but I didn't ask him. I wasn't sure I wanted to know.

The Traveler came to his feet as if by magic, just suddenly standing. "I don't think we could be more astonished if Anita had conjured a dragon from thin air. She has tamed our Asher and paid no blood for it." He glided to the open floor space. "Yvette is not so easily sated." He smiled at her as she rose to her feet. "Are you, my dear?"

She ran her hands through Jason's hair as she glided past. He jumped as if she'd stung him, which amused the hell out of her. She was still laughing when she turned with a swoosh of white skirts and held her arms out to him. "Come to me, Jason."

He huddled in on himself, curling into a little ball of arms and elbows and knees. He just shook his head.

"You are my choice, my special one," Yvette said. "You are not strong enough to refuse me."

An awful thought occurred to me. I was willing to bet that

Jean-Claude hadn't covered rotting on people as a no-no. Jason might not recover from another embrace from the messily dead. I leaned into Jean-Claude and asked, "You did cover torture, no outright torture, right?"

"Of course," he said.

I stood. "You can feed on him, but you can't rot on him."

She turned cool eyes to me. "You have no say in this."

"Jean-Claude negotiated for no torture. Rotting on Jason while you feed is torture to him. You know that. It's why you want him."

"I want my bit of werewolf blood, and I want it exactly the way I like it best," she said.

Richard said, "You can feed off of me."

"You don't know what you're offering, Richard," I said.

"I know that Jason is mine to protect, and he can't endure this." He got to his feet, splendid in his new tux.

"Has Jason told you what happened to him in Branson?" I asked. Jason had been having a forced tryst with two female vamps when they began to rot. They turned into long-dead corpses while he was still lying naked with them. It was his worse nightmare, almost a phobia now. I'd witnessed the event, even had those dead hands on my body when I waded in to to rescue him. I couldn't blame him for being terrified.

"Jason told me," Richard said.

"Hearing about it isn't the same thing as being there, Richard."

Jason had hidden his face against his knees. He was saying something low. I had to kneel to hear it. He was saying, "I'm sorry, I'm sorry, I'm sorry," over and over and over. I touched his arm, and he screamed, eyes wide, mouth open in astonishment.

"It's okay, Jason. It's okay." Richard was right. Jason couldn't do this.

I nodded. "You're right, Richard."

"No," Padma said. "No, the Wolf King is mine. I will not share him."

"I will take nothing less than a shapeshifter," Yvette said.

Jamil stood.

Richard said, "No, it's my job to protect Jason, not yours, Jamil."

"It's my job to protect you, Ulfric."

Richard shook his head and started undoing the black bow tie. He undid the top few buttons on the pleated shirt, baring the strong, perfect line of his neck.

"No," Yvette said. She stamped her foot, hands on hips. "He is not afraid. I want someone who's afraid."

In my head I thought, he will be afraid. He'll be very afraid. Notice I wasn't jumping up and offering myself in Jason's place. I'd seen this particular show. I had no desire to star in it.

"And I have my own plans for the Ulfric," Padma said.

The Traveler tsked at them like naughty children. "It is a fair offer, Yvette. The Ulfric himself for one of his lesser wolves."

"It is not the potency of the blood I want. It is the terror."

"It is too generous an offer for someone who is not council," Padma said.

"Do they always squabble like this?" I asked.

"*Oui*," Jean-Claude said.

Near-eternal life, frightening power, and they were petty. How disappointing. How typical. I touched Jason's face, made him look at me. His breath was coming in short gasps. I touched his hands; his skin was cold.

"Jason, if she didn't rot on you, could you let her feed?"

He swallowed twice before he could talk. "I don't know."

A truthful answer. He was terrified. "I'll go with you."

He looked at me then, looked at me and not at the screaming in his head. "She won't like that."

"Fuck her. She can take it or leave it."

That got me the ghost of a smile. He gripped my hands where they lay on top of his. He nodded.

I looked at Jean-Claude still sitting by us. "You're not being much help."

"I too have seen the show, *ma petite*." He was echoing my thoughts so closely, I wondered whose thoughts were which. But what he was saying was frightening. He wouldn't offer himself to Yvette, not just to save Jason.

I stood up, drawing Jason to his feet. He clung to my hand like a kid on the first day of kindergarten afraid Mommy would leave him alone with the bullies.

"If you give your word of honor that you won't rot on him, you can feed off of him."

"No," Yvette said. "No, that spoils it all."

"It's your choice," I said. "You can have Richard, if Padma will let you, but he won't be afraid. You can rot on him though, but you won't get Jason's horror of you." I moved so she could see him clearly.

Jason flinched but stayed standing, but he wouldn't or couldn't meet her eyes. He stared at me. I think he was actually looking down my dress. But for once I didn't make him stop. Distraction was just what he needed. Knowing Jason, I wasn't surprised that a peek-a-boo show was what he chose.

Yvette licked her lips. Finally, she nodded.

I led Jason towards her. He was dressed for his own peek-a-boo show. He was wearing a pair of leather pants dyed a blue two shades darker than his eyes. The pants looked painted on, sliding seamlessly into boots dyed to match. He wore no shirt, only a vest that matched the pants, fastened with three leather thongs.

He stumbled as we entered the cleared space. Yvette glided towards him, and he hung back. Only my hand kept him from bolting. "Easy, Jason, easy."

He just kept shaking his head, straining against my hold on his wrist. He wasn't exactly struggling, but he wasn't cooperating either.

"It's too much to ask," Richard said. "He is my wolf, and I will not see him tormented."

I looked at Richard, proud, arrogant. "He's my wolf, too." I released Jason's wrist slowly and put a hand on either side of his face. "If this is too much to ask, say so, and we'll do something else."

He gripped my wrists, and I watched him collect himself. I watched his hard-won control fill his eyes, his face. "Don't leave me."

"I'm right here."

"No," Yvette said, "you cannot hold his hand while I feed."

I turned to her, Jason so close our bodies touched without hands. "Then it's over. You don't touch him."

"First you tame Asher. Now you seek to tame me. You have nothing I want, Anita."

"I have Jason."

She hissed at me, all that careful beauty breaking down and

showing the beast inside. She snatched at him around me, and he jerked back. She pawed at him like a cat, and I kept my body between them, moving us into the center of the circle. I felt Jason's back hit the wall, and I grabbed Yvette's arm.

"Feel his terror, Yvette. I can feel his heart pounding against my back. My holding his hand won't make him unafraid. Nothing I could do would make him not fear your touch."

Jason hid his face against my back, hands sliding around my waist. I patted his arm. His body was one throbbing beat as his heart, his blood, pumped through his body so hard I could feel it. His terror rode the air like a hot, invisible mist.

"Agreed," she said. She backed away to the center of the cleared floor. She held one pale hand out to us. "Come, Anita, bring our prize."

I slid in his arms until I was leading him by the hand again. His palms were sweating. I led him to stand with his back to her. He gripped my hands in both of his. His hands trembled. He stared at my face as if it were the only thing left in the world.

Yvette touched his back.

He whimpered. I drew him into me until our arms were touching, our faces only inches apart. I had no words of comfort. I could offer nothing but a hand to hold and something else to think about.

Yvette trailed her fingers around his shoulders until she came to the thongs that tied the vest. Her hands brushed the front of my body as she fumbled with the ties. I started to step back, and Jason's hands sang with tension. I stayed where I was, but my own pulse was beating in my throat. I was afraid of her, too, afraid of what she was.

She had to slide her hand around his waist to get the last tie, molding her body against his back. She licked his ear, a quick flick of her pale pink tongue.

He closed his eyes, bowing his head until our foreheads touched.

"You can do this," I said.

He nodded his head, eyes still closed, forehead still touching mine.

Yvette ran her hands up his back under the vest, then curved

them around to his naked chest, running her nails down his flesh
in a quick rush.

Jason gasped, and I realized in that instant that it wasn't just
fear. He had slept with her before he knew what she was. She
knew his body, knew how to bring him to passion as only a
lover can. She'd use that against him now.

Jason drew his face back from mine. He looked at me, and
he seemed lost.

She shoved the vest up around his shoulders and licked a
long wet line up his spine.

He turned his face from me, so I wouldn't see his eyes. "It's
all right if some of it feels good, Jason."

He turned back to me, and there were other things in his eyes
beside fear. I'd been more comfortable with the fear, but he was
the one hurting.

Yvette knelt and did something low on his back with her
mouth. His knees buckled suddenly, taking us both to the floor.
I ended up flat on my back with Jason on top of me. I had one
leg free, which was a help and a hindrance, since it put him
perfectly on top of me. I could tell his body was happy to be
there. I wasn't sure about the rest of him. He was making small
sounds low in his throat.

I scooted out from under him enough so that his groin wasn't
pressing mine and I could sit up to see what Yvette had done
to him. There were fangs marks low on his back near the spine.
The blood beaded on the blue leather like it had been Scotch-
garded.

His arms locked around my waist. "Don't leave me, please."
His cheek was pressed against my waist. The tension in his body
made my heart thud.

"I won't leave you, Jason." I stared at Yvette over his body.

She was kneeling with the white skirt pooled around her, as
if a wandering photographer would be coming by. She smiled,
and it reached her eyes, filling them with a dark, joyous light.
She was enjoying the hell out of herself.

"You've fed. It's over," I said.

"That wasn't a feeding, and you know it. I've tasted him, but
I haven't fed."

It had been worth a try. She was right. I knew she hadn't fed.
"Then just do it, Yvette."

"If you had let me rot, then it would be quicker, but I want his terror and his pleasure. That takes longer."

Jason made a small sound, like a child crying in the dark. I looked out at Richard. He was still standing, but he wasn't angry with me now. There was real pain in his eyes. He'd have rather it be him than Jason. Like a true king he'd have taken the pain.

I smelled forest, rich and green, leaf mold so wet and new it made my throat tight. I stared at Richard and knew what he was suggesting. We'd had our little fight about the munin. He'd truly thought I was safe from them because I wasn't a shapeshifter. He hadn't known the marks I shared with him would put me at risk. But now it had possibilities. Not channeling Raina, I never wanted to do that again, but the power of the pack. Their warmth, their touch—that could help.

I closed my eyes and felt the mark open like curtains parting in my body. Jason raised his head, staring up at me. His nostrils flared, scenting me, scenting the power.

Yvette ripped the vest down his back like it was paper.

Jason gasped.

She licked along his body, then suddenly her mouth closed over his ribs. I saw the muscles in her jaw tense as Jason's body spasmed against me. He collapsed against me, hands scrambling along the floor as if he didn't know what to do with his them, or with his body.

Yvette drew back leaving neat red holes. Blood dripped from the wound. She licked her lips and smiled at me.

"Does it hurt?" I asked Jason.

"Yes," he said, "and no."

I started to raise him up.

Yvette put a hand in the middle of his back. "No, I want him on the ground. I want him below me."

I smelled the sharp musk of fur. Jason tried to look at me, but Yvette forced his head down into my lap. She used him to support her body while she peered into my face. "What are you doing?"

"I am his lupa. I call the pack to his aid."

"They cannot help him," she said.

"Yes," I said, "they can." I slid down, wriggling under Jason's body. The little black dress ended up about waist level. Everyone was getting a great view of the hose and undies. Good that everything matched. But I could see Jason's face. I could feel his body a little more than I wanted to. But it was his eyes I wanted, his face. I wanted him looking at me.

I'd never tried missionary position with a man exactly my height. The eye contact was incredibly intimate. He gave a nervous laugh. "I've had fantasies like this."

"Funny," I said. "I haven't."

"Ooh, too cruel." His spine bowed, body pressing against mine. Yvette had taken another taste. The fear was back in full force, filling his eyes with panic.

"I'm here. We're here."

He closed his eyes and took a deep breath. He drew in the scent of leaves, and fur, and dark places full of bodies that all smelled like pack. And Yvette struck again.

Jason screamed, and I raised myself up enough to see that the vampire had pulled a strip of skin loose so it flapped. Blood poured down his skin.

Jean-Claude came to the edge of the circle. "That is torture, not feeding. It stops here."

"No," Yvette said, "I will feed."

"Then feed," Jean-Claude said, "but do it quickly before our patience is at an end."

She crawled up his body, putting her weight on top of his, grinding me into the floor. The leather stitching over his groin was ground so hard against me that it hurt. His breath came in quick pants, fast and faster. He was going to hyperventilate.

"Look at me," I said.

Yvette jerked his head back by the hair. "No, look at me. Because I will hurt you, Jason. I will haunt your dreams."

"No," I said. The power swelled inside of me, and I spit power into her pale face. Blood flew in a long, shallow cut down her cheek.

Everything froze. Yvette raised a hand to her bleeding cheek. "How did you do that?"

"If I said I wasn't really sure, would you believe me?"

"No," she said.

"Then believe this, bitch. Finish this now or I will cut you up." I believed it when I said it, even though I wasn't sure I could ever repeat the performance. Only master vampires could cause cuts like that from a distance. I'd never even seen Jean-Claude do it.

Yvette believed me. She leaned close enough that the blood from the cut dripped onto Jason's blond hair. "As you like, *putain*; but know this, I will not put him under. For this—" she showed the cut to me by a turn of her face—"he will suffer."

"Ain't it always the way," I said.

She frowned at me, not the response she was expecting apparently. I put a hand on either side of Jason's face, forced his eyes to meet mine. There was puzzlement under the fear now, because Jason knew I'd never done anything like what had just happened to Yvette. But we couldn't say, golly, gee whiz, how'd I do that in front of the bad guys?

Yvette shifted until her body was pressed along the length of Jason's. He moved against me. There was nothing between Jason and me but the leather of his pants and some satin. My body reacted. It was my turn to close my eyes so he wouldn't see. Maybe it was the physical reaction, but I was suddenly drowning in the scent of fur, and the warm, close knowledge of his body. The munin was here in a warm, building rush.

I lifted my face and kissed him. The moment our lips touched, the power flowed between us. It was a binding of a different sort, better than with Nathaniel, and I knew why. Nathaniel wasn't pack.

Jason didn't kiss me back at first; then he sank into my mouth, into the warm power, and the power grew until I could feel it like a small hot wind across my body, across our bodies. The power flowed over Yvette and made her cry out. She plunged fangs into Jason's neck. He screamed into my mouth, body stiffening, but the pain rode on the warm, building power and was washed away.

I could feel Yvette's mouth like a siphon, sucking the power away. I thrust it into her and sent her reeling from us, drunk on more than blood.

Freed of Yvette's body, Jason moved against me. He kissed me as if he'd climb inside and pull me around him, and I kissed him back. I'd welcomed Raina's munin, and I didn't know how to turn it off.

I felt his lower body react, felt him come, and that was

enough to help me swim back into control. What a nice embarrassing moment to be driving again.

Jason collapsed on top of me, panting, but not from fear. I turned my face away so that I wouldn't catch a glimpse of anyone gathered around us. Yvette lay on her side near us, curled into a ball, blood trailing down her chin. She licked the blood, almost halfheartedly as if even that small effort were too much. She spoke French to me: "*Je reve de toi.*" I'd heard a version of this before from Jean-Claude. She said she'd dream of us.

I heard myself say, "Why do the French always know exactly what to say at times like this?"

Jean-Claude knelt beside us. "It is genetic, *ma petite.*"

"Ah," I said. I had trouble meeting his eyes with Jason still sprawled across my body.

"Jason," I said, tapping his bare shoulder. He said nothing, just rolled off me to lie on the floor, closer to Yvette than I'd have ever thought he'd be willing to get.

I suddenly realized that my skirt was still up around my waist. Jean-Claude helped me sit up while I wiggled the dress down.

Richard knelt with us. I expected a scathing remark. I'd certainly given him enough ammo for one. He surprised me by saying, "Raina, gone, but not forgotten."

I said, "No joke."

"I'm sorry, Anita. When you told me, I didn't realize it was an almost complete melding. I understand why you're afraid of it now. There are things you can do to keep it from happening again. I was too angry at you to believe it was this bad." A look crossed his face, part pain, part confusion. "I am sorry for that."

"If you can keep that from happening again, apology accepted."

Padma was suddenly looming over us. "You and I will dance next, Ulfric. After the show your lupa gave us, I am more eager than ever to taste you."

Richard glanced at me, then at Jason and Yvette, both still lying on the ground as if any movement was too much. "I don't think I'm that good."

"I think you underestimate yourself, wolf," Padma said. He offered Richard a hand, but he stood on his own. The two men were almost the same height. They stared at each other, and I could already feel the power flaring between them, testing each other.

I lay against Jean-Claude's chest and closed my eyes. "Get me out of here before they start. I can't stand to be near this much power so soon." He helped me to stand, and when my legs wouldn't hold me, he scooped me up in his arms, holding me effortlessly. He just stood there holding me, as if expecting me to protest.

I put my arms around his neck and said, "Just do it."

He smiled, and it was wondrous. "I have wanted to do this for a very long time." Was it romantic to be carried in his arms at last? Yes. But when Jason managed to stagger from the floor, the front of his blue leather pants was stained, and that wasn't romantic at all.

51

PADMA AND RICHARD faced each other just out of reach. Each was letting his power out like a lure at the end of a line, to see who took the bait first. Richard's power was as it always was, an electric heat. But Padma's power was similar. More than any other vamp I'd been around, his power was warm, alive, for lack of a better word. It did not have the electric shimmer of Richard's, but it had heat.

Their power filled the room as if the very air were charged with their energy. It was everywhere and nowhere. Richard's power bit along my skin, drew a gasp from my throat that Jean-Claude echoed. Padma's power flared along the skin like being too close to an open flame. The two energies combined were almost painful.

Rafael came to stand beside us. Jean-Claude was still holding me in his arms, which lets you know how shitty I was feeling. The Rat King wore a very ordinary navy blue suit, white shirt, understated tie. His black loafers were polished to a gloss, but he could have been going anywhere, from a business meeting to a funeral. Yeah, it had the look of one of those suits that only came out for deaths and marriages.

"They feel evenly matched," he said, "but it is a lie." He said it softly as if just talking to us, but we were close enough that Richard could hear. "He did much the same with me; then he crushed me."

"He didn't crush you," I said. "You won."

"Only because you rescued me."

"No," I said. "You didn't give him the wererats. You won." I touched Jean-Claude's shoulder, and he put me down. I could stand. Yippee.

"Very impressive, Ulfric," Padma said, "but let's see just how impressive you can be, shall we? Thank you, Rafael, for spoiling the surprise. I will return the favor someday." The gloves, as they say, were off. Padma's power thundered through the room. I staggered, and only Jean-Claude's hand kept me from going to my knees.

Richard screamed and did fall to his knees. We were just getting the backwash of Padma's power. Richard was getting the full treatment. I expected him to do with Richard what he'd done with me, but he didn't. He had other plans.

"Change for me, Richard. I like my food with fur."

Richard shook his head. His voice came out strangled, as if the words were being dragged through his throat. "Never."

" 'Never' can be a very long time," Padma said. I felt his power like insects marching over my skin, ants with red-hot pokers taking bites. It was what he'd done to the wereleopard, Elizabeth, when he punished her.

Richard didn't writhe on the floor like she had. He said, "No." He got his feet under him and took a staggering step towards the vampire.

The burning got worse, the red-hot bites closer together like a continuous sheet of tiny fires. I made a small sound, and still Richard stood. He took another staggering step.

The rush of power stopped so abruptly that the absence of pain brought Richard to his knees nearly at Padma's feet. His breathing was loud in the sudden silence.

"Pain will not bring you to me," Padma said. "Shall we dispense with the games, Ulfric? Shall I feed now?"

"Just get it over with," Richard said.

Padma smiled, and there was something in his smile that I didn't like. As if he had everything under control, and everything was going as planned.

He stood behind Richard and dropped gracefully to his knees. He smoothed his hand down the side of Richard's neck, turning his head to the side for a good clean strike. One arm slid across Richard's chest, pinning him to his body; the other hand pressed his face to one side.

Padma leaned over him and whispered something in his ear. A spasm ran the length of Richard's body. He tried to break free of Padma, but the vampire was amazingly quick. He slid both arms under Richard's, fingers clasped behind Richard's neck. A classic full Nelson. Richard's struggles ended with him on the ground and the vampire on top of him. If it had been a wrestling match, Richard would have been pinned, lost. But no referee was coming to say "time."

"What's happening?" I asked.

"I warned Richard," Rafael said, "but he's always been so strong."

"What?" I asked.

"He is calling Richard's beast, *ma petite*," Jean-Claude said. "I have seen him do it before."

Richard's body spasmed so violently, his head hit against the floor with a sharp crack. He rolled on his side, but the vampire stayed on him, whispering, whispering.

"Did he manage to call your beast like this?" I asked Rafael.

"Yes."

I looked at him.

He stared at the show, not meeting my eyes. "He called my beast like water pouring over my skin, then drained it away. He did it over and over, until I passed out. I woke as you found me on the rack, being skinned." His voice was neutral as he told it all, as if it were a story about someone else.

"Help him," I said, turning to Jean-Claude.

"If I enter that circle, Padma will use it as an excuse to challenge me. If it is a duel, I will lose."

"He's baiting you, then," I said.

"He is also enjoying himself, *ma petite*. Breaking the strong is his greatest joy in this existence."

A scream poured from Richard's mouth. A scream that ended in a howl.

"I'm going to help him."

"How, *ma petite*?"

"Padma can't challenge me to a duel, and he can't call my beast. Touch makes the marks stronger, right?"

"*Oui.*"

I smiled and started walking towards Richard. Jean-Claude didn't try to stop me. No one did. Richard had managed to get to his knees with the vampire still molded to his back. Richard's eyes were amber wolf eyes, and he was close to panicking. This near, I could feel his beast like a huge shape just below the surface of some dark lake. When it broke the surface, it would take him with it. Rafael seemed to have accepted his loss, but Richard wouldn't. Richard would take the defeat and beat himself with it.

"What are you doing, human?" Padma asked, staring up at me.

"I'm his lupa and his third. I'm doing my job." I held Richard's face in my hands, and that was enough. The physical touch was all it took to strengthen his control. I felt his heart slow, the pulsing of his body ease. I felt that great shape sink back into the depths. Richard drew on my mark like a drowning man with a rope, coiling it around himself.

"No," Padma said. "He is mine."

I smiled at him. "No, he's mine. Whether we like it or whether we don't, he's mine."

Richard's eyes bled back to their normal brown, and he mouthed the words, "Thank you."

Padma stood in a rush, so quick it was almost like magic. He grabbed my wrist, hard enough to bruise, and I said, "You can't challenge me, because I'm not a vampire. You can't feed off of me, because I can only play victim once tonight, and Asher was my once."

Richard lay on the floor, one arm braced so he wasn't actually lying down, but I had a flash of how bone-weary he was, so tired, so weak.

"You know our rules well, Anita," Padma said. He jerked me close to him, bodies almost touching. "You are not vampire, or food, but you are still his lupa."

"You going to try and call my beast?" I said. "You can't call what's not there."

"I felt your power with the little werewolf." He raised my hand to his face and sniffed along my skin like he was smelling some exotic perfume. "You smell of pack, Anita. There is something in you to call. Whatever it is, I will have it."

"She is not part of the bargain," Jean-Claude said.

"She interfered," Padma said. "That makes her part of this bacchanal. Do not worry. I will not hurt her. Too much."

He leaned into me and spoke low, soft. It was French, and I didn't speak enough French to follow it. I caught the word for wolf, and power, and moon, and I felt the power rise inside of me. It was too soon after Jason. The power was too close to the surface, too near. Padma called to it, and I didn't know how to stop it. The power burst over my skin in a hot wash. My knees buckled and he caught me, as I collapsed against his body.

Richard touched my leg, but it was too late. He tried to strengthen my control, as I'd done for him, but I didn't have any control yet. Padma called and the munin answered. I was channeling Raina for the second time in an hour.

The power filled my skin, and I stood, pressing my body into Padma, staring at him from inches away. The power wanted to touch someone, anyone. It didn't care. I cared, and I had enough control this time to refuse it. I said, "No." I pushed away from him, falling to the ground as I did it.

Padma followed me, touching my hair, my face, as I crawled away from him. "The power is sexual in nature, a mating urge perhaps. How very interesting."

Jean-Claude said, "Leave her alone, Master of Beasts."

He laughed. "What do you think would happen if I kept calling her beast? Do you think she would give in? Do you think she would fuck me?"

"We will not find out," Jean-Claude said.

"If you interfere with my fun, then it is challenge between us."

"That is what you have wanted all along."

Padma laughed again. "Yes, I think you should be killed for the Earthmover's death. But I cannot kill you just for that. The council has voted that down."

"But if you kill me in a duel, then no one will blame you, is that it?"

"That is it."

I huddled on the floor, hugging myself, trying to swallow the power back, but it wasn't going anywhere. Richard crawled to me, touching my bare arm. I recoiled from him as if his touch had burned, because I wanted him, wanted him in a way so raw and primitive it made my body hurt.

"Don't touch me, please."

"How did you get rid of it last time?"

"Sex or violence, the munin leaves after sex or violence." Or healing, I thought. Though that had been sex, too, in a way.

Padma's power rode over us like a tank, a tank with a spiked tread. We both screamed, and Jean-Claude screamed with us. Blood poured from his mouth in a red rush, and I knew what Padma had done. I'd felt him try to do it to me. He'd shoved his power into Jean-Claude and opened it, burst something inside of him.

Jean-Claude fell to his knees, blood spattering the white shirt. I was on my feet without thinking, standing between Padma and Jean-Claude. The power burned along my skin. My anger fed it as if it truly were a beast.

"Get out of my way, human, or I will kill you first, and then your master." It was like standing inside an invisible wall of fire and pain to be this close to Padma now. He'd weakened Richard, then me, done something to the marks. Without us, Jean-Claude could not win.

I stopped fighting the energy inside me. I embraced it, fed it, and it spilled out of my mouth in a laugh that raised the hairs on my arms. It wasn't my laugh. It was a laugh I'd never thought to hear this side of hell.

Padma grabbed me, a hand on each arm, lifting me off my feet. "I am allowed to kill you if you interfere with a duel."

I kissed him, a soft brush of lips.

He was so startled for a second, he just froze; then he kissed me back, locking his arms behind my back, still with my feet dangling off the ground. He raised his face enough to say, "Even if you fuck me here and now, it won't save him."

That laugh spilled from my lips, and I felt a darkness fill my eyes. That cold, white part of me where there was nothing but static and silence, the place where I killed, opened up inside my head, and Raina filled it. I remembered the feel of Nathaniel's heart in my hands, the moment I'd realized I could kill him, that I wanted to kill him, more than I wanted to heal him. So much easier to kill.

I locked my arms around Padma's neck and kissed his mouth. I shoved the power into him like a sword. His body stiffened, arms opening, but I was holding on now. His heart was slick and heavy. It beat against the power like a fish in a net. I crushed the power around it. He fell to his knees and screamed into my mouth. Blood flowed in a warm gush, filling my mouth with the warm salty rush of it.

Hands pulled at me, tried to tear me away from Padma. I

clung to him, legs wrapped around his waist, arms around his neck. "Back off or I'll shatter his heart. Back off now!"

Thomas fell to his knees beside us, blood trickling down his chin. "You'll kill me and Gideon."

I didn't want to kill them. The power began to slide away, buried in regret. "No," I said it out loud. I fed the power on my anger, my outrage. The munin swelled and filled me. I squeezed Padma's heart—gently, slowly.

I laid my face against his cheek and whispered, "Why aren't you fighting back, Master of Beasts? Where is that large, burning, power of yours?"

There was no answer but his labored breathing.

I squeezed a little tighter.

He gasped. "We could die together," he said in a voice wet with his own blood.

I rubbed my cheek against his face. The blood from his lips smeared along our skin. I'd always known that blood was a turn-on for lycanthropes but I'd never fully appreciated the appeal. It wasn't so much the feel of the blood as the smell of it. Hot, sweet, flatly metallic, and underneath, the scent of fear. He was so very afraid. I could smell it, feel it.

I raised back from him enough to see his face. It was a mask of blood. Part of me was horrified. Part of me wanted to lick him clean like a cat with a bowl of cream. Instead I gave his heart a little extra squeeze and watched the blood flow faster from his mouth.

His power built in a warm wash. "I will kill you before I die, lupa."

I held him and felt his power begin to build, still weakened, but enough to do the job. "Are you still a good Hindu?" I asked.

His eyes showed confusion.

"How much bad karma have you accumulated this turn of the wheel?" I gave a quick lick over his mouth and had to put my forehead against his and close my eyes to keep from doing what the munin wanted. What Raina would have done if she'd been here. "What would be punishment enough for your evil deeds in the next reincarnation, Padma? How many lives would it take to balance this one turn?"

I drew back enough to see his face. I had enough control

again not to clean his face with my tongue. Looking into his eyes, I knew I was right. He feared death and what would come after.

"What would you do to save yourself, Padma? What would you give? Who would you give?" I whispered that last.

He whispered back, "Anything."

"Anyone?" I asked.

He just looked at me.

Jean-Claude was sitting up, cradled in Richard's arms. "It is still a duel until one is dead. It is within our rights to insist on finishing this."

"Are you so eager to die?" the Traveler said. "The death of one is the death of all." He stood above us and a little back as if he didn't want to be too closely associated with us. Too bloody, too primitive, too mortal.

"That is a question for Padma to answer, not me," Jean-Claude said.

"What is your price?" Padma asked.

"No more punishment for Oliver's death. He lost a duel, it is as simple as that." Jean-Claude coughed, and more blood spattered from his lips.

"Agreed," Padma said.

"Agreed," the Traveler said.

"I never wanted them dead because of the Earthmover's death," Yvette said. "Agreed."

Asher said, "The Earthmover earned his death. Agreed."

Jean-Claude held his hand out to me. "Come, *ma petite*. We have our safety."

I shook my head, laying a kiss on Padma's forehead, gentle, chaste. "I promised Sylvie that everyone who raped her would die."

Padma's body jerked, reaction at last. "The woman you can have, but not my son."

"Do you agree to that, Traveler? You, who Liv calls master now. Do you give her up so easily?"

"Will you kill him if I refuse?" he asked.

"I gave Sylvie my word," I said. And I knew that would mean something to them.

"Then Liv is yours to do with as you see fit."

"Master," she said.

"Silence," the Traveler said.

"See, Liv, they're just monsters." I stared down into Padma's bloody face and watched fear fill his eyes like water pouring into a glass. I watched him look into my face and see the emptiness. No, for the first time I wanted to kill. Not for revenge, or safety, or even my word, but just because I could. Because in some dark part of me it would be a pleasure to crush his heart and watch dark blood pour from him. I'd have liked to blame it on Raina's munin, but I wasn't sure. Maybe it was just me. Maybe it always had been. Hell, maybe it was one of the boys. I didn't know and it didn't matter. I let the thought fill my face and eyes. I let Padma see, and fear filled his face, his eyes, because he understood.

"I want Fernando," I said softly.

"He is my son."

"Someone must die for his crimes, Padma. I would rather it were him, but if you won't give him to me, then I'll take you in his place."

"No," Yvette said. "We have been more than generous here. We have let you kill a council member and go unpunished. We have given you back your traitor and our new toy. We owe you nothing else."

I looked at Padma but I spoke for the Traveler's ears. "If you had just insulted the vampires of this city, then it would be over and you would owe us nothing. But we are lukoi and not vampires. You called our Geri to your hand and she came. You tried to break her, and when she would not bend you tortured her. You tortured her when you knew it would not give you the lukoi. You dishonored her for no reason, other than that you could. You did it because you expected no reprisal. The Master of Beasts thought our pack was beneath notice. Pawns in a larger game."

I released his heart, because if I hadn't, the munin would have killed him. I shoved the power deeper into him. I shoved it hard and fast until he screamed. Gideon and Thomas echoed the scream.

Padma collapsed backwards onto the floor with me riding his body.

I rose up, hands flat over his chest, legs straddling his body.

"We are the Thronos Rokke, the Throne Rock people, and we are no one's pawns."

Fernando knelt just outside the circle. "Father," he said.

"His life or yours, Padma. His life or yours."

Padma closed his eyes and whispered, "His."

"Father! You can't give me to her. To them!"

"Your word of honor that he is ours to punish as we see fit, even unto death," I said.

Padma nodded. "My word."

Damian, Jason, and Rafael just suddenly appeared around Fernando. He reached out to his father. "I am your son."

Padma would not look at him. Even when I crawled off him, he curled on his side away from Fernando.

I wiped blood off my chin with the back of my hand. The munin was leaving, draining away. I could taste blood all the way down. I rolled onto my side and threw up. Blood does not improve the second time around.

Jean-Claude reached out to me and I went to him. The moment his cool hand touched mine I felt better. Not a lot, but some. Richard's hand touched my face gently. I let them draw me into the circle of their arms. Jean-Claude seemed to gain strength just from my touch. He sat up a little straighter.

I glanced over to find Gideon and Thomas doing much the same with Padma. Blood poured from all of them, but only Padma's eyes were still haunted by fear. I'd pushed him to the edge of the abyss. Pushed us both. I'd been raised Catholic and I wasn't sure there were enough Hail Marys in the world to cover what was happening to me lately.

52

FERNANDO TRIED TO make a break for it but he was outmanned. Or would that be out-monstered? They bound him with silver chains and gagged him. The last was to stop his constant begging. He just couldn't believe his father had betrayed him.

Liv didn't fight. She seemed to take it almost resignedly. What seemed to surprise her most was the fact that I didn't kill them both where they stood. But I had other plans for them. They'd insulted the pack. It would be pack justice. That was sort of a group activity. Maybe we'd invite the wererats and have a cross species jamboree.

When they were led away, a silence so deep and wide that it thundered in the ears filled the room. Yvette stepped into that silence. She was smiling and lovely, fresh and beautiful on Jason's blood and our mingled power.

"Jean-Claude must still answer for his traitorous ways," she said.

"What are you babbling about?" the Traveler said.

"My master, Morte d' Amour, has accused him of trying to start another council in this country. A council that will steal our power and make us but laughable puppets."

The Traveler waved it away. "Jean-Claude is guilty of many things but that is not one of them."

Yvette smiled, and the smile was enough. She was going to say something bad. "What say you, Padma? If he is a traitor, then we can execute him for it. He can be an example to all others who would dare usurp the council's power."

Padma was still on the ground, cradled in the arms of his two servants. He still wasn't feeling too good. He stared at our little group. We were still huddled on the floor, too. The six of us

were not going to be dancing tonight. The look in Padma's eyes
said it all. I'd humiliated him, scared the hell out of him, and
forced him to give up his only son to sure death. He smiled,
and it wasn't pretty. "If they are traitors, then they must be
punished."

"Padma," the Traveler said, "you know this is false."

"I did not say they were traitors, Traveler. I said *if* they were
traitors. If they are traitors, then they must be punished. Even
you must agree to that."

"But they are not traitors," the Traveler said.

"I use my master's proxy to call a vote," Yvette said. "I
think I know what three of the votes will be."

Asher came to stand near Jean-Claude and us. "They are not
traitors, Yvette. To say so is a lie."

"Lies are very interesting things. Don't you think . . .
Harry?" She held out her hand as if it were a signal and Harry
the bartender joined her. I didn't think I could be surprised anymore tonight. I was wrong.

"I see that you know Harry," Yvette said.

"The police are looking for you, Harry," I said.

"I know," he said. At least he had trouble meeting my eyes.
Didn't make me feel much better, but a little.

"I knew Harry was one of your line," Jean-Claude said, "but
he is truly one of yours."

"*Oui.*"

"What is the meaning of this, Yvette?" the Traveler said.

"Harry leaked the information to those awful fanatics so they
would kill monsters."

"Why?" the Traveler asked.

"My question exactly," I said.

"My master is frightened of change, like many of the old
ones. Making us legal is the most sweeping change we've ever
been threatened with. He fears it. He wants it stopped."

"Like Oliver," I said.

"*Exactement.*"

"But the vampire killings didn't stop it," I said. "If anything,
it's given the pro-vamp lobby a boost."

"But now," she said, "we shall have our revenge, a revenge
so bloody and awful that it will turn everyone against us."

"You cannot do this," the Traveler said.

"Padma has given me the key. The Master of the City is weak, his link to his servants weaker still. He would be easily killed now if someone would challenge him."

"You," the Traveler said, "you could challenge Jean-Claude, but you could never be Master of the City, Yvette. You will never have enough power on your own to be a master vampire. Your master's power has made you try to rise above your station."

"It is true that I will never be a master, but there is a master here who hates Jean-Claude and his servant. Asher." She said his name like it was planned.

He looked at her, but he seemed startled. Whatever she planned, he didn't know about it. He stared down at Jean-Claude. "You want me to kill him while he is too weak to fight?"

"Yes," she said.

"No," Asher said, "I do not want Jean-Claude's place, not like this. Beating him in a fair duel is one thing, but this is . . . treachery."

"I thought you hated him," Yvette said.

"I do, but honor means something to me."

"Implying, I suppose, that it doesn't to me?" She shrugged. "You're right. If I could be master of this city, I would do it. But I could live another thousand years and I will never be a master. But it is not honor that stops you. It's her." She pointed at me. "There must be some alchemy in you that I do not see, Anita. You bewitch every vampire that comes near you and every shapeshifter."

"You've had a big taste and don't seem too taken with me," I said.

"My tastes run to things even more exotic than you, animator."

"If Asher will not take the city as Master, then you cannot control the city's vampires. You cannot make them do some terrible deed to the humans," the Traveler said.

"I did not trust Asher's hatred to make our plan work. It would have been useful to have control of the city's vampires but it is not necessary. The carnage has already begun," Yvette said.

We were all silent, staring at her, all of us thinking one thing.

I said it out loud. "What do you mean, it's already begun?"

"Tell them, Warrick," she said.

He shook his head.

She sighed. "Fine, I will tell them. Warrick was a holy warrior before I found him. He could call the fire of God to his hands, couldn't you?"

He wouldn't look at any of us. He stood there, this huge figure in shining white, head down like a little boy who's been caught playing hooky.

"You set the fires in New Orleans and San Francisco, and here. Why no fires in Boston?" I asked.

"I told you I began to feel stronger the longer I was away from our shared master. In Boston I was still weak. It wasn't until New Orleans that I felt God's grace return to me for the first time in nearly a thousand years. I was drunk on it at first. I was deeply ashamed that I burned down a building. I did not mean to, but it felt so wonderful, so pure."

"I caught him at it," Yvette said. "I told him to do it other places, everywhere we went. I told him to kill people, but even torture wouldn't make him do that."

He did look up then. "I made sure no one was injured."

"You're a pyrokinetic," I said.

He frowned. "I was given a gift from God. It was the first sign of his favor to return to me. Before, I think I feared the Holy Fire. Feared it would destroy me. But I do not fear my own destruction now. She wishes me to use God's gifts for evil use. She wanted me to burn down your stadium with all the people inside tonight."

I said, "Warrick, what have you done?"

He whispered, "Nothing."

Yvette heard him. She was suddenly beside us, white skirts swinging. She grabbed his chin and forced him to look at her. "The entire point to burning the other buildings was to leave a trail of evidence that would culminate in tonight's little sacrifice. A little burnt offering to our master. You burned the stadium as we planned."

He shook his head, blue eyes wide, but not frightened.

She hit him hard enough to leave her hand in a red outline on his cheek. "You holy-rolling bastard. You answer to the same master that I answer to. I will rot the skin from your bones for this."

Warrick stood very straight. You could see him preparing for the torment to come. He stood shining and white and he looked like a holy warrior. There was a peace in his face that was lovely to look upon.

Yvette's power surged forward and I got just the faintest backwash. But Warrick stood there untouched, pure. Nothing happened. Yvette turned to all of us. "Who is helping him? Who is protecting him from me?"

I realized what was happening. "No one's helping him, Yvette," I said. "He is a master vampire and you can't hurt him anymore."

"What are you talking about? He is mine. Mine to do with as I see fit. He has always been mine."

"Not anymore," I said.

Warrick smiled and it was beatific. "God has freed me from you, Yvette. He has finally forgiven me for my fall from grace. My lusting after your white flesh that led me to hell. I am free of it. I am free of you."

"No," she said. "No!"

"It seems our brother council member was limiting Warrick's powers," the Traveler said. "As he was giving you power, Yvette, he was keeping it from Warrick."

"This is not possible," she said. "We will burn this city to the ground and take credit for it. We will show them we are monsters."

"No, Yvette," Warrick said. "We will not."

"I don't need you for this," she said. "I can be monster enough on my own. I'm sure there is a reporter out there somewhere that I can embrace. I'll rot in front of his cameras, on him. I will not fail our master. I will be the monster he wants us to be. The monsters we truly are." She held out her hand to Harry. "Come, let us go find victims in very public places."

"We cannot allow this," the Traveler said.

"No," Padma said. He pushed to his feet with Gideon and Thomas's help. "We cannot allow this."

"No," Warrick said, "we cannot allow her to tempt anyone else. It is enough."

"No, it is not enough. It will never be enough. I will find

someone to take your place at my side, Warrick. I can make another of you. Someone who will serve me for all time.''

He shook his head slowly. ''I cannot allow you to steal another man's soul in my place. I will not ransom another man into the hell of your embrace.''

''I thought it was hell you feared,'' Yvette said. ''Centuries of worry that you'll roast in punishment for your crimes.'' She pouted at him, exaggerating her voice. ''Centuries of listening to you whine about your purity and your fall from grace, and the punishment that awaited you.''

''I no longer fear my punishment, Yvette.''

''Because you think you've been forgiven,'' she said.

He shook his head. ''Only God knows if I am truly forgiven, but if I am to be punished, then I will have earned it. As we all have. I cannot allow you to put another in my place.''

She came to him, trailing fingers across his white tunic. I lost sight of her behind his broad back, and when she came back around she was rotting. She trailed decaying hands down his white suit leaving black and green globs, slimy trails like obscene slugs. She laughed at him with a face covered in sores.

Richard whispered, ''What is happening to her?''

''Yvette's happening,'' I said.

''You'll return to France with me. You'll continue to serve me even though you're a master now. If anyone would make such a sacrifice, it is you, Warrick.''

''No, no,'' he said. ''If I were truly strong and worthy of God's grace, then perhaps I would return with you, but I am not that strong.''

She wrapped her rotting arms around his waist and smiled up at him. Her body was running to ruin, leaking dark fluids over her white dress. Her rich pale hair was drying out before our eyes, turning to crinkling straw. ''Then kiss me, Warrick, one last time. I must find your replacement before dawn.''

He encircled her with his white robed arms, hugging her against his tall body. ''No, Yvette, no.'' He stared down at her and there was something almost like tenderness on his face. ''Forgive me,'' he said. He held his hands out in front of him.

Blue fire sprang from his hands, a strange pale color, paler even than gas flame.

Yvette turned her rotting face to look behind her at the fire. "You wouldn't dare," she said.

Warrick closed his arms around her. Her dress caught first. She screamed, "Don't be stupid, Warrick! Let me go!"

He held on, and when the fire hit her flesh she went like she'd been doused in kerosene. She burned with a blue light. She screamed, and struggled, but he had her pinned to his chest. She couldn't even beat at the flames with her hands.

The fire bathed Warrick in a nimbus of blue, but he didn't burn. He stood there yellow and white surrounded in blue fire, and he did look like a saint. Something holy and wonderful and terrible to behold. He stood there shining and Yvette began to blacken and peel in his arms. He smiled at us. "God has not forsaken me. Only my fear kept me in thrall to her all these years."

Yvette twisted in his arms, tried to get away, but he held her tight. He dropped to his knees, bowing his head while she fought him. She burned, skin peeling back from her bones, and still she screamed. The stench of burning hair and cooking flesh filled the room, but there was almost no smoke, just heat building. Making everyone in the room move back from them. Finally, mercifully, Yvette stopped moving, stopped screaming.

I think Warrick was praying while she shrieked and writhed and burned. The blue flames roared almost to the ceiling, then changed color. They became pure yellow-orange, the color of ordinary flame.

I remembered McKinnon's story of how the firebug had burned once the fire changed color. "Warrick, Warrick, let her go. You'll burn with her."

Warrick's voice came one last time. "I do not fear God's embrace. He demands sacrifice, but he is merciful." He never screamed. The fire began to eat at him, but he never made a sound. In that silence we heard a different voice. A high-pitched screaming, low and wordless, pitiless, hopeless. Yvette was still alive.

Someone finally asked if there was a fire extinguisher. Jason said, "No, there isn't." I looked at him across the room, and he met my gaze. We stared at each other and I knew that he knew exactly where the fire extinguisher was. Jean-Claude, whose hand I was still holding, knew where it was. Hell, I knew where it was. None of us went running. We let her burn. We let them both burn. Warrick I would have saved if I could have, but Yvette—Burn, baby, burn.

53

THE COUNCIL WENT home. We had the word of two members that we would not be bothered again. I wasn't sure I trusted them, but it was the best we were going to get. Richard and I are meeting regularly with Jean-Claude, learning how to control the marks. I still can't control the munin, but I'm working on it, and Richard is helping me. We're trying to be less nasty to one another. He's gone out of state for the rest of the summer to finish work on his master's degree in preternatural biology. Hard to work on the marks from that big a distance.

He's approached the local pack there for possible lupa candidates. I don't know how I feel about that. I'm not even sure it's Richard that I would miss. It's the pack, the lukoi. You can always find another boyfriend, but a new family, especially one this strange, that's a rare gift. All the wereleopards have come on board my bandwagon, even Elizabeth. Surprise, surprise.

The leopards call me their Nimir-Ra, leopard queen. Me and Tarzan, huh?

I gave Fernando and Liv to Sylvie. Other than a few pieces that Sylvie kept for souvenirs, they're both gone.

Nathaniel wanted to move in with me. I'm paying for his apartment. He seems lost without someone to organize his life. Zane, who recovered from his gunshot wounds, says that Nathaniel needs a master or a mistress, that he's what the S & M crowd call a pet. The term means someone who is a step below slave, someone who can't function alone. I'd never heard of such a thing, but it seems to be true, at least for Nathaniel. No, I don't know what I'm going to do with him.

Stephen and Vivian are dating. Truthfully, I'd begun to assume Stephen liked guys. Shows how much I know.

Asher stayed in St. Louis. Here, strangely, he's among friends. He and Jean-Claude reminisce about things I'd only read about in history books or seen in movies. I suggested Asher see a plastic surgeon. He informed me that the burns could not be healed because they were caused by a holy object. I said, what does it hurt to ask? When he got over the shocking idea that modern technology might be able to do something his own wonderful body could not, he asked. The doctors are hopeful.

Jean-Claude and I did christen the bathtub at my new house. Picture white candles glowing everywhere, the light gleaming on his naked chest. The petals of two dozen red roses floating on the surface of the water. That's what I came home to one morning at about three A.M. We played until dawn, when I tucked him into my bed. I stayed with him until the warmth left his body and my nerve broke.

Richard is right. I can't give myself completely to Jean-Claude. I can't let him feed. I can't truly share a bed. He is, no matter how lovely, the walking dead. I keep shying away from anything that reminds me too strongly of that fact, like blood-drinking and low body temperatures. Jean-Claude certainly has the keys to my libido, but my heart . . . Can a walking corpse hold the keys to my heart? No. Yes. Maybe. How the hell should I know?